continued . . .

RAZED

Shiloh Walker

B

BERKLEY SENSATION, NEW YORK

THE BERKLEY PUBLISHING GROUP
Published by the Penguin Group
Penguin Group (USA) LLC
375 Hudson Street, New York, New York 10014

USA • Canada • UK • Ireland • Australia • New Zealand • India • South Africa • China

penguin.com

A Penguin Random House Company

RAZED

A Berkley Sensation Book / published by arrangement with Shiloh Walker, Inc.

Berkley Sensation Books are published by The Berkley Publishing Group.
BERKLEY SENSATION® is a registered trademark of Penguin Group (USA) LLC.
The "B" design is a trademark of Penguin Group (USA) LLC.

For information, address: The Berkley Publishing Group,
a division of Penguin Group (USA) LLC,
375 Hudson Street, New York, New York 10014.

ISBN: 978-0-425-27390-6

PUBLISHING HISTORY
Berkley Sensation mass-market edition / December 2014

PRINTED IN THE UNITED STATES OF AMERICA

10 9 8 7 6 5 4 3 2 1

Cover photo by Getty Images.
Cover design by Rita Frangie.
Interior text design by Kristin del Rosario.

For Haley . . . hope you don't mind me using and abusing your anecdotes . . . it just went so well with what I needed in Keelie's story!

Thanks to Buddy at Tattoo Charlie's in Louisville for answering some questions that came up as I wrote the book.

For everybody who asked from day one if I'd tell more stories about the brothers . . . here we go.

As always, to my family. You are my everything. I love you.

Thanks to Libby Rice for the help with
understanding some basic info on patents.

Thanks to Sara Thorne for some with Italian.

And as always, Nicole . . . thanks for always
helping with the legal end of things.

Chapter One

1. *Stop worrying so much about the future*

2. *Call Roger and tell him off*

3. *Flip off the next photographer you see*

4. *Get a tattoo*

5. *Have a torrid affair with a hot guy*

6. *Ask that hot guy if he'd maybe like to marry me . . . up in Alaska*

Keelie Jessup ran her finger over the warped pages of the journal and couldn't help but smile.

The battered copy of *Wreck This Journal* lay in a place of honor on a table near where the wedding cake sat, waiting. That wedding cake looked more like a work of art than anything edible. But if she knew anything about Abigale Applegate—no—Abigale Barnes, then that cake would be as delicious as it was beautiful. A caterer now, Abigale knew all about finding the absolute best and yummiest of creations—or making them herself.

The newlywed Abigale Barnes was on the edge of the dance floor with Zach. Keelie assumed what they were doing might be called dancing, but it was more like swaying as they stared at each other. They might as well be off on their honeymoon—completely alone in the world, lost in each other.

Neither of them looked like they had eyes for anybody else.

A tug of envy twisted at her.

Not because Abby had Zach, really.

One thing had become painfully clear over the past few weeks. Keelie felt a lot of things for Zach, but she didn't have the kind of feelings for him that Abby did. She'd thought she did. She'd *wanted* to, had hoped he'd realize he felt the same.

Then she kissed him.

She'd got as much *wow* out of that kiss as she did when her buddy Javi gave her a hug. Those rare, infrequent hugs. Physical contact wasn't really up her alley and Javier, more than most, seemed to pick up on it.

No. She wasn't in love with Zach, but who could look at those two and not envy the magic they obviously had? The insanity was that it had taken Abby this long to see it.

Shrugging off that tug of envy, she grabbed a pen and flipped through the journal. There was a space where other people were invited to draw in the journal. It had sat in Steel Ink for a while, the tattoo studio she co-owned in Tucson with Zach, but she hadn't felt right doodling in it then.

Now, though, she had something in her head.

She bent over, braced one elbow on the table as she sketched.

The cartoon images were clearly Zach and Abby and she had fun making them look a little more gah-gah than they already were.

"You're good."

She jumped a little, looking up to see Zane Barnes towering over her. Zane, the oldest of the Barnes brothers, stood there watching her, his eyes unreadable behind a pair of glasses she secretly found terribly sexy. Okay, secretly she found him terribly sexy. All five of them were beautiful, really, from Zane down to the youngest sibling, Sebastian.

Forcing a smile, she looked back at the sketch, gave a few final touches, and then straightened. "Thanks. It's just for fun."

She glanced down at it and then gave the newlyweds a smirking smile. "You gotta admit, it's pretty dead-on, though."

Zane laughed. "Pretty much." Then he held out a hand. "Dance?"

Her heart froze. Dance. With him.

For some reason, he always made her a little nervous. Those blue green eyes of his—*beautiful eyes*—made her feel like she had no shields, nothing between her and him and he could see all the flaws and holes and mistakes she'd made. And man, were there mistakes.

She hesitated, probably too long, because he started to lower his hand.

Impulsively, she caught it. "Yeah. Sure. I . . . ah. Look, I haven't danced in . . ." She stopped to think. *Shit. That long.* "I think the last time I danced with anybody was in high school."

"Well, I'm not going to be a great partner for your first dance." He led her out on the dance floor and tugged her in close. "My brothers used to taunt me for how clumsy I was."

She let him catch her hand in his, her breath trying to hitch in her chest as he slid his free arm around her back. He moved with a little too much ease for her to buy the clumsy bit, though. She tipped her head back, had to appreciate the fact that she actually *could*. She'd worn heels with her dress and with those heels, she stood six feet. Zane still had a good five inches on her.

His gaze rested on hers. Normally, silence didn't bother

her at all, but normally, she wasn't moving on a dance floor with a guy. She didn't know if *normal* could really fit in here. She was in a dress. She was in heels. And she was dancing with Zane.

Since thinking about it made her even more nervous, she had to break the silence. "So what happened to them getting married in Alaska?"

"I think Abby decided it was easier to have a wedding—especially a *fast* one—for two hundred people if she actually had the wedding here." A faint smile curled his lips. "Never let it be said that she doesn't have her share of common sense. They decided to have the honeymoon there instead."

Keelie shuddered. "I don't get it. A honeymoon in Alaska. Sounds cold."

"Nah." He shrugged. The muscles under her left hand glided and shifted and she realized her mouth had gone a little dry. *Nice muscles*, she realized. *Really nice.* "It's early fall. It will be getting cooler, but it won't be bad. Besides, they've both always wanted to go. It's beautiful up there."

"You've been."

He lifted a brow.

"Your pictures. You mentioned it." She shrugged self-consciously. She wasn't about to mention that she sort of stalked him online. It wasn't like he didn't have a blog. It was easy to follow him through the pictures and posts.

"Yeah. Had a freelance thing there not too long ago. Didn't pay much, but it was worth it just to go." The black-framed glasses he wore caught the light, hiding his eyes from her for just a moment and then they swayed, the angle changing.

Her breath caught.

He wasn't looking at her eyes.

His gaze was on her mouth, something hot flashing in the blue green depths. Her heart slammed hard against her chest and without even thinking about it, she licked her lips.

Then he blinked.

She felt like the air had been knocked out of her. *Whoa—*

Unconsciously, her hand tightened on his.

Dragging her eyes away, she stared out over the dance floor, looking back at Zach and Abby.

Her heart started to slow.

"He's where he belongs."

Swinging her head up, she met Zane's level gaze. Blood rushed up to stain her cheeks. Well, hell. Of course Zane knew. Zach and his brothers were tight, but there was no denying he was closest to his older brother. She had the urge to pull away, find a dark corner and just hide until it was polite to leave. The reception had only been going on for forty-five minutes. They hadn't cut the cake. Too early to leave yet.

Besides, she wasn't about to make a habit of cutting and running just because she was uncomfortable. It wasn't an easy habit to break, after all.

Mentally bracing herself, she confronted Zane's stare. "Trust me, I'm well aware of that. That I didn't figure it out earlier just means I'm an idiot. But then again, I wasn't blind to it for what . . . fifteen or twenty years?"

"Give or take." Zane smiled a little. "When something is always there, it's easy to overlook it."

She blew out a sigh. "I guess."

"So you're okay with . . ."

His words trailed off.

Blushing, she focused on his throat. It was easier to do that than to look at him now. She took a deep, slow breath and then wished she hadn't, because suddenly she was aware of something almost painfully intense—Zane Barnes smelled really, *really* good. "Okay? Yeah. It's not like I have much say in it." She darted a look up at him. "I'm going to make a startling observation here and just say I assume you know I kissed him. It was stupid. But I figured something out almost right away—even if those two somehow decided they weren't right for each other, it wouldn't matter. Kissing Zach was like kissing Javi. There's nothing there. If I felt what I thought I felt, there should be something there, right?"

* * *

It took more restraint than Zane thought he had not to pull her closer.

He didn't know he had that kind of self-control. He'd been doing just fine up until she'd given him a quick, almost nervous glance under her lashes and he felt something arc between them.

He knew that sensation, all too well.

He'd been feeling it burn on *his* side almost from the first time he'd seen her.

Need. Lust. Plenty of it.

But Keelie was oblivious.

Suddenly, though, she wasn't quite as unaware.

Of course, it *would* happen at his little brother's wedding.

And it would happen *now*—when they were talking about that kiss that caused the first real fight between Zach and Abby.

"Something there," he murmured, splaying his fingers out wide across her slender back, feeling the smooth, elegant line of her spine under his palm. Her dress, the same pale blue as her left eye, stopped three inches above her knees and clung to her slight curves like a lover, rising high on her chest, the sleeves long and tight. It was smooth under his hands and all he could think of was peeling it away and tasting the skin underneath.

Of course, he'd had those fantasies about Keelie for a long time.

"Yeah," he said, nodding, like he wasn't thinking about seeing her naked. Having her under him. Over him. Kneeling before him. Sweat started to bead along the back of his neck. "I guess there would have been."

Hunger. Heat. Kind of like what he was feeling now.

"You okay?" Keelie cocked her head. "You look kind of hot."

"Yeah." He needed to get away from her—probably for the rest of the night, he decided.

"Me, too. Wanna go outside?" She'd broken away, although her left hand was still gripped by his. "They'll cut the cake soon, but I need to get away from the noise for a few minutes anyway."

Outside.

Not a good idea.

But he wasn't about to say no.

The French doors spilled golden light outside and they moved into the warm night, leaving the noise and the laughter behind them. Keelie didn't go to one of the tables set up near the doors, though. She let go of his hand and kept right on walking, down the steps and into the night-dark garden.

The hotel set up on the outskirts of town was an old, elegant sprawl, the gardens designed for Tucson's desert climate. Zane moved in her wake, trying not to stare at her ass, but he was having a hard time with it.

"That's better," she muttered, finding a bench and dropping down on it, her moves all easy, boneless grace. She stretched out her legs and rotated one ankle.

He dragged a hand down his face.

He should have stayed the hell inside.

"I haven't worn heels in months. You'd think I'd remember how torturous there are. I don't know why we put ourselves through this," she said, eying the glittery, sparkling spikes on her feet with acute dislike.

"Well, whatever the reason, please know that men across the world appreciate it."

The words escaped him before he realized he was going to say them.

She shot him a look and then she started to laugh.

"Yeah. Y'all wear them awhile and then maybe that will mean a little more."

"Hell, no." He moved in restless circles around the small, semiprivate square, listening to the distant sound of music, keenly aware of the woman so very close.

"How long are you in town?"

He shot her a look. "A few days."

He checked his watch. "I should go in soon. They plan on doing the cake around seven ten. I've got to get pictures."

"Oh. Crap. Right." Keelie stood up. "I forgot you were handling that."

He shrugged. "I've already gotten a lot and they left the party packs out for the guests to get some pictures, too. Abby already fussed at me to make sure I have fun, too. A twenty-minute break isn't going to hurt me." Standing out here staring at Keelie was going to do him a lot of damage, though. He wouldn't sleep without seeing her in that dress, without dreaming about peeling it off.

She passed by him and another jolt of her scent went straight to his head.

His cock tightened. *Just once . . .*

A yelp of pain jerked him, and his dick, back to planet Earth. He caught Keelie right as she would have toppled.

She crashed into his chest.

Five feet nine inches of sleek, strong woman. Automatically, he braced her weight with his arm around her chest.

"Are you okay?" he asked, his voice rough. His heart started to race. She was so close.

Her mouth . . .

"Ah . . ." She licked her lips.

His gaze dropped, tracing the damp path her tongue had just taken.

A groan ripped out of him.

Just once.

Keelie didn't know what she'd expected when she'd kissed Zach a couple of months ago. A chorus of angels, an explosion of stars . . . something. Anything would have been nice.

But there had been nothing.

Now, though . . .

Her brain kicked off as Zane's mouth brushed against hers. It was a soft, almost questioning touch. As if he sought permission.

Curling her hands into the lapels of his suit, she sucked in a breath as he lifted his head.

Permission granted! She might have shouted it, except she couldn't breathe.

Instead, she did what he'd done, focused her attention on his mouth, and that seemed to convey the message just fine, because his head lowered once more.

At the same time, one big hand came up, cradling the back of her skull, and she shuddered as his tongue stroked along the seam of her lips.

Stars exploded behind her eyes.

Zane Barnes kissed her and stars exploded.

There might have even been angel song, but how could she tell? She heard nothing over the roar of her own blood rushing in her ears.

He nibbled his way along her lower lip, traced her upper lip with his tongue, taking his slow, sweet time, before he did anything else. By the time he deepened the kiss, she was clutching at him in desperation.

Then he slid his tongue into her mouth.

Her knees buckled and she sucked in a breath. At least she tried. That single action drew him deeper into the kiss and she wanted to sob from the pleasure of it as he tightened his hold on her.

She felt the world spin around her and then a rough brick wall was pressed to her back, while Zane's chest was a hot, solid presence against her front. Trapped now, she arched. That drove her farther against him and she whimpered in pleasure as that single move had him brushing back against her.

So very close.

She throbbed.

That teasing contact left her pulsing and throbbing for more. She didn't know if she could handle any more.

Stop. A logical little voice in her brain whispered. *You should stop.*

Like hell. Awkward, she pressed closer to him and the hand gripping one hip tightened ever so slightly. *More.* She wanted *more.*

As though he'd heard her, he started to guide her, a slow,

easy motion that met his, and her breath stuttered to a halt as their movements had him passing *right* over her.

She tensed, jerking her head back and driving it against the brick wall. A sharp breath hissed out of her.

He did it again.

Pleasure twisted inside her and she felt it gathering in her core. He did it again and she started to moan, shuddering.

"Keelie . . ."

His lips trailed down her neck, but she didn't hear him, didn't hear anything as he continued to rock and move against her. Blind, she hooked one knee over his hip and swiveled against him. *I need I need I need . . .*

"Zane! Hey, Z!"

She didn't even hear it.

Blood pounded in his head.

The sound of one of his brothers calling for him was one of the most unwelcome sounds he'd heard in a long time.

Keelie's eyes were blind.

What in the hell was happening?

Lifting his head, he looked around, spied the narrow dip in the brick wall, and he twisted, taking them inside it. The solid weight of her in his arms, the feel of her body against his was heady, a wonderful pleasure, one he didn't want to give up.

"Zane . . ." She whispered his name as he turned her around, tucking her back against his chest.

"Shhh . . ."

He could feel how close she was. Her entire body had gone rigid. He wanted to pull her skirt up, tear her panties away and sink inside. But he'd be damned if the first time he made love to her happened *here* . . . like this.

Still, her body trembled, a fine subtle tremor that came from deep inside. When he lay his palm on her belly, the muscles jumped at his touch. Slowly, he slid his hand down and toyed with the hem of her skirt. "May I?" he whispered, pressing his mouth to her neck.

"What?" The question was a thick, velvety caress.

He slid the tips of his fingers up. "Let me do this," he said softly. His cock jerked in jealous demand. It had better ideas, but that wasn't going to happen.

She didn't say anything, but neither did she pull away, so he slid his hand higher, the clinging material of her skirt rising up. He reached her panties and she was already wet. He could feel her through the damp material. Slipping his fingers inside her underwear, he circled her entrance and waited.

She bucked against him, a ragged noise escaping.

Off in the distance, he heard somebody shout his name again. One of the twins. Shit.

He covered Keelie's mouth with his free hand, keeping the pressure light. She bit his palm and then turned her face toward him. "Zane, please . . ."

Mindless, he pushed two fingers inside her slick, tight passage.

She moaned, turned her face back into his hand so that the sound of it was muffled.

"You're so damn wet. So tight . . ." he muttered, his mouth to her ear. He spread his fingers wide, twisted and felt her body clamp down on him. He did it a second, then a third time. She tightened around him, riding his hand.

This was insane.

She cried out as he flicked her clit with his thumb and he snarled against her neck as her strangled cry was smothered against his hand. She moved on him desperately. He arched against the curve of her ass, wished they were alone somewhere, anywhere, just so he could push her skirt up and sink his cock inside her, hear those broken cries instead of silencing them.

She went rigid.

The firm nub of her clit throbbed, swollen under his thumb. He pressed and circled it even as he thrust his fingers deep, hard.

She came with a weak, broken little moan.

He wanted to catch it with his mouth.

Even as she went limp against him, he heard the voice again.

Too close this time.

"Damn it, Z. Where the hell are you?"

Keelie froze, blood rushing to her face, scalding her skin as the world came crashing back.

What the hell?

Between her legs, she throbbed.

Her ankle ached—

Shit. Her ankle.

"Let me go," she whispered, turning her head away from Zane's hand.

He hugged her against him instead and she winced as he turned his head, shouting. "Give me five damn minutes, Travis."

Travis. Son of a bitch. I just let Zane get me off while one of his brothers was out here looking for him.

Shame twisted through her and she tore away from him and then had to bite back a yelp as her weight hit her injured foot. Glaring at him in the scant light, she said, "You should go. It's probably time for the pictures."

"They aren't going to start until I'm there anyway," Zane said, his voice soft. "What's . . . Keelie. Wait."

She batted his hands away. "Would you go? If your brother shows up here, he's going to figure out you were . . . we were . . ."

"That was Travis. He'll give me five minutes, unlike the rest of them," Zane said, his eyes lingering on her face.

She looked away.

"What's wrong?"

"Nothing." She swallowed the knot.

"Bullshit." He moved in.

If she could have walked away, she would have. But her ankle was screaming at her and she felt like she was going to cry—not just from her ankle, either. She didn't entirely *know* why. She just knew she felt like she was falling apart.

Frozen, all but trapped there, she went rigid as he reached up and touched her cheek. "I guess . . . shit." Zane looked away, his hand lowering when she flinched. "I'm sorry."

Then a low, raw laugh escaped him. "Even saying that feels like a lie. I've wanted to kiss you for so long, I can't even remember a time when I *didn't* think about it anymore. But you clearly didn't want me to. For that, I am sor—"

"Stop." She forced the word out, made herself look back at him even though her head was spinning from what he'd just said. *I've wanted to kiss you . . .* Her heart started to thud against her ribs and she got that same, lightheaded rush she'd felt when he first put his hands on her. *Don't. Stop. Be logical.* "If you think I didn't want you touching me, then you clearly don't know much about women."

His eyes came back to hers.

That intense, soul-searing gaze left her feeling naked and vulnerable.

"Then what's wrong?"

How did she even explain that? Her gaze dropped to his mouth and to her dismay, she thought about reaching for him again, dragging him against her. Her hands curled into fists and she kept them locked at her sides to stop herself from doing just that. "I don't even remember the name of the last guy who made me feel like that." She met his eyes unflinchingly despite the fact that the blush on her face might have lit up the night sky. "Let's just say it's been a while. I prefer it that way. Then you go and put your hands on me and my brain leaks out. Your brothers, your parents, people I've known for years are just a few yards that way and I'm over here losing my mind because I can't think about anything but finding a flat surface."

His jaw went tight. "Vertical works for me."

Her knees went weak. "No." She licked her lips, ignoring the way her body screamed at her in denial. "That's . . . I don't do this, okay?"

For a long, taut moment, he just studied her and then he backed away.

She stared at his back as he turned toward the path.

Pride warred with pragmatism as her ankle continued to throb.

But she didn't have to say anything.

Zane stopped before he'd even taken a step.

"Your shoe broke," he said softly, crouching down and picking up something from the ground. He held out his hand and she grimaced at the sight of the sparkling heel in his palm.

"I noticed." She glanced down at her ankle to avoid looking at him.

She practically *felt* him follow her gaze—felt it, like a burning caress.

"That . . . doesn't look good."

Her ankle was already starting to swell. "No. It really doesn't."

With her foot elevated, Keelie sat at one of the tables nearest the dance floor. Those were the "reserved" tables and her chair had been angled so she could see the dance floor, as well as the table piled high with presents . . . and Zane.

Too easily, she could see Zane.

Her abdomen went all tight and hot every time she saw him.

He'd picked her up like she'd weighed nothing, carried her inside.

When everybody was rushing around, he disappeared and returned with an icepack for her ankle.

Now, long after the cake had been cut and distributed, she was still trying not to look at him.

He'd gone into what she decided was his *work* mode, focusing on snapping pictures from every imaginable angle—and some she hadn't imagined.

He'd long ago shed his tuxedo jacket and she couldn't help but notice just how well he filled out the white shirt underneath. The bowtie hung askew around his neck and she found herself thinking about how much fun it would be if she could tug it off, unbutton the shirt the rest of the way—

"I can't believe you twisted your ankle at my wedding."

Keelie jerked her head away from Zane, focused on Abby.

"Better me than you, right?" The words popped out without her even thinking them through and then she winced. "That . . . sounded kind of shitty. Sorry."

"Oh, no." Abby grinned and dropped down into the seat next to Keelie. "I absolutely agree. Although I'm really sorry it happened—cuz that looks painful—I'd much rather you twist your ankle here than me." She gave Keelie a dry look. "I appreciate that sacrifice."

Keelie tipped her glass of champagne in Abby's direction. "It's the least I can do."

Zach came up behind Abby and pressed his lips to her brow. "Can we leave yet? Can we leave yet?"

Abby turned her face to his. "You're awful. You just asked that ten minutes ago."

"I meant it just as much then as I do now." He cupped her face, stroked his thumb over her lips. "You look beautiful."

A dreamy smile curved her lips.

"You two are killing me."

Keelie glanced up at the sound of Javi's voice as he settled in the seat next to her, his wife taking the other one. "Javi, be nice," Aida warned, her eyes dancing with humor in her round, friendly face. She smacked her husband in the arm before propping her elbow on the table and resting her chin on her palm. "The two of them are adorable."

"Adorable?" Sebastian, the youngest of the Barnes brothers, joined them in that very moment. He studied his older brother for a long moment and then shifted his attention to his new sister-in-law. "Yeah. I guess I'd say they looked adorable."

There was an edge to his voice that Keelie didn't quite understand.

Zach glanced up at that very moment and Keelie caught the sharp blade of warning in his blue eyes. He opened his mouth, but before he could say anything, the twins joined them. Travis smacked a hand across Sebastian's head. "Behave, kid."

Then he grinned over at Keelie. "He's upset that for once, he's not the center of attention."

Keelie studied Travis for a moment, then shifted her eyes to his twin, Trey. "Yeah, I'm sure Sebastian's ego is getting a beating tonight." Sebastian shot her a devious grin, but before he could say anything, she looked back at Zach and Abby. "He'll survive, though. Zach and Abby just look too sweet tonight. He might be a hot commodity in Hollywood these days, but right now he can't hold up against . . ." She paused and waved her hand at the couple. "That."

At that moment, Abby glanced away from Zach. "If everybody keeps calling Zach *sweet* and *adorable* he's going to find somebody to arm wrestle just to prove his manhood."

"I don't need to prove my manhood." He pressed his face to her neck and then groaned as Abby pushed him back. "Can we leave now? Can we leave now?"

"Hush!" Abby said, but there was laughter lurking under the words. "This is my wedding and I'm going to enjoy it."

Zach leaned in, murmured something to Abby that had her face going red.

"Killing me," Javi said again, his voice mournful.

"You're not kidding." Sebastian rolled his eyes and turned away. Over his shoulder, he said, "I think I need another beer."

Zach opened his mouth. Abby jabbed him in the side. *"Behave,"* she whispered.

At the same time, Aida looked at Javi. "You hush. You'd think you don't remember *your* wedding night."

Javi slid his wife a sly look. "Maybe I don't. You wanna remind me, *mi corazón*?"

Aida shook her head, but the look in her eyes spoke volumes.

Being surrounded by happy people suddenly made her feel that much more acutely alone.

"Zach, not to interrupt whatever dirty thoughts you're

whispering to Abby," Javi said, "but I promised my baby I'd ask—hey!"

"Not now, Javi," Aida scolded.

"But they'll disappear for two weeks," Javi said, rubbing his side where Aida had elbowed him. "I told Evie I'd ask."

"Javi . . ." Aida said, her tone full of warning.

"It's okay, Aida. Javi, what's your baby girl need?" Zach asked, his tone teasing.

Their baby girl was fifteen, not really a baby anymore, but Javi still insisted otherwise. He gave his wife a smug look and leaned forward. "She's trying to raise money for a workshop she wants to attend over the fall break—it's a few months away but they have to get it worked out early. It's in DC and it's up to the student to raise the funds. We agreed we'd cover half, but if she really wants to do it, she has to raise the other half."

"How much does she need?" Abby asked.

"She's raised fifteen hundred. She needs another five— and no, I don't want you covering all of it. She was going to ask you herself, but her asthma was too bad for her to come tonight."

Travis whistled between his teeth. "A workshop that costs four thousand and they think students have that kind of money handy?"

"Some of the kids at her school do—or their parents do." Javi shrugged. "She's lucky—when I was her age, only way I'd have that kind of cash would be if I stole it. We can help with half. A lot of the kids, though, they want to go, and according to their teacher, it can open a lot of doors, but half of them won't be able to attend."

Keelie looked up. "What's the workshop for?"

"Something in the science field." Javi shrugged. "Evie wants to be a physicist. It's still a pretty rough field for girls, she says. Not that they can't do it, but . . ."

"A bunch of sexist morons don't always want girl cooties messing it up," Keelie said, snorting.

"Yeah. Kind of like you do with tattoos." Javi winked at her. "What's up with that?"

"Javi, you're just jealous that some of the girl cooties are smarter than your cooties," Zach said. His eyes bounced off Keelie's—that was the same way he'd looked at her for the past two months. Her heart ached a little over it, but she'd done it herself. "Hey, Z."

Even as he said it, before she even saw Zane, her skin was prickling.

Awareness streaked through her as he moved into sight, camera shielding his face. Automatically, she averted hers so that all he caught was the fall of her bangs.

"You've been taking pictures all night," Abby said. She nodded to the seat behind Keelie. "Why don't you sit down? Call it quits for the night."

"Gotta make sure I get enough pictures." He continued standing, so close it made her burn. And want. And wish.

Keelie felt herself growing all the more self-conscious. Her skin heated. She licked her lips, thought she could still taste him there, despite the champagne she'd had.

"Like you ever *don't* get enough pictures," Zach said, smirking. "Sit. Talk. Interact with the human race, Z."

There was a moment of silence, and then she heard a shift behind her as he sat. Her skin started to hum. Oh. Man. This was so not good. Was she going to feel like this every time—

"What?" She jerked her head up, looking at Aida, who was making a clucking sound.

"You look beat," Aida said.

Travis chose that moment to come around the table and crouch down in front of her. "You've been taking the ice off every twenty minutes, right?" As he asked, he lifted the ice pack away, studying the mottled, swollen mess of her ankle.

"Yes, Doctor Travis," she said.

"Smart-ass." He shook his head. "Everybody's a smart-ass."

"Like you're one to talk." Zane's voice sounded tight. So tight, everybody but Keelie turned their head to look at him. Travis paused, his fingers gentle on Keelie foot and lower leg.

"You okay there, Z?" Travis asked mildly.

Zane snorted and in the next moment, he sounded like his normal self, cool, almost remote. "Just pointing out the obvious, Travis. You still like playing doctor with the pretty girls, little brother?"

"Who doesn't?" Travis gave Keelie an easy grin. "You were able to put weight on it earlier, right?"

"Yeah. It just hurt like a mother—" She clamped her mouth shut, glancing over. Trey, Travis's twin, had his little boy here, but Clayton was out on the dance floor. With the flower girl. As soon as she noticed it, Zane did as well, and he was already moving in to take pictures. She gave Travis a brilliant smile. "Yes. It just hurts."

He grunted and bent his head back to what he was doing.

She bit back a yelp when he pressed down, but he noticed anyway. He gave her a grim look. "You need to get this looked at."

"I'll be fine." She shrugged and tried to pull her foot away.

"That's what you're thinking now." He rose and moved back to the seat he'd claimed a few minutes earlier. "What are you going to do when you can't stand on your feet in three or four days? You're covering for Zach for the next couple of weeks, remember? Get it looked at before it gets worse."

She glared at him. "You're an accountant, not a doctor."

"True." He smiled at her. "But I'm an accountant who has an interest in many things."

"That's just how he excuses being a nosy bastard," Trey said. He tipped a water glass at her. "I'm more honest than he is. I'm just a nosy bastard, period."

"Honey, you do need to get that looked at," Aida said, peering at Keelie's ankle. "That has to be killing you."

"It kinda hurts." She managed a tight smile. "But I'm okay."

"No, you're not. And don't worry, Travis. I'll make sure she sees a doctor." Javi scowled at her when she would have argued. Then he kissed Aida's temple. "Come on, baby. Let's get our stuff and get her home."

"No—" Keelie started to protest, but they were already up and moving, the two of them a united front she couldn't possibly argue with. Sighing, she contemplated the issue of getting herself from here to the car.

"I'll bring her out," a soft, steady voice said from behind.

Her heart dropped out.

Oh. Hell.

Her skin started to burn.

Her mouth went dry.

Slowly, she turned her head as Zane knelt at her side.

His gaze locked with hers.

"You ready?"

Her composure threatened to shatter.

No.

Forcing a smile, she said, "Sure. Doesn't look like anybody is listening to me anyway."

Chapter Two

Three months later

"I am not taking dating advice from *you* two."

She honestly couldn't believe she was going out on this stupid blind date as it was. Part of her kind of wished she was still in the stupid airboot she'd just been able to take off a few weeks ago. She hadn't planned to take Travis's advice, but the next morning, her ankle had hurt even worse, so she'd given in, afraid she'd broken something.

If only.

Instead of a broken bone, she'd messed up the ligaments in her lower leg. The technical term was a *high ankle sprain*. She called it hell on earth. Instead of six weeks to heal a broken bone, she'd spent six weeks in an airboot everywhere she went, and another month in it if she was going to be on her feet for any more than a few minutes—which was most of the day for her.

On the other hand, though, that boot had been a *great* excuse to get out of things she didn't want to do anyway. *No, Javi . . . I don't really want to go to the barbecue so Aida can try to fix me up with her brother. I can't, see . . . it's too annoying to hobble around and you know I hate to have people waiting on me. No, Ani, I don't want to hang out at the club with you and hook up with some guy. Besides, I'd spend most of my time at the bar anyway, watching you dance, me and my stupid ankle. You go, okay?*

Anais, one of the newer employees at Steel Ink, had caught Keelie in a moment of weakness. They'd gotten to be good friends and somehow, the cute, quirky blonde had known just when to strike.

Now Keelie just wished she could find a way out of this. She hadn't had a date in over a year and she'd be just fine to keep it that way, too. Okay, so maybe she *was* a little lonely and maybe she did wake up thinking about—

Stop it. She'd spent the past twelve weeks trying to forget that night existed. That was, in part, why she'd agreed to this stupid blind date. But that didn't mean she'd take dating advice from Javi and Anais. She'd listen to them on some things, sure. She went over tattoo design ideas with Javi all the time. And she'd let Anais talk her into the hoop she currently had piercing her left nostril.

But she'd said hell to the *no* when Anais suggested other piercings and in no way was she listening to *dating* advice.

She paused to shoot the two of them a dirty look before turning to study her reflection in the mirror affixed to the wall in her work area. A date. What in the hell had she been thinking?

Answer?

You weren't. She'd just reacted.

Anais had caught her at a weak moment—she'd had another brain-destroying, bone-melting dream about Zane and she'd been lying in the bed, half dying from the need burning inside her. It had been ten in the morning and, like she had a sixth sense, Anais had called. Dangled this blind date in front of her. *He's great, Keelie, I promise . . . he's sexy. He's got a steady job and he's not a dweeb. Come on. Friday night. Say yes.*

Keelie hadn't thought.

She'd just replied.

She'd just said yes.

She'd said yes, and judging by the lead weight in her gut, the entire thing was going to be a disaster. It was too late to call it off now, though. She'd feel like a heel if she up and told Anais to call the guy and bail ninety minutes before she was supposed to meet him.

Brushing her hair back, she gave herself a thorough study and decided she looked fine. She wasn't out to knock anybody dead, but she looked good. She'd come dressed for the date, and it was a damn good thing; her last appointment had gone way over.

The girl had shown up thirty minutes late and then proceeded to change her mind four different times . . . *I can't do this tattoo, no, I will, no, I won't . . . I can't put it* there*!*

The entire process should have taken maybe an hour and Keelie should have been done by four, out of there in plenty of time. She might have even worked up the nerve to call Anais and bail if she wasn't *looking* at her. But right here? In front of her?

She couldn't do it.

Anais was adamant that this guy was just *amazing* and he was just about perfect for Keelie. Keelie's thoughts on that were *yeah, right*. Then her brain had zoomed in on one man in particular—tall, lean, a serious face, and eyes that you could never really read.

Except she'd read them . . . once.

Her mouth went dry even thinking about that one time.

That one time she didn't let herself think about.

She and Zane. That was insane; and in no way was he perfect for her.

Besides, the *last* time she'd thought a guy was perfect for her, look how wrong she'd been. She'd thought Zach was perfect for her and he wasn't. Now there was a wedge between them and it was all her fault. For all she knew, he probably thought she still had something going for him. Would it make it better if she said something to him along the lines of *kissing you was kind of like kissing my pillow*?

Possibly. But it would also . . . well. She had a feeling it might also sound insulting.

She didn't know. She was *really* good at insulting people without meaning to. Normally she didn't let it bother her. But when people mattered? It kind of sucked.

"Keelie? Are you even *listening*?"

She met Anais's wide blue eyes in the mirror and smiled easily. "Nope."

Dating advice. From Anais. *Not happening.*

"Look, you need *some* help," Anais said.

Help? Oh, honey you have no idea. But the kind of help Keelie needed didn't come in the form of dating advice.

Cutting her friend a dark look, Keelie pushed her platinum-blonde hair back from her face. It was streaked with chunks of black and her roots were starting to show. She needed to do a touch-up. Sometimes she thought about going back to her normal color, but then reality realigned.

Noooo. She didn't want to go back to that girl she'd been. Not even in the most superficial of ways.

Maybe instead of the white and black, she'd try something different. Red. Vibrant murder red and maybe a streak or two of blue.

"Would you pay attention?"

Rolling her eyes, Keelie folded her arms over her chest and met Anais's gaze. "Sure. Just what kind of *help* do you think I need?"

"When was the last time you went out with anybody? For that matter, when was the last time you *kissed* anybody?"

Keelie rolled her eyes and busied herself with digging around in her purse. "I haven't gone out on a date in a year, Ani." She wasn't going to touch on the question of kissing. Her knees went a little weak thinking about it. "That doesn't mean I need dating advice. I don't think it's changed *that* much. And for the record, the last moron I went out with? That fell more under the definition of *hot mess* than anything else."

Anais arched her eyebrows. "Ohhhh? And what happened?"

Keelie jerked a shoulder in a shrug. "Old history. But trust me, it falls in line with my luck as far as guys go. Part of the reason I don't have a lot of interest in dating."

"Guy was a dick," Javi said. "Thought he could get free ink and when Keelie didn't jump on that idea, he up and went to the bathroom—or that's what he claimed. Then he just ditched her there. She saw him slipping out the front door."

"You're shitting me." Anais looked at him, then at Keelie.

Keelie shrugged. "This is how my luck runs. Either I think I like the wrong guy, or I go out with somebody who seems like a decent guy and he's a jerk."

"Having a couple of bad dates doesn't mean you should just give up." Anais hopped up on the counter and grinned at Keelie. "So when was the last time a guy knocked you off your feet? I mean . . . *really* . . . knocked you off your feet?"

Three months ago. The answer was instantaneous. But she kept it to herself.

"Ani, I haven't had a date with a guy who knocked me off my feet in forever. Trust me." And that wasn't a lie. Zane had knocked her off her feet, stolen the breath right out of her and made her come harder than she ever had in her life. But they hadn't been out on a date—before that night, he'd never so much as kissed her. Oh, he'd asked her out, but she never really thought he was that serious. It was like an afterthought.

He's asked you out since *then . . . those aren't afterthoughts,* a sly little voice inside her whispered.

Her hands went slick. No. They weren't. But the thought of going out with him terrified her. She couldn't explain why.

"Okay, so you've had some lousy luck. You know what that means, right?" Anais looked like a cherub, big blue eyes, rosy mouth, round cheeks, blonde curls that were one hundred percent real. She didn't go without a date unless she chose to, and that didn't happen too often.

"Yes." Keelie gave her a brilliant smile. "It means I should just give up this whole relationship idea."

"No." Anais rolled her eyes. "It does not mean that."

"Sure it does." Keelie held up a hand. "Last year's bad date . . ." She ticked off a finger. "There was a guy before that who decided my tats meant I was crazy kinky and he shoved his hand up my skirt. So I punched him in the middle of the restaurant and the cops were called *and* he lied *and* I had to explain it all to the cops *and* half of them didn't believe me."

"What the fuck?" Javi demanded.

Keelie gave him a dark look. "Don't ask. I didn't want you threatening to kill him. I handled it."

She looked back at Anais. "Then there was this guy I thought I *did* like . . . I made a move on him, it was a disaster—" She ticked off another finger, acutely aware that Javi had developed a fascination with the ceiling. Anais was new here, and didn't know about the mess Keelie had caused with Zach and Abby. "He was involved with somebody else and I almost messed that up. See? Bad luck. I'll give this guy a shot, but I'm not expecting it to be a rousing success."

Anais looked away, her shoulders slumping. Keelie felt like she'd kicked a puppy and so she groped around, looking for something to say to make it better.

But Javi spoke first, his voice soft, "Keelie, maybe that's the problem."

"What's the problem?"

"You go into it expecting there to be problems. Guys ask you out and you shoot them down before the sentence even gets out. The few who managed to get the words out, it's like you've already written them off." Javi shrugged. "If you go into this expecting him to be a jerk, expecting this be a failure . . . that's probably what's going to happen. Just don't expect anything. You don't know him. It's hard to know what to expect from a guy you don't know."

Keelie made a face at him. She wouldn't, under any circumstances, admit that he made sense. Nor would she admit that he might have a point. Maybe she did go into things expecting most of the guys she met to be something less than . . . well. Anything decent.

She'd stopped looking for the good in people a long time ago—only after they'd proved it existed did she let her guard down.

Aware that Javi was still watching her, she lowered her brows and gave him the stare that would have had most men backing away. "What?"

Javi only shrugged. "When was the last time you actually thought about giving a guy a chance? Ever liked anybody well enough to just relax and talk to him?"

"Well, that's easy." She fluttered her lashes at him. "I talk to you daily, honey. But the thing is, you're married. You went and broke my heart with it, too."

"Very funny." He rolled his eyes. "Seriously, can you name *one* guy who you don't automatically put at arm's length? One guy who doesn't automatically make you shut down?" Then he added, "Besides anybody who works here. We all get a pass."

Well, yeah. She could. But she sure as hell wasn't *naming* him.

Aware that Javi was watching her, she managed a casual shrug.

"There are a couple, yeah."

"Okay, then. Give this guy the same benefit of the doubt you give them." Javi grinned at her. "You don't need to be looking for the man of your dreams—"

Her bark of laughter all but rang around the room. Javi ignored her and continued. "Just talk to the guy. See if you like him. The only thing you've got a right to expect is that he treat you well. He's got the same right to expect that of you."

Anais grinned and nodded. "Exactly, Javi. Give him a chance without assuming the worst."

Bracing her hips against the counter, Keelie stared down at the toes of her boots. *Give him a chance without assuming the worst.* She jerked a shoulder in a shrug. "I guess I can do that."

Assume the worst was pretty much her motto in life, but it hadn't exactly made for the *best* life, either. Her life was damn lonely. Damn empty. It had seemed even more so the past few months, too.

Yeah. Fine. Mentally, she decided she'd try it. Once.

"That's the spirit. Also, Keelie? Don't get drunk."

Jerking her head up, she stared at Anais. "Don't get drunk?"

Even as Keelie said it, a shiver raced through her, drawing her gut tight with dread. Oh, she most definitely *wouldn't* get drunk. She rarely let that happen anyway, and never with a stranger.

"Yeah. Not that I've ever seen you drink more than a beer or two, but definitely don't get drunk on a blind date." Leaning forward, she stared at Keelie, face completely serious. "Now, you should probably order a beer. Because you'll relax a little and, Keelie, sweetheart, you need to relax. Actually, you should probably get laid, but that's for another night."

Covering her face with her hand, Keelie muttered, "I knew I didn't want dating advice from you two." She was *not* going to discuss sex with Javi standing right there. She wasn't. Absolutely not.

"Hey, this isn't bad advice. Besides . . . you know how bad an idea it is to get drunk around a guy you don't know."

An ugly headache started to pound at the base of her skull. Yes. Keelie knew full well how bad an idea that was. But all she said was, "That's why I don't generally *drink* when I'm going out on a first . . . or even a second or third date." She didn't drink much and when she did, it was only within the company of friends.

Anais waved a hand. "Just order a beer at the bar. That's all you need. One drink. You'll loosen up a little. Now . . . the most important thing . . . and I mean it, this is serious shit—"

Keelie lifted a brow. "You understand the concept of serious, Ani?"

"Absolutely. But only in reference to men and metal." Anais *did* take metal seriously. As the only piercer they had on staff at Steel Ink, that was a good thing. She excelled at her job. And the men definitely loved her. "Now, are you listening to me or not?"

"I'm all ears." And she was. Considering that Anais actually looked halfway serious, Keelie wanted to know just what her friend considered *serious*.

"So am I."

Keelie shot Javi a look. Part of her suspected she should make him leave. There was no telling what would come out of Anais's mouth. She had no filter. *None*. But Javi was like a brother to her and if what Anais had to say was going to embarrass *her*, it would likely embarrass Javi, too. Keelie believed in sharing the misery.

Unaffected by Javi's presence, Anais pinned Keelie with a wide, direct stare. "Listen, no matter what, no matter how hot you think this guy is—and he is hot, I've seen him—no matter how hot he is, you can't give him a blow job on the first date."

The bell over the front door jingled, shattering the silence that had fallen after Anais's declaration.

She might have said something—anything—to ease the embarrassment crawling through her.

But then she heard a familiar voice.

"Hey . . . anybody around?"

That embarrassment exploded and, suddenly, she had a hard time breathing. Her heart raced. Blood crashed in her ears. Her hands felt hot and sweaty.

"Did you hear me, Keelie?" Anais asked, lifted a brow. The hoop there caught the light, shining back. "No blow—"

Blow jobs. She clapped her hand over Anais's mouth just as Zane Barnes appeared in the doorway. Yes. It was exactly who she'd thought it was. Anais was going on about blow jobs and now—

An image formed in her mind. Full-blown, so detailed it might have actually happened, and larger than life.

Stop it, she mentally shrieked. *Stop it right now.*

Like it had happened yesterday, she could feel his hands on her, the way he'd covered her mouth as she came, muffling her cries, the way he'd twisted his fingers inside her, playing her body like he'd been born to do just that. His mouth on hers.

And now she could see herself on her knees. In front of him.

Oh. Hell.

His gaze came to hers, lingered.

Oxygen drained out of the room—he had some bizarre effect on the atmosphere, because when he was around, she couldn't breathe. That had to be it; she refused to admit she just got that stupid around him. Her chest hitched and she forced herself to take in a slow, careful breath.

His lashes swept down low over his eyes and then he shifted his gaze to Anais and the way Keelie was gagging her. "Am I interrupting?"

"No." Keelie pasted a wide, fake smile on her face and jerked her hand away from Anais's mouth.

Zane arched a brow.

"Oh, we're good," Anais said, that angelic smile on her face. "I'm just giving Keelie a hard time. It's so easy with her."

Keelie wondered how easy it would be to tie the woman up, gag her, stuff her in a closet for a while. Anais was tiny. Keelie stood five nine. It probably wouldn't take much.

Her heart continued to pound and her hands were still sweaty, and when she looked back at Zane, his eyes slid to hers, dropped to linger on her mouth, shooting another blast of memory pulsing through her. Her mouth started to tingle.

"I . . . ah . . . I'm heading out soon. Need to wrap things up out front." It was a bald-faced lie but if she stood there so close to him for much longer, she was going to embarrass herself. Especially since she now couldn't stop thinking about Zane. And blow jobs. And his hands on her.

She edged around him and cut into Zach's office. Once inside, she shut the door and pressed her back to it. Eyes closed, she whispered, "Just shoot me now."

* * *

Zane gave himself ten seconds to stare after her as she headed down the hall. Ten seconds, because if he didn't, he'd be looking for her the entire time he was there, and he knew it.

That was how it went when you had an obsession. Zane should know.

He'd been dealing with this one for going on three years now and it had only gotten worse since the night of Zach's wedding.

He'd thought that *finally* something would happen, but she seemed to dodge him even more now than she had before. Before he'd kissed her, she'd just smiled and shrugged it off anytime he'd asked her out. Since then, he'd been a little more determined, and all it had done was make her retreat in on herself.

He was getting frustrated.

And pissed.

He could almost accept the fact that she'd had a thing for his brother. At one time, there'd been millions of girls fawning over the former TV star. Zach had grown up in front of the camera, growing from a skinny kid to a teenage heartthrob in his part as Nate in the sitcom *Kate + Nate*. He'd met Abby there. Met her, fallen in love with her. Even after the show had ended, the public obsession had continued. Paparazzi still hounded Zach and his face graced more than a few fan websites. Zane was definitely used to women looking past him to his famous younger brother.

Keelie wasn't some faceless woman who'd never met Zach, but she'd also told him that when she'd kissed Zach, she hadn't felt anything.

So he could *almost* accept that.

It was hard because Keelie, out of everybody else, was the one woman Zane wanted.

She was also totally oblivious.

Or at least she had been. Seemed to be.

He wasn't sure how she felt now, but he knew how *he* felt. He couldn't get past this want he had for her.

It had steadily gotten worse, too.

"How's it going, Z?" Javi asked.

Zane swung his head around, but before he could answer, Javi spoke again, and this time, his voice split the air.

"Ani, what the hell are you *doing*?"

The blonde had Keelie's phone and was grinning maniacally as she punched things in.

Zane didn't know her. He assumed she was the new woman Zach had hired to do piercings . . . or something. He shuddered mentally at the thought, but gave her a smile as she looked up at him. She had a hoop through her eyebrow, a stud in her left nostril, and there were more hoops and studs going up her left ear. In the right ear, she had a simple diamond that winked at him in the light.

She was cute. She'd be perfect for the project Zach had asked him to start, too.

Except she might not live through the night after Keelie found out she'd messed with her phone.

"That is Keelie's phone, isn it?" Zane asked, arching a brow at her.

The girl nodded, still grinning.

"She's going to hurt you, Ani," Javi warned. "What are you doing?"

She shrugged, a guileless smile curving her lips. "Oh, just helping Keelie out a little. Relax, Javi." She paused whatever she was doing on the phone and held out a hand to Zane. Her nails were a vivid, bright green. "Hi. Anais."

"Zane." He shook her hand. "Zach's brother."

"I can tell." She lifted a brow and looked him over from head to toe. It was a thorough study, one that would have left him uncomfortable if he hadn't spent more than a few years working around models who liked to do the same thing.

He returned her frank stare with a level one of his own.

She flashed him a grin and resumed toying with the phone.

"Girl, you are playing with fire. Keelie is going to get

you," Javi warned. "She's crazy private. But don't worry. I'll make sure they play something pretty at your funeral."

"Oh, lighten up." Anais rolled her eyes. "She's not as scary as all that."

Zane blinked, looked from Javi to Anais and then back. "Ah, how long has she been here?"

"Not long enough." Javi flashed him a wide smile. "She'll figure it out, right?"

Zane cocked his head. "What kind of flowers do you like? I'll make sure to bring them to the viewing."

"So uptight, guys." Anais just sighed and shook her head. And merrily continued to have her way with the phone, her curls bouncing around as she bobbed her head to some unheard tune.

Javi just sighed and swung his head around to look at Zane. "Zach ain't here."

"Where—" Zane's question was cut off by a peal of laughter from Anais.

"Oh, man. That's hilarious. One of her ringtones is "Never Say Never" from Justin Bieber. *Justin Bieber*—for real. I'm going to rib her hard about that."

"You have fun with it." Javi gave Anais a look that might have been pity.

"Where's Zach?" Zane interrupted before they could start again.

A soft sound came from behind him and he shifted, watched as Keelie came back into the room.

From the corner of his eye, he saw Anais casually lay the phone down, out of Keelie's line of sight. Amused, he slid his gaze back to Keelie as she said, "He's not in right now . . . day off."

"What?" Zane frowned.

Keelie's mouth, so lush he'd had probably a thousand dreams about it, bowed upward. He remembered how it felt under his, how it tasted. His cock twitched in warning.

Keelie's mismatched eyes glinted with amusement. "A day off. He takes two days off a week now. He made Abby start doing the same thing."

"I didn't think Zach knew what a day off *was*."

"He didn't." Javi smirked, folding his arms over his chest. "He used to have a day off scheduled but ninety percent of the time? He ended up here anyway. Not now. He's like some old married dude. That ball and chain wants some of his time."

Keelie jabbed a finger in Javi's gut as she walked by. "I don't know who you should be more worried about—Zach, if he hears you calling Abby a ball and chain, or Abby."

Javi puffed out his chest. "Ain't like I'm worried."

"Uh-huh. And when was the last time you called Aida a ball and chain?" She slid her eyes back over to Zane. Her eyes drove him crazy—they always had, but it was worse now, because he knew how they looked when they were fogged with heat. One brown eye, the color of dark chocolate, the other a pale, icy blue. Those eyes gleamed with humor, and there was an echo of a smile on her face as she looked back at Zane. "Did Zach know you were coming by?"

From the span of a few heartbeats, his mind went blank. Then he kick-started himself back into gear and shrugged. "I told him I'd be in sometime this week or next. He had a project he wanted me to help with."

Keelie's head tilted, her eyes narrowing. "Oh. Yeah. You're helping jazz up the website, do a better portfolio." Then she wrinkled her nose. "Of course, a fifth grader with a camera and Flickr could build a better portfolio than we have now."

"Be nice, Keelie." Javi sighed.

"I *am* being nice. Otherwise I would talk about how Zach was a freaking moron to actually pay for that hack job." She shrugged, her gaze skittering back to Zane before bouncing away.

"You're nicer than I am. I told him he was a fucking idiot." Zane tapped the folder he held against his leg. "He was supposed to get some information together for me. Mind if I check his office? I had an estimate, some screenshots that I printed out of what we can do in the timeframe he had in mind."

"If he's pushing too fast, ignore him. I'll handle it. But yeah, go on in." Keelie nodded toward his office. "I'm leaving, but Javi will be around until closing time. If you want to poke around in Zach's office and see if you can find whatever, go ahead. You might be better off just calling him and asking him where it is. When it comes to that sort of thing, he rarely thinks to tell me shit. If you let me know ahead of time when you need something, I'll make sure to have it ready."

But then I can't surprise you when I come in, he thought. Instead of saying that, he just nodded.

"Okay. I'm heading out in a minute." She turned around and headed down the hall.

He made a valiant effort not to eye her ass, but damn. The skin-skimming jeans she had on made it hard. Instead of the sleeveless shirts or fishnet tops paired with tanks that she normally wore, she had on a lightweight red sweater, and her skin, soft and pale, glowed against it. He'd caught another glimpse of the elegant tattoos along her collarbone and he wanted, so very badly, to peel that soft red sweater away and press his mouth to each one. To learn those slight curves and go to his knees—

"You going to go see if you can find whatever?"

"Yeah." He glanced at Javi. The man had a faint smile on his face.

Zane felt a dull red flush creeping up his cheeks and he headed down the hall before Javi could say anything. The last thing he needed was for Javi to run his mouth to Zach.

Zane was still trying to get things moving with Keelie. He didn't need his brother getting in the way.

It wasn't hard to find what he needed. Zach had been a disorganized mess growing up, but running his own business had forced him to learn some manner of order. Zane found the list of clients and the pictures he'd hoped to use in a file marked *Z*, along with roughed out notes of what they'd talked about for the online portfolio Zach wanted.

He took the file and left the disk in its place along with a sticky note.

Here are a few ideas for you and Keelie to go over. Filled it in with pics of you or Javi, since that's all I had to work with, but you'll get the idea. If both of you like it, we can build from here.

Some of Zach's tattoos had been done before he opened Steel Ink, but the designs were his own. He'd been drawing for as long as either of them could remember and he'd come up with the designs that had later been inked onto his flesh. But quite a few of the tattoos on Zach had been done by Javi or one of the artists here. If Zach could find a way to tattoo himself, he'd probably do it.

Zane folded the list of names and tucked it into his pocket, hitting the main area of the tattoo parlor about the same time as Keelie. Trying not to look at her, he pulled his phone out of his pocket and sent Zach a text. *Took the file. In town a few days—maybe we can grab lunch tomorrow and go over some of the ideas I have in mind. Later.* He sent it and kept his focus on the door ahead, painfully aware of Keelie, that pretty red sweater, the scent of her flooding his head.

"You in town long?" she asked.

He jerked a shoulder. "A couple of days."

He lingered. Because he'd lied. He hadn't come to Tucson just to see Zach. He could have handled most of this online, set up the new site, emailed the templates, gone over things with Zach and Keelie in a conference call.

It would have been easier . . . cheaper. The trip back and forth between here and Albuquerque wouldn't break him, but he was going to have to start being more careful about money in the future. None of that mattered, though.

He was here because he had to try. Again. Try to get Keelie to give him the time of day.

Behind him, he heard Anais talking to Javi, but he didn't

hear a word they said. His heart beat in heavy, dull thuds against his ribs and he kind of hated the fact that his hands had gone a little damp. She made him feel like a damn high school kid again. She made him feel stupid. And she made him want more than he'd ever imagined wanting.

Now if he could just get her to admit she felt something, too, then maybe it wouldn't be so bad.

Phone in hand, the strap of her purse hanging between her breasts, she shot Javi a narrow look. "Remember, you promised to bail me out if this goes to hell."

"Relax. *You* said you'd give him a fair shot. So do it. But if you have problems, just text me, okay?" Javi slumped in the chair behind the counter, staring at the TV. It was damn slow for a Friday. Which was good since Zach was off for the day and she was bailing.

She turned around just as Zane started to push through the door.

She really wasn't in the mood for this date. She glanced at her phone and tried to think up an excuse—*Stop it.* She kicked herself mentally. She'd said she'd go through with it.

She started to follow Zane out the door, focused on putting one foot in front of the other. *Just do it. Just get it over with.*

She never even noticed that Zane had turned around until she slammed into his chest.

Her phone clattered to the floor and his arms came up to steady her. Wide-eyed, she stared up at him as a slow blush started to crawl up her cheeks.

Man. She really got clumsy around him.

Sensory memory slammed through her. Her hands automatically gripped his arms, her nails biting into his biceps. Her heart started to race and her breathing sped up.

He's so damn pretty . . .

Zane grasped her arms in return to steady her, and his body pressed close to hers. That was all it took to have her libido flare to burning, aching life. It had been dormant up until he'd kissed her a few months ago, and now, here she was, practically ready to tackle him and rub herself against him, and hold him tight.

Long legs pushed against her own and she had to tip her face back to see him. The thick black fringe of his lashes hung low on his blue green eyes, half shielding his gaze. His hands remained on her arms, steadying her, and it was embarrassing as hell to realize she actually needed that for a minute because her knees felt just a little too weak.

Sucking a breath, she eased back from him. "Sorry about that," she said.

"My fault." A muscle pulsed in his jaw and he let go, stepping back. "Since you're done for the night, why don't we grab something to eat?"

He'd asked her, a dozen times over the years. And in the past few months, it had been probably at least half that. She'd never once said yes, although recently, she'd been more and more tempted. It was just that . . . he scared her. So much.

Keelie didn't even know why.

The word *yes* danced on the tip of her tongue.

Yes . . .

Reality crashed in before she could give in. "I can't." She swallowed and looked away. "I've . . . I've got a date."

Tension slammed into the air. She backed up, looking around and spying her phone, her purse on the floor. She grabbed her phone, shoved it into her back pocket, and hooked the strap of her purse over her shoulder.

From the corner of her eye, she saw Zane watching her.

"A date." He drew the word out slowly, almost like he wasn't familiar with it. "You're seeing somebody."

A muscle pulsed in his jaw.

"No." She closed her eyes, rubbed at her temple before looking back at him. "Ani set it up . . . it's a blind date. I was . . . shit. It's just a thing."

"A thing." He nodded, bent down. She saw another phone on the floor and realized he'd dropped his as well. He pocketed it without even looking at it. "Sounds like a blast." Without saying anything else, he headed off down the street.

She thought of the times before, not even six months ago, when he'd drop by and tease her, flirt with her, ask her out . . . she thought about his hands on her at the wedding, the way he'd kissed her.

She thought of the question Anais had thrown at her.

When was the last time a guy knocked you off your feet?

That guy was walking away from her.

"Zane!"

He glanced back at her.

"I'm sorry. I'd . . ." She blew out a breath. "I'd rather be going out with you. I just . . ."

A faint smile quirked his lips. "Yeah. Sure." Then he shrugged and kept on walking. "Some other time, maybe."

Then he was gone, turning the corner and disappearing out of sight.

But did he mean it?

She just didn't know and suddenly, that thought bothered her. A lot.

It had been twenty minutes since he'd walked away from Keelie.

Parking was shit around here on a Friday night and it had taken him close to ten minutes just to get to his car, but had he left?

Nope.

He was leaning against the hood of the rental and contemplating the blue sky. No, what he was really contemplating was how much he wanted to figure out where Keelie was, so he could shove his fist down some poor bastard's throat.

Jealousy really didn't sit well with him, but it was chewing him up nonetheless.

A date.

She had a date.

He'd asked her out a good six times, maybe more, since that kiss and she'd said no each time.

And now she was going out on a blind date.

"What am I doing?" he muttered, tugging off his glasses. He squeezed the bridge of his nose as he pondered that question. He couldn't get her out of his head, the taste of her out of his blood.

The very feel of her was now imprinted on his skin and he could hear the echo of her moan when he lay alone in his bed at night.

She was out with another guy, somebody she'd never met.

Maybe he should just move on.

Except that was why he was *here*. Because he wanted to move on.

He was tired of spinning his wheels. He was almost thirty-five and at some point, he needed to get serious about the things that mattered. Namely, his photography.

Last week, he'd told the owner of the bar where he'd worked for nearly a decade that he was quitting.

Jake had thought he was joking, but Zane was serious.

He had started looking around, hoping to find a decent spot to set up his own place. No more random shoots when somebody got his name via friends or word of mouth.

He wanted to see his name out there with the masters.

But in order to do that, he had to start focusing and *building* a name. So he was going into business . . . as a fucking photographer. He'd shot his brother's wedding. He definitely didn't see himself as a wedding photographer, but he had to start somewhere. With the portfolio he had already started, and the wedding would build on it.

He had connections—you couldn't spend any amount of time in this field and *not* have them. He'd reached out, talked to some other photographers, including some guys who knew their shit way better than he did, and he at least had a focus, and a direction. He thought.

Although he'd look at a few places in San Francisco, he was almost positive he'd be settling down here, in Tucson. Because of Keelie.

He was ready to get serious about more than one thing, but was he wasting his time here? With her?

Lowering his hand, he tipped his head back to stare up at the sky, but there were no answers for him. Of course, it was hard to really think any of this through because he kept seeing Keelie out with some nameless, faceless—

"Never Say Never!"

He jolted at the sound of the music blaring from his phone.

Scowling, he pulled it from his pocket and then groaned. Sliding his glasses back on, he stared at the phone as the alarm continued to play.

Over and over.

He turned the alarm off and couldn't help but notice the label for the alarm: *Have a drink or two—*

That was all there was room for.

Shoving off the car, he muttered, "Clearly, fate is out to fuck with me today."

Keelie's. He'd grabbed Keelie's phone.

They both had iPhones, both used a plain black Otter-Box. He needed it because he dropped it all the time, especially when he was out hiking. He hadn't thought to make sure he had the right phone. Apparently neither did she.

And . . . she had a picture he'd taken as her wallpaper. The haphazard blog he used where he posted pictures had downloads set up for just that sort of thing.

It hadn't escaped his notice that she seemed to like his photography—she had some of his prints in her workstation and she'd emailed him a couple of times over this print or that one. Still, it was kind of weird, seeing one of them on her phone.

Personal, somehow.

Looking at the calendar message, he rubbed the back of his neck.

Apparently that was what Anais had been doing with Keelie's phone. Because no way in hell would Keelie be setting up reminders to have a drink.

He tapped the reminder to dismiss it, but the entire calendar came up and all of the reminders were right there for him to read. Yeah. It had been Anais, all right.

Have a beer or two tonight. But don't get drunk. Love . . . Anais.

That one might have made him smile.

Don't expect anything . . . just have fun. Love . . . Anais. That message was supposed to come up at seven fifteen, roughly an hour from now.

Don't expect anything? Hell, what kind of loser was she seeing? Keelie had every right to expect *plenty*. A nice guy. Somebody who'd look at her and realize how amazing she was. How funny. How beautiful. And that there was a kind heart under that ball-busting exterior. She deserved somebody who'd make her melt when he touched her, like she had with him, and somebody who'd be careful with her, because she needed it.

She deserved so much.

Don't expect anything?

"Shit," he bit off, and eyed the phone, fighting the need to throw it down and forget he'd seen it.

If she wasn't going to go out with him, fine. He'd have to deal with that. But if she was going to brush him off, couldn't she do it for somebody who at least *deserved* her?

But all of those thoughts fizzled to a halt and then died in a furious fire as he processed the seven forty-five message.

Don't give him a blow job tonight. I don't care how hot he is.

Zane started to see red. Or maybe it was green. All he knew was the jealousy was going to kill him as he stood there, thinking about some faceless, nameless bastard who might be on the receiving end of Keelie's attention.

That wide, lush mouth sliding down somebody else's skin, closing over—

He clenched a hand into a fist. "Stop it," he told himself, tearing his eyes away from the screen. He shoved the phone into his pocket and focused on blanking his brain. "It doesn't matter."

He couldn't think if he was tormenting himself.

Although . . .

He spun around and drove his foot into the hubcap and then slumped forward, hands braced on the hood of the car.

For one long moment, he stood there, jealousy an ugly, breathing monster that rolled down his spine.

Okay. He needed to figure out where she was, get his phone back. Then get settled in for the night—preferably with a six-pack so he could blur out those images and try to sleep.

He started to head back to Steel Ink, but before he made it five feet, he realized he didn't need to go anywhere.

If he had her phone, she probably had his.

Plus, she was probably halfway to wherever in the hell she was meeting this loser she was seeing.

Chapter Three

As she was climbing out of her car, an unfamiliar ringtone shattered the night air.

Something haunting and beautiful—it sent shivers running up her spine and it was unlike anything she'd ever
heard in her life.

It was most definitely *not* her ringtone. She'd told people
she used it because it was too annoying for her to miss—
"Never Say Never" did kind of stand out. The truth was, she
just liked the song. She didn't like anything else by that
annoying kid, but she liked that one.

And if that wasn't her ringtone . . . grimacing, she pulled
the phone out and saw *her* number on the display. Her number. With a groan, she answered just before the call probably
would have gone to voice mail. "We picked up the wrong
phones, didn't we?"

"Appears so," Zane said, his voice neutral. "Where are
you? We can trade."

"You . . ." She sighed and pushed her hair back from her
face, eying the neon sign flashing in front of her. "Look, you
don't have to do that."

"Well, I need my phone. You probably need your phone, especially if you're out on a blind date. Are you meeting whoever soon?"

She checked her watch. "Fifteen minutes." She'd gotten here early so she could follow through on Anais's advice. It wouldn't be a bad thing to have a drink. She was going to try not to go in there expecting the guy to be an asshole, too. There was no question about it—the guy could be Jeremy Renner–hot and she wasn't giving him a blow job.

All in all, she had every intention of following through on Anais's advice. Then she'd tell her friend to never set her up on a blind date again. Once that was done, she'd figure out a way to maybe call Zane, ask him out. Except he was on the phone with her now.

"So where are you?" he asked, his voice cutting into her thoughts. That voice, low and deep, the timbre of it stroking against her senses and making it hard for her to concentrate. "It will be easier for me to run it by than for you to meet me anywhere."

She named a popular Mexican restaurant and gave him the address. "Think you can find it okay?" She tried not to think about the fact that now she'd at least have something to look forward to in a little while. And maybe the blind date wouldn't show, and she could ask Zane to stay. How awful was that?

"Yeah, I know where it is. Abby loves their prickly pear margaritas. I end up eating there almost every other time I'm in town." There was a pause and she heard a car horn before Zane said, "I'll probably take about twenty or thirty minutes to get there, though. That's if traffic docsn't suck."

"That's fine. Sorry, Zane."

No, she thought, as the line disconnected, *I'm not. Not really.*

An hour.

Zane still hadn't shown up.

That was bad because if she had her phone, she would have already been out of there.

The *great guy* Anais had paired her up with—or according to one of the guys *she* knew—wasn't great. At all.

He was actually worse than all of her previous dates in recent memory, combined. Well, except Todd. Todd hadn't been bad. He'd just been boring.

This guy—*Call me Hawk*—was one of those jackasses who thought all his tattoos and his Harley and his habit of talking down to everybody around him made him a badass.

He'd attempted to order for her.

He'd attempted to tell her which beer she should try, since he was something of a beer aficionado. Not that he'd used that word.

He'd erroneously deduced the meaning behind her tattoos and when she'd told him, *Sorry, that's not what the roses are for*, he'd laughingly said, *So you're just into flowers?*

He was a dominating, domineering egotistical son of a bitch and she was more than a little tempted to throw the pitcher of beer he'd ordered in his face.

Jackwagon.

She'd give him credit, he'd managed to keep his eyes off her tits, but when one of the college kids she knew from the shop stopped by to ask her about doing another tattoo, he'd stood and gone all menacing. *Don't you see me talking with the lady?*

The kid had laughed it off and kept talking.

If Keelie hadn't intercepted, she suspected the son of a bitch might have tried to take a swing at the kid. Tayvione was a twenty-year-old jock with more muscles than sense, but he was a nice kid. Nice, but that wouldn't stop him and his friends from jumping into a mess if *Hawk* decided to pick a fight.

Because Hawk went through his life looking for trouble.

Keelie had avoided trouble most of her life just by realizing what trouble looked like.

An asshole who tried to pick a fight with a kid wasn't her idea of a *great guy*.

And if Zane would just—

"So. When you want to go out again?"

She gave him a tight smile and reached for her Coke. Now was the fun part. "I don't think that's a great idea." *Hawk . . .* like hell she was calling him that name.

His face underwent a slow, subtle change. She pretended not to see as she flagged down the waitress. "Can we get our checks? Split the ticket." She'd already mentally calculated her food and had a twenty in her pocket. Once the bill was paid, she was out of there. She'd call Zane from the road.

As the waitress disappeared, Hawk leaned back in the seat, eying her, his dark gaze slitted and glinting.

"What . . . did I do something wrong?" He smiled, and it was a good effort, she had to admit. "I don't mind picking up the tab, ya know. My mom raised a gentleman."

Yeah? Then why didn't Ani set me up on a date with him? She barely managed to keep the question behind her teeth. Out loud, she said, "I usually pay my way on the first date."

If a date tanked, she always paid. Otherwise, she went with the flow. There was just no way she was letting a guy like this buy her anything—even a peppermint from the dish up front. He'd want something in return. Men like him just *did*. She'd learned that lesson a long time ago.

The waitress came by and deposited the ticket and Keelie had the money out before she could disappear. "Okay, Hawk. Thanks. You have a good night."

She didn't bother lying and saying she had a good time.

Keelie didn't see the point.

Traffic sucked.

Zane almost sent her a message, several times over, but figured she wouldn't want to be bothered during the date. That made him want to chew nails, but again, he had no reason to be angry.

He might not be able to help being jealous, but he could

damn well deal with the anger and he'd keep it under control if it killed him.

Climbing out of the car, he surveyed the parking lot. The battered VW Bug she drove was parked near one of the lights, so she was still—

The sound of a scuffle caught his ears.

Then, a low, angry voice.

One he knew very well . . . and not just because he'd heard Keelie tell people off more than once.

He'd heard that voice in his dreams. He dreamed of hearing that voice as he crouched over her body and sheathed himself inside her. He'd heard that voice gasp out his name as he slid his hands over her body.

He'd heard her angry.

He'd heard her amused.

He'd heard her aroused.

But he'd never heard her like this . . . scared.

He took off running and rounded the SUV near her Bug just as she wheeled around and slammed her foot into the side of a man's head.

The guy's mouth went slack and he stumbled, shaking his head as he slammed into a Jeep a few feet away. He shook it off quick, too quick, and shot out a hand.

Zane grabbed the back of Keelie's jeans, jerking her backward.

She yelped as she crashed into him, driving her elbow into his stomach. Half expecting it, he tensed his muscles just in time to avoid totally losing his air and managed not to be winded as he eased her aside. Her gaze flew up to his, but he didn't look at her. He was totally focused on the man in front of them.

Big bastard. Mean. The high school bully who'd never quite learned that he couldn't have everything he wanted— Zane knew his type better than he cared to admit.

"Who the fuck are you?" The guy's lip peeled back from his teeth. "What did you do, text Clark Kent or something on your way out to the car, babe?"

"You want to turn around now," Zane said softly. "You want to turn around and walk away. Otherwise, you won't be walking anywhere."

"Yeah?" He took a step forward and drilled a finger into Zane's chest.

Mentally, Zane calculated. The guy only had an inch or two on him, but he outweighed Zane, a good twenty pounds of solid muscle. He stood there like he knew how to move—probably knew how to throw a punch or two. In a straight-out fight, it could get ugly. Zane had gone through more than his share of straight-out fights.

Then he saw the glint of silver flashing in the man's hand and he stopped worrying—he just moved.

One minute, Hawk was standing there.

Keelie barely even processed what happened, Zane moved so fast. He'd dodged to the side and struck out low with one leg—she'd seen that. Then there was a wet, sickening crack and Hawk crumpled to the ground. Furious, pained noises left his throat and his leg stuck out at an impossible angle. Keelie barely managed to snap her jaw shut before she swung her head around to stare at Zane.

Cool and collected Zane, with his horn-rimmed glasses and serious smiles.

He stood there, watching Hawk with a dispassionate gaze, then he shifted and kicked the knife her way.

Hawk lay there panting, glaring at Zane. "You fuck! My knee."

"You better count yourself lucky the knee is all I broke." He pulled his phone out and then scowled.

No. That was *her* phone.

He held it out and they traded.

Words burned on the tip of her tongue.

Words like *thanks*.

Words like *I didn't know you could do shit like that*.

Words like . . . *whoa*.

If you'd asked her earlier, she would have said, *I don't like the tough guy act.*

But right then, her heart was racing and she was having a hard time seeing anything but Zane.

He punched in a number and lifted up the phone.

"I need to report an attack, please."

She closed her eyes. Great. He was calling the cops. Of course, this shithead was going to have to go to the hospital, thanks to the busted knee.

"You asshole! You calling the fucking cops?"

Hawk went to get up but went down with a screech when he tried to put weight on his leg.

Zane ignored him, still talking into the phone.

A few seconds later, his eyes came back to Keelie's face and she swallowed.

"I had it under control, you know," she blurted out.

A shutter fell across his eyes and he inclined his head. He didn't say anything. He didn't do anything.

And she felt like an idiot.

"I'm fine, Ani."

"You're not fine!" Anais all but wailed into the phone.

Keelie fisted a hand in her hair, leaning against her car as she watched the paramedics finish loading that jackass Hawk into the back of an ambulance. His real name was *Jethro*. That made her smile a little. Jethro Bush.

And Jethro Bush was still cussing and giving everybody in sight the death stare.

Asshole.

"I am fine," she said once Anais had paused to take a breath. "I had it under control and all, but if it makes you feel any better, Zane is apparently some sort of Superman under those glasses of his and—"

"Zane?" Her tone changed, and Keelie could have groaned. "Zane was there?"

"We ended up getting our phones mixed up and he was

just bringing mine to me. Great timing, too. Anyway, Zane was there and it all worked out. Okay?"

There was a pause and then Anais sighed. "Okay. Is . . . is there anything I can do?"

Distracted, she glanced over at the cops and her gaze landed on Zane. He stood there, relaxed and easy, hands hanging loose at his sides, head dipped down as he listened to whatever the female officer was saying—she was petite, her head barely reaching the middle of Zane's chest.

And she was smiling at Zane.

That smile *really* pissed Keelie off.

"Keelie!"

She mentally kicked herself and jerked her attention away from Zane. "No, honey. There's nothing you need to do . . . except . . ." she trailed off, wondering the best way to put this. Blunt. She'd just be blunt and straight-up. Keelie didn't know any other way. "Look, Ani, I know you mean well, but let's not try the blind date thing again. I can handle my social life on my own, okay?"

There was a heavy, sad pause and then Anais sighed. "Keelie, I'm sorry . . . I just . . . you stay home all the time. You work on art and stuff and you do tattoos and you read. That's not a life."

"Maybe it's not your kind of life, but it works for me." She worried her lower lip for a minute. "I'll figure it all out on my own, okay?"

"Okay. You're not mad at me, are you?"

"Nah."

A few minutes later, they hung up and she was left standing there watching a pretty cop flirt with a quiet, sexy photographer. And that quiet, sexy photographer stood there, smiling in that solemn way of his. Of course, he couldn't just shut the woman down, could he?

Keelie scowled and forced her gaze away. She had no business getting jealous, not when she'd been out on a date—yeah, it was the date from hell, but she had been out on a date. Not to mention she'd turned him down more than once or twice.

That didn't matter, though. It still burned to see him turning that slow, serious smile on somebody else.

Zane let himself into Zach's old loft. The place was empty since Zach and Abby had started living together. Collapsing against the door, Zach pulled of his glasses. Pinching the bridge of his nose, he counted to ten. Ten didn't do it. Neither did twenty.

Fury and frustration and worry warred inside him, a bubbling, burning brew that just wouldn't go away.

Shoving off the door, he put his suitcase on the floor close to the bedroom and kicked off his shoes. He could still see her, like her face had been captured on one of his fucking cameras, pale skin, eyes glinting—the blue eye all icy with fury while the brown one was practically glowing and shooting fire. Her pretty mouth had been flattened out to a tight line and she had looked perfectly ready to do whatever in the hell she had to, while that roughneck son of a bitch stood over her, ready to hurt her in so many ways.

Zane knew all about people who liked to hurt.

It was a secret he'd kept to himself for a long time, one he didn't plan on sharing, ever, but he knew far too much about the kind of mindset that made a person want to hurt.

But he was just supposed to ignore that.

Because Keelie *had it under control* . . .

"Fuck that," he muttered.

He headed down the hall and hoped like hell Zach hadn't managed to get most of his shit moved into storage.

An hour later, muscles limp and lax as putty, his mind was almost clear.

The weights hadn't helped much. He hadn't expected them to.

The treadmill had helped some but he'd only been able

to do three miles before he gave up. Running nowhere fast never seemed to do much to burn off any sort of energy for him.

The heavy bag had helped.

Now his hands were sore, his thighs were screaming at him, and he almost felt like he could sleep.

Of course, every time he closed his eyes, he still saw Keelie.

Saw the way that bastard had been moving in on her, the way Keelie had stared at him after he'd taken the guy's knee out. The way she'd studiously avoided looking at him *after* she'd told him *I had it under control* . . .

Translation: *I don't need your help.*

Too fucking bad, because he didn't regret that. Not at all.

Just thinking about it was enough to make his muscles knot back up, so he pushed it out of his mind.

It was over.

It was done.

He'd say something to Zach and the guys at the shop would make sure to keep an eye out in case the guy came back around looking for her. Nothing much for him to do, since Keelie hadn't really wanted him involved in the first place.

Like he was just supposed to . . . what? Stand there?

"You're doing a first-class job of not thinking about it," he muttered, dragging a hand down his face as he headed out of the little gym Zach had set up.

He needed a shower. Needed to put some food in his belly and then he'd collapse.

There wasn't anything in the fridge but there was some canned ravioli and boxes of macaroni and shit in the cabinet. Zane had to take a minute to be glad his brother had the appetite of a twelve-year-old because, otherwise, Zane might have just gone without food all night. He wasn't going anywhere without some sleep.

He opted for the ravioli. Dumping the thick, gooey mess into a bowl, he shoved it into the microwave and dug out some ibuprofen from his bag. The way he was going, he would need another bottle before he headed home. His head hurt, his hands hurt . . . his heart—

He closed his eyes.

He really, *really* needed to take some time and think this through before he committed to moving here. Yes, he needed to move on with his life and focus. Yes, he wanted to try and . . .

He swore and slammed a fist onto the counter. He didn't even have the balls to say it out loud. He wanted to take a chance on making something happen with Keelie. He knew as well as he knew his own name that she felt something. But feeling something and being willing to take a chance on it were two different things entirely.

If he moved here and she never took that step, then what?

"Then you deal," he said softly, forcing himself to acknowledge that very reality. But he couldn't keep hiding away from it because he was afraid.

It was time to start thinking about all the things he could have, all the things he wanted . . . all the things he'd always wanted.

Things he'd never have if he just kept dreaming, instead of reaching.

A little while later, showered, tired, and pissed, he made his way back out into the living room. He wasn't going to sleep. Not yet.

Get dressed. Coffee . . . caffeine rarely had much effect on him anyway. Then he could spend the next few hours going blind on the classifieds. Sooner or later, he'd be tired enough to sleep, he figured.

If he lucked out, he'd find something he could use for his studio around here. That was the plan, at least. He'd have to check out San Francisco or his mom would never let him hear the end of it. He had no desire to move back to California. He spent enough of his life there—the first eighteen years—but he'd go through the motions to make Mom happy.

In his gut, though, he knew where he needed to be. Right here, in Tucson.

This was . . .

Somebody knocked.

Scowling, he eyed the clock on the wall.

Past midnight and, other than Zach, nobody knew he was here. Cautious, he grabbed his phone as he moved closer to the door.

"Zane. Open the door. I know you're up."

Keelie—

He managed, barely, to keep from throwing the door open.

So much for putting her out of his mind.

He even managed to paste a bland expression on his face when he opened the door.

It was harder to keep that expression, though, when Keelie's gaze dropped from his eyes to his chest.

He should have grabbed a damn shirt. Self-conscious, but determined not to show it, he stood there as she cocked her head to the side, studying the tattoo he'd let Zach put on him years ago. It was an owl in flight and it started midway across his chest and continued up, one wing spreading over his shoulder, the body stretched out along his torso, with the tail feathers ending down his side. Maybe not the typical tattoo for a guy, but if he was going to have one, he figured it might as well be something he didn't mind staring at every damn day for the rest of his life.

Normally, he didn't mind at all if women stared.

Keelie was a different matter entirely, though. Her interest seemed to waver between professional and personal, her eyes narrowing as she studied what felt like each line, each feather. But at the same time, a pink blush settled along her neck, climbing higher and higher, and her eyes glittered.

His cock was standing at attention by the time her gaze moved back up to meet his.

He turned away. Shirt. Needed. Now.

"Zach?"

"Yeah." He headed down the hall, letting her come in and

shut the door. "He's about the only one who would have a chance of talking me into it. He needed the practice and the portfolio and all that jazz. You know how he is."

"I've seen that design before. Zach has it pinned up in the gallery." She paused and then added, "I didn't realize it was you."

"That's because it's just the tattoo."

He grabbed his suitcase from the floor and hauled it onto the couch, unzipped it. Unlike Zach, he was organized down to the nth degree and had a neatly folded polo in hand in two seconds flat. He pulled it on and zipped up the suitcase before looking at her. She was studiously looking elsewhere, that pink blush lingering on her cheeks, and, even from five feet away, he thought he could see the mad flutter of her pulse.

"What's wrong?"

She swung her head around, a frown twisting her lips. "What makes you think something is wrong?"

He ran his fingers through his hair and sighed. "Keelie, it's past midnight. You're here. I doubt you're here to chat. So it makes sense that something is wrong."

She grimaced and pulled out her phone, checking the time on the display. "Shit. I didn't . . ."

She trailed off and sighed, moving deeper into the loft and dropping down on the couch with the familiarity of somebody who'd done so more than once.

Jealousy pricked at him, yet again. How often had she been over here to see Zach? Not that it even mattered. Zach had never been for her. It was starting to feel like Keelie wasn't for him, but that didn't erase the envy.

His gut knotted up and the dull headache that had started to fade came roaring back to life. Just being around her somehow made him feel like that stupid, goofy kid he'd been in middle school before he'd shot up a few inches and grown into his hands and feet.

She shifted, slid him a quick glance from under her lashes.

His blood pulsed thick and hot, his cock jerking in demand as memories swam up to the fore. He could remember her shooting him that same nervous, shy look more than once, could remember the taste of her mouth, the satin of her skin under his hands.

Out of self-defense, he seated himself at the bar. Far away from her, tucked behind a barrier, where she wouldn't notice, even if she had been inclined to look.

"You going to tell me what's wrong?"

"Nothing's wrong," she said, her voice weary.

Then she looked over at him. "Except for the fact that I'm a total bitch."

He blinked.

"Ah . . ." *Where did this come from?*

"Look, you don't need to respond to that, okay? I know how I am and I know what I'm like. But I was a bitch to you earlier and it's been eating at me ever since I left the restaurant. I was driving by on my way home and saw the lights— for a second, I thought somebody might have broken in, then I saw the rental car parked out front, realized you were here."

The words were coming out of her hard and fast, like she had to get them out *now* or she'd lose them. Zane stayed silent, staring at the surface of the bar. He was hard-pressed, though, not to go over there and cover her mouth with his, cut off that pointless flow of words. She had no reason to apologize to him.

Except for the fact she felt like she needed to.

So he stayed quiet.

"You helped me out of a bad spot, and I know that, I'm sorry . . ."

She finally wound down, huffing out a breath. "I'm sorry, okay?" She smoothed her hands down the front of the black jeans she wore and then stood up. "So, are we good?"

From under his lashes, he studied her.

Good?

No. They weren't. He couldn't see her without wanting things that he just couldn't or shouldn't want, but that wasn't her fault. Instead of saying that, he shrugged. "Sure. We're fine. But there wasn't any problem on my end anyway."

Well, there *were* problems, but he was too tired, too messed up just yet to go into them.

Too likely to haul her against him and finish what they'd started out in the garden a few months ago. Better to wait. Yeah, much better.

She nodded. "Okay."

She started for the door. Because he couldn't stop himself, he slid off the stool and trailed along behind her, torturing himself with the scent of her. The sight of her . . .

Chapter Four

"Okay." She said it again, heading toward the door. "We're good."

She *hated* that he'd pulled the shirt on.

She wanted to have the nerve to go to him, splay her hands wide across a chest that was more delightfully muscled than she could have imagined. Wanted to learn the lines of that tattoo, wanted to learn the feel of his body, the taste, the warmth.

She wished she was the kind of woman who could do that.

It was stupid, really, because sex should be easier than this.

It wasn't like he wasn't attracted to her. She knew he was.

But nothing about this was easy. It was even harder, actually, knowing that he *was* attracted. It made it that much more terrifying.

Sex had never been easy for her. Relationships just never worked and she couldn't find it in her to trust anybody enough to really open up to them.

Either the guys were looking for an easy time, or they wanted something more and she couldn't give that.

Life was easier without those complications, so she sim-
plified. It was her and her vibrator if she really needed it.
Otherwise . . .

But right now, she had this ache inside that was unlike
anything she'd known. To top it all off, Zane was looking at
her with that polite distance in his eyes. It was like that heat
from a couple of months, even a couple of hours ago, had
never existed and it was a bruise on her soul.

Was it because she'd said no when he asked her out?

Was it because she'd been such a bitch earlier?

Both?

Miserable, she shrugged her shoulders, now uncomfortable inside her skin. She hated this. Hated feeling uncertain
and needy and confused and . . . hell. She couldn't even put
her finger on what she was feeling inside, but she knew she
hated it.

He was behind her. She could feel him, a quiet shadow
that somehow managed to heat her skin even though he was
easily four feet away. All silence. No more smiles, no more
teasing.

We're good?

Like hell.

Feeling empty and hollow, she spun around and glared at
him. "Bullshit."

He lifted a brow and cocked his head, the light reflecting
off his glasses and making it impossible for her to see his
eyes. Beautiful eyes. He had the most beautiful blue green
eyes and now he looked at her like they were strangers.

It pissed her off that she suddenly felt uncomfortable
around him. It hadn't been like that before he kissed her.

No, she didn't want to undo that kiss, but she didn't like
that she'd lost that easy connection and she didn't like that
she'd hurt him and she didn't like standing there and not
knowing what to say.

Most of all, she hated that she'd wasted the past three
months and she hated knowing that if she didn't do something, *now*, while she was hovering on this tenuous brink
where her emotions ran just a little too high, she was likely

to go back to that place where she let caution control everything she did, and every choice she made.

Closing the distance between them, she tipped her head back and stared at him, all but daring him to move back. If she couldn't find her confidence around him, then she'd fake it. She was fine with that.

She'd been faking it for most of her life anyway.

"Bullshit," she said again. "Things aren't good . . . so what's the problem?"

He didn't react. Not at all. There was a faint smile on his mouth. She wanted to feel that mouth pressed against hers again.

His lips moved and she had to concentrate just to understand his words. "No problem, Keelie. I thought we just established that. You should go home. Get some sleep."

"If I want to go home, I'm capable of doing that, deciding that on my own," she said.

"Okay, then. Just what do you want?"

What leaped into her mind in that very moment was so far from acceptable, it wasn't even funny. Mouth dry, she had to fight the urge to clear her throat and she almost found herself backing away, but wasn't that stupid? She was the one who'd walked over to him to begin with. Something hungry and hot moved through her. It left her muscles feeling all limp and lax and she had to lock her knees to stay upright.

"Well?"

She blinked. Dragging her eyes from his, she focused on the simple, dark blue cotton of the polo he'd pulled on. She could still see the lines of the owl on him, never mind the shirt. No common tribal tattoo on him. Nope, he'd gone for something different—she could picture the way the wings stretched out across his body, the intricate detail of the feathers, the fierceness on the owl's face, claws opened and extended. All of it done on a body a hell of lot more nicely muscled than she would have expected.

"Glad we cleared all that up," Zane said, his voice wry, thick with deprecation. "Look, I'm tired and—"

She reached out, laid a hand on his chest.

He stopped talking and the muscles in his body went taut. His eyes flashed and she lifted her head, stared at him. He watched her and her heart lurched up into her throat as their gazes met.

Slowly, she lifted her other hand up. Her fingers twisted in the sturdy material of his polo, and through it, she could feel the heat of his body.

"Keelie," he said quietly, reaching down to close his hands over her wrists.

She felt her pulse accelerate at his touch. Her breath lodged in her throat and she had to force herself to breathe.

Don't do this. This isn't smart—

She was tired of being smart, though. So tired of being careful and shutting herself down.

Just once . . .

With her heart drumming in her ears, his hands gripping her wrists, she leaned in and kissed him.

Her heart stuttered as her mouth touched his, driven by memories of those few stolen moments, a kiss that still burned through her memories, drawn by emotions she didn't entirely understand.

His mouth was firm under hers and he tasted like coffee, like sin, and she wanted to wrap her body around him and never let go.

Zane hadn't moved, not even a little.

But she wasn't stopping . . . not yet. Not when her heart was racing like this.

The only time she'd ever felt like this had been the night of Zach's wedding, when Zane had kissed her.

Before that, the only other time she'd come close had been when she had a really good vibrator, and she'd finished reading a really dirty book. Then she could *almost* get this hot. Almost.

She eased in closer, nipped his lower lip.

Zane groaned against her mouth, the sound ragged and low.

Startled, she pulled her head back, but before she'd even moved an inch, he cupped her head and pulled her toward him. "Open your mouth," he muttered, and then he sweetened that request, nibbling along her lower lip and flicking at the entrance of her mouth with his tongue. "Open for me, Keelie . . ."

She opened on a shuddering sigh and then gasped as the room spun around her. The unfinished brick wall was rough against her back, but that just added another level of sensation. Zane had his mouth on hers and then he angled her head back and she opened for him, and when he pushed his tongue inside her mouth, she thought she just might die.

Except the pleasure didn't stop there.

He rested one hand on her hip and dragged her lower body in closer to his.

Against her belly, she felt the hard, firm pressure of his cock and against her thighs, she felt the solid length of muscle and it wasn't enough.

Nowhere near.

She was burning for him, dying for him.

Cool, strong hands, just a little callused and just a little hesitant, slid under his shirt, and as Keelie stroked her palms up his back, Zane was almost positive he had died. At some point during the night, he'd just died and now he was experiencing the closest thing to heaven he'd ever know.

Or maybe it was just a dream.

Her teeth raked over his lip and he shuddered, tearing away from her to press his face against her neck.

"Zane . . ."

He squeezed his eyes closed.

Slow.

He needed to slow the hell down.

His cock gave an insistent jerk. *Slow down? No. I don't think so.*

But Zane wasn't going to be led around by his dick. The last time he'd let his dick—and his emotions—totally control the situation, Keelie had used that as an excuse to widen the distance between them, and he'd be damned if he gave her that chance now. That chasm would turn into the Grand Canyon and he was struggling to close the distance as it was.

Keelie's fingers slid higher along his spine, her touch cool on his skin, the slightly rough calluses a sensation more erotic than anything he could have described.

"Zane?"

He lifted his head, saw the expression in her eyes. Doubt, need. The doubt . . . fuck, he'd have to figure out how to handle that. The need . . . that would lay him low.

Lowering his mouth to Keelie's, he caught her lower lip between his teeth. Tugged. "Open," he said against her lips.

Slow, he told himself again, practically screaming it. Bracing one fisted hand against the wall, he covered her mouth with his own, shuddered as she arched against him. Sensation raced through him from head to toe as she sucked lightly at his tongue.

He nudged her thighs wide, settled more firmly against her.

A tremor rippled through her body, the long slim body he held against his own. Zane fought the urge to pull away and tear every last shred of her clothes away from her.

Instead, he slid one hand under the hem of the skimpy red thing she probably called a sweater and felt the smooth silk of her skin against his palm. She shivered a little as he stroked higher and when he pulled back, she made a disappointed sound against his lips.

Lifting his head, he looked down at her, absently reaching up to nudge his glasses into place. Then he cupped her cheek in his hand. Her lashes drooped low, shielding her gaze.

"What are we doing?" he asked, his voice gruff.

Does it matter? Get back to doing it.

The problem was, it mattered way too much.

That slow flush crept up her neck and, now, standing this close to her, he could see that it started down low—if he had to make a bet, he'd imagine it started on the delicate slopes of her breasts and crept its way up. He wanted to have her naked in front of him so he could see that blush pink her breasts, her neck, right before he kissed her again.

For a moment, he didn't think she'd answer and then she angled her chin up, met his eyes dead-on with that cocky attitude she so often showed everybody.

"Isn't it kind of obvious?"

He pressed his thumb to the wide, soft curve of her lower lip.

Eyes on that curve, he said, "So . . . what? You here looking for a quick fuck, Keelie?"

She jerked, tried to pull away.

He didn't let her, leaning his weight more heavily against her although he knew full well he might be tasting his balls, bloody and broken, in his throat in a moment.

"Back off," she bit off.

"No." He dipped his head, rubbed his lips against hers, and when she averted her head, he skimmed them along her neck. "I'm just trying to see the picture that's so obvious for you. I mean, I've been trying to get you to go out with me for . . . hell, three years now, if I remember right."

Three years. Eight months. Two weeks? Not that he was counting, really.

When she did nothing, said nothing, just watched him with those inscrutable eyes of blue and brown, he leaned in and buried his face against her hair. Black and white again, the chunks of black framing her face.

"What's this obvious thing I'm missing, Keelie?" he asked.

Then his eyes just about crossed, because instead of outright answering, she twined long, long legs around him and arched, pressing the heat of her sex against him, and rocked. "This . . ." That pink flush rode her cheeks, hotter now, brighter, while her eyes practically glittered at him. "This. Isn't it obvious what's going on?"

Zane couldn't help it. He caught her hips in his hands, his fingers digging into the curve of her ass as he leaned into her and rocked against her, hard, fast. Once, twice.

She shuddered and met him. And when he stopped, she whimpered.

He slid a hand up, closed it over her throat. The mad beat of her pulse against his palm drove him insane. He wanted to cover that fragile bit of skin with his mouth and bite down, suck on her skin until she shivered and whispered his name.

Instead, he said, "There are a lot of names for what this is. A quick fuck, like I mentioned. Keelie, that's easy, and either one of us can get it anywhere. I'll be honest . . . that's not what I want from you."

She stiffened in his arms, the long, strong legs she'd wrapped around him easing down until she was standing on her feet before him. He already missed the solid warmth of her weight.

Her voice, when it came, was hard and flat. "Fine."

Humiliation burned in her.

Rejection turned her blood to ice while her skin shrank down about two sizes too small.

She wanted to sink into the floorboards, turn into something thin and vaporous so she could just disappear.

Pushing against his chest, she focused on the navy blue polo. "Then how about you let me go, huh? My mistake."

The hand on her throat didn't move.

It should have felt threatening.

But the feel of him touching her just made her melt that much more . . . and it was now a heavy ache inside because he—

His lips brushed her ear.

"You want to know what I want from you?" he asked, the words velvet, stroking over her like a caress.

Keelie closed her hands into fists to keep from reaching for him. He was messing with her. It pissed her off—and, to her disgust, it hurt. It almost felt like a betrayal, too, because she hadn't expected to see this in Zane.

"Back off," she warned, putting an edge into her voice and preparing herself to *make* him back off. So what if he had some moves on him? He hadn't seen *her* moves yet. Not really.

"I want . . ." He slid his hand down from her throat, to rest on her chest, fingers spread wide where it rested above her heart. "This."

The simplicity of the gesture stunned her into passivity.

She held still as he lifted his head and stared down at her.

She blinked, not moving, as he continued to stand there, his hand on her chest. "I want five minutes of your time . . . over a cup of coffee. An hour for lunch. I want you to pick up the phone when I call, talk with me for a while," he said, staring into her eyes while the blue green of his gaze cut into her.

Then he leaned in and pressed a hot, open-mouthed kiss to her chest, just above the neckline of her sweater. "I want to peel your clothes away, learn each and every one of these insanely sexy tattoos . . . and the reason behind them. I want to know what makes you laugh, and I want to know what makes you mad. I want to know what sort of book you're reading whenever I'm in the office—I've asked, but you always toss it down when I walk by and you never answer me."

His breath was a caress on her flesh and she broke out into goose bumps.

Her heart raced and she couldn't even begin to understand why there was a knot in her chest.

Then he lifted his head and caught her skull between his hands, leaning in to lightly brush his lips over hers. "You see, Keelie . . . I want a lot more than a quick fuck from you. But every time I try to get even five minutes of your time," he murmured, each word low and raw, "you pull away. The one time you actually *did* talk to me? That was three months ago. At the wedding. You gave me five minutes and then I put my hands on you and since then, you've run even harder, even faster. So maybe you can understand why I'm a little leery about just what is going on here."

Quick as a wish, he was gone, standing five feet away,

and she slumped against the wall, her knees weak as she stared at him.

Her heart lurched, lunged inside her chest, and the voice of common sense told her one very simple message.

Time to go.

Except everything *else* compelled her to stay.

He leaned one shoulder against the wall, his face in shadow, those surreal blue green eyes a wicked, hungry glitter in the dim light. "So, can I ask again or are you just going to leave? What exactly is going on here?"

"Are you *trying* to piss me off?" she snarled, coming off the wall. She was achy and hungry, confused and cold. Her hands itched to reach for him and at the same time, she thought the easiest thing—the *smart* thing—to do would be to just leave.

"No." He blinked and when he looked back at her, his eyes were once more unreadable behind those horn-rimmed glasses. "But then again, sometimes, Keelie, you're really easy to piss off and you probably know that."

She curled her lip.

Zane smirked.

"The bottom line is this . . . if you want casual sex, I'm not where you need to look." Zane said it bluntly and his eyes held her as he spoke, the words so matter-of-fact, it was like he had this conversation every day of the week.

Casual sex? She wanted to break out into hysterical laughter. She kept it locked inside by curling one hand into a fist so tight, her nails bit into her palm.

He shoved off the wall and paced closer and her pulse hammered back into that dangerously fast territory as she held his gaze. "Even if I hadn't kind of outgrown that a while back, I'm not going to sleep with somebody who works with my brother. Who is friends with my brothers . . . who I kind of consider a friend myself. Things get . . . messy there. Especially when I'm already too damned attracted anyway."

Her breath caught.

His eyes dropped, lingered on her mouth.

"But you also keep giving me this idea that I'm not worth your time, either," he mused. "It's getting really confusing, Keelie."

He reached out.

She caught his wrist.

Against her fingers, she could feel the slow, steady rhythm of his pulse.

Five minutes of your time.

Those words spun around in her head as she stared into his eyes. She had a bad, bad feeling she was in over her head here.

Licking her lips, she stared at him, uncertain what to say, what to do.

Leave. Think it through. Or don't. Just don't say anything and don't talk to him and he'll get the point. You'll be nice and safe—

She shut that babbling voice up through sheer will alone.

She was so tired of being *nice and safe*. It was so lonely.

But she didn't know what to do.

His lids drooped, shoulders rising and falling on a sigh— something about it sounded despondent, almost like she'd felt inside when he pulled away from her only minutes ago.

He tugged on his wrist. "It's cool, Keelie. Why don't you—"

"There's a coffee shop," she blurted out, still gripping his wrist, tightening her fingers until he'd have to force it if he wanted her to let go.

His eyes widened, then narrowed on hers.

A knot swelled, then lodged in her throat, and she had to force the words past it. "Across from the shop. There's this place. They have coffee."

He cocked his head and, if she wasn't mistaken, some of the tension seemed to drain out of his body and then, without her quite realizing how he'd done it, he twisted his wrist and freed it. She froze as he reached up to cup her cheek, his thumb pressing to her lower lip. "What about this place that serves coffee, Keelie?"

"I was thinking about going there. Tomorrow." No. She

hadn't been. But she wasn't sure what else to do, what else to say. "Maybe you could meet me there."

For the longest time, Zane thought maybe he'd forgotten how to breathe. He also thought maybe he was having an auditory hallucination. Brought on by lust, lack of sleep, lack of decent food—or maybe botulism. Had that ravioli been tainted and he was sick and just didn't realize it? *That* would explain why he was hearing what he thought he'd just heard.

Easing in closer, he narrowed his eyes.

On the off chance he *hadn't* made this up, he said, "So, this place. You want me to meet you there. For coffee."

"Yeah." She angled her chin up.

It made him want to bite her, kiss her, hug her, cuddle her. That cocky, almost brash exterior . . . what did it hide, he wondered? Sweeping his thumb across her mouth, he murmured, "And just why are we meeting for coffee? You just like caffeine?"

"If you're going to be an asshole," she started.

He cut the rest of her words off with his mouth.

She'd answered his question. He'd just wanted a chance. Now, taking advantage of her already parted lips, he slanted his head and licked the inside of her mouth, sliding one hand up to cup her cheek, angling her head back.

With his other hand, he cupped her hip. Only her hip, because it would be so very easy to try for more.

Everything inside him pushed for that.

But he wasn't going to rush this.

Not this, of all things.

He slid his tongue along hers, growled when she caught him and sucked him just a little. Dark, dirty little thoughts raced through him as he imagined her doing that to his cock. His fingers tightened on her hip and she swayed, leaning closer.

The sound of her moan pierced the fog and he forced himself to end the kiss, bit by bit. His heart was racing when it was done and his muscles were tight with the urge to grab, take . . . *keep*.

Swallowing, he reached for some level of control. His voice was only the slightest bit rough when he said, "So. Coffee. What time?"

Personally, he wouldn't be opposed to her just being there when he woke up. They could wake up together, go for coffee later . . . but that wasn't the way to go and he knew it. Still, it was a sweet, sweet fantasy.

"I have to be in at noon. So I guess a quarter after eleven." Her face was flushed. Her eyes glittered.

One day, he thought.

One day, he'd get her in front of a camera—and every last picture would be just for him. He wanted to capture this look on her face, that slow, sleepy hunger and that glint of lingering . . . temper? Frustration? He couldn't quite name it, but it just added to everything that was her, everything that drove him crazy.

"Quarter after eleven." He went to uncurl his hands, let her go. He'd walk her down to her car. Come back up here. Pace until the heat in his blood cooled.

But even as he tried to coax his hands into letting her go, she reached up, traced the rim of his glasses. "Just how well can you see without these?" she asked.

That glint in her eyes made him leery.

Sliding his hand from her cheek down, he gripped her narrow hips in both hands, studied her. "I can't," he finally said, shrugging.

"You can't?" she asked, lifting a brow.

"Well, if whatever I'm looking at is about a foot in front my face, then yeah, I can see it. If I squint. Farther than that? It's blurs, lights, blobs." He shrugged. "So, basically . . . without them, I can't see."

A slow smiled tugged at her lips as she reached up, slid them off. "Guess it's a good thing we're in here, huh?"

Automatically, he squinted, barely managed to focus on her face. And then he didn't even bother as her lips slid against his.

Warning . . . warning . . .
She kissed him, light and soft.
Then she made her way over to his ear.

She didn't know what drove her.

Maybe it was the weight that still rested in her chest, that burn of rejection, or the knot in her throat.

Or maybe it was the look in his eyes when he'd seemed to think she was pushing him away.

She wasn't good at this.

She'd spent too much of her life hiding . . . from everything. From people, from friends, from emotion. It was just easier not to really let herself feel. The perfect example was what had happened with Zach—she'd thought she felt something real there, and not only had she been wrong, she'd hurt him, and she'd hurt Abby.

Emotions were just too messy and she didn't understand them.

But she needed to give him something.

At the same time, she wasn't ready for anything else.

She rubbed her nose along the column of his throat, the scent of him flooding her head, making her knees feel just a little weak.

Rising up on her toes, she pressed her lips to his ear.

"The last time I had a quick fuck . . ." She drew the word out, felt him shudder against her as she traced her hand down his chest. "The last time I had what could even be called *casual sex* was . . ." She bit his ear, the way he'd done to her earlier, and then continued. "It was . . . well. Never."

Then, before he could respond, she backed away, fast. She put his glasses down on the far end of the counter and headed off. "See you in the morning."

She heard him mutter something behind her as she opened the door.

Then she heard him shout her name, a clatter, then a curse. Grimacing, she glanced back, but kept on going.

She was too nervous, too uncertain to handle anything else tonight.

If this was taking the coward's way out?

Well, okay then.

She was a coward.

She hit the Down button, staring at the door, waiting for Zane to come out.

He didn't and when she slid out of the building a minute later, she told herself the funny ache in her chest wasn't disappointment. She really, *really* wasn't up to handling any in-depth discussions, and her very limited sex life was one of those.

But still . . .

She heard her name coming from overhead.

Wincing, she glanced up.

The feel her of her hand on his chest, her breath ghosting along his neck, did a very good job of fuzzing his brain and making him forget that glint in her eyes.

Then she closed her teeth around his ear and Zane pretty much surrendered the idea of even *trying* to think.

Until she whispered in his ear.

The words bounced around.

The loss of her body pressed to his was a visceral one and he reached out, but she was already gone.

He saw the blur of movement, scowled, even those words finally connected in his brain.

The last time I had a quick fuck, the last time I had what could even be called casual sex was . . . It was . . . well. Never.

Son of a bitch. He lunged forward, determined to . . . to what?

He didn't know the answer to that, but she wasn't dropping that on him and then just disappearing.

But even as that thought processed, he crashed into a barstool, sent it slamming.

"Damn it!" He slid his hand blindly along the counter,

searching for his glasses. Five seconds. If he didn't find them in five seconds, he was grabbing his spare pair—*bingo*.

He jammed them on his face, mentally calculated the time. She was already out the door.

He hit the window in the bedroom and jerked it open.

There she was.

"Keelie!"

She glanced up at him. The loft was on the top floor, but the building wasn't a tall one. He was only four floors up and could see her face just fine. A faint smile danced on her lips, but he couldn't quite read that smile. "You are a brat," he finally said, uncertain what to say besides that.

Now that smile widened. "Please don't tell me you're just now figuring that out, Zane."

Then she waved and opened the door of the car. "See you in the morning, Z."

He clenched his hand on the window sill while hunger burned, his cock pulsed, and his mind raced.

And despite all of that, he found himself smiling.

It had taken three damn years, but tomorrow, he was having coffee with Keelie Jessup.

Chapter Five

Keelie fell into bed a little after one.

She was up by seven, went for a run, came back, and spent more than forty minutes in the postage stamp–sized box that was laughingly called a bathroom by her landlord.

She liked her landlord.

His name was Bob and unlike the previous owner of these squat, boxlike apartments, he actually listened when the tenants had complaints or problems, and he did what he could to fix things.

But he couldn't do anything about the size of the bathroom.

The only thing she could do was move.

Keelie wasn't moving.

She showered, scrubbed, plucked, waxed, and when all of that was done, she stood in front of the small square that served as a mirror. With a scowl on her face, she leaned in and studied herself.

"It's coffee," she said bluntly.

I want five minutes of your time . . .

The ghost of his voice, so soft and deep, stroked over her skin.

No. It was a lot more than coffee and she knew it. Which could explain why she'd spent forty-seven minutes in the bathroom primping. She hadn't done any of that for the blind date with—gag—Hawk. And she wasn't even done.

She'd hauled out her makeup. Not the everyday stuff that she put on just for work, but the kind she'd bought as an indulgence and rarely wore.

A bottle of perfume she'd picked up waited on the counter.

She was already mentally debating just what she should wear that would look good without coming across as too much, considering she had a day of work ahead of her.

"It's coffee," she muttered again, feeling stupid.

But it wasn't *just*.

She was giving him five minutes—and then some, and she wasn't going into it with her guard up and plans for the entire thing to go absolutely nowhere. She'd already dropped her guard, jumped on it with spiked boots until what remained lay in tiny little pieces on the floor—that had happened when she leaned in and whispered a soft, personal secret in his ear.

She'd let him in.

Keelie didn't let *anybody* in.

She hadn't ever opened those doors to anybody . . . not Anais, not Javi, not Zach.

She hadn't let anybody in in so long, she wasn't sure if she'd even remember how. Except she'd done it.

Blowing out a breath, she studied the solemn-eyed woman in the mirror and then, before she could change her mind, she reached for the makeup kit.

This was, after all, a little more than coffee.

Before she'd managed to unzip the metallic blue bag, the landline rang.

Frowning, she put the bag down and moved out into the narrow hallway, eying the phone on the end table.

That phone might ring once or twice a month, and more often than not, the calls were telemarketers. She ended those calls by putting the handset on top of the nearby radio and blasting the speakers. She was on a *Do Not Call* list for a reason.

She didn't give out the landline number. Period. Everybody, and she meant everybody, had the cellphone.

The caller ID display read *Private Caller*.

She grabbed it, hit the Power button for her radio, already prepared to blast away the sales pitch.

"Yeah?"

There was no answer.

Scowling, she lowered it, eyed it, then put it back up to her ear. "Hello?"

With no response yet again, she disconnected.

She really would have preferred to hear a telemarketer over that dead air.

Two hours later, with the call shoved to the back of her mind, she left the house.

She'd donned a modified version of what she considered her "work" uniform.

Zach and the other artists, all guys, wore short-sleeved T-shirts and jeans. Sometimes Javi mixed it up with bowling shirts worn open over a T-shirt.

At times Keelie went for the same, but more often than not, she veered toward a more punkish look. Yeah, she was conservative with it and it wasn't particularly her *personal* style, especially outside of work, but it suited her when she was at the shop, especially when it came to highlighting her tattoos. And since tattoos were her bread and butter, it all worked out fine.

Plus, she liked the image she made when she pulled on a fishnet top over a skintight tank—or if she was really feeling moody, she'd just pair that fishnet with a bra and her jeans. The motorcycle boots were pretty much her ideal footwear, comfortable to walk in, easy to move in, and paired well with whatever else she decided to wear. All of that was part of the reason she'd agreed to let Anais do the piercing about two months back. She'd never really thought about it before, but Anais had told her it wouldn't be a bad idea to showcase her work, and none of the guys had been open to it, so why not?

And she didn't mind at all how the little hoop looked.

Today, she'd worn her boots with black-and-white striped tights and a denim mini. She wore skirts to work; it wasn't a big deal. Instead of one of her fishnet tops, she'd pulled out a lacy one. The lace skimmed her curves, gloved her arms all the way to her wrists. The burnout pattern let her tattoos peek through and she'd pulled on a tank to wear under it. It wasn't that different from what she usually wore, and perfectly fine to wear for . . . coffee.

"Coffee." She licked her lips as she opened the door of her car, but even as she went to climb in, she heard a child's wail. Her spine went stiff and then fury punched as that girl's cry was drowned out by a woman's bellow.

"Annie, shut the fuck up! I'm tired—"

Curling her hand into a fist, she turned her head, stared at the neighbor's house.

A few months ago, a young married couple, Tara and Nolan, had moved in.

They had two little girls. Annie and Megan. Megan was barely over a year, toddling around on sturdy little legs, too often in dirty clothes with a diaper that needed changing desperately. Annie was two years older, with long, tangled curls and she was more prone to hide than anything else.

And right now, she was crying.

As another angry shout rose from the house, Keelie checked the driveway.

Then she breathed out a sigh of relief. The busted-up green Chevy truck was there. So Nolan was home.

A moment later, she heard him, his voice a low murmur compared to his wife's angry shout.

"Don't you tell me to shut up!" Tara raged.

More words from Nolan, too quiet to be heard, and then their door busted open. "Why don't you go fuck yourself, Nolan? You think it's so easy? Why don't you stay here with them then?"

Tara came stumbling out in a pair of fleece pajama pants and a tank top, her feet bare. Her eyes shot to Keelie and then away as she headed off to the car.

She was inside a moment later, gone before Keelie could manage to loosen the fist she'd made.

She looked back at the apartment, saw Nolan standing there.

He held Annie in one arm, rocking her.

But he wouldn't look at Keelie.

He'd stopped being able to look people in the face a long time ago.

It wasn't really weird that Zane got to the coffee shop a good thirty minutes early. Not really. Not in his opinion.

He had things to do while he was in town, after all, and later this evening, he was meeting up with Zach to check out a few places. No reason why he couldn't start scoping out some sites on his own, right?

Nope.

No reason at all.

Of course, all of that would be more plausible if he actually spent a little more time bent over the classified ads instead of staring out the window toward Steel Ink.

He didn't let any of that get in the way.

He had an obsession.

He knew it.

He worked with it.

He and this obsession, they'd settled into a comfortable fit. It had been three years, after all. He was more comfortable with his obsession over Keelie than Zach had been with Abby, after all. That was what he told himself.

He hadn't even spent the past decade-plus dealing with it, letting a million chances slide by.

Never let it be said that the competitive thing was something that brothers outgrew.

As a truck drove by, cutting off his view of the tattoo studio, he blew out a breath and focused once more on the paper in front of him. He actually *had* managed to skim a column or two, nixing everything he saw with the exception of one.

He knew from experience how much room he was going to need and he'd already drawn up a business plan. Most of the ads were for properties either way too big, way too small, or way out of his price range. But there was one that had the right amount of floor space and the price wasn't too bad. Now the question was how did it look and where was it?

He circled that one ad, moved to the next column, glanced up at the street.

Get a grip, he told himself, forcing his gaze back down to the paper.

Then he looked to his watch. Eight 'til. He still had twenty-three minutes. He needed more than a grip. He needed to punch himself.

It took every last bit of his mental focus, but he managed to plow through another column and he found a second location to check out. It was on the high end of what he could afford, but he'd look. Just in case.

The bell over the door jangled, but he set his jaw. He'd just checked his watch. It was only three minutes after. Still had a few more—

"You're already drinking your coffee."

He lowered the pen. Slowly, he looked up, and he managed not to swallow his tongue as his gaze caught, then hung, on a pair of striped tights that curved over endless legs. The skirt probably wasn't indecent—not really. It was just those legs of hers, so damn long.

And if he kept staring, he was likely to start this off wrong.

Instead of letting himself drool over the black lace, the pale skin he could see gleaming through, he met Keelie's eyes.

"I have a confession to make," he said as she dropped into the seat across from his. "I'm compulsively early for almost everything and I can't smell coffee without bolting back a cup almost immediately."

"Hmmm." She lifted a brow and then leaned in, eying his cup. "You're not done bolting."

"Yeah, well." He took the cup, drained it, and put it down. "That's not my first cup, either."

"Really?" Now she smiled and he wanted to die a little. She'd slicked her mouth with a color that hovered between red and purple and he wanted to cover that wide, mobile mouth, taste her, kiss her until she couldn't breathe and then start all over again. "So just how early did you get here?"

He made a show of checking his watch, calculating the time. "Maybe a little before ten thirty." An hour early.

"That compulsive, huh?"

He shrugged. "I've got business in town anyway and I needed to read the paper." He tapped his hand on the one spread out in front of him. "I had to leave the loft to find a paper."

"Yes. You would have to leave the loft . . . even when Zach lived there, I doubted he had a regular paper delivery."

Zane flashed her a grin. "Zach wouldn't know what a regular paper delivery was."

"Bullshit." She shrugged and glanced around. "He gets the paper delivered to the shop. He loves the comics."

"Point taken." He stood up, gestured to the counter. "I'm empty. And we're meeting for coffee. What do you drink?"

"Black. Just black." She glanced up at him, a quick smile on her face, then looked down.

The tattoo on the curve of her neck, that large, exotic rose stood out in stark relief against the soft, pale cream of her skin and he wanted to bend down, press his mouth to her, right there, where the petals were forever frozen just before bursting into full bloom.

Slowly, she shifted her gaze to him, studying him.

Coffee.

Right.

Why in the hell had he said he wanted five minutes for a cup of coffee?

As he turned away, Keelie blew out a breath. Absently, she reached up to touch the rose inked onto her neck before focusing on the paper in front of her. The words blurred and ran together in front of her, but that was okay.

If she was staring at the paper, she wasn't staring at Zane.

She'd stood outside on the sidewalk a good two minutes doing nothing but that before she'd come inside.

He'd been completely focused on what he was doing, that was for certain.

From the corner of her eye, she shot him a glance.

Her breath caught as she saw him looking at her.

Nerves jangled in her belly and she tried to figure out just what she was supposed to do. Smile? Nothing?

But he turned away before she could figure it out. That was a relief.

This is stupid. Brooding, she stared at the paper, eyes catching on one ad, circled in red. Why was she nervous, really? It wasn't like she and Zane had to go through that stupid *get to know you* stage.

They did know each other.

He was a photographer, worked in a bar.

Although she had no idea why he did the bar thing, considering the pictures he took. She wasn't too into photography, but she haunted the blog he updated irregularly and she'd actually joined Instagram *only* because he was on there. He had thousands of followers, too. Like ten thousand–plus, if not more. He'd had pictures featured by major media outlets and she'd had her breath knocked out of her more than once just by staring at the images he'd taken.

With that kind of talent, she didn't know why he didn't live behind his camera.

"Here you go."

He put a cup in front of her and she looked up, caught off guard.

Blue green eyes studied her thoughtfully as she took the coffee, lifted the lid to let steam escape. "You look like you're thinking hard."

She shrugged, not about to tell him she was brooding about how weird this all felt, or that she didn't understand why he spent time mixing drinks when he ought to be out trotting the globe and amazing people with the images he captured with his camera.

"Decided you're not in the mood for coffee after all?"

There was a weird edge to his voice and she slowly lifted her eyes, met his. Normally, she couldn't read a damn thing when it came to Zane, but just then, she thought maybe she saw something in the back of his eyes—something that might have echoed the nerves she felt.

Slowly, she lowered the coffee and leaned forward. Hooking one leg around the leg of her chair, she chewed on her lower lip, tried to figure out what to say, how to say it.

Keelie didn't know how to do this. She was blunt. She was very often a bitch and she didn't know, or care to learn, all the subtle ins and outs of conversation that so many people used. She'd seen subtext and polite conversation used to hide some of the ugliest of lies and that was when she'd stopped trying to be felicitous.

It was easier to just not say anything . . . or to say what she felt.

It had taken her a very long time to get to the point to where she could start speaking plainly about her feelings. Silence had been easier.

But silence wasn't going to cut it here.

"This feels . . ." She ran her tongue around her teeth, decided that *maybe* she should take a little bit of care with her words. *Stupid* wasn't going to win her any points here. "It feels weird, sitting here like this."

"Yeah?" He slumped in his chair, gaze locked on her. He looked relaxed, calm.

She knew he was anything but.

"Why is that?" he asked softly.

"Because this is like . . ." She rolled her eyes and looked around. "It's basically a date. Right?"

Now a grin tugged at his lips. "If we have to label it as something, I guess so. But I really wish you would have let me make our first date something a little better than a cup of coffee, Keelie."

Blood rushed up, heating her face. She suspected that if she looked in the mirror, she'd be glowing pink just then. "Stop," she said, narrowing her eyes. Then she shrugged. "That's the thing. It's a date. A first date. And we're in a coffee shop and I don't know what to say. It's like . . ."

She paused, chewed on her lip. "On first dates, people spend half the time trying to get to know the other person or maybe decide if they even *want* to."

"And in some cases, they kick their date in the head." He tipped the coffee cup he held in her direction. "I hope this date ends better than your last one did."

She made a face at him. "I think we're safe there. But here's the thing. We already know each other. So what do we talk about?"

"Well. We know some things." He put the coffee down and leaned forward.

Another stupid thing—why did her pulse have to sky-rocket like that when all he did was close his fingers around her hands and lift them up? Maybe the kiss he brushed against the back of her right hand could explain the skip in her pulse, but just him touching her?

"We know some things," he said again, his gaze on her hands, his thumb rubbing back against her skin. "That doesn't mean there's not a lot left to learn."

Maybe that was why she was nervous. If they got to know each other, didn't that mean she'd have to figure out if she'd ever talk about . . . her brain shied away from the secrets, the subterfuge, the shadows that made up too much of her.

His lips brushed over her knuckles. She looked up, met his eyes.

Felt the air in her lungs die.
The way he watched her . . .

If she kept looking at him like that, it was going to
cause problems, Zane decided. They were in the middle of
a coffee shop. Not the ideal place for him to knock the table
out of the way, pull her into his lap, and figure out how to
peel those sexy, striped tights away without letting her go
once he had her in his arms.

Since that wasn't really an option, he folded the paper
and tucked it to the side, taking his time with that mundane
task just so he'd have a few more seconds to level out before
he looked at her again.

"See, there's the thing . . . we've known each other for
three years, but like I said, I don't know things I want to
know." He shot her a look.

"Like what?" She looked wary now.

"Well, the books, for one. You're always reading. What
do you like to read?"

Her eyes narrowed. "Romance."

He scratched his jaw. "Okay."

"What . . . no comments?"

"Keelie, have you met my mother?"

She blinked. "Well. Yeah. Half a dozen times, easy."

"Thought so." He nodded and leaned forward. "Up until
ebook readers came out? She'd carried a giant purse just so
she could have two books in her bag with her. All the time.
They were always romance. Now, maybe I'd think it was
silly . . ."

That glint appeared in her eyes.

He grinned at her. "Hey, I said *maybe I'd think*—that's
past tense. Maybe I'd *think* it was silly, but I'm smart. Unlike Zach." He winked at her, watched as she settled back in
the chair, some of the tension fading from her body, a
smile flirting with her lips. "Now Zach had his fun poking
at those books. Not when she was around. Or at least, he
thought she wasn't. He was sixteen, had a couple of friends

over. He started poking at the books, had one of them and was reading it aloud. Mom walked in just as one of his friends grabbed a pillow and started to kiss it. Because, yeah, romance, pillows, and kissing just go together."

Keelie snorted.

"Hey, we're talking teenage boys. We don't always think in ways of logic. So she's standing there and the boys stopped laughing, Zach looks like he was caught with his hand in the candy jar while his friend dropped the pillow, looked back, saw Mom. I'm leaning against the wall at this point, enjoying my front row seat. Mom just picked up her book, tapped it against her hand as she looked at him, then the rest of them. She just shook her head and walked out. Dad was right behind her and he gave them all the saddest look before he said, *Boys, I'm going to save you a lot of trouble. If you want to make a girl mad . . . insult what she reads.*"

Zane rubbed his finger along the table, eying the business cards and bits of art tucked under the protective sheet glass. "Now the boy who'd been kissing the pillow? He started to laugh, then he said, *Like I'm ever going to go out with a girl desperate enough to need romance books.*"

"Oops." Keelie pursed her lips.

"Yeah. That pissed me off. Zach started yelling at him. My dad, though, he just laughed. Told him if he thought my mother read them because she was desperate, then he was welcome to keep on thinking that. My mom graduated at the top of her class from UC Berkeley. She planned on being a lawyer—then she met my dad and fell in love with him. She had me, and she said from then on, the only thing she wanted was to be with us. But she's a smart woman, could have done just about anything she wanted. Probably could have had anything she wanted." He paused, and the smile that softened his face tugged at everything in her. "I guess she did have what she wanted, after all . . . she wanted us. To raise a family. That makes us pretty lucky. Anyway, she reads romance because she enjoys it—anybody who wants to challenge her on that? They do it at their own peril."

"I didn't know your mom went to Berkeley." The words were soft, spoken to the coffee cup she held in her hands. Then she glanced up, shrugged. "I read a lot of stuff, but I like romance and urban fantasy the best. The bad guy gets his, you get a happy ending. There's not enough of that in life. Why not find it in a book?"

He had a feeling there was a wealth of meaning in those words. But he didn't push. Instead, he just leaned forward, still holding her eyes. "So . . . we've covered books. We've had five minutes . . . and then some . . . for coffee. There were a few other things I said I wanted last night."

His gaze dropped to her mouth.

And just like that, she felt her heart start to race. He was evil. He was also a hazard to the female species—why hadn't she realized that about him already?

Grabbing her coffee, she took a sip and then another. "You said a lot of things. You didn't ever say what you like to read, though."

He didn't answer.

"Well?" She shot him a look.

"You never asked."

"You're impossible," she said, shaking her head. "What do you like to read?"

"See," he said, a smile spreading across his normally serious face. "This is how we get to know each other. I ask questions. You ask questions. We maybe talk about another date."

She rolled her eyes.

"Books." He braced his elbows on the edge of the table and leaned forward, pretending to ponder the question. "I like urban fantasy a lot. Dark fantasy. Mysteries, suspense . . ."

Then he paused and shot her a wicked grin. "And my mom got me hooked on this one series. Fed me this line about how they were futuristic police procedurals. I got into them because the cop in them was hot."

Keelie started to laugh. "She's got you reading Nora Roberts, doesn't she?"

"Absolutely not." He waited a beat. "It's J. D. Robb. There is a difference, you know."

"Your brothers know you read romance?" She couldn't stop the smirk from spreading over her face as she studied him.

"Look in Zach's desk sometime. He used to have one of them tucked inside."

"No way," she said, gaping at him.

"So far, she's hooked everybody but Seb." He shrugged. "Seb never was much for reading. Says he spends too much time reading scripts anyway and that's pretty much the same thing."

Keelie wrinkled her nose. "Seb probably can't handle reading anything that doesn't have *him* as the focus. The magazines, the interviews . . . movie scripts." Then she winced. "Shoot. I'm sorry. That's . . ."

She sighed and looked away. "I have no brain-to-mouth filter."

He was quiet for so long, she was almost afraid to look at him, but in the end, she made herself.

Zane was still watching her with that same faint smile, although the glint of amusement in his eyes had lessened a little. "I know my brothers, Keelie," he said with a sigh. "Trust me, I know them—and love them—flaws and all. Seb can be a shallow bastard. He isn't always, but . . . yeah. If the book doesn't focus on him or relate to the job? He's not likely to be interested."

"He doesn't have a focus outside of Hollywood, does he?" she asked softly.

Zane looked away, his gaze on something she couldn't see.

When he finally looked back at her, his expression was inscrutable. "Us." Then he shrugged. "He's got us, and that's more than a lot of people in that business can say, I guess. A lot of the people Zach and Abby knew growing up have already burned themselves out—they've already been to three funerals, and not one of them were over fifty. Seb's got solid ties and he's more grounded than he lets on, but he's definitely all about Hollywood."

Then, in a rapid-fire shift, he leaned in, stretching over the table that wasn't much bigger than a dinner plate. "We talked books. We did some of that *get to know you* stuff. Now, maybe we can do something else," he murmured in her ear.

Chills of sensation raced down her spine. Slowly, she turned her head, met his gaze. She went to speak and had to clear her throat before she could. "Okay. Sure."

He opened his mouth, but before he could ask, she fired off a question, all but breathless with it. "So what kind of business do you have in town?"

The nerves in her eyes were so clear, and so . . . *there*, he decided to let it slide. For now.

He eased back, gave her some space. "Looking for space." He shrugged and tapped the paper. "I quit my job. Going to give the photography thing a real go. Looking to set up here."

She blinked, her gaze blank.

He braced himself, uncertain what she might say. So far, he'd faced everything from cautious optimism to outright skepticism.

Keelie stared at him for a long moment and then a smile bowed her lips. "Well. It's about damn time."

The calm, easy confidence in those words hit him like a bolt. Straight to the chest. He sucked in a breath, kept it steady out of sheer force of will. "Hey, I figured I've screwed around long enough."

"You made the move on your own time." She shrugged, looking more at ease.

"That's how I roll." He watched as she toyed with the sleeve on her coffee cup. "Keelie?"

She shot him a look. "Yeah?"

This time, he didn't give her a chance to prepare. He closed the distance, caught her lower lip between his teeth. "I've asked about two hundred times, I figure. Maybe this time you'll say yes."

Say yes . . . she stared at him, blood rushing, all but humming in her veins. And her mouth burned from that teasing, not-quite-kiss.

He hadn't even asked and she was ready to say yes.

"You free for dinner tonight?"

A fist settled in her chest. She had to force the words out around it. "I think maybe we can do dinner."

"Good. Then I can do this."

Her heart started to stutter as he slowly, oh, so slowly, kissed her.

It absolutely wasn't the kind of kiss he should be doing in the middle of a coffee shop, she thought. Because it was the kind of kiss that made her want, made her *crave* so much more.

And then, all thought ceased and all she could do was curl as close to him as she could possibly get. It really wasn't close enough.

Twenty minutes later, she hoped she'd managed to plaster a calm look on her face as she walked with Zane into Steel Ink.

Javi glanced up and then he was on his feet, storming over to her.

"Are you okay? Why the hell didn't you call me? What the fuck happened—"

Knowing from experience those questions would just keep on coming, she stopped him with the most expedient means necessary. She clapped her hand over his mouth.

Dark brown eyes narrowed at her over her hand and she cocked a brow. "Let me answer a question before the next barrage starts," she suggested.

There was a familiar tread of boots and she glanced up, saw Zach in the doorway. His eyes had that guarded look, one she was too familiar with these days, but she tried not to let it bother her.

His gaze moved to Zane and she dropped her hand, focusing on Javi as Zach moved to greet his brother.

"I'm fine," she said, addressing Javi's first question. "I would have called, but there was a phone mess-up and I didn't have my phone and I couldn't remember your number. And to what happened . . ." She grimaced, her words trailing off.

That was when she noticed Zach's curious stare.

The tension that still lingered between them grew heavier. Maybe she'd just explain this all later—

"What's going on?" Zach asked softly.

Blowing out a sigh, she shrugged. "It's no big deal. Ani had me set up on a blind date and it kind of tanked. He was a jerk, tried to get physical."

Zach's brows dropped low over his eyes but before he could say anything, she held up her hands. "I handled it. Both of you know I'm pretty good at taking care of myself. But it wasn't even necessary." She jerked her thumb at Zane. "Clark Kent here showed up. Zach, how come you never told anybody that your brother was some kind of kung fu master or something?"

Zach crossed his arms over his chest. "Let's back the train up a little. I'm still trying to get past the *he got physical* part. Just what does that mean?"

"He put his hands on me." She jerked a shoulder in a shrug, recalled the bruising strength of the man. Everything else was a blur of adrenaline and lights and nerves as she'd slammed her booted foot into his head. She thought she might have smashed her elbow into his face—there was a bruise there so it was very likely.

Blowing out a breath, she said it again. "He got physical. He didn't like that I was blowing him off. Said I was too uptight and why couldn't I chill out and I told him to get out of my face and I'd chill out when I wanted to. So he grabbed my arm and I shoved him. He grabbed me again and I just . . ." She blinked, frowned. "I reacted. I don't even entirely remember what all happened. Then Zane was there, the guy was on the ground. I'm fine, okay?"

Zane placed his hand on her back, stroked up.

That light touch somehow managed to calm her frazzled nerves.

She would have liked to turn to him, press her lips to his neck. But even that was more than she felt comfortable with. She did stay there, enjoyed the warmth of that long-fingered, elegant hand on her back, his thumb stroking back and forth over her skin.

Zach shot Zane a look, a demanding one. *Tell me. Now.* That look said a lot even though he never opened his mouth.

"You heard what she said," Zane said, his voice level. "I'd swung by here yesterday. We bumped into each other, dropped our phones, mixed them up. I figured it out after she'd left, called her. Since she had plans, I said I'd swing by with the phone. I show up and hear her in the parking lot. Come up while the guy was coming at her." He finished with a shrug.

"Tell me you took him apart," Zach said, his voice tight.

"I handled it," Zane responded.

"Ugh." Keelie's groan was loud, full of irritation and disgust. "He's in the hospital, Zach, if that satisfies your manly need for violence. The guy had a knife on him, pulled it on Zane. And that's when I discovered your brother is like Superman or something."

Zane felt blood rush up the back of his neck as she shot Zach another sidelong look. "How come nobody ever let any of us know that Zane had a secret identity?"

A few taut seconds passed. Then Zach sighed and rubbed the back of his neck. "Hell. Z's the one who taught all of *us* how to fight. Everybody is so busy being fooled by the buttoned up shirts and the glasses, they just *think* he's the nice one." Zach speared Zane with a sharp look. "Sometimes I think he should have been the actor."

"No, thanks," Zane said, his voice dry. "You and Seb want to spend half your life strutting around like peacocks in front of a camera? Knock yourselves out. I got better things to do."

"Hey!" Zach jabbed him. "You live *behind* a camera."

"Exactly." He slid Zach a look. "How else do you think I recognize the peacocks?"

* * *

"Well, at least I know why you wanted to meet here," Zach said as he slid into the driver's seat.

"Yeah?"

Zach jerked his shoulder in a shrug. "You were checking up on Keelie. Don't worry. Javi and I will keep an eye on her."

Zane chewed on it for a minute, debated, then decided what the hell. Once he moved here—and he did plan on finding something here, no matter what—Zach would figure it out.

"I wasn't here checking up on her," he said, reaching into the front compartment of his messenger bag and tugging out his prescription sunglasses. He traded them out and tucked away his regular ones before looking over at Zach. "We had coffee."

Zach started the car, his face carefully blank.

But judging by the way his muscles had tensed a little, Zane suspected this conversation wasn't done.

It didn't take thirty seconds to find out just how right he was.

"Coffee. You're in town, the two of you had a nice, friendly cup of coffee sort of thing?" Zach asked, his voice carefully neutral.

"Nope. We had coffee as in I'm crazy about her and I'm doing my damnedest to get her to notice that. I think she finally figured it out, and we had coffee." He decided it was better not to mention that he'd spent the past few months coming up with a plan to put himself in Keelie's path so she'd be all but tripping over him. He didn't mention that Keelie was a huge part of the reason why he'd decided to move to Tucson—not all of it, but a big part of it.

He didn't think Zach's blood pressure could handle it. Instead, he just slid his brother a look and shrugged. "I think it went pretty well."

"You think it went well," Zach muttered. He shoved a hand through his hair and stared off at nothing, his eyes going hard and flat. He jabbed a button and the top of the convertible glided back, the hot, dry wind blowing in. Tipping his head back to stare at the big, blue bowl of the overhead sky, Zach was quiet for a long moment. Then, finally, he said, "You've been crazy about her for years. I know that. You've asked her out about two thousand times. I told you what happened—"

"Make it two thousand and one," Zane said, cutting off Zach before he could go any further. "I asked her out again this morning. She said yes. We're having dinner tonight. So we have to knock off in time for me to be back here to get my car."

Zach swung his head around and Zane stared at his younger brother.

He meant well. Zane knew that.

But all he wanted him to do was let it go.

"Z, you know what happened—"

"Yeah. I know," he said, cutting Zach off. "And if she was trying to slip into your bed, doing anything to break you two up, that would be different. But then again, if she was like that, I doubt I'd be obsessing over her the way I do. Here's the thing—she's not like that and you can't say otherwise. Can you?"

"Of course she hasn't—she's not—shit." Zach started to drum his fist on the steering wheel, focusing his gaze on the parking lot around them. "Look, I just don't want to see you hurt."

"I'm not big on it myself, man. But unlike you, I'm not going to sit around for fifteen or twenty years and hope like hell something happens to change things. If it's ever going to happen, now's the time." He shrugged. "And if not? Then at least I know."

Zach put the car into reverse, but instead of backing out, he said quietly, "And what happens if tonight goes well, then what?"

"Then it does." Zane rested his head on the padded cushion, his mind already spinning forward down that path. "I have to fly out on Monday, even if we do find a place. It will take me a few weeks to move. You already told me I could crash at the loft when I need to. I'll be going back and forth for a little while. I'll ask her if I can call her. I'll ask her out again. If it keeps going well, I'll be happy to know you're nice and annoyed, wondering if every time her phone buzzes at work, it's because I'm sending her texts you'd rather not think about."

Zach shoved the heel of his hand against his eye. "That girl is like a sister to me. Why you gotta do that, man?"

"Hey, I had to take pictures of your wife. Naked pictures."

"A picture fairy took those, remember?" Zach shot him a dark look. Then he sighed grimly. "Let's get this show on the road. You need to get back and make yourself all pretty for your fucking date."

Zane snorted. "Unlike you, superstar, I don't need to make myself pretty for a date. I already *am* pretty."

Chapter Six

It had been exactly ten days since her first date with Zane.

And her second, really.

The coffee thing counted, Keelie had decided.

Especially after that kiss.

Especially since she'd worked up the nerve to take the step.

Yeah, the coffee counted.

So, really, they'd had two dates in one day.

And not even thirty-six hours later, Zane was on a plane out of town. She would have been demoralized, except he'd told her about it that very night.

He had to go to San Francisco so his mother didn't kill him.

He had to pretend to look at a few spots there.

Then he had to do a few photo shoots back home, appointments he was already committed to.

Then he was heading back to Tucson. He hadn't specified *when*, but he was coming back.

She had no doubt about that. He was serious about this. Very serious.

His house was up for sale.

He was leaving Albuquerque and moving to Tucson.

Bent over a sketch for a custom piece she had to do that afternoon, she eyed her phone and wondered if she would come off as completely lame if she called him. Or sent him a text.

She could maybe take a picture—

Her phone started to buzz. She looked up, smiling as a now-familiar ringtone filled her work area.

Sheryl Crow and Kid Rock—"Picture."

And there was a picture of Zane filling the screen. She'd snapped that one, while he was talking to Zach in the parking lot out back. She couldn't even compare when it came to photography, not with Zane, although she knew how to point and shoot.

Still, she'd wanted a picture of him, just him, that was hers and only hers. Of course, even that thought made her feel silly and stupid.

Reaching for the phone, she swiped her finger across the screen and watched as the message bubble popped up.

You doing anything tonight?

She smiled.

No.

She hit Send and then settled down in the chair. Earbuds in, music blaring, she was completely unaware of anything else in the world.

"I bet they're sexting," Javi said, his face straight.

From the corner of his eye, he saw Zach wince, then, carefully, his expression went blank. "What have you got on for the afternoon, man?"

"Just finished up a walk-in. Have a repair job due in this afternoon." Rubbing at his goatee, he looked back down the hall toward Keelie's work area. Although none of the rooms were completely private, they had four walls and were closed off by a set of swinging doors, offering privacy to those getting tattoos of a more intimate nature. The only room that was completely private was the piercing area where Anais worked, although as of yet, she hadn't talked Zach into letting her do anything more intimate than a naval piercing.

She kept calling him uptight.

Personally, Javi was with him on that. He didn't want to think about a man getting his dick pierced or a woman getting a piercing in anything close to her hoo-haa—Aida had taught him that word. But some people were into that and Javi wasn't opposed on principle. It was just that his balls shriveled up and died a little every time Anais talked about Prince Edward piercings or clitoral piercings and all sorts of other piercings.

He had a feeling that was why she persisted.

Just for the hell of it.

Same reason he was yanking Zach's chain right now. It was fun.

"I gotta say, I never would have thought I'd see the two of them making eyes at each other, but that look on her face, *amigo*," Javi said, heaving out a theatrical sigh. "I'm telling you, he's gone and done something to her. I used to think *you* had a way with women, man. But Zane's got you beat if he's done that to Keelie."

"Whatever," Zach muttered, red creeping up his neck, spiraling past the tattoos.

Javi bit back a grin.

"You think he's gonna start visiting more often?" he asked, watching as Zach bent over the design in front of him, sketching with a little more intensity than necessary.

"For fuck's sake." Zach threw his pencil down and shot him a look, his blue eyes aggravated. "Don't you get enough of this watching those soaps you love with Aida? No, he won't be visiting more often. Z's moving here. As soon as he gets things settled in Albuquerque."

For a few seconds—only a few—Javi was speechless.

Then he caught the back of the chair across from Zach and hauled it out, dropping into it and leaning forward.

Zach was already bent back over the sketch.

"Moving. As in *here*? *Mierda*," Javi muttered. "That went and got serious quicker than I thought. No wonder you're all twitchy."

"Hell." Zach sighed and leaned back in his seat, his eyes glinting. "I'm not twitchy. Or if I am, it's because you're needling me. But Z's not moving here over Keelie. Or not . . ."

Zach blew out a breath, crossing his arms over his chest. "Maybe she's part of it. I don't know. But he quit the bar where he worked. He's making a go of his photography."

"Really?" Javi grinned. "That's awesome, man. He's good. Real good. He oughta be . . . like on magazines, in museums or shit."

"He has been." Zach slanted a look at him. "He could be a hell of a lot bigger if he'd just focus on it."

There was something unsaid at the end of that sentence, though. Javi had known Zach too long not to catch it.

"But . . . ?"

"He holds himself back. Stays on the side. Always did. He's reaching for it," Zach said, pushing the chair back and rising, gathering the sketches on the desk, staring off at nothing. "Reaching, finally, and that's something. But he always holds back and he can't make this work if he doesn't really let himself go."

"What makes you think he won't?" Javi studied him, seeing the concern, the worry.

"Because he's my brother," Zach said softly. "And I know him. He never really goes all in. Not on anything."

Heart thumping against her ribs, Keelie sat in the arrivals lane at the airport, searching. She didn't see that tall, familiar figure.

So she checked her phone.

The flight status hadn't changed from five minutes ago. He'd landed.

Okay. She flipped down her mirror, checked her hair. It looked like it had four minutes ago.

"Stop it," she muttered, closing the visor and focusing on the flow of people on the sidewalks. He had to get his suitcase, had to deal with all the people. It would take him more than just twenty minutes—

There was a tap at her window.

Adrenaline spiked.

Then, before anything could show on her face, she turned her head. Something loosened inside her when she saw Zane, even as other things clenched, or started to melt.

Zane . . .

She reached over and unlocked the door before climbing out. She eyed him over the top of the battered VW Bug and said, "You are certain you want *me* driving you around? You're barely going to fit in here."

He just smiled, a slow, lazy curve of his lips, and then he curled his fingers toward her.

Her knees knocked together as she walked over there.

It felt like they were moving backward in this whole dating thing—they'd made out, he'd made her climax, and then they'd had coffee, dinner . . . and all she'd gotten out of *those* two encounters were kisses that all but scalded her.

Not that she was complaining. It gave her brain time to acclimate, and she really needed to acclimate. Dating so wasn't her thing, as evidenced by the erratic string of bad dates and her abysmally few unpleasant attempts at relationships since high school.

Very, very few.

By the time she reached the curb where he was waiting, her heart was hammering in her chest and she was way too hot. Not that it was cool out. This was Arizona, after all, but she felt like she'd just plunged into a pool of lava, skin buzzing, burning.

"Hey," she said, stopping only when her boots bumped against his shoes.

He reached up, his hand splaying over her neck. Her pulse jumped, slammed against his palm and she felt her breath hitch, catch.

He still hadn't said anything but she stopped wondering

about that in the next second as he lowered his mouth and pressed his lips to hers.

His tongue slid out, teased her.

She opened for him, reaching for his shirt and curling her hands into it.

He repeated that same light caress, his tongue brushing against her lips. Again, and again, until she whimpered against his lips and tried to take control herself. He slid an arm around her, curved it around her waist, tucking her so tight against him, not even a breath could have separated them.

That was fine.

Who needed to breathe anyway?

His hand twisted in the fabric of her shirt and she felt the light brush of air kiss her back, then his other hand tugged on her hair, tipping her head back, changing the angle of the kiss.

She shivered as he finally—*finally*—deepened that kiss, his tongue pushing into her mouth. She bit down on him, lightly, then sucked. A growl emanated from him and she shivered at the feel of his chest vibrating against her breasts.

Not even two seconds later, he was breaking the kiss, easing her back gently.

"Hmmm." She fought the urge to pout and demand more. Instead, she focused on his mouth as he pressed his brow to hers.

"We keep that up and I might forget we're at the airport," Zane teased. Although he doubted it would take much. His cock pulsed against the zipper of his jeans and he had a feeling the teeth of said zipper might already be imprinted on very sensitive flesh.

It was worth it, especially when Keelie reached up and pressed her finger to his mouth.

"It's your fault." Then she shrugged. "I told you you'd have an easier ride if you had Zach or Abby pick you up."

Then she broke away.

He caught her as she turned, hugging her close, his front to her back. "I'm not much interested in easy."

She leaned back against him, her hand covering the one he'd pressed to her belly. "Seems kind of stupid, seeing as how you don't live here, but I missed you while you were gone." She grabbed one of his camera cases, hefting it easily.

Warily, he eyed her, but he couldn't fault the care she used with it.

It was just . . . well, it was kind of like watching somebody hold a baby for the first time. Well, maybe not a baby. More like a camera that cost eleven thousand dollars. One that he pampered like a baby. Once it was stowed in the trunk, he looked up at her, saw the way she lifted a brow at him. Almost like she knew exactly what he was thinking.

He treated it the same way he always did. He flashed her an easy grin.

Then he grabbed two of his bags and added them to the trunk, carefully tucking his luggage *around* the camera equipment. Once that was done, he slid her a look. "Yeah, well, I miss you every time you're not with me. So I think I've got you beat."

Her gaze bounced away from his.

He headed to the passenger seat, not expecting any kind of response. She hadn't taken off running—yet—that was good enough for him. He'd just keep taking it as it came and wait until she was ready to give him more.

If he had his preference, this dinner would have been at someplace quiet, with soft music, even softer lights, tablecloths, and the kind of service that was pretty much invisible.

If Zane wasn't so determined to make everything with Keelie go *exactly* right, he'd have no compunction, at all, about setting the scene to seduce her.

It was harder than hell to resist that urge, because he had a feeling she wouldn't exactly resist him if he went about seducing her.

But he didn't just want her to fall into bed with him.

He wanted her to fall in love with him.

So instead of someplace soft and quiet, they were someplace bright and loud.

The music was a Mexican pop artist, her voice throaty and appealing, but considering she was almost drowned out by the voices of children, crying babies, and chattering adults, he couldn't really call anything about the place romantic.

Keelie studied the drink in front of her with dubious eyes and then she looked up at him.

"It's pink."

"Are you telling me that you've been in Arizona . . . how long? It's six years, right?" He knew she'd started working for Zach six years ago—he'd actually been there the day she came back for her follow-up interview. Zach had tried to con Zane into letting her do a "trial run" sort of tattoo. The answer had been a flat *hell, no.* Not just because he didn't really want another tattoo, but even just one look at her had made him understand one thing. If she went and put her hands on him for an extended length of time, it was going to cause a noticeable reaction.

She shot him a narrow look. "I moved here about a week after Zach gave me the job. So, yeah. Six years. And what does that have to do with a pink drink? I don't do pink."

"It's not the *pink,*" he said. "It's prickly pear. It's like a southwest thing. Almost like . . ." He paused, trying to come up with an adequate comparison. He grinned at her. "Kind of like Kentucky and mint juleps."

For a moment, something flashed in her eyes.

It looked like . . .

But it was gone before he could really read it.

Then she made a face at him, miming disgust. "Out of curiosity, you ever *had* a mint julep? I think they're nasty. And really, that's a Derby thing, not a Kentucky thing. If we're going to do regional things, choose bourbon for Kentucky."

He studied her for a moment longer, wondering what had

caused that glint, that flash of . . . memory. Pain. Fear. Then he let it go. Now wasn't the time. "Fine, fine," he said, pretending to grumble. "So, it's a regional thing. What bourbon is to Kentucky, this is to here. It's a prickly pear margarita. Try it. You just might like it. Unless you hate tequila. Do you hate tequila?"

"I don't see how anybody can hate tequila." She shrugged and reached out, swiping a finger through the sugar-topped rim of the glass. "I . . ." She pursed her lips and then flicked him a look. "I don't generally drink on first date. Or second dates. Maybe not even third dates."

Then she reached out and took the glass before he could tell her she didn't have to—

Her eyes widened at the first drink.

"Oh." She lowered it, eyed it. Then took another sip. A husky little sigh escaped her as she took a third. "Wow. That's . . . dangerously good."

He remained quiet as she lowered the glass.

When she looked back up at him, her familiar smirk firmly in place, he couldn't find it in him *to* smile. "Now you get to say something like *I told you so*," she said.

"Told you." He looked down at the glass in front of him.

"What . . . don't tell me *you* don't drink them," Keelie said.

He shot her a look.

"If it's a pink thing, I might smack you." She leaned back, arms crossed over her chest. "You just nudged me into trying it."

"You got a reason for—"

"Z?"

His question was interrupted, maybe for the better, by a familiar, and somewhat incredulous voice.

Looking up, he saw Zach and Abby. Smiling, he stood up, caught Abby in a tight hug, but when he turned to Zach, there was a stiffness to him that made him pause.

Zach flicked a look between him and Keelie. "We're interrupting."

Keelie shifted on her chair. "Of course not," she said, her

voice losing that sharp, caustic edge of humor that almost made Zane want to bite her, or kiss her. Both.

Zane had to bite back the urge to say, *Yeah, you are interrupting*, especially when Keelie looked at Abby. "There's room, if you want to join us. Zane made me drink this pink thing. I don't do pink. But it's good."

Abby's eyes widened. "You've never had a prickly pear margarita? Keelie, what is *wrong* with you?"

Zane suppressed a sigh as Abby sank down into the unoccupied seat next to Keelie. Zach was a little slower to settle in the chair next to Zane's, and his body was decidedly rigid.

"What's up?" Zane asked, keeping his voice easy, eyes on the two women, murmuring in that way women had, already lost in conversation with each other.

"Not much." Zach's voice held a weird undercurrent to it. Zane slid him a look.

Zach was staring at the table. "I didn't know you were coming back today."

Running his tongue along his teeth, Zane shrugged. "I finished some things up, got a mover to bring out some boxes and wanted to be here when they arrived. Also brought out some of my camera equipment." He angled his head toward Zach. "Why do I get the feeling there's a problem?"

"No problem." Zach shook his head. Then he shrugged. "Might have been nice to know you were here, but hey . . ."

"Shit, Zach." Zane rolled his eyes and grabbed his drink, resisting the urge to toss it back like a shot of whiskey. He could handle his liquor, but tequila was better off taken in a little slower. He knew from experience. "I planned to call you in the morning. I just got in a couple hours ago."

"It's not a problem."

At that moment, the chatter across the table died down.

Keelie's gaze slid between them. Zane could see the questions she tried to hide.

Abby didn't bother. Her dark brown eyes narrowed. "What's the matter?" When there wasn't an immediate response, she cocked her head and studied her husband. "Zach, you look like you got a thorn in your paw."

"I do not." There was a definite sulk to his voice.

Abby rolled her eyes. "Whatever, baby. Geez." She studied him for a long, lingering moment and then shifted her attention to Zane.

When she decided not to push it, he could have kissed her. But then again, Abby knew Zach almost as well as Zane did.

Shoving her dark red hair back, she eyed Zane's margarita. "Sometimes you like those and sometimes you don't. Which is it today?"

"Today, I like it." He took another drink, winked at her from the rim, watched as she stuck out her lip in a pout. Then he turned the glass over to her. "But since I'm a gentleman, you can have it."

"You're my very favorite brother-in-law today." She beamed at him and accepted the glass.

"Today," he said wryly.

"Well, yeah. Yesterday it was Trey because he let me read his book early. Of course, I'll probably hate him by the time I'm done. He's going to make this one another tearjerker," Abby said, shaking her head. She took a sip of the margarita and then shot Keelie a look. "You ever read any of Trey's stuff?"

"A couple." She shrugged, shooting Zane a deprecating look. "He likes to make people cry. I'm not really good with the tearjerker books, but he's a great storyteller."

Trey, one of the twins, was a writer and yes, tears seemed to come with the territory as far as his books went. "Trey's a great storyteller. You realize, you're not required to like his books just because you know him. I've liked a few of them, the rest of them, I told him he needed to add some rainbows or lollipops or something, just to keep me from slitting my wrists with the pages before I was done."

Zach continued to sit there, brooding, and Zane decided he'd just leave him to it.

"He's not that bad," Zach snapped, his voice sharp.

"Hey," Abby said, her voice soft. "Ease up, baby. Trey knows his work isn't for everybody. *You* couldn't finish the last one. I remember you were sniffling when you passed it off to me."

Zach set his jaw and lapsed back into silence.

Zane wondered if he'd get through this meal without throttling his brother.

Well, this sucks.

The few sips of prickly pear margarita she'd taken, combined with the few bites of food she'd forced herself to eat, were doing a weird little lurch and twist in Keelie's gut and she had to make a practiced effort breathe slow and normal.

Nerves always made her stomach upset and if she let herself get *too* upset, she just might puke up what little she had inside her. And wouldn't that just take the cake?

The real bitch was that everything had been going *fine*.

She wasn't even sure just what had gone wrong—well.

That wasn't entirely true.

She watched as Zane and Abby talked—familiar, easy conversation that bespoke of two people who had a long history with each other.

She knew what had gone wrong—this weird tension had hit when Zach and Abby showed up.

She just wasn't sure why.

Feeling a pair of eyes cutting into her, she finally leveled a look at Zach. Under the table, she clenched one hand into a fist. That was the only outward sign she allowed of the turmoil crashing through her though, the one he couldn't see.

As he continued to look at her, she just lifted a brow.

He jerked his gaze away and the table started to vibrate a minute later as he drummed on it with his fist.

Wonderful.

She eyed her food, everything sitting in her gut like a leaden weight, but there was no way she could try to eat more. They'd been here for over an hour. The drink in her glass had long since gone to ice. Abby had eaten most of her food, but neither Zane nor Zach had eaten much.

Somehow, even though she was the one who'd been on the date, she'd managed to make herself the third wheel.

She didn't even know *how*.

When there was a lull in the conversation, she leaned over and murmured to Abby, "I'm not feeling too hot. Can you maybe give Zane a ride home?"

Abby studied her with shrewd eyes. "I have a feeling I know why. Why don't we—"

But she didn't wait for an answer. Digging the money out of her purse, she dropped enough cash on the table to cover the bill and the tip. Ignoring the intense way Zane's gaze cut to her, all but searing her, she rose. "I'm not feeling great. I need some air. Zane, Abby said she can get you home when she and Zach head out. I'll bring your stuff by in a little while."

"I don't think so," Zane said, rising, his voice low.

"Please." She stared at him, unable to explain the awful, vicious ache in her chest.

"We don't mind running you to the loft later, Z." Zach shot her a smile, but it was brittle around the edges. "See you in the morning, Keelie."

She gave him a short nod and then headed for the door.

She heard a chair scrape behind her.

Then Abby's voice.

She didn't know if she'd get out of there without him following her or not.

"Give her a couple of minutes," Abby suggested, catching Zane's hand.

"We were on a date," Zane half snarled.

"Yeah." Abby gave him a sympathetic smile before she turned a hard glare on her husband. "Then we ruined it."

Zach looked up at that. "Hey, we didn't ruin it. She invited us to join them, Abs."

"And if you hadn't sat there pouting because your brother

called the woman he likes before you, then I suspect Keelie wouldn't have left, feeling like *she* had done something wrong, instead of you, you big baby," Abby shot back.

"Nobody made her leave." Zach sat up, his voice edged.

And loud enough that more than a few people glanced their way.

"No." Abby shook her head. "But you sure as hell didn't do anything to make her feel like she should stay. It was *their* date . . . and you successfully made her feel unwelcome. Happy . . . *sugar*?"

"Enough," Zane said quietly. He eyed the money Keelie had tossed down. The server appeared in the next moment and he checked the bill. She'd calculated it pretty much to a T, including the tip. Gathering up the money, he turned it over and then stood. "If it's all the same to you, Abby, I'll pass on the ride. I'm just going to call for a cab."

"That's stupid, Z." Zach stood up, eying him narrowly. "Cab fare from here to the loft will be insane."

Zane just turned on his heel and strode out of the restaurant. They weren't far behind him but at least he didn't have to worry about offering free entertainment to the patrons if Zach didn't get off his back. An annoying little tic pulsed in his temple and he reached up, rubbing at it as he pulled his phone out of his pocket, opening the browser to search for a cab company.

"Come on, Z . . ."

Slowly, he looked up, met Zach's gaze. "I'm calling a cab," he said quietly.

"Sounds good to me." Abby leaned in and kissed his cheek and then turned to her husband. "Come on, Zach."

"We're twenty minutes away from the loft. We pass by it on our way home." He stood there stubbornly, hands jammed in his pockets.

"If I get into a car with you right now, I have a feeling I'll have my hands around your throat by the time the ride is over with." Zane shot him a sharp-edged look. "We'd have to make Abby drive. She'll get pissed at me if we get blood all over one of the cars."

"What in the hell is your—"

"Enough." Abby's voice was sharp, cold as ice, and cut between them. Zach lapsed into silence and his gaze landed on his wife's face. She advanced on him and Zane couldn't deny getting some smug satisfaction from the moment as she jabbed a finger into Zach's chest. "Tell me one thing, Zach. If you get off a plane, who is the first person you're going to call . . . *me*? Or one of your brothers?"

Zach had absolutely no idea how things had gotten to *this* point.

Zane was moving a little too fast—actually, for Zane, he was moving at light speed and Zach was now officially a little worried. And so, yeah, maybe, a little bothered by the fact that his brother—his best friend, next to Abby, hadn't seen the point in letting him know he was coming to town.

But now, not only was *Zane* mad at him, Abby was.

"Well?" she demanded, drilling her finger into his chest again.

"You know I'm going to call you," he said irritably. He caught her wrist. And because he hated when she was mad at him, he started to stroke his thumb over the sensitive inner skin. "You're my wife. I should call you."

She gave him a sweet smile. "And who would you have called a year ago? Two years ago? Five?"

Setting his jaw, he just stared at her. He'd like to argue it wasn't the same.

But then, he looked over at Zane. Behind the lenses of his glasses, Zane's eyes were unreadable. Zane had never been the easiest one to read, but now he was less so.

"Well, fuck," he muttered. Hooking a hand over the back of his neck, he nodded and then turned around, heading off toward the car.

"Don't you think you could maybe say something?" Abby said as she fell into step next to him,

"Why?" he bit off. "If I say much more, he's going to feel like hitting me. I'm mad enough that I'll hit back. We're in public. If we get into a fight in public, my mom will kick both our asses. I'm an idiot and he knows it. He doesn't want me to do anything but leave him alone right now."

Abby sighed. "Sometimes it's amazing men and women can even communicate."

They walked in silence toward the car. Once they reached it, he shot a look back at Zane. He was on the phone, calling for a cab, most likely. Zach felt a stab of guilt punch through him and he looked back at Abby. He'd have to fix the thing with him and Zane, he knew. Eying his wife, he asked, "How mad are you at me?"

She lifted a cool brow. "When are you going to apologize?"

"I'll talk to Z tomorrow."

"And Keelie?"

He looked away. "That, too." And that would be the harder one. He knew how to handle it when he messed up with his brothers. He did it all the time. But how did he handle that one? A few months ago, he might have known. But now . . .

"Believe it or not, slugger, she's still the same woman she was before it happened."

He slid his gaze back to Abby.

She smiled and got into the car.

He joined her, starting the engine.

She reached over, her fingers ghosting over the back of his neck. He leaned into the light touch, relaxed a little as she toyed with his hair. "She's a little smarter, maybe," Abby said, a smile edging into her voice.

"Yeah?" He shot her a look and the glint in her eyes warned him.

"Yeah." She tugged her hand back and fastened her seat belt. "After all, she figured out real fast that you're soooooo not right for her."

"Of course I'm not." He shoved the car into reverse, about as uncomfortable as he'd be if his mother had shown up and started discussing things like . . . birthing rooms and sex education. "I'm your guy. I've always been yours."

Abby caught his hand after he'd swung the car around and pulled out of the parking lot. "Well, there is that. But that's not the exactly what I'm getting at. You're mine . . . yeah. But aside from that . . . you're all wrong. For her."

Zach glanced at her.

Abby settled back in her seat with a faint smile on her face. "I think it's time you get something through your head . . . you're all wrong for her. But I think Zane's completely right."

He opened his mouth.

She shook her head. "Deal with it, baby."

Chapter Seven

The door opened so fast, Keelie suspected he'd been watching for her.

He didn't say anything, just stood back to let her enter, although she hesitated, shifting on her feet in the hallway. "Don't you . . ." She cleared her throat. "Don't you want to get your stuff?"

"Later." He reached out, hooked his hand in the front of her jeans and tugged.

Her breath hitched at the possessiveness of the gesture.

And her heart ached at the storm in his eyes, the glint of anger.

He pushed the door shut once she was inside, but instead of them retreating into the depths of the loft, he blocked her in, arms braced over her head as he studied her face.

"Why did you take off?" he asked, the question blunt.

He was angry.

Do you blame him? You're a basket case and you just showed that facet of your personality in all its glory.

Shoving that insidious little whisper down inside herself, she forced herself to meet his eyes, and she responded in the same tone he'd used. "It's pretty clear I was causing a problem between you and Zach. I decided to remove the problem."

"If you wanted to remove the problem, you should have told Zach to haul his ass out of there," Zane bit off.

"I can't tell your brother to get the hell out." She crossed her arms over her chest.

"Why not?" Zane leaned in closer, so close she felt lost in the blue green of his eyes. "I've heard you tell him that before. You and I were out on a date. He decided to act like a spoiled brat—and for the record, Zach often *is* a spoiled brat—so why not call him on it?"

"He's . . ." She stopped, closed her mouth, shifting her weight as she fought to explain. The problem was, she couldn't really explain why she'd felt so lost, so out of place earlier. "He's family," she finally said. "We were just . . ."

Zane's hands came up and his thumb pressed to her lower lip. "Don't," he said quietly, a thread of steel underlying the words. His voice was velvet, but the warning was there all the same. "Don't say it. We weren't *just* anything. I've been trying to get to this for too long, Keelie. Don't go writing it off. Unless it just doesn't matter to you."

He leaned in, pressed a hot, open-mouthed kiss to her neck.

She shivered, felt the heat of it race all the way to the soles of her feet. She thought she just might melt inside her sturdy leather boots. Melt away into nothing, except Zane's hands were holding her upright, keeping her chained to the world.

His mouth brushed hers now and then he murmured against her lips, "Does it matter?"

She blinked, dazed, as he lifted his head.

"What?" she whispered as he continued to stand there, obviously waiting for an answer.

A hot smile that turned his face into a decadent, devilish delight curved his lips. "When you look at me like that, it makes me want to forget any rules I've ever set for myself," he mused, stroking his thumb across her lip once more.

Keelie closed her mouth around it.

He groaned.

Then he tugged his hand away, pulling her up against him. "Does it matter? Does this matter? Us?"

"Zane . . ."

She bit her lip, uncertain how to even answer that. He seemed to . . . or he *acted* like he'd had feelings for a while, but how did she process that? Trust it? Accept it? Just a couple of dates—and well, yeah, that blissful, mind-numbing experience at the wedding. But she was still trying to get her brain around just being *attracted* to him.

"I'm not asking you to run away to Vegas," he teased, running his lips along her cheekbone. "I just want to know if this matters."

She caught his wrist in her hand. With her heart racing like a mad thing in her chest, she looked up at him. "If it didn't, I wouldn't be here."

"Okay, then." He backed away from her.

Every inch of her mourned the loss, but she managed not to whimper as he held out a hand.

"Should we get your stuff?" she asked.

"Later."

"But . . ." She licked her lips. "The cameras and stuff. I saw how you were eying that one bag. Like it held diamonds or gold."

"Hmmm." He slit his eyes, then nodded. "Good point. Let's go get them. But then you're coming back up."

It was a question that really wasn't.

Smiling, she reached up, touched his cheek. "I'll come back up. We never really did finish our date anyway."

It only took one trip. He trusted Keelie with his precious camera equipment—it was the only option, because if he didn't, he could see her insisting on hauling both suitcases out and lugging them up to the loft. And that thought scraped raw.

Now, after tucking his camera equipment along the top

of the long, wide console table, he went to ask Keelie if she was still hungry—she hadn't eaten much of anything—but he turned at the same time she moved and he ended up with his arms full of soft, slim woman.

Her eyes flew up, met his.

The scent of her flooded him.

A groan rolled out of him and mingled with the soft, shaky sigh escaping her.

"Ah . . ." She licked her lips, shot him a smile. "Sorry."

"I'm not." He tangled his hand in her hair, tugged.

She went still as he slowly, oh so slowly, lowered his mouth to hers.

That kiss at the airport had been sweet, way too sweet, and ever since then, he'd been dying for more.

Although, to be honest, he'd been dying for more even before he'd ever kissed her.

She met him halfway, one hand curling in his shirt, the other dropping to his waist.

Her tongue swirled and rubbed against him, sending a rush of heat pulsing through him. It got worse when she slid her hand under his shirt, her nails scraping against bare skin.

Using his hold on her hair, he tugged her head back, feasted lazily on her mouth, even as he reminded himself to take it slow. Take it easy.

Tugging her lower lip with his teeth, he lifted his head, watched as her pupils spiked, swelled. "You'll drive me crazy at some point," he murmured.

"Like you're not doing the same to me." She licked her lips when he lifted his head, but she didn't look away.

Instead, she held his gaze as she reached up, trailed her hand across his chest. Then, she did look away, but somehow, as her focus sharpened and intensified, it made his blood start to pulse and pump harder. She slid one finger across his chest, as though tracing something through his shirt.

"I kinda want to see that tattoo again," she said, darting a look up at him.

"Ah . . ." Fire seemed to sizzle through his brain, spread out until it was licking through his veins, his synapses, everything inside him, burning him from the inside out.

All from a couple of words, and that look in her eyes and the slow, lazy stroke of her hand down his chest. As it stroked lower, he caught her wrist.

"You realize this is playing with fire, right?" he murmured, rubbing his lips against hers. "Touching me makes me forget what I'm doing, where I am . . . who I am."

The smile that bloomed on her mouth was pure and lush sex, a promise, in and of itself, although there was something almost shy about it. The combination was enough to drive him to his knees and he remembered those whispered words . . .

The last time I had a quick fuck, the last time I had what could even be called casual sex was . . . It was . . . well. Never.

"I really don't mind that at all." She tugged her hand free, and he slowly let go, watching her. She continued on that slow, lazy path down his chest and he could feel the bunch and jump of his muscles under every touch, feel his cock pulse in tandem with his heart, and he wondered just how much of this he could handle without either turning caveman or just losing it in his jeans like a teenager.

She caught the hem of his shirt and he held still as she dragged it up.

His glasses got caught in the material and he scowled, untangling them before sliding them back on. A faint blush settled on her cheeks and he lifted a brow. "I'm not missing this."

"Missing what?"

"Any chance to look at you." He trailed his fingers along the neckline of her shirt, eying the faint flush visible through the designs of her tattoos. "I've always wondered . . . when you blush . . . just how low does it go?"

Her breath caught and he lowered his hand, relaxing against the stool, curling his hands around it so he didn't grab her.

"You wonder weird things, Zane," she murmured.

"No. I wonder the kind of things a guy wonders about a woman he really, really wants."

He was going to turn her into mush if he kept this up. Determined to distract him, she laid her hands on his chest. Against her right hand, she felt the hard *bump bump bump* of his heart.

The light burned overhead and she sighed in satisfaction as she gave into the urge to study the tattoo at her leisure, the feathers, the wings as they swept up and curled over the canvas that was Zane's body. The owl's face, done in such detail. "He must have had one hell of an image to use when he did this," she murmured.

"A picture," Zane said, his voice a little rough.

She slid him a look.

His lashes lay low over his eyes. Her fingers flexed and she felt his chest rise raggedly under her touch.

Slowly, she lowered her gaze, stared at her hands. Her left one lay over his nipple. Her own were puckered into hard, aching points and she wanted, *needed* to feel something other than the silk of her bra rubbing against them.

Slowly, she stroked her thumb over the flat, brown circle of his nipple, listened to the ragged rasp of his breath.

"Hmmm . . ." Slipping him a look, she did the same on the other side.

"Damn it, Keelie."

She stroked her hands down lower, feeling the ridged planes of his torso, his ribs, his belly. Wow. He was—

His hands grabbed her waist and her sudden, startled cry was lost against his mouth. Her hips landed on the edge of the island, but she barely processed that, her hands automatically going to the sleekly muscled shelf of Zane's shoulders. His tongue licked at her lips, demanding entrance, and she opened, unable to do anything else.

He moved in closer and she parted her legs, instinctively seeking to get nearer, but when she would have gripped him with her knees, he stopped her. "Don't," he rasped against her mouth. "I'm . . . shit. I'm already this close to losing it here."

He lifted his head and her heart tripped, then started to race at the look in his eyes.

Nobody had ever looked at her like that.

It wasn't just desire.

It was something deeper—it was . . . everything.

His hand came up, cradled her face, his thumb sweeping across her lower lip. "You'll drive me nuts."

"It's only fair," she said, forcing the words out, fear starting to whisper through her. It was an unfamiliar fear, though. The fear of actually *believing* in those promises she saw in his eyes.

"Yeah? How is that?" he murmured, his mouth pressed to her neck, unaware of the thoughts racing inside her.

"You're driving me crazy, too. Fair is fair, right?"

He chuckled, the sound vibrating through him.

"Fair is fair, huh?"

She jolted at the feel of his hand on her waist. "If fair is fair, then maybe I can . . ."

Stop. Didn't we just establish that we were going to go slow?

Zane knew that calm, rational voice was only trying to help.

He gave it a minute. *Yes, we did establish that. But that was right up until she looked at me that way, kissed me that way. I'm human.*

She slicked her tongue across her lips, her eyes wide, nervous, the brown one all but black, while the pupil of her blue eye was so large, only a thin rim of color showed.

"Fair is fair," she murmured as he stroked his fingers along the satin of her skin.

A rough breath tore out of him and he paused, closing his eyes. "You . . ." He opened his eyes and then eased his hand higher, splayed wide on her back. "You certain? I don't mind being unfair here for a while longer."

"We can just take it as it goes, right?" Her gaze dropped to his mouth and then she tipped her head back.

A hundred questions, a thousand doubts burned in that gaze and Zane knew the wise thing to do would be to wait. Just wait.

But he spent too much of his life *waiting*.

And if she wasn't ready to call it quits yet? He wasn't going to be the one to do it. So he caught the hem of her shirt, a form-fitting black T, and started to drag it, higher and higher. She sat still as he tugged it over her head, and continued to sit there, even as it hung from his fist.

Zane felt poleaxed.

Elegant. Delicate. He'd expected her to be just that and he still wasn't prepared for it. Her breath came in harsh, heavy little pants that had her breasts rising and falling against a bra that had been designed with one intent in mind—to drive a man insane. Made of rust-colored red satin that shimmered just a little, it was edged with black lace and her pale skin glowed against it. It was one of those taunting little bras that pushed the breasts up and together and his mouth was already watering.

Zane was familiar with the female form and all its nooks and crannies, all those delightful curves. He spent hours capturing all those wonderful curves and lines on camera, obsessed with just how to portray the perfection of a woman's body—and he didn't care if his model was a size zero or a size twenty, nor did he care if they were a dewy-eyed nineteen-year-old looking to make a break or a forty-two-year-old divorcée who needed a better headshot for her website . . . and sometimes the divorcée was looking for more, a picture that would let her see she was still absolutely beautiful.

He loved women, but they no longer had the ability to lay him low.

Unless the woman was Keelie.

With that smart mouth and her distrustful eyes . . . and now he had her half-naked in front of him and his hands were shaking.

Dipping his head, he pressed his lips to the gentle swells

of her breasts, where a knife pierced a rose. He traced the line of a petal with his tongue as her breath stuttered out of her. Her skin felt like silk under his fingertips as he trailed them along the edge of the bra and then higher, along the vivid, beautiful colors of the tattoos running along her collarbone and down her arms.

He'd thought about learning every single line of those tattoos. With his fingertips. With his eyes. With his mouth. Now he had every intention of making that a reality.

A harsh, high sound escaped her as he leaned in, rocked against her. That sound made his blood burn hotter, higher. Her knees came up and gripped his hips. One hand braced on the island next to her, he stared at her, watching as her eyes went glassy, color spilling into her cheeks.

So beautiful.

And so hot . . . She moved against him and he shuddered, biting back a groan. Catching her knees, he guided them back down. He still had to keep some level of control here.

Some.

Although even the thought was becoming laughable.

Letting his gaze roam over her, he studied that rose blooming along the side of her neck, the color a rich shade caught between red and purple. The bud hovered in that space just before it burst into bloom, like it was just waiting for the right moment. He leaned in and pressed his mouth to it, curving his hand along her hip to hold her still as she gasped.

Then he moved down along the rose's vine.

There were butterflies worked into the design, but each of them seemed to hover, almost like they were afraid to take flight. He found each one, kissed each one. Eight in all. The vine led to another rose, this one just below her collarbone. There was an identical one on the opposite side and in the middle of the two roses, there was a heart . . . locked.

He pressed his mouth to the heart and sucked lightly on her skin.

A ragged cry escaped her and he lifted his head.

Her pale skin was flushed and her eyes glittered.

Control fraying, he caught her face in his hands and hauled her closer, slanting his mouth over hers.

She opened for him, her hands coming up to grip his shoulders, nails biting into his skin as he drank from her.

Dying of thirst, for her. Desperate for her.

Keelie.

She wrapped her legs around him again and this time, he banded his arm around her, until there was no room between them, no room, no air. All he could feel was the heat of her. She was already wet, he could feel it through their clothes, and the few threads of control he had left started to snap.

"Zane . . ." Her voice broke.

Snarling, he tangled his hand in her hair and arched her head back, baring her throat. She cried out as he raked his teeth down the soft, sensitive column.

She clung to him, wrapped around him and arched—

A warning chill race downed his spine.

His balls went tight.

Fuck. "Keelie," he muttered, lifting his head.

Her eyes were locked on his, half-mindless, and she squirmed and wiggled, the tension in her body ramping up. A flush swept up her neck and he felt that tension spread out through him even as his cock jerked, throbbed—

He was going to lose it. In his fucking pants, like a kid—

"Please . . ." The whisper ripped out of her, broken and full of need.

Well, hell.

Drawing her back against him, he changed the angle of his hips and moved again, just once—

Her eyes flew wide and she cried out his name, her nails digging into the knotted muscles of his biceps as she came.

Sensation reverberated down his spine as she shuddered and moved against him, still riding the edge of her climax. Zane groaned and buried his face in her neck.

Yeah, the idea of maintaining some level of control had just flown right out the damn window.

* * *

Panting for breath, her head resting on his shoulder, Keelie tried to process just *what* had happened.

Her mouth was dry.

Her heart was racing.

One of his hands smoothed up her back and she shivered. He had rough hands, and the feel of those calluses along her hypersensitive skin was just one more torment.

Just what the hell . . .

"I don't know about you, but I probably need to go take a shower."

She blinked.

As he lifted his head, she went to cross her arms over her chest except *that* seemed kind of stupid just then.

So she kept her hands limp at her sides as she looked at him.

"A shower?" she asked dumbly.

A wry grin twisted his lips, his eyes more than a little unfocused as he glanced down at himself. "Yeah. A shower."

Automatically, she glanced down and then jerked her gaze back up at the sight of the wet stain along the front of his pants.

"What . . . you . . . oh."

He laughed, and when she would have looked away, he hooked his arms over her shoulders. "You went and turned me into a sixteen-year-old boy, Keelie. *I'm* the one who should be all embarrassed and blushing."

"Ah . . ."

He nuzzled her neck and then murmured, "I kind of need a favor."

He sounded . . . softer.

Zane was always so controlled and calm, polite with it, but almost . . . rigid. Now he sounded sleepy and warm and she just wanted to cuddle up against him and sleep.

But he said he needed a favor.

She didn't let herself tense up.

She'd stopped trusting guys—if she'd *ever* trusted

them—a long time ago. There were a very, very few exceptions. But . . . this was Zane.

He was watching her with a patient, almost knowing look and she had to fight the urge to cringe as he reached up and rubbed the bridge of his nose.

"I seem to have misplaced my glasses. Can you help me find them?"

She blinked.

"Is that . . . that's all you need?"

He pushed a hand through her hair. "Well, I'd love to find a way to solve world hunger, but I'll settle for my glasses. For now, at least. And maybe that shower, with you."

It was too warm in the bed, too warm, and too comfortable, and the last thing she wanted to do was move. But the light coming through the windows was shining right in her face.

The light.

That wasn't right.

And the bed . . .

Swallowing, she let her brain process things for just a few seconds. She wasn't in her bed. Okay.

She wasn't naked. That was good.

It was an old terror and one she was starting to think she'd never get past.

But she wasn't at home either—

Memory surged back.

The airport. Dinner. Zane.

Then Zach—

And . . . Zane again. She'd come over to apologize.

I just want to know if this matters.

His hands on her.

Every moment from the past night slammed into her mind, all too clear, the memory of him all too potent. Especially the feel of his hands on her, the taste of his mouth— and the way he'd looked at her.

He looked at her like she meant something.

And he wanted to know if this *mattered*?

How could she possibly tell him that this was starting to matter *too* much?

That he was starting to terrify her, all because of how *much* this mattered?

Her heart gave one hard, heavy slam against her ribs and she thought maybe all the air in the room disappeared as she let herself ponder that very thing—how much *did* this matter?

Oh, shit.

Now her heart started to race, too hard, too fast, and she couldn't pull in the oxygen she desperately needed. Gripping the sheet in her sweaty palm, she closed her eyes tight, squeezed them shut. *Get a grip.* She had to calm down, because if she rolled over and he was in the bed behind her and caught a look at her now, he'd see everything she was thinking, everything she was feeling, and there was no way she could explain away her sudden, inexplicable panic.

She didn't entirely understand it, although she knew the root of it.

There were things she wasn't ready to tell Zane. Not now. Not yet. Maybe sometime. Maybe.

She forced herself to take one slow, shallow breath. When that worked, she managed another and the band around her chest eased. Good. That was good.

Okay. Another breath. Then she popped an eye open. Slowly, she sat up and looked around. The room was empty.

A momentary reprieve.

Swiping a hand through the tangle of her hair, she licked her lips. She could do this. So what if this was the first time she'd ever spent the night through with a guy—and they hadn't even had sex. She could look at him, face him, talk to him.

Because yes, he did matter.

This mattered.

The cold knot of fear in her chest slowly unraveled and a smile spread across her face.

It mattered.

She mattered.

Without her truly realizing how it had happened, one of those ugly little threads of her past shriveled, snapped, broke. The chains that bound her didn't lessen all that much, but it was a start. Maybe just a small one, but that didn't matter.

Keelie had always been good at making do with small bits and pieces.

A second later, the floor creaked and then Zane was there, leaning against the wall, dressed in a white T-shirt and khaki shorts, his face clean shaven, glasses firmly in place.

He looked alert and awake and aware . . .

She just wanted to bite him.

Her mouth started to water.

Heart racing, she stood up and turned to face him. The T-shirt she'd slept in fell halfway down her thighs, but she still felt exposed. Of course, standing there half-naked, facing this guy who had rocked her straight in the most explosive orgasm of her life wasn't exactly going to make her feel steady.

"Morning," she said, tripping over the word.

He lifted a brow and then a slow, easy smile curled his lips. "Good morning, Keelie. I called for some food. There's next to nothing here and I'm starving."

She licked her lips. "Ah, that's . . . well, I have to . . ."

"In a hurry?" The bland look on his face made her feel foolish.

She'd spent the night. He'd made her come. Apparently, she'd done the same for him. Then they'd showered. And they hadn't had sex. She almost felt sort of cheated. If she was going to feel all guilty and awkward, couldn't they have at least had sex?

"No." Nervous, she shoved her hair back. "I'm not in a hurry."

He came toward her. "Good."

She held still as he reached up, stroking a finger across her lower lip. When he went to lower his head to kiss her, she averted her face. "I haven't brushed my teeth."

"I don't care." He caught her lower lip, bit her lightly.

Her heart did a slow, lazy roll in her chest as he caught her close and smoothed his hands down her back, tucking her up against him. Then he just held her. One hand curved along the back of her neck, cradled her up against his chest, while the other curved along the small of her back.

Closing her eyes, she sighed and leaned against him.

He felt so warm.

It was possible to be cold for so long that you simply *forgot* you were cold, she realized. And now, pressed against his warmth, she felt something almost painful—those cold places, slowly thawing. It hurt, even as something sweet and blissful spread through her.

Tears pricked her eyes and she pressed against his chest.

She needed a few minutes alone, before she started to cry right there.

"I need a minute," she said, and it took every bit of will-power she had to give him an easy smile.

His hands fell away and she kept her movements fluid and her steps unhurried until she was in the bathroom. Then, after she'd shut and locked the door behind her, she leaned against it as that tingling, painful ache spread throughout her entire soul.

Staring at her reflection in the mirror, she sighed.

"I think you're in trouble here, Keelie."

Zane had a lifetime of practice when it came to hiding his emotions. If his parents had any idea of some of the shit he'd hidden from them, some of the secrets he never planned on sharing with anybody . . . well. Suffice it to say that things wouldn't be pleasant if any of that came out. His mother would never let him hear the end of it and she'd maybe go on a maternal rampage, even now, more than twenty years later.

But he'd kept secrets and he'd kept them well.

He'd hidden his feelings and hidden them well.

Now he had to do it all over again. The door opened and

Keelie came out, still wearing the T-shirt she'd slept in. It was his and he was going to bronze it, or maybe sleep with that damn thing, because it would smell like her . . .

"Can I borrow the shirt?" she asked, tearing him out of his fantasy.

He blinked. "Ah. Yeah." Okay. Keelie walking around wearing his shirt did something to his brain that just wasn't conducive to conversation, but he managed a fairly normal smile as he picked up his coffee. "There's coffee."

Keelie gave him a grateful smile. "I need it."

Her hands closed around the cup and she lifted it up to her lips.

He watched, practically mesmerized as she took a sip. A soft sound, somewhere between a moan and a sigh, escaped her.

His dick hardened.

How in the hell could she get him worked up just by drinking coffee?

Blood throbbed, pulsed in his veins as she took another sip and then moved over to the bar. The worn cotton of the T-shirt he'd given her slid over her slight curves. The fabric was all but shapeless from years of use, wearing it to the gym, on hikes, but the body under that shirt was anything but shapeless. Her shoulders, the line of her back, how she settled on one of the stools.

"So . . ." she drew the word out. The seriousness of it managed to break through the cloud in his head.

He settled on the stool next to hers, then caught her waist, hauled her into his lap. She yelped and then grabbed his hands, twisting her head around to look at him.

"Our date was shot to hell," he said, staring into wide, startled eyes.

"Well . . ."

Dipping his head, he caught her lower lip, bit down.

She shivered against him.

"It was shot to hell. But I'll have you know, I didn't punch Zach. I wanted to."

When he lifted his head, she blinked at him. "Ah . . . just where are you going with this?"

"I'm just explaining that I didn't hit him, even though he was a stupid asshole."

Keelie lifted a brow, an elegant arch over the pale blue of her eye. "Zane, from what I understand, you *enjoy* hitting him. I doubt y'all need reasons to fight. But I appreciate the self-control."

He reached up, stroked the tip of his finger across her eyebrow. "We have to try the date thing again. Since last night flopped."

"Well." She shifted on the stool, wiggling around until she could wrap her arms around him.

His brain went into a slow, complete meltdown as she draped her arms around his neck, her hip tucked against his cock. But that wasn't the worst. A fist reached up, grabbed him by the throat as she settled her head on his chest. "I don't think it was a total flop. Not really. The end of the night wasn't so bad, was it?"

Closing his eyes, he rested his head on hers. *Hell. I love you.*

The words almost escaped him then.

But he knew she wasn't ready. She thought she hid it, but he'd seen the fear, the nerves. He wasn't going to risk scaring her now. "No," he murmured. "The rest of the night wasn't so bad."

He settled his hand on her hip, fighting the urge to grab her, hold on tight, so tight she'd never be able to get free. "Still. We should have that real date. Without my brother. Without Abby. No interruptions. How about I make you dinner . . . here."

"Dinner." She lifted her head, studied him. "You cook?"

Stroking a finger along her cheek, he smiled. "Yeah. I cook. You'd probably be amazed."

"Anybody who can do anything more complicated than mac-n-cheese or a pizza from the freezer amazes me."

"Please. I passed that level before I was in high school.

Mom made sure of it. Only one of the boys failed the mom test—Seb." He curved his hand over the back of her neck. "Zach got stuck on anything more basic than breakfast, but Trey and I do pretty well. And Travis . . . well, he could give Abby a run for her money if he really wanted to."

"Then maybe you should have Travis cook." She gave him an innocent smile.

He bit her lip, licked her. "No. It's just us."

Chapter Eight

"I like the third one."

The tension in the air was thick enough to cut with a knife, but Keelie was focused on ignoring it.

So far, Zane and Zach were doing the same thing, although Zane had his hand on her spine as the three of them studied the web templates Zane had put together for Steel Ink's new site.

Web design wasn't particularly Zane's milieu, but he'd designed his own and if he did this one, he'd be able to showcase the photographs he'd be taking to their absolute best. It was, in short, a good starting point, he'd told Keelie when they met at the shop.

And she didn't care if it was his ideal job or not—she'd get on her knees and beg if it would get them something better than the eyesore they had.

Looking over at Zach, she lifted a brow. "What about you?"

He shrugged, eyes narrowed, as he stroked his thumb along his chin. "Torn between the second and third. The first one is out."

"Agreed." She nodded. "You'll have people pulling it up on their phones. I do. Plenty still don't like the mobile layouts. I think that will be the easiest to still get a good layout on a phone."

Zach shot Zane a look and he nodded. "Both will have a mobile layout but some people just don't like it that way. The second template isn't going to show up as well if somebody is trying to view it on a phone, or even a tablet."

"Yeah, I guess." Zach nodded. "Fine."

Zane hit a button and the images spread across the wall changed from templates to tattoos, but they weren't the basic pictures currently displayed on the website or out in the shop. "These are what we've got so far. I can do more while I'm here. Maybe you can offer a discount to those willing to let me get some shots either while the designs are being done or right after, whatever, if you want to build a larger gallery to display." Several images, all professional, all beautiful, flowed across the screen. "I've got images of you, Javi."

He paused and looked at Keelie. "We need a few for the female customer base."

She made a face at him. "I don't do pictures."

"Don't trust me?" He lifted a brow.

"I don't like seeing my face out there."

He shrugged. "Nobody said your face had to be on them. I can focus solely on the designs. People would never know it was you. Like . . ." He stopped and showed a cute little dragonfly, perched on the pale white curve of a woman's hip.

A soft growl escaped Zach. "When did she let you take that?"

Keelie glanced at Zach and then Zane, saw the glint in his eyes. "Aw, come on, man. You know Abby is like my kid sister. I told her we needed to get some images for the women's gallery. She was in her swimsuit when I took it. Relax."

"Fuck you," Zach said, shortly.

Zane just smiled, a cool twist of his lips before he shifted his attention back to Keelie. "What do you say? The rose on your neck, maybe? I guarantee nobody would see your face."

She shrugged restlessly. "I don't know. Maybe."

He let it go at that and started breaking down the equipment. Keelie went to head out, checking the time on her phone. Fifteen minutes before her first appointment. She had to get out of here, away from Zach and this awful tension. She had time enough for a cup of coffee—

"Keelie."

She paused in the doorway, looking back at Zach.

He was staring at his desk, his shoulders rigid under his Darth Vader T-shirt. "Yeah?" she said, trying not to let anything show in her voice.

Zane stood off to the side, his movements a little less fluid, a little sharper than they usually were.

Zach didn't say anything immediately.

Instead, he came out from behind his desk. Nudging Keelie back in his office, he shut the door and leaned against it, hands jammed into his pockets. Then, in a rush that had the words tripping over each other, he said, "I was an ass last night and I'm sorry. I shouldn't have fucked up your night and I wanted to apologize to both of you."

Keelie nibbled on her lower lip. Then she shrugged. "Okay." She eyed the way he continued to bar the door. "I've got an appointment soon and I need coffee."

Zach lifted his head, stared at her. "Are we okay?"

She sighed. "Zach . . ."

"I'm serious. Are we okay?"

Uncomfortable now, she looked away. "Sure we are."

"Are we?" He continued to stare at her and, feeling like a coward, she made herself look back at him. "It doesn't feel like we are."

"That's because neither of us seem to know what to say to each other anymore," she said softly. "That's my fault. But—"

"Maybe it's our fault." Zach glanced at his brother and then back at her. "You're like a sister to me and you . . . well. You threw me for a loop, but that doesn't mean I had to keep spinning, even after you went back to acting normal. I'm the one who kept putting the distance between us."

One of those little knots in her heart started to unravel. Moving forward, she reached out.

He didn't take her hand.

He caught her up in his arms and before she could prepare herself, she was trapped in a hug so tight, she couldn't breathe. But she didn't really care. She hadn't realized how much she missed this. Missed her friend, one of the first she'd really let herself have—let herself count on. Eyes burning, she pressed her face against his chest as she wrapped her arms around his waist and hugged him back.

Zane didn't say anything, even as she slid out the door.

Once more, Zach shut the door and then he stood there, staring at the large black-and-white block tiles for a long while.

After a few minutes, he looked up, opened his mouth. Then he closed it without saying anything.

Zane moved to the battered leather chair and dropped into it.

Zach's eyes went devilish.

"When Abby came back after we had that fight, we had sex in that chair. I thought about bronzing it, but figured I'd keep it here so I could look at it and remember whenever I was in a bad mood."

Zane pinched the bridge of his nose. "I'm pretty sure your germs are gone by now, man. Although I'll be sure to let Abby know you're sharing details of your personal life." He watched as Zach went white, waited a few seconds. "Or maybe not. I'd hate to have to see her get arrested over your sorry ass."

"What I want to know is why everybody thinks *you* are the nice one of the bunch," Zach muttered, throwing himself into the chair behind his desk.

"Maybe because I somehow managed to grow up?" Zane shrugged.

There was no answer but the silence between them was no longer so strained.

A minute or two passed and then Zach looked over at him. "If Keelie doesn't offer to let you do the pictures on her own, let it go."

Zane frowned.

"I mean it," Zach said, his voice low, brows coming to-gether in a hard line over his eyes. "She's weird about hav-ing pictures taken and it's not just because she doesn't like having them done. If she doesn't offer, don't ask. I'm asking you to let it go."

Studying his brother's face, Zane found himself fighting a world of questions, his curiosity biting at him.

But he nodded.

They'd found a peace and they were fine, but now wasn't the time for the questions.

"Okay." He nodded again. "Okay."

"Thanks." Zach propped his booted feet on the desk, swiping his phone from the edge. "I'm on until four, but there were a few places Abby wanted me to show you if you had time. Do you?"

"I've got some." Zane shrugged. "Anything in particu-lar?"

"Two places. One of them . . ." Zach grimaced. "I think she just likes the space herself. But the other one? Yeah. I can see it. She said it fell in your price range and it's in a decent area of town. Sounds like it's got enough space for you."

"Okay." Rising, he shot the chair a look and then shook his head. "You better not tell anybody else about that chair, man. Abby will kick your ass."

Zach flipped him off. "Wanna do dinner tonight?"

On his way to the door, Zane shook his head. "We can try lunch tomorrow or something. Since you kind of shot last night to hell, I'm cooking for Keelie tonight."

He paused before he opened the door, looked back.

Zach had a grim look on his face. "I am sorry."

"I know that. I'm still trying to figure out what the hell the problem was, though."

Zach's gaze moved to his. "If I could figure it out as easy as that, I'd . . . well. Maybe I'd tell you. But nothing has felt right with you, or Keelie, for a while. What happened . . ."

"It was a kiss," Zane said, his voice brusque. "And I hate to tell you this, Casanova, but I don't think you rocked her world. If that's what it took for her to understand you're not for her? Fine." As Zach's gaze moved to his, Zane opened the door. "Doesn't mean I didn't want to hit you over it."

"Didn't rock her world." Zach chuckled. "And have you?"

Zane snorted. "Fuck you, man."

He found Keelie in the front of the shop.

She had on a pair of black-and-white striped jeans that clung to her long, slim legs—they were so tight, he imagined he'd have to peel them off her. He was even fantasizing about doing just that. It was a pretty beautiful fantasy, too. He would take his time, watch each inch of skin as he bared it, the curls between her thighs—

"Hi, Zane!"

He looked up as a petite, pierced version of Tinker Bell appeared in front of him. Anais, with the rings running from her lobe to the curve of her left ear, a rainbow of glittery makeup on her eyes, and a wide, wicked smile, popped in front of him and smiled.

No. That wasn't a *smile*.

She beamed.

It was the first time he could remember meeting somebody who actually *beamed*.

She was pretty damn cute.

"You need to let me take your picture for the website."

She grinned at him. "I don't have any tats that these guys have."

He nodded at Keelie. "Make an appointment with her."

"She let me give her *one* piercing. An *easy* one. Hardly

any poking at all." Anais spread her hands out wide. "If somebody is going to poke me with a needle over and over, shouldn't I get to do the same?"

Zane scratched his head, squinting one eye as he pondered that logic. "Well. You've got more skin to tattoo than she has places to pierce."

"There are always plenty of places to pierce."

"Ani, you talked me into the one. That's it," Keelie said from the counter.

"These people are so uptight." Anais heaved out a sigh. "I tried to talk Zach into a Prince Albert and he went white."

Zane fought the urge to cover his cock protectively. He kept his expression blank only because he recognized that look in the woman's eyes. He had four younger siblings. He knew *exactly* when somebody was saying something just to get a rise out of him. "Well, considering what and where that goes, that's probably something he'd have to talk over with Abby."

"She'd enjoy it." Anais winked at him.

"Yeah. You try talking *her* into that," Zane advised.

Anais heaved out a sigh. "You're no fun. I say all of this to Zach and he starts acting like I'm trying to make him into a eunuch."

Grinning at her, Zane fought the urge to tug on one of the wide, buttery yellow curls. "The problem is that's the main reason you do it."

"You're onto me." Anais grinned and moved out of his way, throwing herself onto the long, low couch that ran along the length of the window.

Zane made his way over to Keelie. She glanced at him. "Onto her, huh?"

He braced his hands on the counter on either side of her. "I'd rather be on you."

She went red, that blush that fascinated him so much spreading across her face. Her eyes narrowed. "You've known me long enough to know how mean I am, right?"

He grinned.

"Good. Don't start. Not here."

"You're no fun." He dipped his head and nuzzled her neck. "You smell amazing."

She shivered.

Her hands came up and he braced himself in case she tried to push him away, but all she did was curl her hands into his shirt as she turned her face toward him. "I kind of prefer the way *you* smell," she whispered, her voice low, erratic. Then she sighed. "You have to go. You distract me and I've got an appointment."

"I'm going. I need to go to the store and I saw some ads for a few houses I wanted to look at anyway." He didn't back away, though, curving one hand over her hip, the silken warmth of her skin calling to him. "You and Zach—you going to be okay?"

He lifted his head so he could study her face.

"Yeah." Her lips bowed up. "We will be, now."

"Good." He brushed a kiss over her lips and backed away just as the door opened.

She slid him a smile and then moved past him. "Hey, Little Tom. You ready to finish up today?"

Zane glanced back over his shoulder as he headed for the hall.

Then he shook his head. *Little* Tom was so damn tall, Zane would have to tip his head back to meet his gaze. The guy had to be seven feet and his shoulders were probably almost half that wide.

And he blushed when Keelie smiled at him.

In the back of the shop, he paused by the table where Zach and Javi were bullshitting.

"Heading out?" Zach asked.

"Yeah." He glanced over at Javi. "Hey, man. We need to set up a time so I can get some more shots. You talk to Aida about letting me get a few of her?"

Javi rolled his eyes. "She keeps brushing me off. You oughta come by, talk to her, *amigo*."

"I'll call."

"Oh!" Javi winced and looked over at Zach. "Man, Aida, she's gonna kill me." He went over to the hooks hanging by the door, grabbed a worn leather bag and pulled it down. "I was supposed to give you this a week or two ago."

"Javi, your brain isn't attached to any other part of your body," Zach said, accepting a battered envelope.

"Sure it is. It's attached to my—"

Zane lifted a brow as Javi clamped his mouth shut. "What, you're behaving now?"

"I told my lady I'd try to mind my manners better." Javi shrugged.

Zach looked up from the card. "I didn't have anything to do with this."

"Don't bullshit me, man. I won't tell the school."

"I didn't."

Curious, Zane reached over and plucked the card from Zach's hand. Zach didn't stop him and Zane read the feminine script quickly.

Zach and Abby,

We heard from the school about the anonymous fund set up for the kids who didn't have the money available for the trip. Now the entire advanced group is able to go to the workshop in DC. While they weren't able to give us names, I have a feeling I know who is responsible. You all made it possible for Evie to go, but it was so very kind of you to provide the funds for the other kids as well. Thanks so much.

Aida

Zane slid his brother a glance. Zach shrugged. "I didn't do it. I'll ask Abby, but I don't think she did it, either. She would have mentioned it."

Zane handed the card to Javi. "Well, whoever did it, that was pretty nice of them. This was the thing you were talking about back at the wedding, right?"

"Yeah." Javi stared at the card, hard. "I . . . seriously, man. It wasn't you, boss?"

"No. I . . ." He paused as Keelie jogged in, grabbed a bottle of water. "Please tell me Little Tom isn't feeling queasy again."

"Nah. He's just thirsty." She paused, looked at Javi and Zach. "What's up?"

Javi waved the card at her. "Somebody set up a fund for thousands of dollars at my baby's school. We thought it was Zach and Abby, but they say no. I dunno who else could have that kind of money. It would be like fifty grand or more, and they said they'll renew the grant as deemed appropriate." His face brightened. "Hey . . . hey! Sebastian! He was there!"

"No, he wasn't." Zane shook his head. "He'd wandered off by then. And hate to say this, pal. If he'd done it, he'd have his name all over it. In bright, sparkling letters."

Keelie took the card, read it. Then she shrugged and passed it back. "What does it matter who did it? I gotta get going. If I take too long, Little Tom *will* get queasy." She flashed a smile at Zane.

It hit him, right in the gut.

She was gone before he could give in to the need to grab her, plant a hard kiss on that pretty mouth.

"The big guy." Zane ran his tongue across his teeth. "He gets queasy."

"He passed out on Keelie once." Javi shoved the card in his back pocket and grinned at Zane. "Was sitting up in the chair and Keelie had to hold him there when he started to slip out of it. She threatened to kill me if I took a picture of her."

"You're an ass, Javi," Zach said, sighing.

"Yeah. That's why you love me."

"So have you hit anyplace since you got in town?" Zach asked.

It was two hours earlier than planned, but some of Zach's appointments had cancelled. That worked out better really, because Zane hadn't had time to figure out what he wanted to cook and he still needed to do that, go to the store. This would take up an hour or so and then he'd be free to focus on Keelie.

"Nope." Zane swapped out his regular glasses for sunglasses as Zach climbed inside the convertible. Zach had the top off and the sun seemed way too bright and it was way too high in the sky for Zane's liking. But then again, it had taken him until two a.m. to fall asleep. Being curled around Keelie's naked body had been both pleasure and pain—he hadn't wanted to miss a moment of it. "I did some driving around earlier, but I was looking at houses."

"Houses. You can use the loft, you know. It's paid for. Save you money while you're building the studio up." Zach scowled, his hair already escaping the band he'd used to pull it back. "You need to be careful how much money you go throwing around."

Zane managed not to laugh, although it was hard. The idea of Zach lecturing him on money was hilarious.

"I appreciate it, but I got it under control."

"I'm serious." Zach gave him a narrow look before he pulled out of the parking lot. "The first couple of years are rough for small-business types. And I had money to fall back on."

"Zach? I appreciate the concern, but I got this." He slumped in the seat and squinted as the sun proceeded to shine directly in his eyes. "Just two places, right?"

"Yep. We can hit the one farthest out first—it's the one I think Abby just likes because she likes it." Zach grinned. "If that makes sense."

"Since when you do you make sense?" Zane swiped through a recipe website on his phone, careful to keep it angled away from his brother. He might have to put up with some razzing from his brothers over the fact that he knew his way around a kitchen—and enjoyed it—he wasn't in the mood to listen to Zach's ribbing him about digging around for ideas on what to make for dinner.

"I ran that idea for the discount thing by a couple of my regulars. They like it. You going be here long this time?"

Zach hit the road, driving like he'd spent most of his formative years as a stunt double, not a child star on a sitcom.

Zane set his jaw and managed not to brace himself as Zach took a corner at a speed that really should have sent them spinning out of control.

"You realize they have speed limits for a reason, right?" he said calmly. "And if you hit anybody going this fast, you're going to do damage."

Zach grimaced and slowed down. "I'm not going to hit anybody. And you didn't answer me."

"A few weeks this time. I'm waiting for my stuff to get here, put what I don't need in storage. I had a call from my real estate agent—somebody made an offer on my place, sounds serious."

"That was fast. Is it fair?"

Zane shrugged, eyed the road, decided it was safe to look away. "Yeah. It's a little lower than I'd like but the economy sucks." It was also more than Zane had paid, but he'd been adding on and upgrading, so he was coming out on top. Plus, the house was paid off. Maybe Zach had money coming in from the show and syndication, but Zane actually understood the language of *money*. The game of it. He'd paid his house off two years ago and once he moved here, the only real debt he'd have would be the studio.

Unaware of Zane's thoughts, Zach shrugged. "That happens. Just remember you can use the loft as long as you need it."

"Thanks," Zane said, smiling a little. He eyed a marinade that popped up, wracked his memory—he'd seen Keelie tear through a steak at a cookout over at Abby's once. That could work.

They reached the first place and even though Zane could see why Abby liked it even from the outside, he knew it wouldn't work.

Climbing out of the car, he met Zach's gaze.

It was a modern, sprawling building done in desert tones of beige and sand, with a pretty garden that surrounded the perimeter, ornate windows and doors. Everything flowed and fit. And it also screamed *female*.

Zane ran his tongue along his teeth.

"It looks like Southwestern Barbie has some property available for lease," he said.

"Yeah. She'd be your landlord."

In that very moment, the door opened.

Zane closed his eyes at the squeal of delight that came from the door.

"Zach!"

Oh, yeah, he thought as a long, stacked blonde came rushing down the steps. Big round breasts pressed against a fitted, designer T-shirt and jeans gloved lush hips and long legs. Her feet were clad in shiny silver sandals, teal nail polish on her toes.

She flung her arms around Zach.

"Hi, Leslie." Zach turned his head and grimaced at Zane. "Abby didn't tell me you were the other tenant here."

"Didn't she?" The woman pulled back and smacked a loud, delighted kiss on Zach's mouth. "Silly her! I'm part owner, too!"

Zane smiled at her blandly as she looked at him.

Zach cleared his throat. "Zane, this is Leslie. Abby met her through the wedding circuit when Leslie used to plan weddings."

"Oh, that was ages ago. I'm a massage therapist now." She smiled at him and held out a hand. And her eyes slid over him so thoroughly, he had the feeling she could have gone out and bought him a set of clothes . . . and underwear, from that look alone. "So. Are you the one who needs to rent some space?"

No. No. Absolutely not. The words leaped to Zane's lips, but he managed to give the woman a polite smile. "Right now, I'm just looking at my options."

And this wasn't one of them.

"She did that to be mean," Zane muttered as they pulled away thirty minutes later.

His head was still spinning from the incense and the scent of candles that had pervaded the air.

"She probably did it to get back at us for something. What, we may never know." Zach sighed, glanced in the window.

Leslie with the big breasts and sweet smile and unexpectedly gentle humor wasn't anywhere in sight. She'd taken Zane's honest statement—*I need space for a photography studio and I don't think this will work*—with good grace. When she'd pushed for why, he went with a diplomatic response, and not the *Southwestern Barbie* one he'd given Zach.

A lot of people have issues with scents, and the incenses, the candles here—I'm worried it would bother them. I have to keep this in mind.

She'd nodded, completely okay with that.

Then she wished them luck.

They'd left her massage parlor behind with a quiet sigh of relief, and she'd offered both of them a free session.

Zach, of course, was welcome to bring Abby for a couple's session.

"Couples massages," Zane said, pondering the idea as they drove to the other location. "Is that a romantic thing?"

"Abby thinks so. We did one in Alaska." Zach shrugged, shot him a grin. "I was just laying there thinking about how much I hated having a guy put his hands on Abby while she was naked. He was gay, but I still didn't like it. She should have had the woman."

"Abby might have requested to have him." Zane was never one to miss the chance to needle his brother. "You and Seb have a big following, ya know. She probably knew he was gay and didn't want him thinking anything while he had his hands on you."

Zach opened his mouth. Shut it. His hand started drumming on the console between them.

When he didn't say anything after a minute, Zane pushed him. "What, no comment?"

"Go fuck yourself, man." Zach just sent him a look, rolling his eyes. Then he nodded at the building in front of them. "We're here. Abby knows the current owner. She said he's willing to let you in, if you want. Might be able to swing it today, if you have time. Not sure how long it would take."

Zane looked away from his brother, a comment on his tongue.

But it died as he took in the building in front of them.

Whoa.

Zach shoved the car into park and Zane was out of the car a split second later, almost forgetting his bag. He swapped out his glasses as they neared the building and he lingered at the windows, staring inside as Zach put in a call to Abby.

"I figured that was a yes," Zach said as Zane moved to the other window.

"What's a yes?" he asked, distracted. The floor space looked perfect, he thought.

"You want to look inside."

He stopped, looked at his brother and then back at the building. Then he grinned. "Yeah. I wanna look inside." He went back to staring in through the glass while Zane went back to talking.

"Well, you're in luck," Zach said a minute later. "He was having lunch with Abby and a couple of her friends. He's on his way over."

Zane looked over at his brother.

Zach shrugged. "He's a wedding photographer. They all spend a lot of time together around here. He's moving out of state soon, but they're pretty good friends."

A few minutes later, Zane was inside, pacing the floor while Zach, Abby, and the owner—a slim, short Asian-American chatted near the front.

Gleaming hardwood floors.

Lots of windows.

An angled slope of a ceiling that caught Zane's eye the minute they came inside.

This was perfect.

He didn't even have to look at anything else.

Yeah, he'd be in bride-to-be central with Abby's catering place a few doors down and the wedding dress boutique across the way, but that wasn't a problem. He already figured he'd be doing some of that for a while anyway, so what better place to be?

He just wouldn't make bridal photography his sole focus when he did his advertising—or as he set up things here once he started designing everything inside.

Here.

The idea settled inside him, anticipation curling through him.

Yes.

Here.

It really was perfect.

Twined with that anticipation was a bit of nerves though and he blew out a breath, rubbing the back of his neck. He really was doing this.

"Wishing you hadn't quit your job?"

At the sound of Zach's voice, he glanced over at his brother.

"I quit because I was ready to do it," he said, shrugging.

"Safety net's gone, though." Zach hooked his thumbs in his pockets. "Now it's all up to you. You gotta push now, make it work."

Zane studied his brother with narrowed eyes. Zach didn't really look much different from the pretty-boy actor he'd been years ago. Well, except for the longer hair, the tattoos that climbed up his arms, and his face was a little leaner, a little harder.

Sometimes, though, he was still every bit as annoying—or worse.

"Wow. I'm gonna have to work?" Zane drawled. "Shit. Why didn't anybody tell me that? Here I was thinking spending anywhere from eight to ten hours a night on my feet was easy. Not to mention the grabby hands some of those pretty ladies get, especially after a few tequila shots."

"Z, wait . . ."

The apology was already there in Zach's voice. Shaking his head, he looked back at Zach. "Man, I know how to work. I know how to work for what I want. I just never wanted it enough until lately." He paused, the rest of it trembling there, but finally, he just said it. "Not all of us were as lucky as you, Zach."

Zach's jaw went tight. "Lucky?"

"Yeah. Lucky . . . and I'm not talking about Abby, although, son, you hit the jackpot there and fuck the fact that it took a while to happen." Zane walked over to the exposed brick wall. Off near the front, he could hear Abby and the owner talking—Conan. While they continued to chat, Zane lifted a hand and pressed it to the brick, imagined seeing some of his prints hanging there, framed.

"You're lucky," he said after a moment. "You always had a picture in your head. Once the show stopped, you had a goal. Everything you wanted was always right in front of you, crystal-clear . . . right in focus. Me? Every time I tried to zoom in, it just got harder and harder to see it. It took this long to actually make it clear in my head. But just because it took a while doesn't mean I don't know how to make it work, pretty boy."

"Is it clear now?"

Turning, he met Zach's eyes. "It's more clear now than it's ever been. Why else would I be here?"

Not all of us were as lucky as you.

It was something of a rub to realize that guilt was still there. Zach had thought he'd gotten over it a good ten years ago, at least. More. Even fifteen years ago. He'd left Hollywood behind. There was no reason he couldn't leave behind that guilt, too.

But it wasn't as easy as all that.

They thought he hadn't noticed, but he had.

More than once, some asshole reporter would shove a microphone under the nose of one of his brothers with those obnoxious questions . . . *What's it like living in the shadow of such a famous brother? What's it like knowing that your brother's talent is what made it possible for your family to have such a good life?*

Yeah, those reporters could screw themselves sideways, a dozen times over. His brothers had either ignored the questions or laughed them off, because they were all close, they all loved each other.

Oddly enough, it was Zach who hadn't been able to brush them off.

It was Zach who felt guilty when somebody would make a jab at one of his brothers. Every last one of them was talented. Trey with his books, Seb and the way his star was just taking off—Zach's was all but gone and he was fine with that. Travis had turned out a little more serious than Zach would have expected, but he was a good man, worked hard. And Zane . . . everybody's protector, the one who took care of all of them. He thought nobody saw it, but they all did. And he stood in the shadows with his camera, capturing secrets some people didn't even realize they had.

They didn't live in anybody's shadow.

And here Zach was, tooling away his life in a tattoo parlor. He was damn happy with the way his life was going. He had peace now, privacy, the ability to live his life without worrying how it would affect others. He wouldn't give it up for nothing.

It was what he'd wanted for a long time, and he was doing just what he'd wanted.

Yeah, he was lucky.

He was also an idiot—

"If you don't tell me what's bothering you, I might not share this with you."

Looking up, he watched as Abby crossed the floor.

She had a plate in her hand and he had to smile as she settled on his lap, one knee on either side of his hips. She had a giant brownie and the smell of it had his stomach growling.

"Maybe I'll just take it," he teased, trying to brush aside the brooding thoughts.

She laid the plate on the couch and cupped his face. "Tell me you didn't fight with Zane again. And don't try to brush this off. Don't lie and say nothing's wrong. I know you too well."

If anybody could say that, it was her. But for the longest time, he didn't say anything. "Have I had it easy, Abby?"

She frowned, sliding her arms around his shoulders as she studied him. "What?"

"You heard me." He slumped deeper into the couch, studying her from under his lids. "Have I had it easy? I mean, the two of us both know that Hollywood isn't exactly the dream gig plenty of people make it out to be, but it wasn't like my parents went crazy with it. They kept my life pretty normal. They were—*are* good parents. I have some great brothers, didn't have to fight my way through school, and I knew what I wanted almost from the beginning." He stroked his thumb across her lower lip. "The hardest fight I've ever had was for you."

She arched a brow. "Are you implying something there?"

"Hell, no." He tugged her closer and caught her mouth, a punch of lust crushing through him as she opened for him. A soft hmmm of pleasure rose in her throat and he swallowed it down. Slowly, he broke the kiss and cupped her cheek, looking into the brown eyes that knew him so well. "You were worth every day, every week, every year I waited. I'd go to hell and back for you if that's what it took. It's just that . . ."

"Is this about Zane?"

Sighing, he closed his eyes. "I told him he didn't have a safety net anymore. He'd up and quit his job and he'd have to start working hard." He looked back at her. "Then he told me that not everybody was as lucky as I was."

For a moment, Abby didn't say anything.

Then, she straightened up, laying one hand against his cheek.

"Zane's not afraid of working hard," Abby said, her voice soft. "He's afraid of not being good enough. He had to get rid of that safety net. Otherwise he won't ever see just how amazing he is."

Zach covered her hand with his. "I know he's amazing. I've been telling him to quit bartending for years, but . . ."

"Now he's done it. Why aren't you happy?"

"I am," he said. Then he closed his eyes, realization hitting him. "I . . . I just don't know what's going to happen if it turns out he can't make it. He's walking away from everything. Selling his house. Giving up a job. Trying to make a living on something he's only played at. What if it doesn't work? Then what does he do?"

"He tries harder." Abby hugged him. "Zach, baby. It's sweet that you're worrying about your big brother like this, but Zane has a game plan. He's thought things through and he's got a sound business model. He'll be okay."

"A sound business model." The words had made him shudder the first time Abby had put them on the table in front of him. "Does he even realize how hard running a business is?"

Abby pressed a kiss to his ear, chuckling. Then she settled down on the couch next to them and reached for the plate—and the giant brownie. "Zach, I was the one who helped *you* figure out a business model, remember? Zane is ten steps ahead of where *you* were after you'd been in business on your own for six months. He can handle this." She cut off a bite with the fork and held it out to him. "You seem to forget who you're talking about, slick. This is Zane. He handles everything, remember?"

"Yeah." Despite himself, he chuckled. "He does."

Then he sighed, slid a hand up her knee. "I guess that's what's bugging me. Maybe I have had it easy . . . and he fights, pushes . . . handles it. He ought to have more than just . . . *handling* it."

Chapter Nine

Zane had the Realtor's number in his pocket.

He had a figure in his brain.

He had dinner to cook.

Or, well, he had steaks to marinate and a salad to deal with, because the rest he wasn't doing until Keelie was over here.

Keelie . . .

His brain was full and all it took to make those thoughts die was that one thought of *her*.

He'd be picking her up in a few hours and just thinking about that made his skin go tight, his cock start to ache, and his heart start to thud.

Since he couldn't get through what he needed to do if he was mentally jacking off, he pushed those thoughts out of his head as he parked the rental car.

Dinner.

He'd deal with dinner. Putting up the groceries he'd grabbed.

Mundane stuff.

He even managed to make it all the way to the top floor

by thinking about that mundane stuff. Then one of the bags he was juggling started to slide out of his grip. Swearing, he tried to scramble everything together before the elevator door opened, and he'd almost managed it, too.

The booted foot stopped the door from closing. "Z, you know, Mom said you'd outgrow that clumsy thing," a wry voice said.

Zane grimaced and shot a look up.

The sight of the man in front of him would normally make him smile.

Normally.

But he wasn't feeling social enough to deal with another brother. Especially not Travis. The son of a bitch saw too much.

If it had been more than five years ago, just about everybody else on the planet would have had an impossible time figuring out which twin they were looking at.

Zane hadn't had that problem, not that he'd let on.

The twins were identical, right down to the mole each of them had just a little below and to the side of their right eye. Side by side, you could tell it was in a slightly different spot—and Denise Barnes alone knew which was which by the position of that little discoloration.

But then Trey's wife had died and that had caused a change in him.

Zane had always been able to tell, because Travis looked at things in a weird sort of way. Zane couldn't define it really. He just noticed it because while *he* looked at people and places and things the same way he'd look at them if he was going to photograph them, Travis looked at them like he was trying to figure them out.

Life was one unending puzzle for Travis Barnes, although he hid that facet of his personality behind the sly humor that had matched his twin's.

Eying his younger brother, Zane managed to get the bags back into position as Travis scooped up the few items he'd dropped.

"Trav. Long time no see," he said, somehow making it to his feet, the bags precariously balanced in his arms.

"Yeah. All of three months. You got to kiss the bride and I got shafted there because my nephew insisted I take him to the bathroom." Travis lifted a brow as he studied the bags. "You have your hands full."

"As always, your powers of deduction astound me, kid. You must make a killing in the accounting field—that very fascinating field."

Travis snorted out a laugh and reached out, grabbing one of the bags. "Hey, it's more fun than you think. And some women think it's a hella sexy. One even asked if I could fingerprint her."

Zane stared at Travis. "Fingerprint her."

"Yep. Cuz that's what a forensic accountant does. We fingerprint balance sheets and 1040s and W-9s." He gave Zane a sober look. "Didn't you know that?"

"You need to start talking to women who have actual brains in their heads." He tried to imagine his genius brother spending his life fingerprinting balance sheets and tax forms. "Maybe at least look for somebody with an IQ higher than her bra size," Zane muttered, shaking his head. He unlocked the door and then started to swear as another bag went on a downward slide.

"Your grace astounds me. How can you tote around cameras that cost ten grand without dropping them, but give you groceries and you're all thumbs?" Travis took another bag and came in after Zane, kicking the door shut. "At least you don't come home with a black eye once every other week all because you were in the way of somebody's elbow during basketball."

Zane grimaced, studiously keeping his gaze averted. Yeah. There is *that*. "I'll have you know I only drop stuff once a week and twice on Saturdays now. Just out of habit." Dumping the bags on the island, he looked at his brother.

Trey and Travis—the twins—were a couple of years younger than Zach. Out of all of his brothers, Travis was the one he saw the least. It was the job—and no matter what Travis said, it still sounded boring as hell. But it kept him busy and hc traveled a lot. Consulting, according to Travis.

"What brings you to Arizona?" he asked.

Travis shrugged and started to unpack the bags. "Just visiting. I have to head to Europe for a while, wanted to see everybody before I headed to Virginia. I'll hang with Trey a few days, then disappear. Hey, did you hear he was doing a thing at a bookstore in a couple of weeks?"

"Ohhhh . . . yeah." Zane ran his tongue around his teeth. Trey hadn't done anything book-related, well, other than writing, since his wife's death several years earlier. "I about had a heart attack over that one. Mom mentioned it when I was in San Francisco a few weeks ago. And the conference a few weeks after? Who in the hell blackmailed him into that?"

Travis shot him a grin. "Mom? That's my best guess." He shrugged. "I called him to rib him about it, but he wouldn't say much. Clay keeps asking to go visit Mom and Dad . . . and I think he's trying to adjust to the little guy starting school soon."

"He'll be fine," Zane said.

They both knew he wasn't talking about the kid.

Trey had all but shut down. His entire focus was the boy and that boy was moving closer and closer to starting school.

Trey didn't even like leaving the kid with a babysitter. It was going to rip a hole in him to send that kid to school the first day.

Hell. The first *month*.

"Will he?" Travis asked, his voice soft as he took the cloth sack and crumpled it into one big fist. His blue eyes stared at nothing. "Everybody keeps saying he'll be fine. He's not fine. I talk to him and I hear his voice and I know— *he's not fine*. He's twenty-nine years old and he's so far from fine I don't even know where to start. He's locked up inside himself. He's been like this for years and I saw it coming, but I thought . . ."

He stopped and stared up at the ceiling. "Fuck," Travis

muttered. "Mom saw it coming. I told her to leave him alone. He'd work it out. But he's just gotten worse."

"He *will* be fine," Zane said again, despite the knot of worry. "Something is going to happen that will jar him out of that empty place where he goes and he'll be forced to open his eyes and look around. You'll see."

"I hope so." Travis didn't look convinced. "There was this . . ."

Then he stopped, shook his head. "That his business anyway." He shrugged, looking away. When he looked back, it was like the tension of the past moment had just disappeared. "So, you're here. Why are you here and not in Albuquerque? I was going to crash here. I guess I can flop on the . . ."

He paused and then eyed the box he had in his hand. "Or maybe not."

Zane caught the box of Trojans Travis tossed his way.

"Got plans, Z?" A wide, wicked grin split his face. "And here I was thinking I should worry about you *and* Trey. I guess not."

"Seeing as how you were too afraid to even *buy* your first box of condoms when you needed them? I think I can do without your concern, kid," Zane advised, heading out of the kitchen. He put the box in the nightstand and turned around to see Travis loitering behind him.

"Condoms in the nightstand." He turned and looked back into the kitchen, a thoughtful look on his face. "I don't tend to do a lot of cooking on my own—it's just me most of the time. But it seems to me you've got the goings for a some-what nice meal in there."

Zane was quiet for a minute and then he pushed past his brother. "Zach and Abby have room at their place. I can give them a call. Or I can—"

"I can find my own room," Travis said, his voice mild. "Now be quiet. I'm thinking here . . . although really, there's not much to think through. Either you're big on wishful thinking or she finally decided to put you out of your misery."

Zane grabbed the olive oil he'd bought and put it in a cabinet near the stove. "Last time I was in town, I stayed at this nice little hotel on the outskirts of town. Quiet. Kind of run-down but it had a killer view. Give me a minute and I'll remember the name."

"What time will Keelie be here?"

Zane shot him a dark look. "Can you just shut your mouth? For maybe the next month—also, it wouldn't hurt if you could fail to mention this. To everybody."

"Now that kind of silence will cost you." Travis grinned.

"Oh, kiss ass." He flipped him off and then stared up at the sky. "Just what do you want?"

Cheerfully, Travis said, "I'll hold it in reserve. Don't worry, I'm not as demanding as the others are. I'm not going to mess with a hotel, though. If I can't inflict my presence upon you, I'll just go crash at Zach's house. Abby will cook breakfast."

"Do that." Despite himself, he couldn't keep the sharp edge out of his voice.

Travis caught it. Narrowing his eyes, Travis cocked his head and waited.

Zane ignored him.

And Travis just waited.

Now this was why Travis pissed him off.

The son of a bitch should have been a psychologist or a cop or something, the way people spilled their guts to him.

Finally, he turned and crossed his arms over his chest, stared the younger Barnes down. "Zach is a mule-headed son of a bitch."

"You say this like it's news," Travis pointed out.

Zane didn't comment for a long, long moment. Staring off into the distance, he brooded, debated. Then he started to talk.

Travis said nothing until Zane had finished. Zane started with the kiss Keelie had laid on Zach months ago—Zach hadn't told anybody but him—and he finished with the visit to the space Zane thought he just might try to buy to use for his studio.

When he stopped talking, Travis pushed off the counter and went to the fridge, opened it. He studied the sadly lacking contents and pulled out a beer. "Zach has been lucky," he said after a minute. "We all have, in one way or another. But Zach . . . yeah, he always knew what he wanted, where he was going. He worked for it, chased it. Doesn't see how hard it can be for others, but that doesn't mean he doesn't deserve what he has."

"I know that," Zane said tiredly. Rubbing the back of his neck, he shoved off the counter. "I just . . ."

Travis slid him a look. "He's just worried. He shouldn't be. If anybody can make something work, it's you. He'll figure that out. It's probably just because you're grabbing for everything at once. You don't do anything fast and all of sudden, you quit your job, you're moving, you're selling your house . . . Keelie."

"I think I can handle it," Zane said mildly.

Travis absently stroked his thumb across the neat goatee he'd grown over the past year, his eyes still staring over into nothing. "It's not about you handling it. He wants you to be happy. With the job, with Keelie. With everything."

"That's why I'm doing this." Zane shrugged.

"I know. He'll figure it out, too." Travis took a long pull of his beer and then leaned back against the counter. "So. Keelie. You took long enough."

Zane snorted. "You're not exactly one to comment about my lack of social life. When was the last time you were serious about somebody?"

"Never." He shrugged and focused on Zane. "But it's not like I've got a job that actually allows for it. I travel all over the place and I never really meet anybody. But, hey, it could be worse . . ."

A sly grin lit his face and Zane lifted a brow at it, a mix of curiosity and dread mingling inside him.

"Yeah? How is that?" he asked.

"I could been floundering at the door, fighting to get my damn dick in my jeans because the zipper is stuck while some ditzy extra is trying to understand why I'm panicking over the sound of somebody calling my name at the door." Travis took another drink from the bottle and lowered it, sighing in satisfaction, a devilish grin on his face.

The word *extra* had Zane cocking a brow.

"Just what has Sebastian gotten into now?"

A gleam appeared in Travis's eyes. "He forgot Mom was coming over a few weeks ago—she let herself in and if she hadn't pulled a mom thing and started picking up some his clothes, fussing at him in the middle of it, she would have walked in right while he was having some one-on-one time with some cute extra they hired for the new action flick he just finished shooting."

"And what's this thing about his zipper?"

"Now that's the best part," Travis said, laughing. "I think fate was giving him a much-needed reminder to come down to earth—Mom said she heard him yelp all the way across the house."

"Oh. Son of a bitch." Zane damn near clapped his hands over his cock protectively. And Travis stood there laughing about it. "Kid, you are evil."

"Yeah. You tell people that all the time. Nobody believes you." Travis's blue eyes gleamed as he said it.

Zane eyed the apartment in front of him, still not quite able to make this place *fit*.

Keelie lived here.

And it didn't fit.

Zach's loft—or his *old* loft—wasn't exactly *luxury*, but it was pretty sweet. Yeah, maybe Zane's little brother still had money from the TV show, but he'd also mentioned that Steel Ink turned a decent profit. Hadn't the first few years, but most small businesses struggled at first.

It was doing well now, though. Zach talked about it enough, with enough pride in his voice, that he knew the place did well.

Javi made decent money—he was talking about the bike he'd just bought and was working on restoring. He'd had the money to pay half the fee needed to send his daughter on an expensive workshop to DC.

They had a couple of full-time artists and Zach was even talking like he might open a second location in Phoenix.

The place was doing pretty well.

So why was Keelie living somewhere that looked like it was going to fall down around her ears?

This place . . . it didn't fit. Or rather, it was like she'd *made* it fit. He frowned as that idea settled itself in his mind. It settled there, took root, and he couldn't push it aside. Sighing, he climbed out and looked around, eying the car next door, propped on cinderblocks. There was somebody attempting to clean some graffiti off the door and he nodded at Zane. "Hi there."

"Hey." Zane smiled as he headed for the door.

Screaming broke out in the other building and from the corner of his eye, Zane saw the man dealing with the graffiti lift his face to the sky, like he was praying for patience.

A second later, the front door flew open. A skinny man— just barely old enough to be called a man—came out, his jeans riding way too low on his hips. On his heels, there was a woman, and when he turned around to glare at her, the woman slapped him. "Is that the fucking best you can do? I give you two fucking kids and you make a lousy two hundred a week?"

Zane looked over.

"Yeah. That's the best I can do."

"Why isn't there any money left now? Where did it all go?" the woman demanded.

"Bills. Water. Electricity. The sitter. My truck," the guy said, without looking back.

"We don't need a fucking sitter!"

"We do if you're drinking when the kids are here."

The door in front of Zane opened.

He swung his head around and, for a minute, the screaming coming from the other apartment faded away. The spit dried in his mouth and he went still.

Keelie stood there, and if she'd struck him across the

head with a two-by-four, it might have had about the same impact. There was a faint smile on her lips—lips painted a dark, lush red. Her eyes were shadowed, dark, made up in a way that complemented both the blue eye and the brown. Her head cocked as she studied him, a fringe of black falling down to frame her face. The rest of it was scooped back, leaving the elegant line of her neck, and the brilliant color of the tattoos there unobstructed.

Her shoulders and arms were bare. Ruched silk clung to her torso, dipped low over her breasts. The blouse ended at her hips and a skirt of midnight started, only to end a few inches later, revealing legs that just went on and on.

Zane found himself envisioning grabbing that cloth, dragging it up . . .

"Are you ready?"

Her voice startled him out of the daydream and he jerked his gaze upward, met her eyes. "Ah . . ."

She lifted a brow.

"Sorry." Zane had to clear his throat, feeling pretty much like he had when he'd shown up on the doorstep the first time he'd actually asked a girl out—and she'd accepted.

The yelling picked up next door and lines appeared near Keelie's mouth. Zane held out a hand. "Looks like you've got your own live reality TV show living right next door."

"Yeah." She glanced over and then looked back at him. "Wouldn't be so bad if it wasn't for her. He busts his ass. She up and disappears with his paycheck half the time." She jerked a shoulder in a shrug. "The good news is . . . they aren't the worst neighbors I've ever had."

"What's the bad news?"

She lifted a brow. "Listen to them. Do I need to expand?"

"Good point."

She glanced past him, sighing. "The cops will be here in a minute."

"Cops?"

"Yeah." She angled her head to the other building. "That's my landlord. He's on his phone. Fifty bucks says he's calling the cops."

He had nothing to say to that. As the yelling next door got louder and louder, he stepped aside and gestured to his car. "You ready? I'm starving."

Just brilliant.

Keelie settled into the passenger's seat with a mental groan. Before Zane had managed to shut the door, she caught the wail of sirens. She'd been right—her landlord *had* called the cops, it seemed. Rarely a month went by when this didn't happen with Tara and Nolan. She glanced in the mirror, watched as Tara hit her boyfriend—or whatever Nolan viewed himself as these days—punching bag seemed more apt.

He took it like a champ, his head swinging from the force of the blow, but all he did was stand there. She saw him spit something—it looked like blood—on the ground and then he turned away.

Tara kept screaming, the sound muted by Zane's car.

If Nolan would see the light and maybe press charges against Tara one of these days, he could probably fight for custody of the kids, maybe even win. Battery wasn't a charge that belonged solely to the male persuasion, something that Keelie had seen with her own two eyes, and she'd seen it a *lot* since those two had moved in. There was rarely more than a week or two when the poor kid didn't have either his eye blackened or his mouth swollen, thanks to his lady's attention.

But he wouldn't leave.

Cops came peeling around the corner as Zane pulled away from the block. "Is this just a typical Saturday night?" he asked softly.

"Nah. This is actually fairly quiet." She gave him a grim smile. "Once she went after him with a lead pipe."

"You're kidding me."

"Nope." She shrugged, thought about the baseball bat she kept tucked behind her front door for just such occasions. She'd even hauled it out once, threatened to use it.

The cops had let her go with a warning. The fact that they knew all about Tara probably had plenty to do with why Keelie hadn't gotten arrested for assault. That, and the fact that Nolan's forearm had been broken from the first blow Tara had laid on him with that lead pipe.

Tara had pled guilty to assault but she'd ended up doing only three months and then she was back home. That had been when their oldest was six months old.

If Nolan had left then . . .

"And he's still here," Zane said, shaking his head.

"Because of the kids." Keelie glanced up at the apartment, but the little girls were nowhere to be seen. Thank God for small favors.

"He's not helping them any."

"No." She slid him a look. "He's not. He ought to just take them and go." Blocking out the familiar flash of lights coming up behind them, she focused on Zane. "So . . . you told me you were making me dinner."

A smile curled his lips. "Yes. I did." He caught her hand and lifted it to his lips. "And I told you that you just might be amazed."

"You're doing that on a fairly regular basis, Zane."

He chuckled. "Just wait."

Chapter Ten

"So . . . favorite movie?"

She eyed him over the steak and cut another bite, popped it into her mouth and chewed before she spoke. "I'm eating. Be quiet. I want more."

Zane laughed. "Hey, you were the one you grumbled a few weeks ago that we weren't the typical *get to know you* thing. We're here, nobody is going to interrupt. Ideal time, right?"

She rolled her eyes and looked down at her plate. "The steak is almost gone."

"I guess I should have bought bigger steaks."

She rested a hand on her belly. "Maybe." Sighing, she leaned back in the seat, feeling just a little too full. "Although I already ate too much." Reaching for her wine, she eyed him narrowly. "Favorite movie, huh? *Addams Family*—the one they did with Anjelica Huston and Raul Julia. Only the first one, though." She waited for a comment.

"Yeah?" All he did was cock his head and study her. "Why?"

She sipped at her wine, feeling a little self-conscious

now. "Hard to explain." Lowering her glass to the table, she shot him a look and shrugged. "It was one of the last movies I saw with my dad before he died. I mean, they were crazy and all, but they were . . . happy. They loved each other. Gomez and Morticia . . ."

"One of the greatest romances in all of Hollywood." He smiled, looking amused.

Cocking an eyebrow, she said, "Make fun and I won't help you with the dishes."

He pushed his chair back and came around to kneel down next to her. "You're not helping me anyway. But I won't make fun. I like the movie, too. The first one was the best, if you ask me." He pushed her chair out and then dipped his head, lowered his lips to kiss her knee. "I took Italian because of that movie."

Well, damn. "You're kidding."

"Nope." He slid a hand up her thigh, his fingers toying with the hem of her skirt. *"Cara mia . . ."*

Something hot and liquid spread through her as he leaned in and murmured to her in a language that secretly turned her into mush. That was *another* reason—one of her early movie crushes had been none other than Gomez. So she was weird. So what?

As Zane caught her ear between his teeth and tugged, she shivered.

Then he whispered, *"Ti voglio piú di quanto abbia mai voluto un'altra donna."*

She curled her hands into fists while her mind struggled to translate. She thought maybe he told her he wanted her. Maybe. But he could have been reading a grocery list for all she cared. "That sounds a little too practiced to be your typical high school language requirement."

"I didn't just speak it in high school." He kissed his way across her cheek, slanted his mouth over hers.

For the next few seconds, nothing else in the world seemed to matter. His tongue caught hers, toyed, tangled, while his hands slid under the hem of her short, tight skirt and moved up to trace the edge of her panties. Liquid heat spread through her and if he hadn't kept her knees pinned in place with his body weight, she thought she might have wrapped herself around him like a vine and started to rock in sheer, desperate hunger.

His hand rested on her side and he slid it up.

Yes, please!

But all he did was move it up to rest on her throat, easing back.

"I spent a year in Italy. A year in France."

She blinked up at him, confused for a minute. Then, slitting her eyes, she leaned back. "You've been to Italy."

"Yeah." He brushed his thumb over her lips. "It's beautiful."

"I think I hate you."

He chuckled. "Now, don't say that . . ."

He caught her mouth again, nibbling her upper lip, then her lower one, until she sighed in longing, opening for him. When he tried to pull away this time, she caught his head and pulled him back to her. He growled, hungrily, against her lips, taking her mouth with a harsh, deep hunger that left her panting.

Then he was gone.

Bemused, she stared at him as he started to clear the dishes.

"Have you ever been out of the country?" he asked, his tone conversational as he stacked up their plates, carrying them with a dexterity that left her eying him with more than a little consternation.

"You look like you've waited a few tables in your day."

"I have." He winked at her. "In Italy. And you didn't answer me."

Sticking out her tongue at him, she gathered up the rest of the dishes, just a few pieces of silverware and the napkins, following him to the sink. But when she tried to help, he caught her by the waist and lifted her onto the counter. "No. You're not helping," he said. "Unless you want to help like this."

He poured her another glass of wine and pushed it into her hand.

"How is that helping?" she asked, staring at the wine for a minute before looking at him.

"Hate to waste it, right? I can't have more than a glass of red wine or it gives me a headache."

She snorted and took a sip. "Yeah. I've thought about it. I just . . ." She shrugged and looked away. "Never have."

For a minute, the sound of running water filled the room. He didn't say anything until he started to wash the dishes, and when he did speak, his voice was soft. "I've thought about a lot of things. For a long time. Put them off for too long. Sometimes waiting only makes it harder."

"Don't I know it," she muttered.

But it didn't matter. There were some things she'd never do. Not because she didn't want to. She wasn't going to explain all of that to Zane, though.

Zane wondered if she knew how much those eyes of hers showed.

Most people probably didn't see the secrets.

Zane looked for secrets, though.

Studied them, even.

Hers were sad ones, painful ones.

One of these days, he hoped she'd share them, but he wasn't going to push her on it. Not yet.

After he'd finished with the dishes, he dried his hands and moved to stand in front of her. She was still toying with her wine and he reached out, took the glass. He sipped at it, put it down. "You ready to go home or did you want to stay longer?"

Her gaze came up to meet his.

"Unless you planned on kicking me out for a rousing night of partying with your brother or something, I wanted to hang around for a while," she said, a smile kicking up the corners of her mouth.

"Well." He braced his hands on the counter by her hips, pretending to mull it over. "Zach stopped being an ass. I reckon we could hit the bars with a bunch of college kids . . . nah. I've done that."

She chuckled and reached out, curling her hands around his neck. "What did you wanna do, then?"

"Movie?" He didn't reach for her. He wanted to. Wanted to push that skirt up, peel that shirt away. He thought maybe she might be naked under the silk. Maybe. But he kept his hands planted flat against the counter.

Keelie's gaze dropped to his mouth.

"I'm not in the mood for a movie."

"You sure? Zach still has Netflix. We could probably find *Addams Family*."

"No." She licked her lips and leaned in, pressing her mouth to his neck.

He curled his hands around her waist then, wondered if she felt the same subtle shake he'd just felt. "What then?"

"Zane?"

"Yeah?" He turned his face into her hair.

"I'm already nervous enough. Can you stop talking, maybe?" The words came out tight and strained, like she'd squeezed them through a straw.

He caught her hand, lifted it to his lips as he leaned back. Her hands were shaking, too, he realized.

"Why are you nervous?" He studied her face.

"Because . . ." She blew out a breath, her gaze locked on his throat. Finally, she looked at him. "I told you I don't do casual sex. Quick fucks. Sex is serious for me."

"Keelie, are you saying you're—"

"I'm not a virgin." She looked away, but not before he saw the haunted, strained look in her eyes. "I just . . . there was a time when I tried to treat it as casual, like it didn't matter. I sucked at it, even then. But I thought it might . . ."

Her words trailed off, but he could tell she wasn't done.

Finally, her shoulders rising and falling on a sigh, she looked back at him. "It was a way to be close to somebody, I thought. Didn't matter if I loved him or not, if he loved me.

It was a way to be close. So maybe I had a few too many flings. It only made me feel worse. So I stopped. Since then, I just . . . sex should matter more than I let it matter. I told myself it would matter the next time."

Her gaze lowered, and her words were ragged as she continued. "Ah . . . you're the next time."

He was quiet.

Too quiet.

She shot him a look, half afraid at the look she'd see on his face.

The moment she looked up, his hands cupped her face, cradling her so she couldn't look away. His mouth brushed against hers, butterfly light. But even as she opened her mouth to deepen the kiss, he slid his lips up along her jawbone. She shivered as he nuzzled her neck, scraped his teeth along her neck.

The arm he had wrapped around her waist tightened and she whimpered, the sound foreign to her ears as she rocked against him. He caught her hips when she would have done it again.

"Easy," he whispered, pressing a quick kiss to her mouth. "We have all night."

"Is that enough?"

The question escaped her before she knew she'd asked it, and she bit her lip as she tipped her head back to meet his eyes. She was tall, standing five nine in her bare feet, and her heels added almost three inches to her height, but Zane still towered over her. In the golden glow that filtered in through the western-facing windows, a look of taut, harsh hunger tightened his face.

"No." He pressed his thumb to her lip, his gaze locked on hers. "It sure as hell isn't. But it's where we start."

There was a heat in those words, a sensual promise that threatened to send her senses into overload. She might have collapsed back completely limp onto the counter if he hadn't caught her up against him.

* * *

You're the next time.

Those words shattered the threads of control that Zane had been working to rebuild. He'd like to give her pretty, sweet words, but something told him that wasn't what she needed, or wanted.

Pulling her up against him, he guided her legs around his waist, dying a little as the warm, wet heat of her settled against his cock. Watching her face, he carried her into the bedroom down the hall. There, dying sunlight streamed through the slits in the Roman shades. If there hadn't been other buildings around them, he would have thrown the material back just so he could see the way the light played over her skin, the way the color of the tattoos spilled over the delicate ivory.

He'd find a place, he thought, somewhere out of the city, just so he could have her in the sunlight.

Soon. Some other time, he'd take her in the sun and trail his hands along those long, graceful limbs, see her pale skin painted gold under the setting sun.

Lowering her to the floor by the bed, he reached and caught the straps of her silken, rust-red blouse and peeled it down.

And realized he'd been right.

She was naked under it, the blouse lined. Her breasts, small and delicate, firm enough to go without a bra. A delicate blush painted her cheeks pink, spread down along her neck to touch the upper slopes of her breasts. Dipping his face, he pressed a kiss to her breastbone, nuzzled her softly.

"I knew you were naked under this. I knew it."

"How?" She blushed even deeper as he cupped her breast and stroked his thumb across her nipple.

"Instinct." He flashed her a grin. "And it was driving me crazy."

The blouse caught around her waist as he turned, sat on the bed and guided her to kneel between his thighs. She was naked from the waist up. Leaning back, he let himself feast on the beauty of her, on the elegance of her tattoos scrolled up her arms, the way they swirled along her shoulders and down her upper chest to stop just above the slopes of her breasts.

He traced the lines of the rose that bloomed on her neck and pressed his mouth to it, male satisfaction rolling through him as she shuddered. He'd needed this, needed to feel her shaking as he touched her, needed to feel how much she wanted him. Was it as much as he wanted her? Could she ever want him that much?

He'd do his damnedest to make it happen, to brand himself on her as indelibly as those incredibly sexy tattoos.

More tattoos started along her sides and he tried to trace them only to get caught in the shirt. "Clearly, I didn't think this through." Easing her back, he stood up and grasped the shirt, pulling it upward. She lifted her arms to help him and he folded it, placed it on the table near the bed, before he went back to stroking his fingers along the tattoos, determined to memorize each and every line, every stroke, every curve, every swirl.

"You act like you haven't seen them before."

He looked up at her, smiling slowly. "The shower doesn't count. I didn't have my glasses, so I couldn't see everything. And you wouldn't let me play." He slid his finger along the vine that started under her left breast. "Now I'm going to play."

She shivered.

It made him smile as he turned her around.

Then he stopped, staring in amazement.

Her arms, torso, belly, and neck were a garden, only her breasts untouched by the vivid color of her tattoos. Delicate roses, tulips, and bright daisies, other flowers he couldn't name swirled and twined up her arms, vibrant bursts of color—some cute, others elegant, all of them beautiful.

The tattoo on her back was different, markedly, from the rest.

It was . . . haunting.

There was no other word to describe it.

And he realized, then, that he'd never once glimpsed it. Even with the clothing she wore, most of it picked out seemingly to showcase her ink, this tattoo had never been displayed so.

It was a tree, a stark, barren tree.

Her upper shoulders were bare, the tattoo ending along her mid-back, the branches of the tree empty, stretching across her back, the trunk following the line of her spine. At her hips, the ink flared out where the trunk met the ground and then, roots.

They trailed along her hips, curved along her buttocks before the ink stopped.

The entire tattoo was done in black, stark against her flesh.

She shivered as he leaned in and pressed his lips to the center of her spine, rubbed them along the edge of one barren branch.

"This is amazing." He brushed his finger along one branch, felt her shudder.

She shrugged. "It's just ink."

"Funny words, coming from a tattoo artist." He stroked the branch in toward the trunk. "Zach didn't do this."

"No. The guy who taught me did it. It was one of my first."

He dipped his head forward to run his lips along another tree branch, one that curved around her side, almost long enough to tease the slight swell of her breast.

"It's terrible to say this, but I'm kind of glad. I don't think I want any of my brothers seeing you like this. Or anybody. Fuck, Keelie . . . you're beautiful. You're like a canvas and every single tattoo is a work of art . . . no. You're the work of art." He sank to his knees, trailing his mouth along her spine, his lips caressing the tree while her body trembled under his touch.

She swayed when he kissed the dip in her spine.

"Zane . . ."

He caught her skirt in his hands, started to tug. "Yeah?"

Her only response was a whimper and the sound of it was

enough to draw that knot of hunger inside him tighter and tighter. After he'd stripped the skirt away, he settled back on his heels, studying the tree in its entirety.

She wore only a pair of icy blue panties that rode low along her narrow hips. The roots of the tree curled along her buttocks, trailing just to the edge of those panties. "Which one was your first?"

Slowly, she turned and he looked up at her from his position on the floor.

As she held out her arm, he shifted his gaze, studied the script.

Storms make trees take deeper roots.

Laying his hands on her thighs, he read it, thought about the tree. And something that might have been anger started to burn inside him. He shoved it down deep before he looked up at her. "Who said that?"

"Dolly Parton." She shrugged. "Had a lot of . . . well, storms, I guess you could call them. A friend told me that once. It stuck with me. Got the tat to remind me that if nothing else, everything I've been through had made me strong enough to handle the shit life threw at me."

Sliding his hand around, he danced his fingers up her spine, he studied her face. "Strong roots?"

"Ah . . ."

He leaned in and nuzzled her navel. "I see nothing but strength in you, Keelie."

She swallowed. He rose, kissing a pathway along her torso as he moved.

Her throat worked as she swallowed. He teased the soft skin there, listened as she murmured, "I dunno. Anyway. I wanted the reminder. And then the roses and all. My dad . . ."

He stilled, straightened to look down at her.

She was smiling a little, a far-off look in her eyes. "He died when I was young. But he liked flowers. We used to have a garden." Then she grimaced. "Weird shit to talk about right now. Anyway, plenty of kids think they have it rough, then, right? It's part of growing up."

Somehow, Zane suspected this went a lot deeper than

growing up. That was for another time, though. He dipped his head, caught her lip between his teeth. "So . . . how are things now? They better?" he asked against her lips.

"Well . . ." She was gasping when he let her pull away. "Lately it hasn't exactly sucked."

"Such high praise. It's going to go to my head." He leaned in, so close their breath mingled. "I think I need to see if I can do better, though. Make things even better."

A lot better. If he could, he'd make her entire world better . . . if she'd let him.

For now, though, he could give her this.

Of course, within seconds, he wasn't thinking of anything but her, his hands on her, and how much he needed to make her burn—the same way she made him burn. Mouth slanted over hers, he tugged her to the edge of the mattress and leaned in, closer, closer, until nothing separated them but the layers of his own clothes and the thin barrier of her panties. Her arms wound around his neck, her mouth parting under his.

Slow . . . slow . . .

Her hands dipped into his hair.

She arched against him, all soft skin, delicate curves.

Slow . . . slow . . .

Her teeth caught his lip.

Slow . . .

She wrapped one leg around his and then he grunted as she shifted so fast and shoved, tripping him so that he fell backward onto the bed. She tumbled forward to land on him and his eyes flew open, staring up at her.

She stared back, eyes glassy as she sat up, straddling him.

He curved his hands around her hips, felt the heat of her burning him through her panties and his trousers. So damn hot. So damn sweet.

"I keep telling myself I should go slow," he said, sliding his fingers under the edge of her panties.

"Yeah?" She leaned forward.

His eyes crossed as she bit him and then pushed her tongue into his mouth.

"I don't know if I want slow," she whispered when she lifted up.

He stared at her. She was blushing, but her eyes were focused on his.

"You should have slow." He stroked his thumb over the heat that teased him, taunted him.

"I'm too nervous for slow."

He shifted then, spilling her onto her back and moving between her thighs. "You don't have to be nervous. We can stop—"

She covered his mouth with her palm. "That's not why I'm nervous. I just . . . I'm nervous. I'll start thinking and that's never good."

He caught her wrist, bit her palm. "I won't let you think, don't worry." Then he guided her to the bed and settled her on his hips. Catching the material of her panties in his hands, he drew it down, baring her to his gaze. Keelie tensed and he leaned in, kissed her hipbone. "Shhh. . . ."

Slowly, she relaxed, and he stripped the material away, tossing it off to the side as he sunk on his heels and sat back to stare. She went to close her thighs and he caught her knees. Pale, ash-brown curls covered her sex, glinting with the evidence of her need, and Zane felt his mouth watering. He gave in to *his* need, bent over her and pressed his mouth to her.

She bucked against him, a harsh cry ripping out of her.

Steadying her with his hands, he slid his tongue along the slit, parting her so he could dip in, take a deeper, longer taste. It exploded through him and, half-mindless, he caught her around the hips.

This. Just this, he thought.

Wordless, sharp sounds came from Keelie and he followed the signs she unconsciously gave him, deeper there, quicker here.

When she exploded, his cock gave a hard, insistent jerk inside the material of his trousers and he felt the first few drops of pre-come leaking free.

"Zane . . ."

* * *

She couldn't think. Couldn't even move.

That was . . . she closed her eyes while her brain struggled to put a name on what that had been. Vaguely, she heard the rustling of material and she cracked open one eye, saw him peeling away his shirt. Her mouth went dry at the sight and she opened her other eye.

The better to stare at you with, my dear . . .

The phrase popped into her head from nowhere and if she'd had the breath to laugh, she might have. But she had no breath, and a split second later, even the thought of laughter died.

He was beautiful. All long, lean limbs, golden skin stretched over tight muscle. He only had the one tattoo, that owl curling over his shoulder and down his chest, the feathers done to a perfection that made the bird of prey almost seem alive.

As his hands dropped to his belt buckle, a mad rush of heat arrowed straight down to her core and she fisted her hands in the sheet.

Damn.

She was really doing this.

Was really here. With him.

The bed shifted and Zane caught her around the waist, wrestling her higher up on the bed and then, his hands cupped her face. "Look at me," he said, his voice raw and rough.

His mouth came down on hers and she froze at the taste of herself on his lips. His hands bracketed her head, refusing to let her turn away and after a few seconds, she didn't even want to, lost in the hunger of him, the heat.

Then the kiss ended and he rose up, kneeling between her thighs.

She heard something tearing and looked down. Any embarrassment she might have felt was gone because the sight of him sheathing himself utterly fascinated her. No. *He* was utterly fascinating. He was thick, his balls lying heavy below his cock and she found herself wanting to stroke her hand down him, close her fingers around him, and learn the feel of him.

The taste of him.

"You keep looking at me like that and I'll be lucky if I last five seconds," Zane said, meeting her eyes. He'd lost his glasses at some point and his gaze was a little unfocused.

"I thought you couldn't see all that well without your glasses."

"I don't need to see that well to feel your eyes on me." Then he covered her and she shuddered at the feel of his cock pressing into her belly. He did nothing else, just lay there, as though he was giving her a chance to adjust to his weight, the feel of him. His lashes lay low over his eyes, shielding that amazing blue green from her. "Tell me, Keelie . . . were you looking at me?"

"I think you already know the answer," she whispered.

"And what were you thinking?" He rubbed his lips over hers.

Gulping, she brought her hands up, absently digging her fingers into the taut, ridged muscles of his back. "I . . . um."

He rubbed his mouth against hers. "That's not an answer." He levered up and started to stroke against her, drawing a shaken, startled cry out of her as the head of his cock moved over her. "I suppose I could just do this until you answer me."

"That's . . ." She arched up, seeking more of that teasing, taunting contact. "That's not nice."

"I'm not very nice." Wedging a hand between them, he closed it around his cock and used the head to tease her clit.

She felt every featherlight touch from her head down to her toes, the pleasure seizing at her as though he was pouring liquid lightning into her veins.

"I'm not the nice one . . . everybody just thinks I am. So . . ." He raked her neck with his teeth and sucked in a patch of skin, drawing the blood to the surface. "Are you going to tell me or do I just do this, and play, and play . . ."

She could feel the promise of another orgasm, hovering

just out of reach, and she wanted to shove him to his back, or twist her hips until one of those teasing glides had him plunging inside her. At the same time, part of her wanted to do the same thing he was doing—tease. She'd never had a lover . . . not really. The thought of playing with Zane, teasing him, was intoxicating.

She sucked in a breath and then met his eyes. She even managed to smile, although it was shaky, and when he did another one of those taunting, slow glides, that hunger twisted through her again and sent a cry ripping from her.

"I was thinking . . ." she gasped out, once she could breathe. "That I'd like to touch you. Almost like what you're doing."

And because Keelie didn't believe in empty words, she slid a hand between them, her teeth sinking into her lip as she sought him out. Her fingers brushed his hand. His eyes narrowed to slits and then he stiffened over her. His other arm went tight, muscles hard as he braced his weight over her.

"Then do it," he muttered against her ear, guiding her hand into place.

Blood rushed to her cheeks but she let him guide her, show her. His hand folded around hers and heat bloomed in her belly as he stroked his cock into her hand. "Tight," he said, his voice rasping over her skin. "That's . . . that's it."

His voice tripped and then he started to surge into her hand.

Her sex clenched and she clamped her thighs together against that burning, aching hunger. Panting, she fisted him as he rode her hand and then abruptly, he snarled.

In movements almost too fast for her to follow, he caught her wrists and pinned them with one hand. His free hand caught one thigh, shoved it high, hooked it over his arm. "Last chance," he said, the words ragged, snarled against her lips. "Say it now or we move past the point of no return."

"We've already done that."

A hard, hungry kiss swallowed her cry as he pressed against her.

That same hungry kiss muffled her whimper as he drove inside and she fought not to flinch.

Too hard. Too rough.

Distantly, he knew he was being too rough. "A minute," he muttered. "Just give me a . . ."

Her body shuddered, her hips rolling against his. Sweat popped out on his brow. "Be still." It was practically a plea and he wasn't ashamed to admit it. He thought he was going to die. She was so tight and she felt so good . . . Then she moved against him again and . . . oh. Hell. "Keelie, just be still and give me a minute. I don't want to hurt you."

Her hands gripped his hips, her nails sinking into his skin. "If you don't do something, *I* will hurt *you*."

"I need to . . ." He swore as she arched against him again. "Damn it, you're too tight. I'm being too rough."

A soft, broken little moan escaped her and she sighed. "It was uncomfortable, but . . . oh." She brought her knee up, pressed it to his hip. "Zane, if you don't do something and soon, I'm going to cry."

His weight braced on his elbows, he studied her. Then, lowering his head, he pressed his mouth to hers. She opened for him, a hot, hungry kiss that he felt all the way down his balls.

As he pulled away, she flexed around him and that milking sensation almost had him whimpering, begging for mercy—or more.

"You're trying to kill me," he muttered as she did it again, then again. Keeping his weight off her, he slid out, watching as her eyes flew wide, then fluttered closed as he stroked back in.

"No. If I did that, we couldn't do this again." A cat's smile curled her lips and she rocked up to meet his next stroke. "And I really, really want to do this again."

Slow, he told himself.

He could do this. He just had to . . .

Her body, that long, elegant body arched like a bow

under his and she started to rock against him harder, her nails biting into the skin of his ass. Gritting his teeth, he reminded himself, *Slow* . . .

She moved under him again and then, with that sexy feline smile still on her lips, she twisted. "That . . ." Her voice was a husky murmur, another caress that threatened to drive him mad. "That right there."

He was still convinced she wanted to kill him.

He shifted and then twisted his hips as he pushed into the wet, welcoming grip of her sheath. She was like a fist, so tight, milking him. Her nipples stabbed into his chest and her nails bit into his skin harder. A harsh whimper tripped out of her and he stared at her from under his lashes.

Her gaze had gone blank.

When he went to withdraw, she clutched at him.

"Keelie." He lowered his head, fusing his mouth to hers as he wrapped his arms around her and rolled to his back.

Keelie gasped, torn between delight and a weird sort of awkwardness as Zane eased her body upright. She braced her hands on his chest and moved, slow at first, each movement tentative as she tried to find a rhythm.

Zane's hands gripped her hips, but he didn't do anything but lie there.

The weak, breathy moan that stuttered out of her sounded nothing like her, but it was. Shifting her position, she twisted, then rocked . . . and just like that, it was easy.

Zane's fingers turned to steel on her hips and she looked into his eyes, watched as that blue green started to blaze. Deep inside, she felt his cock jerk and, unconsciously, her muscles clamped down in response.

"Don't . . ." Zane gritted out, his teeth clenched, neck arched.

"Don't what?" She fell forward, bracing her weight on her hands on either side of his head.

His gaze bore into hers and then she twisted her hips and this time, when she tightened those internal muscles, she did it intentionally. His response was to arch up and drive into her, so deep, so hard. She cried out in response.

"Keelie . . . ?"

"Again." She rocked against him, harder, squeezing him, milking his cock, and he swore, his hands gripping her in an iron grip as he thrust against her hard. Fast. He swelled inside her and she cried out, tensing. Zane tensed in return and then, impossibly, moved faster, her name a growl on his lips.

There—

She would have begged if she could have formed the words.

But she didn't have to.

Zane tangled a hand in her hair and yanked her to him, his mouth sealing over hers. At the same time, he twisted his hips and drove up, using his free hand to hold her tight against him.

Locked together with him, her breath caught, hitched— and the bliss exploded through her, flooding her every pore, overtaking her entire being.

If she'd been one to think along poetic lines, she might have thought she was seeing fireworks.

But all she saw was him.

All she felt was him.

Zane. And that gut-wrenching pleasure as it ripped through her body, and stole the very breath from her.

Chapter Eleven

Keelie lay with her back to him, face pressed into the pillow.

The sweat had dried from their bodies.

He'd forced himself to pull away long enough to dispose of the condom and then he'd collapsed in bed behind her, wrapped himself around her, delighting in long, pale limbs, in the fact that he could move just a scant inch and press his lips to the tattoo that spread across her back.

But even as he studied it, her words rose up to haunt him. *Storms.* The questions twisted, burned in him.

Leaning in, he pressed a kiss to her shoulder and then hooked his arm around her waist.

She sighed and snuggled in closer.

"What happened to your dad?"

She'd smiled as she spoke of him, but that look in her eyes had been one of sadness. Was that the storm she'd spoken of?

She shifted in the bed, enough that she could turn her head to look at him. "I told you . . . he died."

He half expected her to let it go at that, but then, to his

surprise, she rolled over and faced him completely. Lifting a hand, she stroked her fingers along the upswept wing of the owl. "He was out on a business trip with his partner. There was a car wreck. A truck driver—he'd just finished up a long haul and was heading home. Wasn't drunk or anything. Just tired. He went over the line and hit the car my dad was driving. All three of them died instantly."

Zane cupped her cheek, brushed his thumb over her lower lip. "I'm sorry."

"It was a long time ago." Then she scowled. "I don't know why people say that. Eighteen years ago, eighteen months, eighteen days. It still hurts. I still miss him. I remember on graduation day, I looked out, halfway still expecting to see him, camera in hand." A grin curved her lips, a little bittersweet, as she looked up at him. "You and he would have had that in common. He almost always had a camera in hand. I kept looking for him, even though I knew he couldn't be there. I was . . . alone. I had nobody."

"Your mother?"

A shutter fell across her eyes.

"My mom." She rolled onto her back and she snorted. After a moment, she turned her head and stared at him, her face barely visible in the faint light. "You know the term *sperm donor*? Well, in this case, I guess I had an *egg donor*. She wasn't exactly fit for motherhood. I don't remember much about her from when I was little. When they divorced, my father filed for sole custody and won. I was ten when he died. I don't remember anything, but she was fucked up enough that she wasn't considered an acceptable guardian. I ended up in in foster care."

Zane frowned. "Wasn't there anybody else?"

"No." The word was short, clipped. She sat up, drawing her knees to her chest. "There had been arrangements. My dad and his business partner, Otto, Otto's wife Beth, they were all good friends. If my dad died, Otto and Beth were going to be my guardians. But Otto had died, and well . . ." She shrugged. "I ended up going into foster care. I guess

Beth had her hands full. She'd just lost her husband. Didn't want to take care of me and her four-year-old son. I don't blame her."

You should, Zane thought, but he kept it behind his teeth. How could somebody just let an orphaned, scared girl go off into foster care?

Keelie looked back at him, a sad smile on her face. "It's okay," she said, reaching out to push his hair back. "She was young. Grieving. It was a hard thing for her."

"You were a kid. It was just as hard, if not harder on you. And you ended up alone, in foster care."

She shrugged. "Yeah. But foster care wasn't the worst thing that ever happened to me."

"Don't tell me the story gets worse," he muttered, focusing on the ceiling.

An odd, almost strangled tension blanketed the room. Slowly, he sat up and shifted his attention to Keelie. She was twisting her hands in the sheets, over and over.

"Keelie?"

Keelie kept her face carefully blank as she turned away and focused on the wall.

Twilight had fallen and the light streaming in through the narrow slit in the curtains was that surreal shade of pink gold. Almost unearthly. She'd always loved sunsets here in Arizona. Grabbing the sheet they'd kicked off, she wrapped it around her toga-style and moved to the window, brushing the curtains back enough that she could stare outside. She could see the mountains, see the golden gleam of the fading sun.

But the view gave her no peace.

"Talk to me," Zane murmured from behind her.

"You sure you want to hear this?" she asked softly.

His hands closed over her shoulders. She leaned against his heated chest and realized how cold she was. "If I didn't want to hear, I wouldn't have asked."

"Hmmm." She closed her eyes, rested her head against his chest. He slid one arm around her waist and she snuggled into his comforting warmth.

He'd listen. She knew that.

She could tell him. The abbreviated version, the white-washed one.

She could even do what she'd never done—tell him everything.

She wasn't sure she was ready for any of the above, though. Sliding a hand down, she covered his hand with hers.

"Some kids spend so many years in foster care, they just get used to it. Others, they daydream—they spend their time dreaming about a parent—a mom or dad who'll show up out of the blue. I knew my dad was dead, but I had no idea what had really happened with my mom. Not then. I had a caseworker. And . . . there was Mr. Jenkins. He'd come out to see me." She smiled, remembering his smooth bald head and his wide, almost startled blue eyes. "I liked Mr. Jenkins. I didn't really know who he was—why he was there, what he did. But he was always checking up on me. Made sure I had toys or electronics or whatever kids my age wanted . . . for me it was books. Art supplies. He made sure I was happy, or as happy as I could be. Made sure that I had clothes I liked. The caseworkers would change and my foster families would change, but he was always there. I'd even daydream that maybe he was my fairy godfather or something— helping me look for a home. He was there the day she showed up, though. And I figured out real fast he wasn't out there waiting for her."

"Who?"

Keelie angled her head around. "My mom."

"Your mom?"

"Yeah." She looked back out the window. "I'd been in foster care for four years when she showed up, out of the blue. I was sitting outside at a picnic table talking to Mr. Jenkins about school clothes and music and he was telling me about his granddaughter and we were having a nice time.

And then there she was. My mom. I didn't even know who she was.

"My mother," she murmured again. "Mrs. Katherine Marie Vissing."

It had been a punch in the face, seeing the woman climb from the back of the shiny black car. The coat of paint had gleamed so bright, Keelie would have been able to see her face in it. Her mother had stood there, posing, for just a moment.

Keelie could see it now, with the clarity that came from years—and knowledge.

Her mother was many things. Genuine wasn't one of them.

That faint quiver of her lip, the way her eyes had widened. How she'd pressed a snowy square of linen to her lips.

A man had come around the side of the car and wrapped his arm around her and Keelie had been staggered. They were beautiful, like the Barbie and Ken dolls some of the girls she knew liked to play with. Keelie had been more prone to drawing on them or just taking them apart and putting them back together with different pieces—the *Princess of Ireland* doll and her red hair with the body of a doll from Africa. Arms from Asia. Legs from who knows where. Then she'd draw all over them. Crazy little pictures.

Of course, that usually ended up with her getting in trouble—usually just *sweetie . . . we have to talk . . .* discussions, followed by chores where she had to earn money to pay for the dolls.

Sometimes, it had led to calls to the caseworker and visits to a counselor, but for the most part, her experience in foster care hadn't been a bad thing. She was lucky, she knew that.

All of *her* bad luck had started when she went to live with her mother.

"They'd come to take me home," she murmured. "I was fourteen and I'd been living with the same family for almost two years. I liked them. They liked me. We weren't falling apart crazy for each other, but we . . ." She shrugged, thinking of the Huxtables, how the father got up to work the farm and how, sometimes, he'd let her ride out with him in the summer. "We were happy. It was almost a fit. Then my mom showed up."

Zane was almost certain nobody wore a brood quite as well as she did. With her knee drawn up to rest on the wide lip of the window's ledge, her head resting against the window frame, she stared outside, but he knew it wasn't the slow sprawl of the city or the sun-gilded vista of the desert she saw before her.

She was trapped somewhere back in her past.

"I'm sorry."

Keelie swung her head around. "Why?"

"I'm making you sad. I shouldn't have—"

"It's okay." She came over, sat on the edge of the bed. "I mean, hey, it's kind of stupid, isn't it? Girl spends years in foster care and then bam. Gets to go be with her real mom. I ought to be happy, yeah?"

He reached out, covered the hand she'd curled into a fist.

"That depends on the mom."

Her eyes met his.

Leaning in, he cupped her chin in his hand. "My mom is wonderful. Whether she still scares me a little—"

"A lot," Keelie cut in. She arched a brow and said, "I've seen you guys around her. She scares you. A lot. It's almost cute."

He leaned in, bit her lower lip. Since he was there, he kissed her, soft, slow, taking in the taste and just the . . . moment. The fact that he was here with her, that he *could* press his mouth to hers, hear the way her breath caught. Before he could lose his mind to that moment, though, he eased back. "Whether she scares me *a little* or not," he said, "I know the five of us sort of hit a jackpot all around and our parents are amazing. I also know that not all parents are like that. I've seen it with my own eyes."

"Yeah?" She lifted a brow at him, smirking. "Wait. Let

me guess. You know some kids who had to actually work for their own car or something?"

He reached up and caught a hank of her hair, tugged. "Smart-ass."

He turned away, spying a pair of jeans he'd left folded over the foot of the bed. "You got a chip on your shoulder about money, Keelie."

"I've got reasons." Her voice slid into a cool tone.

He shrugged. "I figure you think you do. But a person having money doesn't change one simple fact . . . a person is still a person and some of them are assholes, while some of them aren't. Case in point—Zach has a pretty decent chunk of money. And under most circumstances, he's not an asshole."

He turned back to her, tried not to stare at the way she sat with the sheet draped around her. He wondered what she'd looked like in college—if she'd done toga parties or she'd just curled her lip in that obnoxious, *appealing* way of hers.

"I'll grant you that." She cocked her head.

"Now let me tell you about Abby's mom." He crossed his arms over his chest and leaned back against the dresser, trying to decide just how much he could say here, how much he should say. A lot of this was public record. It wasn't anything unknown. Too much of Abby's life had been made public years ago. She had her own life *now* and she kept it private, but she'd clawed and fought hard to make it that way.

"Did you ever see the show they were in?" he asked.

Keelie shrugged. "Not much. It was winding down by the time I was old enough to pay attention. But I've caught some of the reruns. Cutesy sitcoms aren't my thing, but they are just as adorable now as they were then as kids." She lifted a brow. "It's almost sickening."

"Yeah . . . I could tell how disturbed you were with that *awwww* face so many women make at weddings." He chuckled. "And some people thought there was some chance they wouldn't end up together. So . . . since you watched a few episodes of *Kate + Nate*, I guess you noticed Abby's hair when she was younger."

Keelie rubbed at the bridge of her nose. "I'm not blind."

"Her hair started to change when she was . . . I dunno. Thirteen or so? Abby used to hate her hair," Zane murmured, remembering how they'd all tease her. Everybody but Zach. "She hated it. Then it started to change and you'd think she'd won the lottery. But the producers hated it. Zach had heard them talking about it—he was like a fly on the wall, heard anything and everything connected to that girl. We'd gone to pick her up for a movie and I went with Zach to the door—Abby answered, trying not to cry. She had this plastic cap on her head, a towel around her shoulders. She couldn't go. Her mother had people over to deal with a *problem*—I heard the bitch complaining in the background. She made Abby dye her hair for years. All because the producers thought that the brighter red hair was the only thing that would work for darling Kate."

"It sounds like typical Hollywood," Keelie said, looking away.

"Zach wanted to cut his hair that year—so he did it. On his own." Zane could still remember that butcher job, too. "He all but shaved his head bald and my parents even figured out why. Mom just tidied it up, and even trimmed it shorter right before they were going to start shooting the next season. The director, a bunch of others, freaked out. The director *really* got worked up, started laying into him. Biggest mistake they ever made, because Mom was there. They never did it again. It's different for girls . . . women. Some of the biggest double standards are found in LA. But Zach had the time of his life the first day on set—I always liked to go the first day of shooting. It was a family thing. He walked right up to Abby and grabbed his head, started to shriek. *My hair—my hair . . . Abby, I could only act because of my hair—they'll fire me and the show is overrrrrr . . .* Then he looked at Blanche and pretended to pass out."

"Blanche."

"Abby's mom." Zane shoved away from the dresser and moved across the floor, sinking to his knees in front of the bed. "That one was mild. You should have seen the look on her face when she showed up to get Abby after Zach hit this pervert in the head with a skateboard—it was this guy Blanche was screwing on the side, not that she ever admitted to it. She was *such* a faithful wife, you see. He tried to go after Abby, tried to put his hands on her. Zach showed up at just the right time and bashed him with his skateboard. But of course Abby *misunderstood* . . . Blanche would never bring a man into the house who'd touched a girl *that* way."

"Son of a bitch." Keelie's eyes started to burn. "You're joking . . . no. No, you're not, are you?"

"No." He angled his head. "Not too long after that, the show's popularity started to sag. Zach and Abby weren't as cute as teens as they had been when they were kids. The show was in trouble. They weren't offered as much money. Now Blanche, she was all about money. After the show was cancelled, she had this brilliant idea that she'd get Abby into more serious acting—one of the first auditions she'd tried to push at Abby wasn't much more than a skin flick dressed up as a thriller. She would have been perfectly happy seeing her teenage daughter walk around in next to nothing, acting her way through an orgy, a gang-rape, and then a suicide— Abby hated the script, but that didn't matter to Blanche. Blanche just saw the potential for a check with a lot of zeroes."

Zane rose, turned away. "Fortunately, her dad had a better head on his shoulders and he argued. Unfortunately, he started to lose more arguments and one day, he up and killed himself, left Abby alone."

"I . . ." Keelie blew out a breath. "Shit. I didn't know any of that."

"That glamour girl didn't exactly walk a rose path."

Keelie flushed at the mention of the mocking name she'd used for Abby. "So I see. It sounds like her mom and my mom might have been great pals."

"She liked zeroes, too?"

"You know that song 'Diamonds Are a Girl's Best Friend'?" Keelie shrugged. "Screw diamonds. If you have enough zeroes in the bank, then you can buy plenty of diamonds. Furs. Cars. You name it. Anyway, family court decided they should give my mom a chance. She was older, smarter, looked like she could provide a stable home life . . . blah, blah, blah. Plus, she was married—I even had a ready-made family, a stepbrother and two half sisters. What more could you want?"

Zane came to her and slid his arms around, tucking his chin against her shoulder. She leaned into him and sighed. It felt so good just to be near him. To feel his warmth, his strength. She felt . . . Keelie closed her eyes and let herself acknowledge how she felt here with him. In his arms, she felt at *home*. She felt like she belonged, something she hadn't really felt in years.

"You could want to be happy," he said quietly, stroking a hand up her back and tangling it in her hair. "It's not a bad thing to want, not really."

"Yeah." She opened her eyes and stared out the window. "It's not a bad thing."

Neither of them said anything else.

"I still think you should spend the day with me."

She slid Zane an amused look. "I've got stuff to do."

"I can be stuff."

She laughed a little, but the laugh died as they came to a stop in front of her apartment. "Well," she murmured. "This is . . . different."

Nolan's car was pulled up to the front door and as she watched the door swung open. Nolan came out, the muscles in his skinny arms bulging as he hefted a box into the back.

Zane pulled the car to a stop, his eyes following hers. "Problem?"

"Looks like Nolan is pulling out."

"Is that a bad thing?"

"If he's leaving the kids, yeah." She rubbed the back of her neck and turned her head to look at him. "Their mom has a weird idea of parenting. Smacking them across the face is how you deal with them when they are hungry. Or not feeling good. Or just about anything."

Zane didn't say anything.

And when she climbed out, he was right behind her.

Her heart lurched up into her throat only to still when she saw the two girls snuggled into their car seats.

Nolan paused when he saw her, his young face far too old. Lines bracketed out from his mouth and a vicious, glorious bruise surrounded his eye.

"Keelie." He nodded at her, ignoring Zane.

"Tired of trying to make it work with her, huh?"

His bark of laughter was razor-edged. "There's no making it work with Tara. You and I both know that. I was a fucking moron to think I could. A moron to think I could . . ." He stopped, clamping his mouth shut. "The cops came. She'd just slugged me one when they showed up. Was going to do it again and they restrained her."

"How much had she had to drink?"

Nolan shook his head. "Who knows? I can't do this anymore. Can't let the girls see it. She tried to hit a cop. They arrested her—pretty sure she's in violation of her parole, too."

"Where are you going to go?" She wondered what he'd do, how he'd take it if she offered him some money.

He slammed the trunk door shut and then, slowly, he lifted his head. "I'm going home. Back to my mom's. She . . ." He stopped, shaking his head. "I don't know if she'll want to help me, but she'll do it for the girls. She won't say no to kids."

"Your mom. I didn't know . . ."

He moved around the car. "We ain't talked since I left home, five, six years ago. But she ain't gonna close the door on the kids. I'll tell her about Tara. I'm hoping she can find a way to help me get custody, too."

"How can she do that?"

The look he gave her then was a bitter one. "My mom works for the DA's office. She's a lawyer. If anybody can keep Tara away from the girls, it's my mom."

* * *

She was still staring at Nolan's disappearing car when Zane slid an arm around her waist. "You okay?"

"His mom is an attorney," she muttered, shaking her head. "And he's been living here, dealing with Tara. I don't get it."

"You'd probably have to ask him before you'd understand."

"I don't know if I'd understand even then." She looked around, staring at the apartments, the busted-up cars. She had a reason for being here, although it wasn't as simple as some people might think. Most people were here because they didn't have anyplace else to go.

She was here because . . . well.

She didn't feel like she fit in anyplace else. And this was anonymous. Nobody asked questions here. Nobody was likely to spend a lot of time trying to get to know her, ask questions, or make her feel like she was supposed to share some part of herself or get involved in the community.

She could be as alone as she needed to be.

She only had herself to worry about.

But Nolan had kids. He had other people to worry about. And both he and the kids deserved more. "I don't get it," she murmured.

"Keelie . . ."

Turning her head, she found Zane just a whisper away.

"Go inside." Then he brushed his lips over hers. "Or come back to the loft with me. I don't care. Just don't stand there looking lost."

If he'd used any other tone, maybe if it had been anybody *but* Zane, she would have sneered at him and forced those words down his throat.

Instead, she reached up and laid her hand on his cheek. "I enjoyed last night," she murmured.

His breath was a soft kiss on her lips. "Did you? Enough to do it again?"

She licked her lips and his gaze dropped, lingering on her mouth.

She drew in a breath of air and then he groaned, closing the distance between them.

She brought up her other hand, fisting it in his shirt, feeling the warmth of his skin under it, the strength of his chest, the solid wall of muscle.

"Call me later?" she asked softly, laying a hand on his cheek.

"Damn straight." He brushed his mouth across hers.

A moment later, she locked herself in her apartment. Two moments later, she was wishing she'd asked him to stay.

Chapter Twelve

"Now you realize you're going to have this tattoo . . . forever. Even if you change your mind and decide to have it removed, there are likely going to be marks. You can get it covered up, but that can be costly." Keelie smiled at the pretty, wide-eyed blonde across from her. Said blonde was curled up against her boyfriend. The boyfriend could double as a brick wall in the dead of night and some people would never know the difference.

Keelie had a feeling they'd last all of four months.

The guy had *Dionne's* tattooed around his neck.

The vacuous little blonde clinging to him was terribly sweet. But her name wasn't Dionne.

"I want it to last forever," Channing said, smiling up at the brick wall. So far, he hadn't said anything. He seemed to be riveted to Channing's cleavage.

Said cleavage was pretty impressive, Keelie had to admit. Sighing, she looked down and read the neatly printed words through once more. *My hart belongs to Jason.* She'd brought in a picture of an anatomical heart, pierced with a dagger. Pretty enough—a little weirder than she would have picked for Channing, although the spelling thing seemed totally on key. She looked back at the girl. "You know you spelled *heart* wrong. Is that how you want it?"

"Oh!" Channing's baby blue eyes widened and a blush spread across her cheeks. "Oh, I feel like an idiot. Jason, I almost ruined your birthday present to me."

He brushed his knuckles down the back of her cheek and Keelie found herself studying them, re-evaluating. Yeah, the guy was fascinated by the girl's boobs, but she had seen Javi that entranced by his wife's butt. There was a look in that kid's eyes that made Keelie's heart sigh.

Maybe there was more to this.

"It's okay, Chan. She saw it, right?" He leaned and rubbed his cheek against the girl's and something about that tender little gesture had Keelie looking away. It was almost too personal, she thought. Something that belonged just to the two of them.

Seeing something from the corner of her eye, she looked up, spied Zach in the doorway.

"Oh! Hey!" A wide, happy grin crossed the girl's face when she looked at Zach. "I know you. I saw you in that magazine—you run this place, right? You used to be on TV."

"Ages ago." Zach had that easy, smooth-as-sugar tone in his voice.

"Ages ago." Keelie snorted. "If people had their way, he'd have his face on the screen all the time. He still gets nagged for interviews." She slit her eyes at him when he shot her a quelling look. Figuring he still owed her a bit for that night at the restaurant, she looked at Channing. "You know, before he got married, the producers of *The Bachelor* were always calling him—wanted to get him on their show."

Channing wrinkled her nose. "That stuff is so fake. Nobody finds love on a TV show."

"True." Zach's blue eyes promised retribution. "I'd be a lousy guy for them anyway. My heart's always belonged to Abby."

"She was your costar." Channing sighed, her breasts threatening the decency of her tank top. "That's so sweet."

Then she beamed at Keelie. "You've got great people working here. Especially her. I almost had a word misspelled on my tits forever."

Keelie bit back a snort of laughter and flicked the girl a look. "That's why we check these things, sweetheart. We try to avoid just that."

"Keelie's not just a worker here," Zach said. "She's my partner. You and . . . ah, your tattoo are in very good hands, ma'am."

Keelie bit back a snort of laughter as Zach disappeared. A few minutes later, she finished and turned out the roughed-out font she wanted to go with for the tattoo.

"It's kinda . . . plain." Channing stared at it.

"It's going to be in color, on your skin. And you said you didn't want it too big. The fancier we go, the harder it will be to read."

"Oh." After a quick look at her boyfriend, Channing nodded. "So are we ready now?"

"No." Keelie smiled. "I need a few minutes to get the design and everything ready. If you want to grab yourself some coffee or something from across the street, that would be great. That will give me time to get this finished and get set up."

Shortly thereafter, she was alone in her work area, bent over the design, everything blocked out as she worked. It wasn't too long before she wasn't alone, though, and she glanced up to see Zach loitering in the door.

"So what was she going to have misspelled on her cute self for the rest of forever?"

Pursing her lips, she picked up the design and turned it around for him to see. He came closer, squinted his eyes. "Hart. Nice. Well . . . she could have a thing for deer or something." He settled against the work counter on the far side of her space, arms crossed over his chest, legs stretched out in front of him.

Keelie snorted, then slid him a glance. "I need to get the font done, superstar."

"That will take you all of ten minutes." He shrugged, looking unconcerned. His gaze slid away from her to focus on her walls. Unlike his work area or Javi's, hers was decorated with framed sketches she'd done—nothing she'd do for a client, and she had been asked, often—and a few framed prints. She tensed as Zach paused in front of one, cocking his head to study it. "This is Zane's."

"So?"

"You've had these up awhile."

She jerked a shoulder. "He's talented. I like pictures. Why stare at tattoos I've done? I know what my work looks like."

When he didn't answer, she shot him another glance, but he had just moved over to another picture, studying it.

She managed to get halfway through the design before he came to stand in front of her. "He hasn't bugged you about doing any shots for him, has he?"

She didn't let the tension overtake her body.

It had been years. She shouldn't worry about it so much.

It wasn't that big a deal and she was a different person now, she knew that.

The uneasiness she felt was just a kneejerk reaction and even *that* was starting to piss her off.

Slowly, she pushed the design aside, checking the time. She could take a few minutes. "No," she said, keeping her voice casual. "He hasn't. If he says anything, I'll decide then. It's no big deal, Zach."

When she went to turn away, he caught her elbow.

"You sure about that?"

She looked back at him, studied his blue eyes.

There was something there.

Did he know?

He watched, for a long, long minute and she wondered, the entire time.

But she couldn't tell.

"It's no big deal," she said mildly. Then she smiled. "But if he tries to bully me into it, I'll sure to knock him down to size."

* * *

Hours later, she slid out of her car and studied the ramshackle apartment where she'd lived for the past few years. If books and poetry and all that bullshit could be believed, she should be hearing birdsong and looking at everything through rose-tinted glasses.

That meant her piece of shit accommodations should look a little less shitty. The patchy yard would look like there were possibilities to be had. Windows she'd just cleaned over the weekend should sparkle under the sun, but instead, she only saw how small they were.

Grimly, she shifted her attention to the apartment next door where Nolan had lived with his little girls. He'd promised to call her, and she knew he would.

The apartment where he'd tried to make it work with the girls' mama was still empty but it wouldn't be for long.

Soon, somebody else would move in and Keelie knew she'd watch that cycle of despair start up again.

She'd watched it all play out over and over again for years.

Up until recently, it hadn't bothered her too much, living here, or in other places just like it. But now . . .

"What's wrong with me?" she muttered.

There wasn't an answer. Shoving away from the car, she strode toward her place. She'd only worked until four and now she was off until Monday. It was Zach's weekend to cover the shop and that meant she could just relax.

They were talking about hiring somebody to cover the place on weekends, because Zach wanted more time with Abby, and while she didn't mind working some weekends, she wasn't doing *all* of them—not in a college town.

And Javi had kids, a family.

So that only meant finding somebody else. An assistant manager, maybe, someone they could trust with the place. But they'd have to look for a person, interview. Hire. Train. Decide if they could trust said person . . .

Man.

She didn't even want to think about it.

For now, she'd just think about her weekend off.

And Zane.

Would he call?

Come over?

She headed to the door, suddenly anxious to get inside.

If he did come by, she needed to get the place picked up. She should get her laundry done. There were other things she needed to do, but that would wait until tomorrow.

For the next two hours, she lost herself to the monotonous, mindless tasks. Sweeping, cleaning out the tub, dusting the shelves that held the few items she considered worth anything in her house. She studied the camera resting on the top shelf, stroked a finger down it, smiling in memory. Then she checked it, made sure the cap was on tight over the lens.

After she'd finished cleaning, she gave herself a manicure, removing the deep red and replacing it with a glittery black—the silver flecks shone like stars in the desert sky. Nice.

Nails done, she brooded until the polish was dry and then moved on to her hair. She trimmed it, standing in front of the sink in panties and a tank, handling the task with a familiarity born of practice. While she worked, she debated yet again on dying her hair. She'd had the platinum and black locks for a while and she needed to decide what she was going to do. Soon, because the roots were really starting to show.

Maybe she'd go back to her natural . . .

The phone rang.

Scowling, she brushed the loose bits of hair from her shoulders and walked out of the postage-stamp square that served as a bathroom, down through the hall.

Ring.

Ring.

Ring.

It was the landline and, for some reason, her gut twisted with dread. Less than five people had this number.

Staring at the caller ID, she curled her hand into a fist.

859. She knew that area code. Like the back of her hand. She almost turned away, but then, she grabbed the phone and lifted it up, answered in a voice so cool and calm she didn't even recognize it.

"Hello."

There was a pause, and then a man's voice flowed out. He had a good voice. Soft and low, a faint Southern accent—just a faint one, but familiar all the same.

"Hello. I'm trying to contact Katherine Ann Vissing."

She didn't flinch, didn't let anything come flying out of her mouth. She'd always suspected somebody would track her down one day. What was really excellent was that she could do this without lying. With a slow smile, she slumped against the wall. "Sorry, man. There's no Katherine Vissing here."

"Do you by any chance know her? I was certain this was the right number."

Yeah. I bet you were. Some of the hair she'd cut had settled down inside her tank and she brushed it away as she answered, "Afraid I don't know her. Can't help you."

She went to lower the phone and then stopped as he said, "What about Katie Lord?"

I love you, Katie-did. I'll see you soon, okay?

She squeezed her eyes shut against the memory. "No. Nobody here by that name, either," she said. Then she hung up the phone. Carefully, she put it back down in the cradle.

Stripping off the shirt and her panties, she strode into the bathroom. She turned up the water to high and climbed in, bracing her hands on the wall.

I love you, Katie-did.

Dad.

After twenty years, Michael Jessup Lord's face wasn't very clear to her. But sometimes, some things would bring her father's face into sharp, almost brittle clarity. A certain scent—he'd never smelled fake to her . . . he loved to work with his hands and had spent a lot of time in the workshop he'd had built on the back of the house. He'd often smelled of leather or wood, and more than once, he'd had bandages or stitches, because he was also a capital klutz. That's what he'd called himself: a capital klutz. The smell of leather would bring him into focus, or fresh cut wood. Freshly cut grass, because he loved to spend an afternoon on a riding lawn mower.

"Dad," she whispered, curling her hand into a fist and pressing her brow to the cool, slick tile.

The water beat down on her as the memories—sad and bittersweet—rolled through her.

She didn't climb out until the water ran cold.

Standing in front of the mirror, she stared at her reflection, at the pale oval of her face. Right now, with her hair darker from the water and her eyes grim and serious, she could almost see the echo of somebody she'd spent years trying to forget.

Absently, she reached up, stroked her fingers through some of the pale hair.

If somebody had tracked down her number, then it wasn't going to be long before one of them showed up to actually *look* for her.

She got that.

She suspected she even knew *why*.

But she wanted to be sure.

Forewarned, after all, was forearmed.

With that in mind, she dried her hair and wrapped a thin robe around her body. Her stomach growled demandingly but she ignored it. She wasn't hungry. She hadn't eaten much since dinner last night. Coffee wasn't really a food group, something she'd finally figured out, and all she'd done was peck at the food Zane had offered that morning.

She took a minute to grab her bag, an army-green purse she'd bought at a flea market, and a diet Coke from the fridge. Then she settled down on the couch with her laptop and her cellphone.

She started the search even as the phone started to ring.

When he came on the phone, she had to smile.

She hadn't heard his voice in almost five years.

"Hello?"

"Mr. Jenkins."

There was a pause and then, "Well, hello, Miss Katie."

To her complete and utter humiliation, tears sprung to her eyes. Pressing her lips together, she stared up at the ceiling and tried to will them away.

"Katie?" Paul Jenkins said softly. "Are you okay?"

"I . . . I'm okay. It's really good to hear your voice."

It was almost an hour before Paul Jenkins hung up the phone. It was past seven. When his wife came in and saw him sitting at his desk, she stroked a hand across his naked scalp and sighed. "Now, honey, we talked about this. You might still work on Mondays and Thursdays, but the rest of the time, you're mine, remember? You're retiring soon."

He smiled, nodded. "This one . . . well. It's a special circumstance." Then he tapped the legal pad in front of him. "I'm going to have to get in touch with J. P."

Delia squinted at the paper, read Katie's name. She sighed. "That poor girl. What's going on, baby?"

"Somebody called her, looking for her. She played it cool, acted like she had no idea who they wanted. But sooner or later, somebody will show up. It's her mother."

"Of course it is." Delia rested her hip against the chair, sliding an arm around Paul's shoulders. "Nobody else it could be. It's been well over ten years. Why would they be bothering her now?"

He just gave her a smile.

She slid off the arm and studied him for a minute. "You have one hour," she warned him. "We've got dinner plans and you need to take a shower. I'll be in here to drag you out if you aren't ready."

He was tapping away at the keyboard before she slid out of the room.

He had a good idea of why they were bothering Katie after all this time. More than likely, they'd been looking for quite some time, too. News traveled fast in this area and when it concerned certain families, it traveled even faster.

He still kept his ear to the ground, too. Especially with some people.

Paul had always had a soft spot for Katie.

The call had left her smiling.

If she'd left it alone there, she could have happily gone about her day.

Happily.

Easily.

Paul could have taken care of all of this and turned everything over to her in a nice, neat, impersonal report. It probably wouldn't even take that much time. She knew his son, J. P., and J. P. was every bit as thorough and methodical as his father.

But Keelie had stopped letting other people handle things for her a long time ago.

The one time she'd tried to let somebody *handle* something, a nightmare had ensued and she still couldn't quite deal with the guilt.

No.

She couldn't just let her lawyer take over things for her. She had to poke around by herself and that was why she was huddled on the bathroom floor, nearly thirty minutes later, puking her guts out.

Now, Sheriff Deluca, you understand how it is, surely . . .

She gripped the toilet seat as her head pounded. The echo of her stepfather's voice seemed to come from within her, and all around her.

You know how this sort of thing can happen. Boys will be boys. It just got out of control.

Cool assessing eyes, settling on her. *Katie, can you tell me what happened?*

Her voice breaking, *I already did.*

Katie, let me handle this . . .

Her legs shook as she stood up and made her way over to

the sink. She washed her hands, scrubbing them until her skin was pink and then she did the same to her face. She brushed her teeth until she saw blood on the toothbrush and that was a smack in the face. She wasn't going down that road again.

They'd made her feel dirty, because of what they'd done. She wasn't doing this again.

Carefully, she put the toothbrush back in its place and then she rinsed her mouth out.

She left the bathroom, feeling like her legs were going to give out under her, but she refused to cling to the wall or reach for any other form of support.

She was stronger now.

She'd made herself stronger and she had to remember that.

Once she was back on the couch, she reached for the laptop and started to read. This time, she made it all the way through and then she read it a third time.

When she was done, she scrolled back to the top, but instead of reading, she stared at the image of her stepbrother.

She was still staring at it when the phone rang ten minutes later.

"Hello?" She answered her cellphone woodenly, without even looking at the display. She knew who it was by the ringtone and if she'd thought it through for even a split second, she wouldn't have answered at all.

"Keelie?"

She closed her eyes at the sound of Zane's voice. "Hi."

He was quiet for a few seconds and then asked, "What's wrong?"

"Nothing," she said, her voice brusque. "I'm just not in the mood to talk right now. I'll call you tomorrow."

Then she hung up, and went back to staring at the picture.

* * *

Zane lowered the phone, stared at it.

The weird, hollow ache in his chest—he tried, for a minute, to pretend it wasn't hurt.

But then he wondered what was the point?

Nobody had the ability to hurt him the way she did.

He'd known, going in, that this wasn't going to be an easy relationship. Here was just the first hurdle.

Okay.

So he'd wait until tomorrow.

But he sure as hell wasn't going to stay inside all night, either. The longer he did that, the longer he was going to brood. And think about calling her.

Grabbing one of his camera bags, he checked inside, got an extra battery, his tripod. He was halfway to the door when he stopped and headed back toward his equipment, and took the old Leoto his grandfather had given him years ago. It had been his first camera and it was still his baby, even if it was a dinosaur compared to some of his equipment.

Right then, he was in the mood for the old, the familiar.

It was too late in the day to do any hiking, but he could head out of town. Do some shots out in the desert.

Empty his head for a while.

Convince himself he wasn't thinking about her.

Yeah.

That wasn't going to work.

Because he knew he would be thinking about her . . . thinking, and wondering just why he'd heard that underlying thread of pain in her voice.

Just what had happened between this morning and now?

Chapter Thirteen

Keelie woke up on the couch, sometime near nine.

She hadn't gone asleep until nearly three and the table was littered with notes.

Links to various articles, dates, names.

She had no doubt that Paul would dig up all of this information if she asked—he probably already *knew*, but she had to see it for herself.

Boys will be boys . . .

That voice echoed in the back of her mind, a mockery. "Fuck you," she whispered, rolling her stiff, aching body into a sitting position. She rubbed at her tired eyes and made herself look around at the small, tired little apartment.

Abruptly, a surge of anger burned inside her and she swiped her hand out, sending the notebook, her notes, the laptop, all of it flying off the table.

Rising, she started to pace the small square of her apartment, feeling like the walls were closing in around her.

"Why am I *here*?" she muttered, shoving her hands through her hair, fisting them.

Paying a penance, when he'd been the one to commit the crime.

More than a decade later, and she still carried that guilt.

But she knew why.

Eyes closed, she lifted her face to the ceiling while the memories slammed into her.

She was still fighting with them when the phone rang a few minutes later.

She didn't even consider ignoring it. She couldn't stand the thought of being alone in her head if she didn't have to.

"Keelie!" Zach's voice was a rush in her ear. "Look, I'm desperate. Javi is sick—some bad chicken—that's what he says, I bet he's hung over, but he has an appointment today and I need your help."

She opened her eyes, something that might have been relief slipping through the knots that bound her heart, her throat. "Zach . . ."

"It's somebody from the base. They ship out to Iraq at the end of the week. He wanted to finish the tattoo first. I can't even come close to Javi's style. You can. It's important to the guy, Keelie. I tried to explain, but . . ."

Slowly, she turned to look back at the mess she'd sent flying to the floor. "I'll be there. What time?"

"You're my favorite person right now. Thank you. Appointment is in an hour and a half," Zach said, his voice heavy with relief. "We have the pics, the coloring they'd wanted to go with. This was the last visit. Thanks. Thanks a lot. You're the—"

She disconnected and stood up, walking away from the memories that seemed to mock her.

The sight of Keelie had Zach wincing.

Okay, Javi had sounded rough.

Keelie looked worse.

She was pale, her eyes glinting like chips of glass in her face and she pushed past all of them without saying a word. If he was a smart man, he would have gotten out of her way.

Like Anais did—she clearly was smart.

She'd given Keelie a wide-eyed look and then turned away. Clearly, she wanted no part of this.

The new artist he'd hired recently, Rusty—a giant of a man with dark red hair and a bass grumble instead of a voice, beat a fast retreat.

But Zach wasn't smart. Slowly, he made his way down the hall and peeked into Keelie's work area. She was leaning against her counter, staring at the wall.

Her gaze whipped to him.

"What's wrong?"

Keelie looked everywhere but at him.

"Nothing." Her shrug was jerky, erratic. And her voice was thin, almost ghost-like.

"Yeah. You really look like *nothing* is wrong." He hooked his thumbs in the front pockets of his jeans. She looked . . . dangerous. Sharp. Edged, like if somebody got too close, they'd find themselves bleeding and might not even understand why. "You didn't have a fight with Zane, did you?"

She cut him a look, the pale blue of her left eye turning to ice. "If we did, you'd have a reason to celebrate, right?"

"No, I . . . shit." He clamped his jaw shut on the words that automatically jumped to his lips. He probably deserved that. Waiting a few more seconds until he knew he could be level before he answered, he said softly, "Both of you matter to me. He's my brother. I love him. You're like a sister to me and you know I love you. So if you're happy, that's all that matters. Keelie, something is wrong. I just want to . . ."

She sighed and turned, resting her hands on the counter. The muscles in her narrow back, her shoulders went tense, tight, so tight they started to tremble.

A harsh gasp left her and for one awful, terrible moment, Zach thought she might cry.

No. No crying, he thought desperately. Everything in him told him to flee.

But he couldn't.

His movements awkward and stiff, he crossed to her.

Reaching up, he touched her shoulder. She jerked away—or tried.

"Don't," she said, her voice harsh. "I just need to be alone right now."

He sighed and tugged harder, pulling her into his arms. It bothered him to realize she felt fragile. Completely fragile. "No," he said quietly, tucking her head under his chin. "You don't. You spend too much time alone anyway."

"Zach—"

"Stop. If you don't want to talk, don't talk. But something is tearing you up and we both know it. You don't have to be alone with it." He'd spent too many years around Abby not to know what he was dealing with.

A broken sound escaped her and then abruptly, her arms clamped around him.

Zach held her tighter as she started to tremble. "It's going to be okay."

He didn't know what else to say.

Something moved outside the corner of his eye and he looked up, saw Anais. Because it felt like the only answer, he mouthed, *Call Zane.*

She stared at him blankly for a moment and then she nodded.

Sighing, he held on to Keelie as she refused to let herself fall apart.

The morning dawned too early, and too bright.

Zane shoved his head under the pillow and tried to ignore it.

He could have done that happily except his phone started to ring.

After staying out too late, grabbing some night shots that turned out to suck, he'd put in a good three hours on the website he was building for Zach and Keelie.

Now, the last thing he wanted to do was answer his phone.

But it might be Keelie.

So, without taking his head out from under the pillow, he grabbed the phone, answered with a tired, "Hello?"

"Um, you might wanna come in. Like now. Keelie is here and she's all weird and quiet and I think she's crying and Zach thinks you should come in."

He frowned, tried to place the voice. Pushing the pillow aside, he pulled the phone away, squinted at the display. Steel Ink. "Who is this?"

"Anais." She paused, and then added, "From Steel Ink."

"I know who you are," he said, sighing as he sat up. "I just didn't recognize your voice. What's going on . . . you said Keelie?"

"She's crying. Zach wants you here, like now."

Crying—

"I'm there."

He was already heading to the bathroom, the exhaustion gone, chased away by something he couldn't even name.

He barely remembered showering, dressing, or the drive. It was a blur, but one that inched by. All he could think about was getting to the shop. It was Saturday and the drive should have been fast, but it seemed to take eons.

Finally, the narrow lane of Fourth Street opened up and he sped it, hoping against hope for a decent spot to park.

For once, fate or God was smiling on him because he was right there near the store when somebody was pulling out. A miracle.

Arrowing into it, he climbed out and managed to not run into the store.

Zach looked up as he came through the door and if he wasn't mistaken, there was a look in his eyes that might have been relief.

He opened his mouth but Zach held up a hand and looked at the customer who was flipping through a design book. "Why don't you keep looking? Remember, if you see something you sort of like, we can work with you to make it your own. That's just part of the service."

Then Zach came striding toward him, his face grim.

"Did you two fight?" he asked, his voice so low Zane barely heard him.

"What? No. What's going—"

"Not here." Zach closed his eyes, covered them with one hand and then jerked the other to the area behind the desk where the employees usually loitered between customers. "Can you wait for her? She came to cover for Javi and she's working on somebody now. Something is . . . shit. She was practically crying, Z. That's not her. That's not *ever* her."

Instinct told him to go find her. *Now.*

But he just studied his brother for a long minute. "What's going on?"

"If I knew that, I'd . . ." Zach's voice trailed off and he stared at nothing for the longest moment. When he finally looked at Zane, he said quietly, "Something's wrong. She came in pissed—I'm used to her being mad, but not like this."

Not like this.

If he didn't know that Keelie would hate for him to barge in while she was working, he'd have gone to her then. So he took a seat where Javi would have normally been. Sitting down, he stretched out his legs and folded his arms over his chest.

I'm not in the mood to talk right now—

That edge of pain, brittle, encased in ice, had cut into him.

He should have said *fuck it* and just gone to her.

Closing his eyes, he dropped his head back against the wall.

Nothing to do now, though. Not really.

Except wait.

It was a beautiful design.

There were names, nearly two dozen. And between those names, the design she was going to finish coloring in, there was the soldier's cross, the weapon, with a pair of boots and a helmet. She didn't have to ask what the names were for. She hated that there was so little room left on him.

"You ain't asked who they are."

His name was Myke. He was a few years older than her and he stretched out on her chair, all hard muscle and scars.

She glanced down at his face, managed to smile. The work had distracted her enough and he was quiet, so she didn't have to force herself to talk when she didn't want to.

But with that blunt statement, she couldn't ignore it.

"Considering the work Javi started on you," she said, choosing her words with care. "I don't think I need to ask."

He grunted and closed his eyes. "Some people are dumbasses. They still ask."

"Yeah. Well, like you said, some people are dumbasses."

It seemed he'd had enough time to reflect or think or brood or whatever he did when he was quiet. She hadn't had more than thirty seconds of silence when he spoke again. "How did you get into doing this?"

"Tattoos?" she asked, even though she knew damn well what he meant. She paused, cleaning up the blood from his skin. "I'm good at it. When I was a kid, the few times I ever had a Barbie doll, I'd spend more time drawing on her and giving her bad tattoos than playing with her. Got older, had some of my own done but never thought about doing it for a living." The only thing she'd thought about doing was anything and everything that would keep people from *noticing* her. "I did some waitressing, worked retail, other shit. Hated all of it. I was having this big design done on my back and while I was getting it done, I thought maybe this would be a good job."

She didn't tell him *why*.

The first time she'd actually considered it was when she thought about how much her mother would *hate* it. But then she'd started to see the beauty in it. She'd found her own healing, her own form of . . . penance, even.

In ink and blood, images and words on the skin.

It seemed like an act of rebellion to some, or a trend of the times.

Keelie had thought maybe some of the poison she had in her soul had wept out of her with each small bit of blood. Maybe that was why she'd gotten so many the first few years. Purging herself of the poison.

She'd purged herself of some of the poison, found a way to sleep at night. Maybe she could help others. That was when she knew.

Clearing her throat, she continued. "I asked the guy who was doing mine about how to get started in it, what all was involved.

"Anyway, it turned out I had a knack for it. I learn fast, I can come up with my own designs. I'd been working at another shop in Texas for about a year, then started with Zach a few years ago. And let me tell you, it's a lot better than waiting tables."

Before he could ask anything more, she asked a question of her own. "So why'd you join the army?"

He was still talking twenty minutes later when she finished up his piece.

She heard every word, but she doubted she could recall any of it.

If the aftercare wasn't so drilled into her head, she might have forgotten what to tell him. Walking him out front, she made sure to give him the information she knew he'd heard a dozen times, easy.

Now, she could get out of—

"Zane."

He sat behind the counter, eyes half-closed, but at the sound of her voice, he came to his feet in a smooth, liquid movement.

"Ahhh . . ." She looked from him to the client and then shot Zane a look. Hopefully he could figure out what it meant: *Not right now.*

Even though instead of the *alone* time she'd been hoping for just seconds ago, she had a different plan in mind now. One that involved him, her, and lots of hard, sweaty sex. That would give her something to think about—something besides memories she didn't want inside of her.

"Okay, Myke, if you don't have any questions, that's it. Be sure to keep up with the aftercare, okay?" She stared at the man in front of her, instead of the one who watched her from behind the counter.

Myke nodded and held out a few bills. She went to pull out the change and he waved it back. "Keep it."

It was too big of a tip, but she wasn't going to argue. It ought to go to Javi anyway. "Take care of yourself in Iraq."

He was gone a moment later and she clung to the counter for a long moment before turning to look at Zane.

It was oddly quiet in the front area.

Looking around, she didn't see Anais or Zach or Rusty.

Just Zane. Watching her with those calm eyes. It was like staring into the endless waves of the ocean, she thought. He could outwait her and was fully prepared to do it. There was a patience to his gaze, like he knew something was wrong, like he knew she hid something—

Something lodged in her throat. That caged, bubbly tension inside her tried to break out. Spinning away, she went to edge out from behind the counter.

"Hey. Ah, I'm sorry about last night."

He didn't say anything, just moved closer, with that eerie, easy grace.

Her heart hitched a little.

"Okay. So. What brings you here?" she asked, keeping her voice calm, light. Casual, even. She could do this. She could fake it. *Fake it until you make it.*

He stopped in front of her, rested his hands on her waist. She tensed.

"What's happened?" he asked quietly.

Closing her eyes, Keelie tensed her jaw. Then she had to relax it before she could even force the words out. Force the lie out. "What do you mean?"

"You know what I mean, angel," he murmured, wrapping his arms around her and resting his chin on her shoulder. "Something's hurt you. What is it?"

Curling her hands into fists, she tried not to break. There was a trembling that had started deep, deep inside and if it reached the surface . . . "Let me go," she whispered, and her voice shook. "I can't . . . I can't do this here."

"Then we'll leave."

So simple, so easy.

She pulled, half-heartedly, against him as he closed one hand over hers and went to lead her away.

But then she looked up at him.

He met her gaze, his blue green eyes steady behind his glasses, his mouth unsmiling.

She knew, without a doubt, if she reached for him, he'd come.

She knew, without a doubt, if she started to cry, he'd hold her. Those solid, square shoulders seemed to be made for it.

But what would he do if she told him? Would he look away, disappointed in her?

Would he learn about the deception she'd lived the past few years and see her in a different light?

"Stop thinking so hard," he murmured, closing the distance between them and reaching up to cup her cheek. "Let's just get out of here for now. You and me."

You and me.

She and Zane. It was the sweetest thing she could think of just then. Just her, just him.

Slowly, she nodded, and this time, as he went to lead her out of the room, she didn't resist.

Zane thought about taking her home.

But his gut told him that whatever had made her miserable waited for her there.

He thought about taking her to the loft and tucking her into bed. She looked like she'd slept as much as he had and even though the sun still burned high in the sky, she probably needed a good eight hours of sleep. But he saw nightmares and tears and misery in her eyes. If she tried to sleep now, all of that would follow her.

So he drove, no destination in mind.

At least not one that he was aware of.

It wasn't a surprise, though, when he found himself in front of the empty space that he planned to turn into his studio.

If things kept moving, they'd be finalizing soon. Things were moving forward with a speed that almost satisfied Zane's desire to *do* this—*now*.

He'd even gotten the door code. Not that the Realtor knew about it. The current owner apparently trusted Abby, so that trust transferred onto her brother-in-law.

When the SUV stopped, she looked around with a grim expression.

She was pale.

Whatever had put that haunted look in her eyes was something he wanted to kill. He wanted it dead and battered and buried.

"Where are we?" she asked, although the lack of interest in her voice didn't reflect all that much enthusiasm.

"I'm setting up my studio here—made the offer the other day. The current owner accepted." He shoved open the door. "Come on. I want you to see it."

He thought he might have to convince her to go inside, but apparently she wasn't too big on just sitting and brooding. She was out of the car almost before he could shut his door, meeting him on the sidewalk.

But she was closed off, arms wrapped around her middle, her shoulders slumped. Even the tattoos bared by her shirt seemed less . . . vibrant. He didn't pull her against him the way he wanted. Not yet.

He was going to give her a chance to open up, without him pushing. She might not do it. He'd try not to force it. But that would make it hard for him to kill whatever had done this. Batter it. Bury it.

She really brought out the bloodthirsty Neanderthal in him.

"Let's go inside." He grabbed his laptop bag from the back and held out a hand.

It surprised him when she accepted it.

Once in the cool, slightly stale air, he led her deeper inside, away from the windows. "I'm already thinking about the design layout I want to go with."

"You just found this place, right? How did you get things rolling so fast?"

"I didn't *just* find it. It's been a few days." He looked around, rocking back on his heels. "This is the place—I knew it when I saw it. Talked to the previous tenant. His family owns the place. They'd like to sell it, but for now, they're willing to let me take it at the price he was paying for rent. He really wants to move out of the state. I've already got my business plan, everything lined up. I'd been half planning for this for a while and now that I'm done with the *half* planning part . . ."

He stopped and shrugged.

"You're tired of waiting," she finished.

"Yeah. So they gave me the code, let me come in so I can start getting measurements, figure what I'm going to do with the space. I guess Abby vouched for me."

"And he just let you have the code." A faint smile curved her lips. "I swear, you and your brothers. You just ask, and you get. Spoiled."

He snorted. "Yeah, that's me . . . the world is my oyster."

Impatience all but gnawed him with hot, sharp little teeth. Zane had spent the last twenty years of his life acting like this was just a hobby, but now that he was ready to make it something more, he was stuck with *waiting*.

"I put this off too long," he said, intensity burning inside. "I don't want to wait anymore."

Under most circumstances, waiting for anything didn't bother him.

He was the patient one. Everything happened when it was supposed to and him pacing the floors and brooding and bitching didn't do a damn bit of good, so why bother?

The past few months had twisted things up on him.

He didn't want to wait to put his life into motion anymore.

He didn't want to wait to get this business growing.

And he didn't want to wait for . . .

Keelie came to stand next to him and he had to jam his

hands into his pockets to keep from pulling her into his arms and making demands he had no right to make. Asking questions he knew she wasn't ready to answer.

He didn't want to wait for her.

He was a hypocrite.

He'd been nagging his brother to make a move on Abby and here he was, standing next to the only woman who'd ever made him feel much of anything . . . So maybe he hadn't carried a twenty-year torch for her, but he'd known her six years, and even that very first time he'd seen her, he'd felt a pull. It had been another year before he saw her again, and the pull was stronger.

But he still hadn't done anything, not for a couple more years.

Then she'd smiled, shrugged it off. He'd tried again, with the same result, a few months later. Normally after that, Zane would let it go—if a woman isn't interested then she isn't interested, but there was something about *this* woman that wouldn't *let* him let go.

The more he got to know her, the more he *needed* to know.

And he was tired of waiting.

He was closer now than ever, but it still wasn't enough.

He opened his mouth, those questions burning on the tip of his tongue.

Keelie tipped her head back, studying the slanted ceiling set with wide windows. It was one of the features that had caught his eye, although the bare, naked white didn't exactly fit in with what he had in mind.

He'd have to paint it. Maybe in a few years, put a different ceiling in altogether.

"I wonder if you could put a picture up there."

He slid Keelie a look. She still had those shadows in her eyes, but there was a hard glint, almost like she had made up her mind to lock herself away from whatever had crawled out to haunt her. Biting back a sigh, he resigned himself to yet more . . . *waiting*.

She wasn't ready for anything more.

Wasn't really a surprise. A few dates. Phone calls off and on while he was in Albuquerque. A couple of nights that made him sweat even thinking about it.

But that didn't make for a relationship, not in her eyes.

She'd probably take off running if he told her he loved her. Needed her. Dreamed about her. Needed to take away some of the misery of whatever hung around her like an ugly, painful cloak.

He said nothing.

Folding his arms over his chest, he studied the ceiling.

"A picture."

From the corner of her eye, he saw her shrug. "I don't mean like a framed print or anything. That space is huge— it's the first thing you see when you walk in. All that white is kinda distracting."

"No. I get it." He rolled that idea over in his head and looked around, spying his laptop bag where he'd dumped it near the front door. Grabbing his computer, he settled his back against the long wall that split the front from the back and powered up. Keelie sat down just as the desktop came up.

"That owl," she murmured.

He glanced at her.

She reached out, stopping just before her fingers touched the screen. Then she angled her gaze up at him. "That's one of yours."

He shrugged. "Yeah. Took it back when I was a kid. My grandpa was big into birding and nature. He used to take us camping before he died. The others loved the fishing, making s'mores. I loved hearing him talk about everything else. Mom gave me his camera when he died. Man. I loved that camera. It was a Leoto. They don't make them anymore. I carried it almost everywhere with me up until I went to college." He touched his finger to the screen, remembering how his grandfather had taught him how to use the camera, how to grab something more than a few blurry shots of his brothers. "The owl was one of the first good shots I got."

"How old were you? Do you remember?"

To the day, he thought, his mind flashing back to it. Then he shrugged. "When I was twelve."

Sixth grade. Riding his bike home with Shannon Macy. His first big crush.

Sixth grade . . . when he learned one of the most crucial lessons in life.

Running away never solved anything.

"I guess I see why you had the owl put on you," Keelie murmured, resting her head on his shoulder. "Is that when you really got into photography?"

Zane stared at the image.

Let it go. Let it go . . .

"It was before then actually." He flipped open one file, studied a couple of the mountain images, one from Mount McKinley up in Alaska—the snow-covered peak spiking out of the ground to stand guard over a pristine lake, so still you could see the mountain, the sky, the green of the trees reflected in it. "Something like that. You can get murals made from images—they need to be high resolution. This might do it."

He studied the space overhead once more.

It might not be a bad idea.

"So how did you get into this? I can't believe you took a picture that good when you were a kid."

"Yeah." He let his fingers hover over the mouse pad on his laptop and then, before he let himself think about it too long, he went to one file. He kept it on hand for when kids showed an interest in photography. It held his oldest shots, starting from the shaky pictures he took of his brothers, a few of Abby and Zach, then to when he moved to subjects other than people. He scrolled them slowly, letting Keelie see the way he'd caught the childhood of his brothers on film. The pictures had started when he was eight and went from the unfocused pieces to the ones that had helped him land a scholarship.

"Wow," Keelie murmured. "Show me more."

He shifted to another folder, still from his teens, but these weren't ones he showed others. Not ever. He rarely even looked at them himself. Slowly, he felt the tension creep back into the quiet woman leaning against him. Her hand lay on his thigh. He wondered if she realized she'd started to squeeze.

Chapter Fourteen

The pictures were . . . brutal.

Keelie couldn't think of any other way to describe them.

The fact that the subjects were kids made it that much harder and her nerves were already raw. One of them showed a guy—looked like a jock, right down to the letter jacket—leaning into a girl who probably didn't weigh half what the guy did.

That fear . . .

The sight of it drove a spike into Keelie's heart and she fisted her hand tight as she stared at the image.

Around the guy stood a group of boys and their faces were locked forever in masks of laughter.

He'd caught that image of a bunch of guys terrifying a girl, trapped against her locker.

The next image had a girl sitting at a table. She was by herself, lost in a book. A pair of glasses slid down her nose but she didn't seem to notice.

The image after it was the same girl, looking up, startled.

The next ten images, all captured so fast, were of the girl, as that guy who'd pinned another girl against a locker took

this one's book from her and stood around with his friends.
The images were so lifelike, so *real*, Keelie could all but
hear the mocking words coming from his mouth.

Yeah, Price! That's . . .

No, stop! Help!

The memories intermingled and tried to overwhelm. She
shoved them back as she focused on the pictures, watched
as the girl tried to grab her book. The mocking sneer of a
smile on his face made him think of things she never wanted
to remember, but couldn't forget.

*You know how this sort of thing can happen. Boys will
be boys. It just got out of control.*

The final images showed her trying to get the book back,
and that evil little son of a bitch tearing it in half.

The last picture was the girl walking away in tears.

There was another set, a boy in what looked to be a gym
locker room—his tormentor was another guy. The victim
was a skinny black boy, braces on his teeth, and something
about him made her think he'd bump into a wall, drop his
books. He just looked . . . her heart ached. He looked like
the type of kid people just picked on.

There were only three images of him. Him by his locker,
and then four guys bearing down on him.

As two hands came up to grab him, another shoved the
locker open wide.

Do it, man, do it!

She shoved the laptop away and surged upright, her head
pounding so hard, she thought it was going to explode.

"I can't look at these."

Those kids, treated like things.

Boys will be boys . . .

And Zane . . .

Spinning, she stared at him where he sat, legs stretched
out.

"Why didn't you stop them? You just stood there, snapping pictures. Why didn't you help?" Guilt, helplessness,
fury, they all beat and roared inside her. "You just stand
there taking pictures?"

His lids closed, a bitter smile on his lips. Then he opened his eyes and tapped at something on the computer. He turned to face her and placed it on the floor, rising to his feet.

"I don't want to see any more," she bit off.

Katie, let me handle this . . .

She shoved a hand against her temple, tried to shove the voices out, the memories.

"You should look." He was standing back where he'd been earlier, studying the ceiling as though they hadn't just witnessed some of the most casual cruelty imaginable. "You're the only one who is likely to ever see those pictures, other than me."

Curling her lip, she stormed back over to the computer, flinging herself to the floor with enough force that she jarred her bones. She didn't care. That minor pain was *good*. It distracted her from the pain, the misery . . . the *guilt*.

Why hadn't he done something?

Why didn't you . . .

How could Zane had have just—

Her blood froze.

The boy stood in front of a mirror. He held the camera up over his shoulder, angling it at his back. It might have seemed odd, but the outline of what looked like a shoe solved the puzzle very well.

The next picture had him facing forward. His nose was swollen. One eye was black.

He was young, probably twelve years old.

But she knew exactly who he was. Those blue green eyes hadn't changed.

Sucking in a breath, she moved to the next one. She didn't know how much time had passed, but some had. His hair was longer, his shoulders looked a little wider. This time, the picture was fuzzier but the focus of it was a gash, right behind his ear.

She rubbed her fingers together. She'd felt that scar.

Another picture—another black eye. He was older now, maybe by a year or two, and the look in his eyes was angrier.

Picture after picture after picture. Twenty in all, following him up until he was probably sixteen, and that set of images was both the worst, and somehow . . . the easiest. Because the boy in front of the mirror had a smile on his face. Not a happy smile, but the kind of smile you'd see on the face of a man who'd emerged from the lion's den.

Two pictures, one of each hand, showed bloody, busted knuckles.

Another of his face—his lip split, left eye black.

There were bruises on his ribs and she swallowed in horror at the red ring on his neck—she knew what that was from, somebody grabbing you by the throat and *squeezing*.

Shaken, she put it down.

Her hands were so slippery with sweat, they left damp tracks on the surface of it. She slicked them against her jeans as she rose. He still stood with his back to her.

"What the *fuck* was that?"

He didn't move. Didn't say a word.

Striding up to him, she shoved him, planting her hands on his lean back and putting all her strength into it.

He stumbled, caught himself and turned.

She lifted her hands to push him again, her blood roaring in her ears as emotions she couldn't even begin to process ripped through her.

"What the *fuck* was that?" she demanded again.

He caught her wrists, eased them down.

"That was me," he said, shrugging, his voice easy, casual. Like he was discussing the weather.

Tears clogged her throat and she swallowed them down, along with the furious snarl that tried to come out. "Yeah. I got that—looks like you were always pretty, even when somebody was beating the hell out of you. Who did that to you?"

He sighed and pulled her close.

She didn't resist, mainly because she wasn't sure if she had the strength to pull away.

"If I had to be honest, I only remember the names of a couple of them." His mouth—that beautiful mouth and now she could remember the way it had been split open time after time after time—twisted in a self-deprecating smirk. "I was jumped the first time by a couple jerks when I was coming home from school. I was in sixth grade. Decided I was going to sneak to a park and take some pictures—wanted to impress a girl. It was the day I caught the owl. Mom was at the studio with Zach and Seb. Dad was working, and the twins were in the after-school group they always went to. I spent about thirty minutes at the park, grabbed some shots—that owl—and headed back. I was two blocks from home when one of them nailed me with a rock. I crashed my bike. Before I could get up, they were on top of me."

Keelie blinked, then shook her head. "A couple of kids jumped you . . . and you took pictures. *Why?*"

"So I'd remember. Every time I saw them, I wanted to remember what they'd done." He shrugged. "You know those goofy kid movies where they show the kid daydreaming about turning into a superspy or something, coming back and taking out everybody who was ever mean to him? That was me. I had this super-cool TV-star little brother. And I was the gawky geek in glasses who'd just gotten jumped riding home on his bike. I wanted to remember what a wimp I was, who'd done it . . . because I wouldn't be that way forever and I didn't want to forget it."

She reached up, touched her fingertips to the black frames. "I don't see anything gawky here."

"You didn't know me twenty-five years ago." He brushed a kiss over her forehead. "Anyway, I had really good grudge mojo. I bet you know what that is like."

Keelie lowered her lashes, fought the urge to pull away and hide.

He saw too much. Way too much.

Yeah, she carried a grudge very well. Unwilling to think about it, she glanced back at the computer, resting her head on his chest. "That big guy in the pictures . . . was he one of them?"

"Nah. Just another bully. I didn't even meet him until

high school. Those two, Rick and Rodney, were the bane of my sixth-grade year, but that was the worst of it. I worried more that they'd go after my brothers. Once, they actually were messing with Zach and I went after them—something snapped. I knocked two of Rick's teeth out and Rodney had to pull me off. They moved away that summer. Was the happiest day of my life."

"I bet." Feeling helpless and angry, she reached up to touch him, then stopped, curling her hand into a fist. "How did your folks handle it?"

A shutter fell across his eyes. "They never found out."

As he pulled back, her jaw fell open.

"*What?*"

He crossed the floor and picked up his laptop. Over his shoulder, he looked at her. "You heard me. That was the only time they ever did any real damage. I was the first one to get home and I locked myself in my room. Mom got home with Zach and Seb. Seb was still a baby so he was there with her all the time. Dad showed up a little while later with the twins. Zach comes to get me about dinner and I picked a fight with him, let him catch me in the eye."

Keelie pinched the bridge of her nose. "You're telling me that you let your brother take the fall?"

"No. I'm the one who got in trouble." He met her stare levelly, his mouth quirked up in the faintest of smiles. "I elbowed him in the gut and called him a pussy, told him to leave me alone. He was getting razzed all the time about being on the show and some of his friends had been teasing him. It was the exact thing to set him off. He shoved me back and I turned around to hit him in the stomach. That was all it took. He laid into me and I didn't bother to fight back. Mom walked in and pulled him off me."

She stared, speechless, as he walked across the floor and put his laptop up. Finally, her brain remembered how to make words and she was able to sputter out, "Why would you do that? You should have told them about those little assholes."

For a moment, he stood there. Light shone in the glass windows behind him, casting him into shadow as he stared down at the floor. Finally, he turned and came toward her.

"I can give you a lot of reasons. I was embarrassed. I was afraid if they got in trouble, they'd do it again. Or that they might go after Zach—or worse, Trey and Travis." His expression was serious, his eyes grim. "I could tell you that Mom was sick a lot that year—she'd miscarried."

Shock slammed into her and she fumbled for anything to say to him but he didn't even pause.

"It was a girl." He brushed her hair back. "They'd always wanted another child and Mom had hoped for a daughter. This was a girl, and she miscarried. She couldn't stop bleeding. They had to do a hysterectomy. She never did get the little girl she wanted."

Curling her hand over Zane's wrist, she held on. "That doesn't mean they wouldn't want to know."

"Oh, I know that." A mocking smile curled his lips. "I know full well if I were to tell them now, they'd hand me my ass. But I still don't want to tell them. I hid it. All of it."

"How could you hide the fact that you came home with a black eye, and bruises all over you? How do you hide that?"

"The first few times . . ."

"The first *few*."

She curled a hand in his shirt, wanting to shake him, hit him, scream. Something. "The first *few* . . . Zane, how long did all of this go on?" But she wondered why she'd even asked. She'd seen the pictures, the way he aged from barely touching puberty to hovering at the edge of manhood.

"Too long. Or maybe just long enough. I was one of the lucky ones, Keelie. I figured out how to make it stop on my own, and I did it without hurting myself."

"How did you hide it?" She gaped at him, hardly able to believe they were having this conversation. Having this kind of conversation with this man she'd always thought was . . . *smart.* No. Beyond smart, but he'd done something like . . . "I don't get it. Why hide it? How?"

"I already told you," he said gently. "I was afraid to admit it. Ashamed. Embarrassed. I couldn't *let* myself. There's no easy answer to that, Keelie. As to how? I did it the same way I did the first—picking a fight with one or a couple of my brothers." He shrugged. "But then . . ."

He stopped, tension creeping into his body as he moved away. She wanted to go to him, needed to. But she held herself still, arms wrapped around herself. "It happened on set once. One mom had brought her entire family—her daughter had a small part for two or three episodes. I think she was hoping one or two of her other kids would catch somebody's eye."

A sardonic smile curved his lips. "They did, but not the way she hoped. The oldest two were closer to my age. They were two or three years older than me. They were *huge*. I mean like linebacker big. They were giving Abby grief and Zach told them to leave her alone. One of them acted like he was going to push him."

That was it, Keelie realized.

That was the one thing they couldn't do. After all, everybody has a stopping point.

Zane's stopping point was his family.

She hadn't found hers so easily, and by the time she had, there had been damage done.

Rubbing her hand over her heart, she listened as he continued to speak. "He towered over Zach. Almost six feet, and he was just huge. I got in his face, told him to back the hell off. Abby was almost in tears, Zach was ready to beat on both of them. A couple of the crew members saw it, told the kids to cool off or they'd be forced to leave. The kids laughed like they were just teasing and the crew gets back to work, Abby and Zach and I go off to get more pictures— that's the main reason I was there. Then they come at me from behind. I was outside by then and everybody is busy. One of them hit me. I remember that and then nothing for a minute or two. When I sat up, both of them were on the ground, one of them is out cold and the other one was puking his guts up. There was one of the guys who helped out in wardrobe. He looked at me and held out a hand."

"Mr. Miyagi style?" Keelie forced a smile. "Did he turn you into the Karate Kid?"

He glanced back at her, shook his head. "No. I had to beg him not to tell my mom. He was nineteen so that probably helped. Plus . . . he'd been where I was. Knew what it was like. Told me that if I was going to make myself into a punching bag, then I either needed to learn how to take a hit better or maybe find something else to do. His name was Tony."

"So Tony taught you how to fight?"

"Nah." Zane shrugged. "He showed me a few things, then told me to get my skinny ass into the gym, start lifting weights—and he told me about a guy who taught martial arts. I nagged Mom for months before she let me join."

"How old were you when that happened?" She thought of all the pictures, how many times he'd been battered.

"Fifteen."

"And when did you stop being a punching bag? When did you stop being everybody's victim?"

"Everybody's victim?" He turned and looked at her. "That's not what I was. I was the troublemaker who couldn't leave it alone."

"I . . ." She scowled. "I don't get it."

He could see that.

This was more than Zane had wanted to talk about, more than he'd wanted to explain. But there was no way to turn back now. Self-conscious, he went back to the laptop once more, pulled up the two files. He set up the galleries so the images could be pulled up side-by-side.

"That was Haley Klein," he said, pointing to the girl who'd been pinned at the locker. It was weird. He could re-member *her* name. He remembered almost all of the ones he'd captured like this. He didn't remember the ones who'd pounded on him after. "She was in my ninth-grade English class. Super smart. Broke the grade curve. Her mom was . . . well. Her mom had a reputation. Haley got teased about it a lot. That asshole was saying things my mother would *still* smack me over—as she should. I took the pictures. That was the first time I took pictures like that. Then I put my camera up. They never even saw me, not until I blocked them from going after her. He had me up against the locker before I could even think of what to do next. I had more guts than brains at that point. He busted my lip, would have done worse but teachers showed up and he disappeared in the crowd. They asked what had happened—I lied, said somebody crashed into me and I smashed into the lockers on accident. He started threatening me, showing up wherever I was with his friends . . . and I started leaving copies of those pictures of him bothering Haley everywhere. A couple of teachers found them."

Keelie slid him a look, her brow going up. "Clever. Did they know you'd taken the pictures?"

"Probably suspected, but I lied, through my teeth. They couldn't prove it. It's pretty obvious he's not asking her to the spring formal in the picture so the school came down on him. I had a few more of him with other students and every time he showed up around me again, I just started dropping more of them. He got the point. That summer, he ended up getting arrested. He'd jumped a kid near his house but he didn't realize it was a cop's kid."

"Ouch."

Zane flipped to the next set, the girl at the table. "Lisa. I don't remember her last name. She was a year younger than the rest of us, smarter than almost all of us. She got treated like that nonstop. He ended up getting pulled into the office over her—her parents saw the pictures and reported him to the police. He left her alone after that."

Keelie worried the neckline of her shirt.

"That's Malcolm. He was sick a lot. Asthma put him in the hospital a few times and he caught the flu our senior year—it killed him." Zane stopped for a minute, just remembering. Unable to say much more, he just flipped to the pictures of his black eye and busted mouth. "They tried to shove him in a locker. They'd done it before. I grabbed somebody's backpack and swung it, hard enough to knock one of them down. The yelling caught the gym teacher's attention and they had to pull us apart. I'd already been taking classes for a few months so I'd done more damage and, that time, they actually did call my parents but they didn't say anything once they heard what those kids had tried to do to Malcolm."

"Nobody mentioned how they were always picking on you?"

"But they weren't," Zane said softly. He looked at her. "I'd been the victim before. I'd decided I wasn't going to let it happen anymore, and what's more . . . I wasn't going to stand by when it happened to others. If I got hurt, I got hurt. I was bigger, not as much fun to pick on. But when I waded in, that was when they turned on me. I was the troublemaker by that point."

I'd been the victim . . .

Guilt swamped her and she had to turn away while the voices rose up, pealing inside her head like bells.

Stop, Price . . . help!

Katherine, let me handle this . . .

"You're a better person than I was," she said, her voice thick.

She looked back toward the spot where his laptop had been. It was gone, but she could still see the pictures, remember her loathing, and her anger at him. At *herself*. Only he'd done what she'd wished she'd had the courage to do.

"Keelie?"

His hand brushed her shoulder.

She flinched.

He didn't let that stop him.

How surprising. As Zane closed his hands over her shoulders and pulled her back against him, she reached up, covered her hands with his. That one touch managed to both ground her and still leave her feeling so completely adrift.

He pressed his lips to her temple and she shivered, confusion and frustration raging inside her.

"What's wrong?" he asked.

What's wrong . . .

Such a simple question.

Such a complicated one.

She eased away from him, although breaking that connection with him felt like she was ripping out something vital.

Moving to one of the windows that ran the length of the western wall, she pressed a hand to the smooth surface. The heat from the sun warmed it yet did nothing to warm her.

For more than a decade, she'd tried to come to grips with the guilt.

At first she'd tried to hide from it. Then she'd tried to outrun it.

Finally she'd tried to make amends. It wasn't ever going to happen.

You can tell the truth now.

"When I was fifteen, I walked in while my stepbrother was raping a girl. His friends were watching. Egging him on."

Slowly, she turned to face him.

Chapter Fifteen

"Wow. Which one are you?"

Travis Barnes pushed his sunglasses back on his head and studied the blonde leaning against the glass-fronted case. His eyes automatically bounced off everything inside it.

If he didn't *look* at it, he could pretend it didn't exist.

That was how he operated, as far as this went.

He'd seen some messed-up shit in his life and he'd dealt with it all just fine. Hell, Travis had *done* some messed-up shit.

And while he might deny it even on his deathbed, he got a little weirded out over the bizarre, painful, and private places some people chose to get pierced.

He wasn't sure if the pieces displayed in that glass case were intended for some of those weirder places. Zach had once told all of them about a woman who'd come up to him and asked him to look at her clitoral piercing. Zach, of course, had declined. He didn't do piercings, but he knew enough about them—and others—to leave Travis cringing.

Even Zach had been grimacing by the time he finished.

Travis didn't get it.

Why would a woman do that?

Why would a man would pierce his cock?

One reason only, as far as he was concerned. They were insane.

Insanity explained a lot, really.

Insanity was one of the reasons he had a job. Insanity, arrogance, and stupidity. Zach and his crew made a living tattooing and piercing. Travis made a living dealing with insane, arrogant, or stupid criminals. Everybody had their quirks. His just didn't involve shoving metal into sensitive personal bits.

"Well?" The blonde cocked her head and smiled. Her mouth was a pretty, rather delightful bow, Travis decided, feeling a slow stir of interest. "Which one?"

"Which one what?" he asked, smiling back. He moved closer and caught a trace of something almost too intoxicating to ignore. If that was her, it was a miracle she didn't have guys hovering around her like mad.

"You've got to be one of them. You're too pretty not to be." She tapped her finger on her lips, drawing his attention back to them.

Slicked with something pink and shimmery, that mouth didn't need the highlight. But he liked it all the same.

"Well, you're not Zane," she mused. "I know him. And you're not Seb. You're too old, and don't take this wrong, but Seb's full of himself. You look a lot like him, but even if it wasn't for makeup and all that shit, anybody who has ever seen him in an interview can tell that boy is too full of himself. He has so many thoughts going on about himself, it's amazing he can think about anything else."

Travis ran his tongue along the inside of his lip and tried to decide if he should be offended on his little brother's behalf, and then decided it wasn't worth it. Seb *was* an arrogant little bastard. And hell, he understood her question now.

She was trying to figure out which brother he was.

"Well, if you know us that well, then that leaves . . . " Deciding to play, he leaned against the counter and smiled at her. It brought him closer, let him fill his head with the scent of her. Seriously. It was almost a drug.

"The twins." She cocked her head. "I know about the writer, have seen pics of him online. You're not him."

"How can you be sure? We are identical." Travis and Trey had looked, and acted, enough alike to fool their brothers and parents right on up until halfway through college. It wasn't until that point that it was easier to tell them apart. But strangers still had trouble.

"No. He's got sad eyes." She shrugged, one shoulder lifted. "Can't blame him. But you don't have sad eyes."

"Well." Damn. She was good. "I guess I don't have as much reason as Trey does."

"Probably not. However, he has the cutest little boy on the planet. Bet you can't top that."

"No. I cannot." Travis smiled and then held out his hand. "Since by default that only leaves one . . . I'm Travis. The other twin."

"Anais." She wrinkled her nose. "Most people call me Ani, because they butcher the name. It's not that hard, though. *Ann—EYE—ees.*"

He repeated it dutifully, decided it suited her. Ani sounded just a little too ordinary for her. "So. I'm looking for my brother."

"Which one?" She braced her elbows on the counter. "You've got two of them in town. One lives here . . . the other is moving here." She wiggled her eyebrows and added, "I keep hoping Trey will come out here and do one of those book cons. We have all sorts of writer things in the area."

"Yeah, my twin just loves those writer things." Travis kept his face sober as he said it, even though on the inside he was worrying about his twin. Because he didn't want to brood about that, he leaned on the counter and let himself study *Ann—EYE—ees* for another minute.

She really did smell good enough to eat.

His cock stirred, interest spreading through him, and he wondered if she might be up for dinner. Then dessert . . .

She lifted a brow, a smile flirting with that way too sexy mouth, as though she knew exactly what he was thinking.

Yeah, dinner was sounding very appealing. Except he was thinking maybe they could skip dinner and go right to dessert.

But first . . . "Zach or Zane. Haven't seen either of them much since the wedding. Work keeps me busy."

"You'll have to settle for the mean one." Anais nodded her head toward the back. "Zane is out with Keelie. Zach is in back in his office."

Travis squinted one eye at her. "Zach. Zach's the mean one?" Hell. *Zane* was supposed to be the mean one. Zach was the laid back one.

"Yeah." She shrugged. "He's in a mood, but I guess I can't blame him. It's been a lousy day. He's in his office. You can go on back."

He studied her a moment longer, thought about lingering to get more info. He could. It was what he did best. But if he wanted to talk with his brother for a while, then try to talk her into dinner, he needed to get to it.

Besides, if he didn't get the information he needed from Zach, he'd go to the more reliable source. He'd ask Abby.

He was almost to the hall when she stopped him. "If you're in town long, maybe you and I could have dinner."

Shooting her a look over his shoulder, he lifted a brow.

That slow, rolling burn kicked up a little hotter. That tug of interest wasn't really a tug anymore. It had managed to tether itself around him, without him even realizing it, and he was being firmly drawn in.

Yeah. Dinner was sounding like a very, very good plan.

"Maybe we can do that, Miz Anais." He lowered his gaze back to her mouth for a long moment and then turned back, heading on down the hall.

Keelie said the words in a flat monotone.
Her face was blank, devoid of emotion.

Her eyes were anything but.

Zane remained where he was through sheer force of will.

He didn't think anything had ever been as hard as just standing there.

He wanted to go to her, to reach out and touch her, cup her face in his hands as she fought to release whatever poison she'd carried inside her—and it was poison—but something inside him told him that would only make this harder.

So he remained still, and silent.

"She was a friend of mine." Keelie continued to watch him and, now, her eyes all but challenged him.

He continued to wait.

"Did you hear me?"

"Yeah."

She jerked her chin up, her eyes glinting. "Well?"

"Well . . . I'm waiting to hear the rest of it."

"The rest . . ." A low, derisive laugh escaped her. "Just what else do you want to know?"

"How about the entire story?" he suggested.

"Oh, so you're one of them. You like the sordid, dirty, disgusting details." She flung it out like an accusation.

"No." Now he did move, unable to stay away any longer. She flinched and backed away. It was like a slap against his heart but he didn't let it stop him as he caught her arms, pulled her up against him. Pressing his lips to her temple, he murmured, "I want to hear the story—I want you to tell me what happened."

She shuddered. He felt it wrack her body, from her head straight on down.

He held her tighter and she shuddered again. "I already told you. I walked in . . . he was raping her."

"There's more to it than that."

More.

There was more to it. Yes. There was more. So much that she *still* felt sick and dirty inside when she thought about it. Sometimes the dreams found her at night and she'd stumble into the shower and no amount of scrubbing could wash away that kind of filth.

"Keelie."

At the soft, low murmur of his voice, she looked up.

He'd moved toward her. She hadn't even heard.

Now, he stood so close, his shadow had merged with hers and without thinking about it, she reached out. Her hand tangled in his shirt. She felt the heat of him through it. The knot in her throat seemed to swell, trying to choke her.

"I met Victoria—Toria—in art class. She hated being called Victoria. She was . . ." Keelie paused, her hand tightening until her knuckles stood out against her skin. "She was goth before people even knew what goth was, ya know? A regular Wednesday Addams. We had to sit together and at first, I just . . . I hated it. I'd been living with my mom for more than a year and she had me convinced that I was just this cardboard cut-out. I was like . . . you know that movie *Mean Girls*? The Plastics? That was me. I wasn't really *happy* with it." She licked her lips and looked away. "I didn't want to lose everything. Again."

Zane cradled her face in his hands and pressed his lips to her brow.

The gentleness of it infuriated her and she tried to twist away. "Don't," she said, her voice thick and harsh. "Don't. I don't want . . ."

She couldn't even finish the sentence.

"I know."

Curling her hands around his wrists, she dug her nails into his skin, trying to ground herself, trying to find some way to keep going despite the misery and shame that choked her. "She . . . damn it. Toria hated me. She used to razz me, called me a rich bitch, made fun of me . . . we probably would have just kept going right like that all of high school except this new girl came into class." Keelie uncurled her hands from Zane's, and then forced herself to take a step away, then another. "I knew her. I'd met her through one of the homes I'd been in. Part of me felt like I should just ignore her . . . she wasn't part of my world anymore, ya know? But

Clara was always so nice. I was lucky with my foster parents for the most part. The one time I *wasn't* lucky, Clara was the only one there for me. She was bigger, mean. She was always bigger than the other girls—she'd been held back twice and she kind of took on this big sister role with some of us. Me, included. Now she was at this school where most of the students were upper middle class or just plain loaded. There she was, wearing cheap clothes, she needed braces and, to be honest, she was a fashion mess. But I still liked her. She looked at me and it was like . . . I'd found my long lost sister. She saw me and grinned—but halfway to the table the teacher assigned to her, one of the students tripped her. I can't even remember which one of us reacted first. Toria, Clara . . . or me."

Keelie rubbed the back of her neck, thinking of how she'd practically had to hold Clara back.

The guy who'd tripped her had been one of the varsity ball players.

He didn't know it, but Keelie had saved him from complete and utter humiliation when she kept Clara from going after him.

He'd turned away, laughing.

And Toria had upended the pot of ink she'd been using for her calligraphy project onto his shirt. *Oh, wow . . . Lucas, I am soooooo sorry.* She'd blinked kohl-rimmed eyes at him. *I was just so overcome by that display of masculinity—tripping a girl and making her fall. No wonder you're such a popular guy.*

"Toria found us talking after school. I got up and left— Clara was my friend, but Toria was . . . well. She was Toria." If Keelie had just kept to that mindset, Toria wouldn't have been hurt, either. "She started nagging me again the next day."

So you were a foster kid, huh? The state took me away from my dad once—Mom was traveling on business and somebody called CPS because they found out he was leaving me alone at night. Mom freaked. *When did your dad die? Who do you live with now? Were you adopted . . .*

"I . . . I don't even remember how it happened, but one day we started . . . talking. I told her about my dad. About being put with the first foster family . . . then being taking away. The group home. Then the family that almost adopted me, but had to move because the dad lost his job. Then the next family—I loved them. I was with them a long time. But then . . . then my mother showing up. By Christmas, we were talking all the time. By the end of that year, we were inseparable." Keelie looked down at her hands, remembered the way they'd looked, smeared with Toria's blood. "My mother hated her. Couldn't stand her. My stepbrother, my half sisters . . . they were about the same. The weekend after school started back up, there was a party. Both Toria and I were invited. I didn't know he'd be there. Toria didn't want to go, but I liked parties. She didn't like me going alone."

She curled a hand into a fist. "Toria was always smarter than I was."

Zane's hand covered hers.

The silence that fell between them hurt, like knives jabbing into her skin, into her heart with every slow thud.

I don't want to do this. I don't want to do this. I don't want to . . .

The urge to clamp her mouth shut, to take everything back, to hide and lock herself away was almost overwhelming. Because she knew if she stopped now, she'd never move forward, so she forced herself to keep going.

"They had booze there. I didn't know. It was in the punch and I had one glass, then another . . . Toria tried to tell me, but I ignored her. There was this guy and he was flirting with me. I don't remember much." Her thoughts were a blurred rush and her heart sped up, lurching somewhere up in her throat as she recounted what she could of the night. Toria had tried to help. She could remember her own laughter and then, just grey. Nothing but grey, until she was on her hands and knees, somebody half shouting. The smell of vomit. Her shirt was half off and she was on the floor, on her knees.

Then Toria.

Come on, sweetie. We need to get out of here.

She'd stumbled down a hall with her friend and then the darkness faded in and out, tugging her under. When the world stopped pulling its disappearing act, she'd been on her back, in a bed, staring up at the sloped ceiling overhead.

She'd been terrified—and her terror about waking, alone in a strange place, all stemmed from that night. Some part of her was still afraid she'd find herself there, all over again.

The house had been quiet.

"Toria wasn't anywhere around. I got up to find her, confused. I was in a room up on the fourth floor—it was a big house," she murmured, her voice thick.

She looked so lost, Zane thought. He wanted to lock her against him, promise that nothing would ever happen to her, that nobody would ever hurt her, or shake her world again.

But the pain in her now was an old one. How could he fix that?

Sliding his hands up to rest on her shoulders, he just waited. What else could he do?

"I heard the noise on the third floor, started to run. My legs didn't want to work. My throat felt funny. I tried to speak and couldn't. I found the door—heard her scream and I grabbed the vase from the table just inside the room. He hadn't shut the door. Two other guys were watching. Laughing. One held her down, the other had a camera. I smashed the vase down on my brother's head."

She stopped, lapsed into silence.

Her hands clenched into fists, empty ones that tightened then relaxed. "The guy with the camera took off running. The one holding her tried to hit me but . . ." She stopped again and looked up. "I spent too many years in foster homes. I had too many foster brothers—they either taught me how to fight or gave me a good reason to learn how. I broke his nose. Price was groaning and moving around but I didn't wait. I helped her get up and we started out of the house. I took her home. I didn't know what else to do." Ugly, bitter laughter rang through the open space. "I should have taken her to the hospital. We called the cops, but they talked her out of going to the hospital. I didn't even realize how bad that was until it was too late."

Rage started to throb, pulse, beat inside him, a harsh tattoo that had him ready to pummel something. "The cops didn't want her going to the hospital?" he asked softly.

"No." She tipped her head back, stared at him with stark eyes. "My mother had married into a politician's family, you see. The all-American boy, his well-off family. The good ol' boy network clicked in fast. Real fast. I didn't even realize what was going on until later, when the sheriff came to talk to me. It actually should have been turned over to the sheriff's department anyway. It happened outside the county, but Toria had been staying with her dad that weekend. Her mom found out. If I'd called her from the beginning . . ."

A knot settled in her throat, the ache in her chest so hot and heavy. "A lot of *if onlys* in my life. Anyway, the sheriff was the one who tried to handle the investigation. They came to talk to me."

Now, Sheriff Deluca, you understand how it is, surely . . . Her mother's cool, calm voice.

You know how this sort of thing can happen. Boys will be boys. It just got out of control. Her stepfather, while Price watched from the side, his face downcast, his entire body language that of a boy who was being so thoroughly wronged.

And the sheriff, how he'd watched her. He'd known. She knew it, even now. *Katie, can you tell me what happened?*

"What happened?" Zane asked.

"My stepfather paid them off. He convinced them all to be quiet." Keelic's voice was scathing and hot. "Paid Toria's dad and when her mother showed up at the sheriff's office, he was there waiting. How could anybody take her seriously when her father had accepted money? He'd be happy to help make the inconvenience go away."

Nausea roiled, twisted inside her gut, and she stumbled away, her legs stiff, her eyes burning and her hands trembling. *Inconvenience.*

She found the bathroom—it was the first door down the narrow hall and she stumbled inside, hitting the light and bracing herself over the sink. *I won't be sick. I won't be sick.* She didn't deserve that luxury. She knew she didn't.

It was a release she wanted so desperately, but one she wouldn't allow herself.

Her hands trembled and she curled her fingers around the edge of the sink. A shadow fell behind her and she stiffened, slowly dragging her gaze up to meet Zane's in the mirror.

The pity in his eyes dug ugly furrows into her heart. Years of instincts had her lashing out. She curled her lip at him as she stared at him in the reflection. "Don't look at me like that. I don't need your fucking pity. It's not like *I* was the one who ended up leaving school because it was too hard to face people."

Zane moved in closer instead of backing off.

She tensed. She didn't want this—his compassion, that quiet strength. But he didn't turn away, even when she turned around and gave him her darkest, dirtiest look.

"If you want to pretend you're pissed off at me, go ahead." He cupped her face in his hands.

The gentleness of his voice grabbed her by the throat. And then he leaned in, pressed his lips to her temple. Her heart trembled, almost shattered. Planting her hands against his chest, she fought to hold herself back. The sight of Toria's face, the bruises, the marks on her skin. And the battered look on her face the last time she'd seen her . . .

"Why would I be pissed at you? You weren't there. It was a long time ago." She kept her voice flat and even managed to work up a shrug. "It's over. It's done. I lost my best friend over it and she—"

Her voice caught, stuttered, then tripped.

There was too much guilt, too much pain, and too much sorrow. In that moment, it all ripped out of her.

Narrowing his eyes, Zach studied the twin standing in the doorway.

Then he lifted a brow and dropped back into the chair behind his desk. "Well, well. It's like old home week. All we need is Seb and Trey. What are you doing here, you son of a bitch?"

A sly smile lit Travis's face, but all he did was move inside and drop into the leather chair next to the desk. Zach waited a minute, but when Travis stayed quiet, he went back to scanning the spreadsheets on the monitor in front of him. Spreadsheets. They were the bane of his existence. That, and taxes. And inventory.

Maybe Travis being here was like a harbinger.

The accountant. Taxes. Spreadsheets.

It was a trifecta of evil.

After the silence lingered another five minutes, Zach finished up one task. Since he really didn't want to start another, he saved the file and shifted his attention to his brother. "So, you want to tell me why you're here?"

"You don't even sound happy to see me."

Zach snorted. "I already took care of the *Man, where ya been* bit, right? But I know you. If you're in town, it's for a reason. I'd like to know what the reason is."

"You are so suspicious." Travis heaved out a sigh.

"No. I just know you."

Travis shrugged and then slumped farther down in the chair. "Look, I'm just taking some time off from work before I head off to Europe for a while, okay? Might be there for a while." Then his eyes started to gleam. "The pretty lady out front says you're mean. Are you being mean, Zach?"

Zach scowled and grabbed the file in front of him. "Don't flirt with Anais, Travis. I need my employees *not* fluttering about with broken hearts."

"But she's awful damn cute." Travis just continued to smile. Head cocked, he asked, "What's the deal? You're pissed. She's worked up over something—somehow I don't think that's normal for her."

"Ani doesn't have a norm." Zach wanted to shrug it off, but he couldn't. "Don't worry about it."

"So there is something up."

With a thin smile, Zach suggested, "Here's an idea. I'll tell you after you tell me why you had to take off from work." Zach threw it out there, fishing more than anything else. He didn't expect to see that tiny flicker of his brother's lashes, didn't expect to see any sort of reaction at all. But he did. Curious, he braced his elbows on his desk and narrowed his gaze on Travis's face. "So what kind of problems are you having on the job, Trav?"

The phone rang. Zach ignored it.

"Who says I am?" Travis shrugged, his voice easy. He looked at Zach without blinking. His voice was exactly on key and his motions, his mannerisms, everything was exactly as it should be.

But everything *wasn't* as it should be and Zach couldn't figure out just how he knew it. He just did. He wracked his brain, tried to figure out what sort of problem Travis *could* be having, but he didn't know jack shit about what his brother did. Zane was smart. Both Zach and Seb had fumbled their way through school, even managed to pull *B*s throughout honors classes in high school and Zach had held his own in college.

The twins had coasted by doing the absolute bare minimum. They'd aced any test put in front of them, but then they'd gone back to doing what they did best—causing trouble.

Come college, Trey had settled down.

Travis had gotten wilder.

Nobody would know it to look at him, but behind those cool, calculating eyes, that devilish grin hid the mind of a genius. Travis could have gone on to do anything. If he'd wanted to, the man probably could have gone into crazy shit like rocket science or whatever put people on the moon.

But for some reason, he'd decided to do spreadsheets and shit.

Zach didn't quite get that, but whatever made the kid happy.

The problem was . . . Travis wasn't happy. He also held his cards too close to his chest and out of all of his brothers,

Zach knew the least about Travis. He suspected even Trey didn't know as much as he'd like to.

How could he figure out where to poke and prod for a reaction when he hardly knew the man anymore?

Tired of trying to think it through, he dropped his pen and leaned forward, pinning Travis with a dark look. "What's going on?"

Travis lifted a brow. "Who says anything is?"

Zach pushed out from behind his desk, worked through all the plausible scenarios in his head. He could ask, and get shot down again. He could ignore it, and that wasn't much of any option, really. He could snoop, but that might not do any good at all.

There was always the good old-fashioned method of trying to pick a fight, but that had never really worked with Travis. He'd talk when he wanted to talk.

He *might* be able to wheedle something out of him, but that was his only option.

"Look, Travis," he said, keeping his voice nice and level.

There was a knock at the door before he could go any further.

For another few seconds, he studied Travis, and then he raised his voice loud enough to be heard through the closed door.

"Come on in."

Anais come in, eyes wide, her mouth tight.

Slowly, Zach rose to his feet.

"Zach, there's this guy on the phone." She shifted from one foot to the other, licking her lips nervously before she continued. "He's asking about our employees—called looking for somebody named Katherine and I told him we didn't have anybody here named Katherine. He asked for a Katie Lord. I was going to hang up, but then he started asking what the employees looked like. He's kind of weird and I told him to go creep on somebody else, but then he started describing Keelie. I mean, like exactly. Even her eyes."

He sensed more than heard Travis's interest. Keeping his

body between his employee and his brother, he kept her focus on him while Travis sat up and looked back at them. "Did he leave a number?"

"He hasn't hung up," she said softly, shaking her head. "He kinda insists on talking to somebody."

"Okay. I'll take it in here."

Travis waited until Anais had left and then he studied Zach. "Should I leave?"

"Why? It's not like you'll say jack shit. You don't even tell us what's going on in your life." Aggravated, Zach grabbed the phone and leaned back, ignoring his brother to focus on the phone call. "Hello?"

"Hello, Mr. Barnes, I assume?"

"You got that right. How can I help you?"

"I just need a few moments of your time. I'm trying to locate the daughter of a client—she's been missing for a long time and my client is desperate to see her again."

He noticed two things about the caller immediately. One, that smooth, polished voice was just a little too smooth and polished—Zach had learned a long time ago never to trust anybody who put that much work into sounding honest and open. Two, he was trying too hard to drum up sympathy, right out of the gate.

Using your voice could be an art form, something Zach knew well, and this guy definitely knew how to use his. It already had Zach on edge, but he didn't let it show. After all, he was an actor—he might be out of practice, but he damn well knew how to fake a lack of interest . . . or just the right amount of curiosity.

"Yeah? Who are you trying to find?"

"Her name is Katherine Vissing, although she might not be going by that name." The man on the other end of the line paused.

Zach just grunted. "Seems to me if she's not using that name, maybe she doesn't want to be found."

"It's rather complicated, Mr. Barnes." That charm just continued to seep from him. "Can I beg a few minutes of your time?"

"Sure. Why the hell not? Can't say I can help much—my employee just gave me the name you'd called about. I know a couple of Katherines, but Vissing? That's not familiar. By the way, I didn't catch your name." He kept his voice nice and easy and unlike his caller, he knew there was nothing in his voice that he didn't want there.

"It's Gleason. Phil Gleason."

Zach grabbed his pen, scrawled it down on the notepad he used for his sketches and notes. He drew a big block around it so he didn't overlook it.

A shadow fell across him and he looked up, saw Travis studying the notepad before shifting his attention the phone. Zach wondered why but a quick glance gave him the answer. The caller ID. It had flashed up when he'd taken the call.

"Okay, Mr. Gleason." Zach jotted down the number, underlined the area code. Did he know that one? He didn't think so. "Just why do you think I might know this woman you're looking for?"

"I've been looking for her a long time. My sources have led me to think she's in the area, that you might have—might still be—employing her." Gleason's voice was carefully neutral now. Too careful.

Zach's eyes narrowed. "Why don't you just cut to the chase, Mr. Gleason?"

"Katherine is twenty-seven. She might have lied about her age. The name on her identification won't be Katherine. She's five feet nine inches tall and the last time she was seen, she was a hundred and thirty pounds. That might fluctuate some—she's prone to depression and when she doesn't eat, she loses some weight. She's got a very fair complexion and her natural hair color is dark blonde, but it's very likely she's changed it. She does have rather unique eyes—one brown eye and one blue."

Zach's hand tightened on the pencil.

Keelie.

Son of a bitch.

Those first few years she'd come here, part of him had wondered if she was running from somebody. Just something about the way she'd acted, almost like she was looking over her shoulder—waiting for something.

He'd known, really.

But it didn't matter.

Keelie was practically family. *That* mattered.

"I couldn't say if I've seen her or not, Mr. Gleason," he said, the lie coming easily. Whatever the bastard wanted her for, it wasn't a happy mother/daughter reunion. The few times anybody asked about her family, Keelie would get a tight, cold look in her eyes and while Zach might not be super insightful, he knew that look.

He saw it on his wife's face every time her mother was mentioned.

"What do you mean you can't say if you've seen her or not?" For the first time, an edge crept into Gleason's voice, slicing through that nice, slow drawl.

Zach smirked and settled back in his chair, propping his boots up on the edge of the desk. "Well, I mean just that. I've had this place open for several years now. I've had a couple of female employees, and hundreds of female clients. I can't recall the number of women who've applied for jobs. In short, you're not giving me enough information. Tall woman, brown hair, needs SPF 2000 when she goes outside. That could be one of a thousand women I've seen just this year alone."

"You did hear me describe her eyes, didn't you?"

"I did, yes. But again, there's nothing standing out." Zach grimaced and shoved a hand through his hair. "Look, I can talk to my employees and if this rings a bell, I'll have them give you a call."

"Perhaps you can give me their names and I can handle the calls myself."

"Not happening." Zach stood up, braced one hand on the desk.

From the corner of his eye, he saw Travis slip a piece of paper on the desk. In neat print, it read:

Private investigator. From Lexington, KY.

Zach shot Travis a narrow look. Travis flipped his phone over and Zach saw the search results. Travis had just googled the man's name and number. Gleason was the only hit.

"Look, Mr. Barnes. I don't think you understand my position—"

"I don't care about your position," Zach said, cutting him off. "I care about the privacy of my employees, and the privacy of those who come in and out of my shop. I'm not passing names off without so much as a by-your-leave. Now I think this conversation is over."

Without waiting another second, he hung up the phone.

Travis studied him.

Zach ignored him and headed to his file cabinet. It was stuffed too full, crammed with information he should have gotten rid of years ago. It also needed to be replaced and he had plans of parting with it right about the time the world ended, or when the cabinet fell apart. He got attached to things. Like the file cabinet and its crazy designs that he'd do when he got bored or frustrated or distracted.

The bottom file bore a series of lotus blossoms, the kind he'd thought about inking onto Abby's skin, more than once. Then he'd actually gotten to do it—temporary ink—but ink was ink and he'd had his hands all over her soft, naked flesh.

Crouching down, he made himself think about things not related to lotus blossoms and Abby naked. The files wedged in at the back were for his employees—not that Keelie was technically *just* an employee anymore, but as he lacked organizational skills, he knew the information he'd gotten when he hired her would still be in there.

He grabbed the fat folder and had to pry it out. The manila file ripped and he swore, gripping the pages together so they didn't go flying as everything came free.

"You know, you really need to find some way to get some organization going."

He shot Travis a dark look. "You need to find a way to keep your trap shut on how I run my business." Rising, he used his boot to shut the file before heading back to his desk.

He had to flip through quite a few useless files before he

found the one he needed. And it wasn't a surprise that he encountered applications from people who no longer worked there. The first couple of years, turnover had been pretty high.

Keelie's application was down near the bottom.

He plucked it up and started to read.

Nothing popped out, not at first. Her last address had been in Texas.

There were a few references, all from Texas.

It wasn't until he flipped it over and skimmed the info at the bottom that something stood out.

The name she'd put down to call in case of an emergency.

Running his tongue across his teeth, Zach studied it thoughtfully.

"Paul Jenkins," he murmured.

"What's that?"

Zach held it out to his brother. "I don't know. The name she used for an emergency contact. Has the same area code. I'm probably reaching here. It's not like Lexington is a small city, right?"

Travis looked up at him.

"Absolutely you could be reaching." But Travis continued to stare at him and the pressure of that gaze didn't relent.

There was a knock at the door. He looked up. Anais gave him a half-hearted smile. "You look grouchy. Sorry, boss, but your next appointment is here."

After Zach slid out of the office, Travis helped himself to a cup of the shittiest coffee he'd had in a long time. He'd had some really shitty coffee, too.

Then he settled back behind Zach's desk.

The computer seemed to struggle its way back into life and Travis sighed, pinched the bridge of his nose. If he had time, he'd see what he could do about that, but first . . .

He did a quick search on the name Zach had just given him.

Huh. Mr. Paul Jenkins was an attorney. Interesting area of practice.

He eyed the piece-of-shit computer and hunkered down, fingers flying over the keys as he started to dig deeper.

It wasn't really a violation of privacy, not the way he saw it.

Since it looked like trouble was already nosing around, Travis figured the best thing to do was be ready for it.

Forewarned, forearmed, all that jazz.

A crying jag left a woman feeling exhausted and tired and ready to just curl into a ball. A week of sleep might undo some of the damage. The physical damage, never the emotional. Nothing could undo the guilt, or the anger.

A hand smoothed up her spine, settled over the curve of her neck and the fingers started to press against muscles gone tight.

Keelie closed her eyes.

"Are you okay?" Zane asked, his lips moving against her temple.

Such a question. One she had no idea of how to answer. Instead of trying, she shifted on his lap and pressed her face into his neck. The smell of him surrounded her. His arms were warm and strong, his body a firm, hard presence beneath her. Keelie didn't feel like she was going to fly off into nothingness—she couldn't. Because he was there, holding her.

Smoothing her hand up, she toyed with the collar of his shirt.

Sniffling, she tried to blank her mind, but too many memories continued to rage inside.

"I tried to tell."

The words popped out of her before she'd realized she needed to say them.

Zane rubbed his cheek against her hair.

"I went to her mom, told her what I'd seen." She blew out a shuddering sigh and fisted her hand in the material of his shirt. "This was more than a month later and Toria hadn't been to school in over two weeks. I'd heard they were moving. I went over there, told her mom that I'd seen what happened, said I'd go to court. Her mother just shook her head and said it was too late. Toria couldn't fight anymore."

Zane was quiet, saying nothing.

"I didn't understand, but then her mother took me to Toria's room. She . . ." Keelie swallowed, tears burning her eyes as the memory backhanded her. "She was on the bed. Staring outside. It was like the world had ceased to exist. Her mother was homeschooling her for the moment. Toria did enough to skate by and nothing else. I said her name and she looked at me like I wasn't even there. Her father had sold her out. The friends she'd had at school had gone and turned into either statues or they laughed when she went by. I told her mother I'd tell the sheriff, but it was too late."

"You tried. You were a kid, too. Your mother was cutting in, trying to keep you from doing the right thing."

"It doesn't matter." Keelie surged upright and paced away, staring out the windows. A headache pulsed at the base of her head. "She said she'd *take care of it*. I didn't know what she meant, but I was afraid, and Price was there and I . . . I let myself believe she'd do the right thing."

"She was your mother—that's what she *should* have done." Zane's voice was a slap and she flinched at the sound of it.

Now, striding to stand before her, he watched her with burning eyes. "You'd had somebody drug you hours earlier."

Her eyes came to his.

"Didn't you?"

"I . . ." She stopped, blew out a breath. "I don't know. Not for sure. But probably. She saved *me*. And then I wasn't there to help to her."

"You tried." His voice was so full of compassion, it almost broke her. Even as it infuriated her.

Blood roared in her ears as he continued to speak. "She was raped—that's on the sons-of-bitches responsible. You tried to help her. Both of you had done *enough* to save each other, and yourselves. The adults around you should have been there to protect you, to make sure none of that happened—and they should have stood by the both of you. They didn't. They are the ones who failed. Not the fifteen-year-old girl who'd been slipped a couple of roofies and ended up sick enough to pass out."

Keelie flushed from the shame.

"If I hadn't wanted to go to the party—"

"Stop," Zane said, his voice a growl. "If those bastards had been able to act like decent people, none of this would have happened."

She averted her face.

"Does it help?" he demanded, his voice sharp. "Blaming yourself? Does it make him any less capable of doing what he did? Did it fix him? Fix her? Fix anything?"

"Fix anything?" Keelie's laugh was so jagged it hurt her to hear it. It was brittle and broken and when she opened her eyes to stare at him, she had a hard time seeing him past the misery. How did you *fix* somebody like Price? How did she *fix* what had been done to Toria?

He must have seen some of the questions whirling in her mind because he came to her, caught her head between his hands. Pressing his brow to hers, Zane whispered, "You can't. And you weren't to blame. Maybe things would have been different if you'd spoken to the sheriff, and maybe not. But her parents should have pushed to prosecute. You tried to speak for her and her mother decided to take her away. That was her choice. Not yours." He brushed his lips across hers, a gentle kiss. "And you didn't make it happen by going to the party. That's on them, not you. Not on her. It's on them."

She caught his wrists in her hands, squeezed. She wanted to believe that. So much.

"If you could do anything different, now, would you?"

"Yes." She blurted it out, not even having to think about it. If she had the chance . . .

The chance.

Licking her lips, she looked up at Zane as her heart started to pound, hard and heavy in her chest.

If I had the chance . . .

"Price is being investigated," she said softly.

"Price?"

She let go of his wrists and spun away. "My stepbrother. I saw the article online last night. That's . . . that's why I didn't want to talk. That's what set me off. He was accused of assaulting somebody on . . ." She stopped, bit her lip. *On his campaign committee*. She wasn't sure if she wanted to go into that yet. Wasn't sure how to even broach the subject. "A woman he works with," she finished, lamely. "The papers aren't painting her in a nice light. He'll try to talk his way out of it. He'll probably win. People just don't speak up against him. Even if there are others who have had trouble with him, the family buys them off or threatens them."

She swiped her hands down her jeans, her mind racing.

They couldn't buy her off. Any attempt to intimidate her would be laughable. What would they do? There wasn't anything they *could* do. Not to her.

"Keelie?"

She turned and stared at Zane. "I have to go. Now."

Now. Before she lost her nerve.

Chapter Sixteen

"You stupid son of a bitch."

```
Restart in safe mode . . .
```

"I'll show you safe mode." Travis almost slammed his fist into the ancient tower but decided the thing was ready to draw social security. It should live out its final days as pain free as possible. He'd just given it a new lease on life, although what he should have done was sabotage the obsolete piece of shit so Zach would let it go.

"Are you threatening my computer?"

Travis looked up. Zach stood in the door, drying his hands off.

"I'm trying to convince it that euthanasia would be a kindness in its condition. Zach, this thing is five years old. Do you even do routine maintenance on it?"

Zach frowned. "Maintenance? It's not a pool for fuck's sake."

"No." Travis watched him, speaking slowly, the same way he talked to his nephew, Clay, when he went over using

Trey's computer. "It's a piece of technology—that means it needs maintenance and upgrades and updates. That keeps it from running slow and crashing. It's so loaded with spyware and malware, I'm surprised it even works. You haven't emptied the recycling bin in more than a year."

"It gets the job done. Why are you bitching about it anyway? You don't work on it." Zach tossed the rag he had into a laundry basket positioned near the wall and headed around the desk. He stopped when he saw the neat stack of papers. "What's this?"

"Information." Travis grabbed the stack, rolled it into a sheaf and slapped it against Zach's gut. Automatically, Zach grabbed the pages. "Read it. I don't know for sure if that's your connection, but just in case . . ." He shrugged, keeping his eyes on the keyboard as he typed in another command.

It was easier to lie to his brothers if he didn't have to look at them.

It was Keelie.

He'd had to dig pretty deep and go around some walls, but he had found pictures and Keelie looked pretty much the same. She'd been a little softer in the face ten, twelve years ago, but the eyes were the same, the shape of her face.

There were other changes, too, but Travis had some idea of just what might have led to those changes.

Sometimes, the people in your life changed it—and for the better. That was the way it should be.

But too often, those people changed it for the worse.

Keelie had spent some time with people who'd changed her life for the worst.

Whatever *good* changes she'd brought on had been because she'd made them happen on her own.

A harsh noise left Zach, and Travis looked up.

Zach's eyes pinned him in place. "She'll kick your ass for digging this up. What the fuck, Travis? She doesn't need you digging around in her past. I trust her—"

"So do I." Travis cut that thought off right there. "This isn't about whether or not anybody trusts her, man. Whoever is trying to track her down, it's not about a happy reunion. You really want her to think she's got to deal with it on her own?"

"Deal with what?"

The brothers turned as one to look to the doorway.

Maybe it was left over from childhood.

Maybe it was the fact that Zane still seemed to loom over them.

Or maybe it was the grim look on his face, the dark, haunted expression in his eyes.

But Travis kind of found himself wishing he'd just slid out of there. From the corner of his eye, he saw Zach's mouth tighten, realized Zach didn't feel much different.

Travis cleared the cache and shut down the window on the computer before he rose.

"Just talking a few things over with Zach," he said, keeping his voice level. "Was hoping to track you down and have dinner or something, Z."

Zane's quiet eyes studied him and then shifted to Zach.

A few taut moments of silence passed and then he came inside. The door shut behind him and the tension in the air ratcheted up. Zane was still facing away from them as he lifted his hands, shoved his hair back. "Keelie had me drop her off at her car. She needed to go home. Wants to be alone. Me? I felt like grabbing a beer—or five. Thought I'd grab one of you idiots and drag you along. But now I feel like knocking one of you down and pounding on you until you stop lying."

"For the record, I haven't said anything, much less lied." Zach held up his hands as Zane turned around. "I want to get that straight right here."

"Fine." Zane practically chewed the words off. "So how about you just tell me whatever Travis is not telling me."

Travis held still as Zach turned the information over to Zane. He kept his hands tucked into his pockets, debating on whether or not to share the information he *hadn't* printed out, the information he'd just wiped off the computer.

Information that Zach just wasn't savvy enough to be able to pull back up, even if his piece-of-shit equipment *would* cooperate.

In the end, that was Keelie's business. He'd already crossed lines, but everything he'd found was anything anybody halfway decent with a computer could dig up, if they knew how. The fact that it had taken a private investigator this long to find anything was just a sign of how incompetent the investigator was.

Keelie did need people at her back if somebody was digging around for her, the way he saw it. She had people who cared about her.

But caring about her was one thing. Sharing her entire history was another.

"What is this?" Zane asked, his voice neutral. He didn't look at them as he flipped through the information he held, skimming over each sheet before moving to the next.

"Somebody called earlier." Zach crossed his arms over his chest, leaning against the desk and crossing his ankles, legs stretched out in front of him. "Turns out he's a private investigator. Seems like he's digging around, looking for information on Keelie."

Zane's gaze swung up, lasered in on the two brothers standing by the desk. "Please tell me you didn't tell him anything," he said, his voice deceptively soft.

That didn't fool Travis.

Judging by the way Zach tensed, he wasn't fooled either. But he kept his voice easy as he replied, "Nah. Of course not. I'm not in the habit of telling strangers jack about my friends. But the fact that he was digging around about her had me concerned. I pulled out her application—one of the contacts she listed has the same area code."

"Yeah." Zane's voice dripped with scorn. "I can see the cause for concern here."

"Lay off," Zach snapped. "I was worried she had somebody looking to cause her trouble. She's never been an open book and you can tell she's got secrets. If she has trouble looking for her, I'd rather know about it upfront so we can be there to back her up."

Some of the tension drained out of Zane. "That's the only reason you're looking."

"Hell, I'm curious—you know that—but if I wasn't worried she'd have people showing up to cause her shit, I'd leave it alone." Zach jerked up a shoulder and glanced at Travis.

He was going to let it go. Travis already knew. Unless he spoke up, Zach would let their older brother think he was the one responsible, the one who'd unearthed the information Zane now held in his hands. Like Zach *could*.

Skimming a hand back through his hair, Travis shrugged. "I'm the one who dug it up, Z. The private investigator didn't even use her name—called her Katherine Vissing. But the description was spot on, except her hair and that doesn't mean shit. She's had different hair just about every single time I've seen her and I don't see her that often."

Zane narrowed his eyes. Travis didn't let anything show on his face. If any of his brothers would ever see through the smokescreen, it would be Zane. Not his parents, not Zach, sure as hell not Seb, not even his twin. But Zane, because he always looked deeper.

A few seconds passed and Travis let himself shrug. "Look, I spend my days digging around for people who are skimming money and finding various ways to screw people over. I've got a good bullshit meter. It started to spin out of control when that guy fed his lines to Zach."

"Why?" Zane asked, his voice implacable.

"Because he said *a parent* wanted to see her. And I know it's not her father—he died when she was a kid. So if he's being straight, then it's her mother." It was Zach who took that one, his voice just as hard as Zane's. "You ever talk to her about her family?"

A mask fell across Zane's face, a muscle pulsing in his cheek. "A little."

"Then you've probably noticed that she shuts down real fast if you ask her about her parents, especially her mom. So

I'm not buying this line that suddenly her mother wants to reconnect—out of the blue." Zach shrugged, but despite the casualness of the movement, the tension was still there.

Her mother.

Lowering the printouts to his side, Zane managed to keep himself relaxed through sheer will alone. "Her mother," he said slowly. "Somebody called looking for her, saying it was about her mother?"

"He's trying to locate the *daughter of a client*. His words." Zach's gaze was hooded, revealing very little. But everything else about him said he was worked up, maybe almost as aggravated as Zane.

Zane's mind spun, moving to the next logical step. Normally that came easy. He handled logic and plans very well, but what was the next logical step here?

He needed to call Keelie. No. He needed to go see her, first to tell her about the call. Then he wanted to know what this shit was with her name.

Katherine.
Was that her real name?
What the hell?
Wait . . .

He shot Zach a look. "You hired her. You get social security numbers. Wouldn't something weird pop up if the name and social security number didn't match?"

"It did match." Zane shrugged. "Plus, I do the criminal history background. None of that would stop me from hiring—depending on what it was and how I felt about the person. Javi did grand theft in his teens. Did his time, turned his life around. But there was nothing that showed with Keelie. The name checked out, the background was clean."

So that only made it all that much more confusing.

"I got to go." He looked at the information in his hands, then at Zach and Travis. "I need this. I'm going to—"

Zach's phone rang and he pulled it from his belt. "That's Keelie," he said, glancing up. "Do I tell her?"

"No." Zane shook his head. "I will."

Zach looked like he wanted to argue, but he just answered the call.

Keelie swung a look around her apartment, one last look before she locked the door behind her.

The phone rang a second, then a third time, and she was almost relieved. Voice mail—the coward's way out, maybe, but just then, she didn't care.

Then Zach answered.

Shit.

Bracing herself mentally, she plunged in, feet first. "Zach, I hate to do this to you, but I have to bail for a little bit. Hopefully just a week, but something personal has come up. It's urgent and I have to deal with it."

There was a pause, and then Zach said softly, "Are you okay?"

No.

"I'm fine. I just . . ." This was where she fumbled. *I have to go talk to the cops about this guy I know—he's my stepbrother and he's a rapist and I know it and he's done it again.* Not a great thing to drop in on a conversation. *It's a family emergency.* Not entirely a lie. It was family. In her opinion, dealing with that son of a bitch was pretty high up there. In the end, though, none of it felt right. "Look, I don't want to go into this on the phone and I have to get to the airport—"

"Airport?"

There was a rush of noise and the sinking feeling in her gut intensified. Sighing, she shoved her suitcase into the trunk, already knowing the reason behind the silence on the phone.

"Keelie, what the hell is going on?" Zane was on the phone now. His voice was a blade to her heart. At the same time, she wanted to just go to him, tell him what she was doing. Ask him if he could come with her. He would. She knew it without asking. He'd drop everything if she told him she needed him with her. He probably would have done it a couple of months ago when they were just friends—he was the kind of guy who'd offer that to his friends.

But now things were different.

She couldn't do it, though. He was in the middle of trying to get his life where *he* needed it to be.

And she . . .

I want to be part of it, she realized abruptly. She very much wanted to be a part of it, but she couldn't do that until she found a way to make peace with the life she'd dropped like a bad habit.

"Keelie?"

It dawned on her that she'd just been standing there, silent, while he waited. "I'm here," she said as she slid into the car. The pent-up heat was enough to sap her energy. She took a second to roll the window down and then she started the car. "Zane, I have to take care of something. It's . . ."

She squeezed her eyes shut, blocking out the memory of Price's face. The memory from that night superimposed on the pictures she'd seen when she'd done the search on him.

"My life isn't my own," she said softly. "Not yet. You're right, you know. I'm not to blame, and I've let it drag me down forever. You can't even imagine the ways I let it drag me down."

You got a chip on your shoulder about money, Keelie . . .

She might have laughed a little if she thought it wouldn't come out like a sob. Looking back at the building where she lived, she wondered what Zane might say if he knew the truth.

"It changed everything I am—shaped everything I do. And I'm tired of it. But I can't move past it without doing something. That's what I'm going to do."

"You're going back home."

"I'm going back . . . but it's not home. Arizona is." The words felt like a death knell. When she'd left that place, she hadn't ever wanted to go back. Hadn't ever wanted to see the cool, collected face of her mother, or look into the sly, scheming eyes of her stepbrother, the icy mask that was her stepfather. They had done everything they could to convince her to *forget the incident*. The harder they tried, the more trouble she'd caused. She became the poster-child for a *troubled youth*. Bribes of shopping trips, a car for her sixteenth birthday, none of it had worked. She hadn't understood why they'd kept her as long as they had—why they'd even wanted her to begin with.

Not until years later, during one late-night discussion with Paul Jenkins.

That was probably why there was somebody trying to hunt her down now.

She'd save them the trouble. Why not take this right to them?

"Let me come with you," Zane said, his voice low, warm, a coaxing comfort that she so badly wanted to indulge in.

"No." It was one of the hardest things she'd ever done. Even after just a couple of weeks, she was already counting on him to be there. She knew why, now.

He always *had* been there. Just waiting. For her.

She was ready for that now. Ready to see where this led, what would happen.

But she had to free herself first, do this one thing.

"Why?"

"Because they silenced me once. I was too scared, too young, too naïve to know what to do. I'm not that kid anymore, but if I don't take this one step on my own, some part of me is always going to feel like that scared, foolish girl." That admission took all the courage she had in her.

She'd had no courage, no self-confidence, no pride when she left that house, and she hadn't deserved it. It had taken her years to be able to look at her own reflection without flinching.

This one thing might help her finally accept what she'd done. What she'd *failed* to do.

So damn it, she'd do it. Alone.

"How long?"

She closed her eyes against the disappointment, the bitterness in his voice. "I don't know. Hopefully no more than a week. I'll probably have to go back, but at least I'll be able to plan for it better. I'll know more once I get there and talk to whoever I need to talk to."

"And me?" The question was soft, almost uncertain. "Are you going to talk to me and explain this to me?"

She opened her eyes, stared at her reflection. He already knew the worst things she had hidden inside.

She might as well explain the rest of it. But not now.

"I will. Soon."

Chapter Seventeen

The heat of a Kentucky summer sucker-punched her as she left the airport. It was already night, but the air was thick, choked with humidity that already had sweat beading on her brow.

Yeah, that was one thing Keelie hadn't missed about this place.

Well, one of many.

Her rental car waited and she had to smile at the sight of it. After so many years of driving the beater, she wasn't quite so certain how to handle the Mercedes Paul had lined up for her. She fumbled with the key fob for a minute and then opened the door, almost reluctant to climb inside.

Her phone rang as she went to shut the door and she welcomed the distraction, even more as she saw the number.

"Paul."

"Katie."

She licked her lips. "Keelie. That's who I am now. Katie . . ." She sighed and closed her eyes, letting her head fall back against the padded headrest. The seat was almost too comfortable to be believed. "It's Keelie. Katie's been gone a long time."

"You aren't defined by a name, kid. You're defined by what you do."

"And Katie was a kid who hid under the covers, ran away instead of standing up," she said, opening her eyes to stare at the quiet, dark parking lot. She'd locked the doors out of habit and she sat in a cocoon of silence. Easier, she thought. Easier to just sit here and pretend the rest of the world didn't exist. But there were things to do. She had to do them, so she could close this chapter of her life. "I don't hide away anymore."

Paul was quiet, but after a moment, he said, "I knew your dad. Did I ever tell you that?"

Her heart swelled, expanding until it seemed to fill her entire chest. She couldn't breathe, couldn't think. "What?"

"I knew him. Not well, but I knew him. He was attending UK on scholarship and I'll tell you, that boy had fire. He played basketball, but you could tell that it was a means to an end for him." Paul's voice was soft, faraway.

She could all but feel the memories he'd lost himself to. "We didn't get to be friends in school. I was older, focused on finishing law school. He was taking more classes than most kids his age, playing ball. He had his hands full. But he found my name when he was looking for a lawyer to handle his estate, should he need it. We got to be friends then. He came from nothing, your dad. Grew up in a trailer park in Louisville. His dad was a drunk. His mother wasn't much better. He'd lose himself in school, in the library . . . all he wanted was to make something more of himself . . . *for* himself. Then you came along, and all that focus shifted to you."

Her throat went tight. She knew so little about him. Yes, she'd dug around as she'd gotten older, found some information that was public. She'd known he'd played basketball in college, knew he'd gotten through college on a sports scholarship. But the rest, all those personal details—as young as she'd been, she'd never known things like that.

She swallowed around the ache inside. "Why are you telling me this?"

"You've got the same kind of drive your dad had, Ka . . . Keelie. You're his daughter. You found your center. You were a scared kid. And you tried. Don't ever forget that. You tried."

It wasn't enough.

But she had to get past that.

It was time to start blaming the ones responsible—her stepbrother, who was still a monster under the skin, and his parents, for hiding who, and what, he was.

A day rolled by.

Then another.

Zane was back in New Mexico, talking with the Realtor. The couple who'd made the offer wanted to buy. Zane had to get the rest of the stuff out, handle a few more things.

And deal with the Realtor.

"I think we should have pushed for—"

Zane dragged his thoughts away from Keelie. "No. I wanted it done." Turning his head, he met the Realtor's bland brown eyes. What was the guy's name? Zane should know it—he did know it, he thought. But just then, he couldn't think of it. All he could really think of was Keelie.

Getting back to Tucson. Waiting for her.

Brooding when she went another day went without calling him.

Shit.

He yanked his thoughts back to the matter at hand and said again, "It's done. It's not like they're robbing me blind."

Ron—that was his name—Ron went silent, his mouth tightening a bit, but he nodded. "Maybe not. But that other guy was loaded, showed a lot of interest. We could have gotten even more."

"And these people are ready to move forward now." *So I can move on—focus on everything else . . . Keelie.*

Later that night, surrounded by more empty boxes, he stood at the window, his phone on the table next to him.

The phone stayed mockingly silent.

I will. Soon.

He'd kind of expected that to mean she'd call once she landed, got herself in a hotel.

But Keelie hadn't called once. She'd sent a short text when she landed: *I'm here. I'll call in a few days.*

A few days. That didn't really work for him, but what was he supposed to do?

Unsettled by the emptiness inside him, he moved away from the window and sat in front of his laptop. He'd go over the designs he'd been thinking about for his studio for what felt like forever. The shop Abby had shown him had been perfect in more ways than one. It actually fit everything he'd ever wanted to do.

Now he had a place to do it.

He should be all but ready to tear down the walls himself—have sledgehammer, will travel.

Instead, here he sat.

"*Fuck,*" he snarled, scrubbing his hands over his face as she shoved her way into his mind yet again.

How could he focus on anything else going on when she was dominating his every thought?

What was she doing and why was it so important that she couldn't let him know what was going on?

"Get to work. Just . . ." He blew out a breath. "Just don't think about it, okay?"

He booted up the computer but it didn't do anything. Aaaannnndddd . . . wonderful. He'd left it unplugged, and sleeping, so long the battery had died.

Plugging it in, he took a minute to grab a cup of coffee and then he sat back down.

That annoying little message flashed up.

Blah blah blah. Yeah, he'd let the battery go dead. Computer shut down, blah, blah blah. He tapped the mouse pad and then went stiff as he saw the images of the pictures he'd shown Keelie flash up. He hadn't closed the folder and now, there they were.

He looked at the scared, skinny boy he'd been.

Keelie had looked so horrified, and then floored when he'd told her he'd never told his parents.

How in the fuck did a guy tell them that?

How could he tell his brothers?

Hey, Zach . . . you know all the times I picked a fight with you guys, half the time it was to cover up what some shit-head had done to me? Sorry about that.

Except . . .

Swearing, he shoved up and turned away from the computer.

Keelie was off doing God knows what, trying to come to grips with the scared kid she'd once been. Find some way to accept what she hadn't been able to stop.

Here he was hiding pictures of the bruises he'd borne.

Yeah, he'd done it at first because he didn't want to forget.

Most probably wouldn't understand that. But remembering had driven him to get stronger. Faster. It had driven him to make sure his brothers were the same way. Then he'd remembered and looked at others and known how it felt to be the weaker one, the one who couldn't get away. So he'd been driven to step between the victim and the victimizer.

It hadn't even stopped once he left school, either.

All throughout college, even at the bar where he'd worked. His old boss had been pissed partly because he wasn't just losing a decent bartender who'd worked for him for ten years. Zane had been just as good at dealing with the drunk idiots as some of the bouncers—and he'd *enjoyed* it.

Sometimes when he saw that glint in the eyes of a certain kind of guy, he'd remembered how he felt when he'd seen that same light in the eyes of Rick, Rodney, every asshole he'd ever dealt with growing up. And it felt *good* to be the one able to bring them down.

Slowly, he returned to the couch and sat down, staring at the monitor.

He swiped a finger across the screen, moving from one image to the next and the next. Even though the bruises had long since faded, he could almost feel the echo of them, sitting there, staring at those pictures.

He wanted to know why Keelie had gone off to face her demons?

He had the reason right here in front of him.

He carried his demons with him. He thought he faced them by not being the target he'd been.

By not letting others be the target.

But how did he really, truly face it when he still hid from it?

Sighing, he lowered his face into his hands and closed his eyes.

In that moment, he felt brutally old. Brutally exposed. Brutally alone.

The summer sunshine beat down on her shoulders.

She was due to meet Paul in five minutes.

She could have parked right in front of the law office. There had been room. But Keelie needed time to think. Time to breathe. So she'd parked a block down and now, she was trying not to panic. It wasn't working.

She thought she just might sweat through the dress she'd bought for just this purpose.

Yesterday had been busy.

She knew, too well, just how important appearances were so she'd just decided to ride with it. She'd decided to go back to her natural color, pale blonde, and she'd practically felt her jaw hit the floor when she saw how much it cost to pay a professional to get her hair back to the color of her roots—and cut her hair into the short, pixie cut she'd decided to go with.

Her makeup was subtle—even for her. Since she rarely bothered with anything unless she was out on a date, the fact that she even wore any was a sharp one-eighty. The dress had a moderately high neck, although nothing would hide her tattoos. She wasn't going to worry about that. But the sleeves went to her wrists and the material, a pale blue, was thin so she didn't feel like she was smothering. It cut to her upper body before flaring out just slightly at the hips.

She wore a simple pair of taupe heels with a bit of sparkle down the side. She didn't look like the woman who'd spent the past seven years of her life inking tattoos onto people's skin for a living. Not that she was ashamed of what she did, what she planned to do for a good long while.

Keelie Jessup was a damn good tattoo artist and she was proud of it.

But the people she was here to face down weren't going to *see* Keelie Jessup in the same light they'd see Katherine Lord.

Katherine Lord, heiress.

That was who her mother was looking for.

So she'd wear that face, even if it was a mask she was uncomfortable in. Money, appearance, it carried weight here.

Thus the reason she'd let Paul arrange for the rental of the Mercedes. The reason she carried a slim Coach purse instead of the battered, army-green handmade tote she'd used for years.

Spying a familiar form, she quickened her pace, suddenly eager to see the man who'd been a rare bright spot in her life.

At the sound of her heels clicking, he turned his head and it wasn't more than a few seconds before she had her arms around his neck. "Paul." She swallowed against the knot in her chest.

He just hugged her.

After a minute, she drew back and smiled at him, surprised at the wealth of emotion burning in her chest.

He reached up, tapped her nose. "Well. You turned out pretty decent, I must say."

She laughed, the sound watery even to her own ears.

"You went and got older," she said, making a face at him. Really, though, he looked the same. A few more lines on his face, and a few more pounds around the waistline.

But he still had that same kind smile she'd first seen in a

courthouse years ago. She'd been sitting with the child advocate while they waited for her hearing. Paul really hadn't had any reason for being there, but he had been.

It wasn't until years later that she figured out why—he had wanted to be there so she wasn't alone.

It was why he'd showed up every time she had to go to court, why he'd come to visit her, no matter which home she was in, no matter what family they'd placed her with.

She'd always had at least one person who'd cared.

"Thank you," she said, the words slipping out of her before she could stop them.

He cocked his head, puzzled. "For what?"

"For always being around. You might have been the one hired to handle the estate, but you and I both know you went above and beyond your obligations to me."

"Keelie." He sighed, shaking his head. "Sweetheart, I didn't do anything out of obligation. I gave some time to a scared, alone little girl and I started to care for her." He reached out and caught her hand. "More than once, I thought about asking if we could take you, the missus and I. But I worried that might present a conflict of interest with the estate and, more than anything, we had to make sure nothing interfered with that. It was your father's gift to you and we had to protect it. Of course, after that nasty business with your mother and that stepson . . ."

Paul's mouth went tight.

"I got out," she said, squeezing his hand. "Whoever they talked to—"

"It wasn't them." Paul looked up. "It was me. I talked to your social worker, to a few other people I knew. Told them things I probably shouldn't have. But I knew you shouldn't stay there. Your mother . . . now . . . she was not happy."

Keelie felt her jaw fall open, shock rippling through her. "What . . . you . . . ?"

He inclined his head. "You know why she wanted you."

"My father's money," Keelie said, her voice bitter. "Somebody's making calls, looking around for me back home. I know it's her. I know that's why."

"So she's looking for you. We always suspected she might." Paul looked unconcerned. Then he shrugged, averting his gaze so that he stared out over the street. It was mid-morning and early morning commuters were settled into their offices. None of the lunch rush had started. The traffic, both vehicular and pedestrian, was light. "I'm not surprised. The past few years haven't been kind to the Vissing family. They made some poor investments and Price . . . well. Let's say he's got more arrogance than any ten men should have. He's mismanaged more than a little bit of money."

"And he wants to embark on a political career. Lovely."

Paul slid her an amused look. "He'd be far from the first crooked politician, Keelie. But . . . maybe you can throw a wrench into his plans. Maybe he can silence or bribe a bunch of other people, but I don't think he'll have as much luck with you."

Keelie smile grimly. "I'm planning on using more than a wrench. I've got a toolbox full of shit to heave his way."

It was hours later when they finished.

It had been grueling, intense, almost invasive, and she had to explain far too many times why she'd been living under a different name for the past nine years. Why she'd left the state, why her money was managed not by her, but by a lawyer.

Not that Paul was just a typical lawyer.

He was a friend, one she trusted implicitly.

Quarterly, he sent money to her and she put it in an account, although more than once, she'd told him just not to send anything. It wasn't like she needed much. He handled the investments, he handled contributions and bequests, found other areas that he thought might interest her—the latest was a rape crisis center in Lexington. The funding had been pulled in the past few years and the people running it had managed to keep it going through private donations, but they were struggling.

Or they had been. Thanks to an anonymous donation, they were going to be okay.

It was one thing that made her smile when she thought about this place.

Although now, if she let herself hope, she might have another.

The woman Price had attacked, her name was Alice Reyes.

Alice wasn't there.

They met with her lawyer, spoke only with him. He was a sharp-eyed, slim man by the name Howie Franklin and he had listened with keen interest as Keelie detailed why she was there, what had brought her home . . . and why she'd left. The need to distance herself had been strong. Now, the need to see her stepbrother answer for what he'd done, the need to see him stop preying on women was just as strong.

She'd had to sit through it as Howie blasted her with questions, and her temper had been a frayed, withered thing by the time he was done. He'd left her alone with Paul and she'd all but come out of her skin in the twenty minutes they'd been in that room.

When he came back in, he'd put a cup of coffee in front of her and then, dropping the shark exterior, he'd said bluntly, "If I put you on the stand, can you hold up like you just did?"

Now, looking back, she almost wanted to hope.

To believe.

They thought she'd be enough to rock Price.

He'd warned her—it might not be enough to get him behind bars, but Howie wanted him to pay in any way imaginable. They'd go for a conviction and if that didn't work, then they'd hit another way. Civil lawsuits, through the media, anything.

"He's caused this much harm and suffered no consequences because he's in a position of power. Imagine how much worse it will get if he starts climbing that political ladder. We have to shut him down now," Howie had told her.

It was nothing less than the truth. That was why she was here. Maybe if she'd thought to check up on him—

Stop it. She told herself that as she waited with Paul in the elegant, quiet waiting room of the law offices. Howie was speaking softly on the phone. She wondered who he spoke with—Alice? Somebody else?

"Sir, you cannot go back there—"

The voice from the front caught Keelie's attention and she turned her head just in time to see a tall, slim man push past the receptionist with careless arrogance.

His head was averted. "He'll see me. Why don't you bring some coffee back?"

"Sir, he's in a meeting," the receptionist said and her tone dripped with cool professionalism.

"Is he now?"

Even before he turned to look at the room, Keelie knew. Drawing her shoulders back, she braced herself.

His eyes glanced off her without really seeing her. He looked at Paul, eyes narrowing slightly. "Well, haven't seen you in a while, Jenkins."

Then he shifted his attention to Howie.

"Howie, man. You're not returning my calls."

"Mr. Vissing. If you want to speak to me, it's best your attorney set up a meeting." Howie stared at him, his eyes sharp as a blade, although his tone was just . . . smooth. Slick and full of Southern-boy charm.

"No reason for that. Yet." Price smiled and then looked around. "Are you wrapping up here? We really do need to talk."

Keelie stared at him, hard, seeing past the slick exterior, the polished suit, to the arrogant son of a bitch. Her heart kicked up harder, her hand curled into a fist.

Don't. Don't.

She had to be careful, she knew it.

She wasn't going to let him ruin this . . . *again.*

The Vissing family had ruined *enough.*

Don't. Don't.

But she couldn't stop herself from staring at him.

That must have been what did it.

His gaze slid to her, away.

And then back again.

His eyes widened.

His mouth opened in shock.

"Katherine."

Howie said something, but the words were lost in the roar of blood crashing in her ears.

Paul caught her arm. She glanced at him, smiled. All the years of hiding everything, locking it all down inside, rushed to the fore and saved her.

Turning her head back, she studied her stepbrother through narrowed eyes, let a faint, dismissive smirk dance around her lips for a moment before she looked back at Howie. "You'll let me know if there's any other way I can help, won't you?"

"Of course." Howie inclined his head and his eyes gleamed with what she could only describe as a predatory sort of glee.

She'd faced Price.

Faced him, and she hadn't folded.

He wouldn't—*couldn't*—bend her.

"Wonderful." With one more nod, she looked at Paul.

He held out his arm. "My dear."

"Katherine," Price said again, his voice low, but the command there was unmistakable.

She slid him a curious look. He would never know she wanted to hit him. Could even see herself doing it. It would feel so very good.

But that wasn't the ultimate satisfaction. He'd go down . . . for a few minutes.

She wanted to see him go down, publicly, and for so much longer.

"You'll have to excuse us," she said as they walked around him. "Paul and I have so much to discuss."

He shot out a hand to catch her arm.

She'd been prepared and edged back, lifted a brow as their gazes connected once more.

His smile was strained. "I'm sure we do as well. It's been a long time. We should do dinner. My treat."

"That . . . wouldn't be a good idea," she said, shaking her head. "Paul, if you're ready? It's been a long day."

That didn't even touch on it.

Chapter Eighteen

Late that night, she sat on the bed in her hotel room, staring out over the twinkling lights.

There really wasn't that much to Lexington, she realized. Small, really. She'd lived in Dallas for a year, then moved to Tucson.

Knees drawn up to her chest, she continued to stare outside, willing her mind to stay blank.

Paul had called Howie once he had her tucked in the room he'd booked for her. She'd insisted he let her know what Howie said. Howie was a little irritated over Price's unexpected appearance in his office, but he wasn't too concerned.

Yes, now he knew—in advance—that she'd be coming, but the lawyers would have figured that out soon anyway.

Price would go to court.

Alice Reyes wasn't going to give up.

The date was already set.

So far, nothing Price had thrown at her had shaken her determination and, now with the information Keelie had provided, it was just going to be another strike against the asshole.

No, they might not get a conviction and Reyes seemed to get that.

But she wasn't looking *just* for a conviction.

She was looking for vindication and she wanted the world to know what Price Vissing was, wanted the world to understand before people helped put him in office.

The scandal alone would do him considerable damage.

Keelie was betting on it.

Resting her chin on her knees, she closed her eyes. "I wish I could have done the same for you, Toria."

Wherever Victoria Kingsley was, this wasn't going to offer her any justice, but it was the only thing Keelie could give her.

You tried to help her. Both of you had done enough to save each other, and yourselves.

Zane's words drifted to her, and she felt terribly, terribly alone in that moment, in that luxurious suite, surrounded by soft light, sitting on a bed that felt softer than a cloud.

From the corner of her eye, she saw the phone and she reached out, touched it.

Slowly, she traced the edge with her finger.

She needed to see him.

Needed to hear his voice.

Before she could talk herself out of it, she rolled onto her belly.

She didn't dial his number though.

She initiated that annoying FaceTime thing. She needed to *see* him.

Not just hear his voice. She needed to see the elegant lines of his face, those cool, blue green eyes.

Seconds ticked by. Her heart slammed.

Her hands started to sweat.

She almost broke the connection—it was taking so long.

And then, there he was.

Her throat locked up.

Her voice was a tight wheeze when she finally managed to say, "Hey."

A slow smile curled his lips and just like that, the knot inside her chest started to unravel.

* * *

Zane's day had been shit.

The past few days had been shit.

But none of that mattered at the sight of her.

Especially once her lids drooped over her eyes and she gave him that slow smile she seemed to save just for him—almost shy, almost nervous. And it wrapped a fist around his heart every single time.

He stared for a few seconds, let the tension inside him drain away before he even bothered trying to talk.

"You changed your hair," he murmured, stroking his finger over the screen of his iPad, wishing he was touching her instead of that cool, lifeless surface.

"Yeah." She shrugged, a deprecating look on her face. "Doing something where people seem to think it's better if you don't have two-tone hair. It's going to be boring for a little while."

"Nothing about you could ever be boring." If anything, the pale strands, the delicate cut seemed to accentuate her skin, the fine bones of her face. "One of these days, I'm going to get you in front of my camera."

She made a face at him. "Find a better model. I hate pictures."

"You'll break my heart. I'm dying to get a couple of pictures of you . . . just you. Naked."

She caught her lower lip between her teeth, a slow blush rising up her neck before staining her cheeks. A self-conscious laugh escaped and she muttered, "You're a damn pervert."

"No." She had shadows in her eyes. Too many of them, and all he wanted to do was pull her against him, make those shadows go away. He couldn't hold her now. But he could make her laugh. Leaning forward, he craned his head like he was trying to see outside the monitor. "If I was a pervert, I'd be doing things like asking you to take off your shirt." He waited a beat, then smiled. "Keelie . . . would you take off your shirt?"

He could hear the sharp intake of breath, watched the

spike of her pupils. "I knew you were a pervert." Her tongue stroked across her lower lip. "Just why would I do something like that?"

"Because it's been a little too long since I've been able to put my hands on you. Way too long since I've seen you naked."

She laughed, the sound breathless. "You just saw me naked a few days ago."

"See what I mean?" He focused his attention on her mouth. "If I was there, I'd already be working on taking your shirt off. And kissing you. It's been way too long since I kissed you."

"Zane . . ." His name was a ragged burst of sound on her lips, needy and broken.

Then that need exploded through him as well as she leaned back and reached for the hem of her shirt, a skinny-strapped tank top. She peeled it off, slow, oh so very slow, and Zane's cock started to pulse in time with his heart.

Son of a bitch.

This was a game that he maybe shouldn't have started.

She tossed the shirt aside and he groaned. "I can't see you," he muttered.

She glanced down and then shot him a wicked smile. "I can see me."

"Evil little brat." He could see the upper slopes of her breasts, her face. That was it.

It was torture.

It was bliss.

"I want to see you," he said, demand edging into his voice.

She lifted a hand, trailed it across one of the rose vines that climbed up her breastbone. "I miss you," she murmured. "How did that happen?"

Caught between staring at her fingers, so slim and pretty, and looking back at her face, Zane had to clear his throat before he could even speak. "I've been having that problem for the past couple of years, angel. I spend fifteen minutes around you and then I'm gone for a couple of months—the second I walked away I was already missing you."

Her mouth parted.

"Fuck, I need to kiss you," he rasped. "When are you coming home?"

"I . . ." She swallowed, her lashes sweeping down low. "I don't know. I . . ."

Her hand dropped and she looked around, grabbing her shirt.

Her face disappeared from his view for a minute and when she was again on the screen, she'd pulled the tank back on.

"I guess I should tell you what's going on," she said, her voice subdued.

The shift of emotion in her eyes, on her voice was enough to cool the heated pulse of his blood. Cool, not erase. He shifted on the couch, braced his back against the arm as he watched her face. "I wouldn't object," he said. *Please. I'm going out of my mind.*

She watched his face the entire time she spoke, waited for some sign that she'd messed up, leaving him for this.

But when she finished, he just looked down for a minute, then he shifted his gaze upward, a faint smile on his face.

"As much as I hate you not being here, I gotta say . . ." He blew out a breath. "I'm proud of you. This all has to suck, but if you're going to cut those chains you talked about, you're doing it in fine style."

Something warm and sweet shifted in her heart.

I'm proud of you.

How sappy was it, that it made her feel so warm inside to hear that?

She was a grown woman. She shouldn't *need* anybody's approval.

And she didn't.

But hearing those words meant something. It touched something deep inside and for a moment, she couldn't even speak around the ache in her heart.

Clearing her throat, she waited until she thought she might be able to talk without her voice wobbling. Then she said, "Yeah. Well. Part of me feels like it's years too late, but it's something. I don't know if he'll do time, but regardless, this trial is going to happen, and it's going to happen really close to the primary."

"The primary?"

She licked her lips and then met his eyes. "My stepbrother is running for the state senate in Kentucky, Zane."

He was silent a moment, processing that. "Damn. Hopefully this will hurt his platform, huh?"

"Yeah." She chuckled and shifted on the bed, rolling onto her back, holding the phone in her hand. With her free one, she reached up, touched his cheek. "I miss you."

"I miss you." His lids drooped low. "Come home. Soon. I know you have things to do, but once you can . . . come home."

Chapter Nineteen

She left Lexington with about as much fanfare as before—telling nobody.

On her way to Louisville International Airport, she put in one last call to Paul, told him her flight number, when she'd land.

"You're sure I'm okay to go?"

"I've told you a hundred times," he said, his voice patient. "You're fine to leave. We'll call you when we need you."

"I know . . . I just . . ."

"You're not running away," he said gently. "You've got a life, one that's not here. You can make trips back and forth if we need you to and when it's time, you'll come back. It's not time yet."

"Yeah." She eyed the signs ahead of her and nodded. "Yeah. Listen . . . I . . . uh. Maybe it's time for me to take control of that life. A little more on my own. Ah, I mean . . ."

"I'll get started on transferring the funds over into your name."

She didn't even have to say it. He just knew.

"You were the first friend I had, Paul. I don't know if I

ever told you that, but you were. You don't know what it meant to me."

His voice, when he spoke, was husky. "Sweetheart, you were, and still are, one of the sweetest, bravest young women I've ever known. It's been an honor to be your friend." Then he cleared his throat. "You let me know if there's anything you need. J. P. and I are always here when you need us."

She hung up before she started to blubber.

She had enough things on her mind that she couldn't handle the emotional storm of a crying jag.

It would be hours still before she was in Tucson, but between then and now, she had a lot of stuff to think through.

Some decisions to make.

She had to linger in baggage pickup even though when she'd left, she'd only had a carry-on. The shopping trip in Lexington had left her with more clothes than she usually bought in a year.

For the first time, though, she didn't let herself feel any guilt.

Not at the suitcase, not at the nice clothes inside.

Her father had been a man who'd made himself out of nothing.

When he died, he'd left that money to her.

It wasn't money that made people into conscienceless monsters.

People without conscience just did conscienceless things— and if they had money, they'd use it to cover those sins up.

Living like the *little cretin* her mother had accused her of being right before she'd left the Vissing household for the last time hadn't solved or fixed anything.

As far as her mother was concerned, Keelie considered it both poetic justice and irony to donate some of the money toward things Katherine Vissing Price would loathe. She'd done it before—it had been a small thing, really. But it had brought Keelie so much satisfaction. When she'd become

Zach's partner, giving him the money to help expand and upgrade the shop. Other things . . . the rape crisis center. Splurging on sparkling rhinestone boots or funding a group of high-schoolers to go to a workshop in Washington, DC.

She might even set up a couple of funds in her mother's name—having Paul handle everything, of course. And if there were cards or letters that came in, he could forward them on to her darling mother.

The thought made her smile as she lugged her suitcase out. The smile turned sardonic as she tried to figure out how to get the suitcase into the Bug, though. It wasn't going to fit all that well. Zane's smaller suitcase and his camera equipment had been one thing.

This, though?

She managed, after some clever maneuvering.

Then she sat in the car and debated.

Home?

Zane's?

Flipping the mirror down, she studied her reflection for far too long.

The sight of the car sitting in the parking lot of Zach's old building had Zane's heart jump up into his throat.

He sat in his Jeep for a long, long moment and then he climbed out, looking up at the soft glow of the lights.

Tugging out his phone, he eyed it. She hadn't called.

She hadn't texted or emailed.

But Keelie was home.

He managed, barely, not to rush the place and kept his steps slow and measured as he headed inside. He even managed not to race up the steps. He took the elevator. Nice and cool.

All of that nice, cool calm shattered though when he unlocked the door and found her sitting inside, flipping through a magazine.

Her gaze slid up to his.

His heart stuttered to a stop.

I missed you.

I have something to tell you . . . I'm in love with you . . .

Those words tangled in his throat as he crossed the floor.

She sat up as he lowered himself to sit on the low, square chunk of polished wood that served as a coffee table. Keelie met his eyes, that familiar smile quirking her lips.

"How did you get in here?" he asked.

Yeah. Smooth, man. Real smooth.

She shrugged. "I've had a key for ages. Zach? Great guy. A little scattered." Her grin widened. "He locked himself out about once a month. I have a set of keys. Abby. I think he was going to make up a set for Javi, but never got around to it."

"Ahhh . . ." He reached, brushed his fingers through the pale strands of her hair. "Blonde. I like it."

"It's boring. I haven't done anything this boring in ages." She rolled her eyes. "It will work for now. It's . . . ah . . . well. Pretty much my natural color. They had to bleach all the other color out, but I might keep it this way. Who knows?"

He pushed his fingers into the strands. It was so short now that was all he could do. "There's nothing boring about you, angel."

When he tugged her closer, she came.

He didn't kiss her, just wrapped his arms around her. She made a soft little sound in her throat that hit him square in the chest.

Closing his eyes, he pulled her into his lap until her knees settled on either side of his hips. Now he let himself say *some* of the words trapped inside. Mouth pressed to her neck, he said, "I missed you. You were gone too long."

"It was only six days."

"Too long."

She lifted her head and lifted a hand, pressed it to his cheek. "Yeah. Too long." Then she winced. "I'll have to leave again. The trial. All of that."

"I'll go this time."

"Yes." She leaned in and pressed her mouth to his. "You'll go this time."

She nibbled at his lower lip until he opened for her and the hungry little moan went straight to his dick.

He had a desperate need to get her naked. Once he had her naked, tucked under him, he'd feel a little better, he decided. Well, a *lot* better, if she was wrapped around him, wet and hot and as close as they could possibly get.

But even as he went to push his hands under her shirt, she slid back, easing off his lap and holding out a hand. "Can we go for a drive? I want to show you something."

He eyed her hand. It was painful standing up, his cock already a pulsating ache in his jeans. Grimacing, he glanced down and then back up. "I had other plans . . . but for you, anything."

"Why does it seem like you really mean that?"

He hooked one arm around her waist and tugged her against him. He took her mouth, too hungry and impatient to be gentle, and she was panting when he lifted his head.

"Because I do. I've all but been your slave for the past three years, Keelie. You just never noticed."

Her hands were slick on the steering wheel as she drove.

Did he *really* think she could concentrate now?

Really?

I've all but been your slave . . .

With her heart rabbiting in her chest, it felt like she was breathing in syrup, the air thick, heavy. And full of him.

Her VW Bug was too small for him. She'd already started trying to figure out what kind of car she wanted to get—the Bug had been yet one more way to live a life as far apart from the one her mother had lived as possible and she was done with that, but now, with his large body taking up all the space, she had to wonder.

Cramped as it was, driving in this car with him was actually . . . nice.

He grunted as his knee banged the dash and she bit back a smile.

Maybe not for him.

"Where are we going?" he asked after a few more minutes.

She glanced over at him. "Almost there."

He stared out the window, oddly tense, almost strained, ever since they'd left the loft.

Feeling like she had to do something, offer something, she said softly, "I've got some of your pictures in my work area."

Now he slid a smile her way. "I've noticed. The one of the Borealis . . . ?"

Her heart had sighed in wonder when she saw that one. "It's my favorite."

"I took that one thinking you'd like it."

An ache settled in her heart. "Damn it, Zane."

She sniffled.

"Now, what you're *supposed* to say is *thank you*."

She sniffed again. Slowing down at a red light, she shot him a look. Then, she reached across the nonexistent console, hooked her hand in the front of his shirt.

As he came to meet her halfway, the light turned green. She didn't care.

"Thank you," she whispered against his mouth.

He smiled. "You're welcome."

The rest of the drive was in silence, but it only took another ten minutes.

When she pulled up in front of the big, sprawling old house, Zane studied it with some level of bemusement, his gaze lingering on the *For Sale* sign before he looked back up at it.

She wondered what he was thinking, although she doubted he'd have any idea what was in her mind.

"I love this house," she said softly, as they both got out of the car.

He looked over at her.

Tucking her hands into the back of her jeans, she rocked back on her heels and just stared.

"Sometimes, I'm out driving and I'll just come here and look. It's big . . . almost too big, but it feels like a home, ya know?"

She didn't wait for an answer, just started toward it.

He was right behind her and when she took the paved walkway that led around the side, he moved to walk along with her. "I haven't had a home since my father died." She accepted that ache in her chest, accepted it, and realized for the first time she could maybe even learn to let it go. He hadn't left her on purpose. "There were a few times when I was *almost* there, but every time I came close, something went wrong. So I stopped letting myself try to find anything that might *be* home. Even when I left Kentucky, even when I was on my own. I didn't want anything that might be taken away again."

She stopped as the walk opened into a large courtyard.

It wasn't so beautiful now.

But the home had stood empty for more than a year.

She could see it as it should be, as she wanted to make it.

"So I didn't let myself look for a home. I think . . ." She blew out a breath. "I think I'm ready to be done with that."

The house was something, Zane had to admit.

It was also huge, and sitting on what he suspected was prime real estate.

He had money in the bank—or *would*—from the sale of his house, but that didn't mean he could afford something like this, nestled in the foothills of the mountains, with a view that faced out over the desert.

Unless, of course, he gave up on the idea of buying the photography studio instead of renting it. He could own it, outright. He'd been tinkering with the idea. He could do it, with the money from his place, the business loan. It would be tight, but he could make it.

Yet looking at the house that filled Keelie's eyes with such longing, he realized there was no contest.

He didn't need to own a big place for his studio—didn't need to *own*, period. He could rent. Might have to start out smaller, cheaper. He'd have to juggle the figures. The place near Abby's might not work now, but he could find a way to make everything work.

For her.

For her.

Reaching out, he rested a hand on her spine.

"You want this."

She glanced at him, a gleam in her eyes.

"I'm *getting* this," she said.

Then she turned to face him, even as he tried to process that comment.

"I think some part of me knew," she said, her head cocked as she studied him. "Every time you kept asking, and every time I pushed you away. I spent a long time punishing myself."

Fury whipped through him. He tried not to let it show as he reached up and cupped her cheek. "You *weren't* to blame," he said, his voice hot despite his best intentions.

"I know." She covered his hand with hers, pressed lightly. "I know. But that didn't stop me from believing it. For a very long time. I kept myself isolated. I convinced myself I was in love with a guy I *knew* belonged to somebody else . . ." A smirk twisted her lips. "And then, just to twist myself up even more, I threw myself between them, because hey . . . why settle for being miserable, if I can be *utterly* miserable? And you . . ."

Her eyes moved to his.

"You." She moved her hand to his cheek, stroked her fingertips along his cheekbone, his jaw, across his lips. "You looked at me like you saw me. I hated it. Even as part of me wanted to be around you *more*, just because it was nice not to have to hide, or wear a mask, or throw up a wall just to keep people away."

Her eyes roamed across his face and then she turned away. "I think I always knew."

His heart twisted, shifted. There was something burning deep inside, but he was afraid to look too deeply at it just yet.

Not yet.

She went back to staring over the courtyard. He followed her gaze because if he kept staring at her, he was just going to haul her up against him and . . . do what? He didn't know.

The courtyard might look desolate and deserted, but he saw it with a practiced eye, saw the promise of what waited.

He could do this. If he could get the loan. If he couldn't get it on his own . . . he braced his shoulders. Hell. He'd do what he had to. He'd talk to his folks. Zach, if he had to. Pride wasn't shit when it came to her. *This* was the one thing she'd let herself want—

"I need to tell you about my father," she said quietly, moving deeper into the courtyard.

Her words sliced through his own brooding thoughts and he jerked his head up, stared at her.

She wasn't looking at him, her gaze focused now on the slowly darkening sky. "My dad was . . . well. Brilliant. Studied engineering. Wanted to make things. The problem was he didn't have a focus on the *things* he wanted to make. He'd come up with a couple of different ideas—or improvements on current inventions—technology . . ." She glanced over at him. "I don't have his brain. I don't even completely understand the stuff he did. But he was smart. He'd already made his first million before he married my mother. That was why she went after him. She saw that he was going to be rich and she set out to twist him up. She did it. But then she got pregnant . . . she hadn't planned on how *not* fun that would be. She wanted a nanny. He wanted a family."

She turned to face him now. "She left before I was even two. She wasn't happy about it, either. But she'd cheated on him and there was a prenup. Apparently, he'd offered her a lump sum if she just left. There was . . ." She paused, looked down. When she looked up at him, her eyes were vulnerable. "Seems he came home early from a business trip and I was locked up in a closet somewhere. I'd been crying, interrupting her *me* time. Rude of me, right?"

Zane curled his hand into a fist.

"After that, he told her she could take the money he'd

offered her, or he'd see her in jail. She left, signed over custody. If he hadn't died . . ." She shook her head. "Anyway. Right around the time my mom left, my dad and his partner came up with something pretty revolutionary. They'd founded a small camera manufacturing company and it was gaining a lot of attention."

She walked closer, stopping to nudge at a loose stone with the toe of her boot. "They had a lens design that was apparently unique—something my father and his partner had helped come up with."

Lens—

She looked up at him, a faint smile on her face. "My father's name was Michael Lord."

Michael Lord.

Otto Leonard.

Leoto—Zane felt poleaxed, standing there staring at her. "Son of a bitch."

Now the smile split across her face. "Yeah."

He turned away, swiped a hand down his face. "The first camera I ever owned . . . it was a Leoto. That was the one that had belonged to my grandpa. I used it when I took that picture of the owl. I still have it."

"They last forever," she murmured.

"The lenses . . ." He stopped. Then he narrowed his eyes. "The lenses were unique to that company—they held the patent."

"Yep."

"And Leoto was bought . . ." He stopped, scrubbed his hands down his face. "It was bought about ten years ago. For a very fat chunk of change."

When he lowered it, she'd gone back to studying the house.

She glanced back at him. "I didn't get it all. Otto was a full partner. They had bequests. But . . . yeah. I inherited. He'd left his estate to me. It's why my mother came looking for me. She didn't know he'd died until a few years after the fact. Paul Jenkins—I told you about him—he was the lawyer who handled the estate. She fought to get her hands on the money for a long time. It was a losing battle. My dad knew her very, very well."

Zane looked up at the house, then back to her.

"So you're buying this place."

A serene smile curled her lips. "I am buying this place. And all the land surrounding it, if I can manage it."

He squinted, decided he was glad he hadn't mentioned any of the thoughts running through his head. As she came toward him, he went to pull her close, one hand coming around her waist, the other molding the back of her skull. "So I guess I get to be the first to hear the news, huh?"

"Yes." She smiled and leaned in, pressing her mouth to his. "Although that's not the only reason I'm telling you."

She caught his hand and drew him over the patio that led up to the house. There, she leaned up against one of the columns, crossing her long legs at the ankle. Zane tried not to notice just how much leg was left bare under the hem of her snug black skirt, or how the boots rose to hug her legs to the knee. Only Keelie was crazy enough to keep wearing knee-high boots all throughout the year in Tucson, he thought. And able to pull off the look, too. He slid a hand down the satin length of her thigh—he had to touch her. Just touch, that's all.

"I'm telling you," she said quietly, "because this is the start of the life I want . . . for me."

She bit her lip and tipped her head back to look at him.

The last, lingering rays of the sun gilded her skin gold. "I want this place. And I want you."

His hand tightened on her thigh.

His heart tightened in his chest.

Blood crashed and roared in his ears as he stared at her and, for the longest time, he couldn't think, couldn't even breathe.

"Keelie . . ." he whispered. He didn't even know where to go from there. What to say.

What was *she* saying?

He curved his hand over the side of her neck.

"I want a life." She wrapped her hands around his neck.

"I want to make a real one. And I want to try to make it with you."

Her eyes searched his. "Is that okay?"

Shuddering, he lowered his brow to hers.

"Okay?" He gripped her waist, his hands spasming on the narrow curve. "Is it okay?"

Then he hauled her up against him. She wrapped her legs around him and he couldn't help but notice how her miserable excuse of a skirt rose to the very tops of her thighs. "Okay?" he said again, his face against her neck. "I already told you I was your slave. Being a part of your life was the main reason I came here to begin with."

She turned her face to his and he caught her lips, but she didn't let him kiss her. Her fingers rested on his chin. "You came here because you wanted to set up a studio."

"Keelie." He cupped her head in his hands, stared down at her before he slowly, so slowly, lowered his mouth to hers. "I can do that just about anywhere. I came *here* because *you* are here. I love you, Keelie."

She went tense.

"It's okay if you're not ready to tell me yet. You will be. And I'm going to be here. Waiting for you."

He dipped to kiss her and her mouth opened on a sigh.

"Waiting. For you . . ." He said again, after they broke the kiss. "Always for you."

Chapter Twenty

Courthouses were cold.

Keelie remembered that from her youth.

Stupidly enough, she hadn't brought a jacket.

But after another shiver rocked her, something warm, and smelling of Zane, wrapped around her.

She looked up as he sat down next to her.

"You look like you want to puke," he said, a faint smile twisting his lips.

"I feel like it." She grimaced, glad she hadn't let him talk her into eating anything at lunch. Experience had taught her better, though. She'd grown past it, mostly, but in the years after she'd left her mother's house behind, she'd spent months emptying her stomach anytime she got upset. Just one of the many neuroses Katherine Vissing had left her with.

Katherine . . . and Price.

But she was getting better, growing past them.

And once this was over . . . ?

Zane took her hand. "It won't be much longer."

She shot him a look. "I know."

Then she lifted his hand to her lips. "I still want you to tell your parents. I think if I get through this without throwing up, or crying, you should have to. Fair is fair, right?"

He shot her a dark look. "You play dirty."

"They should know." She touched his mouth. "You didn't do anything wrong, either . . . except hide it from them."

"I know that." He sighed, looked away. Then he looked back at her. "You still play dirty."

"I do what I have to." Unable to stay still, she came off the bench and started to pace. It had been almost two months since she'd come here the first time, and she still didn't want to be here.

Those past two months had been a blur.

Zane was almost ready to open his studio.

He'd helped her moved.

They spent more nights together than apart.

She slid a hand into the narrow little pocket of her tailored suit jacket and shot him a look. She had a gift in her pocket, something she'd wanted to give him for weeks.

Now, as he slid off the bench to meet her on the marbled floor, she pulled it out.

She looked down, nerves a tangle inside her.

Then she shoved it at him.

"Here."

He took it, staring down at it for a long moment. He shifted his gaze to her, staring at her through his lashes.

"It's a key," she said helpfully.

"I know what it is." He rubbed his thumb across it.

"I want you to have it."

He cocked his head. "Okay."

He wasn't getting it. This was stupid. She was too nervous.

Spinning away, she started to pace all over again and then she spun back and glared at him. "You could make this easy. I'm standing here trying to figure out how to tell you I love you, that I want you to move in. You gave me pretty words and you made me feel like I matter and I can't do that. Can't you at least—"

The rest of the words were caught against his mouth.

"Oh . . ." She sighed when he finally pulled away.

Oh . . .

He ended the kiss softly, rubbing his mouth over hers before he lifted his head.

"I'm a guy," he said, a sardonic smile on his face. "I don't need pretty words. A key works for me. And you just told me you loved me. I can't think of anything I need more than that."

"Oh. Well, then." She licked her lips. "I guess that's . . . that's good, right?"

He laughed and pulled her up against him. "You're all I need."

"Wow."

The unfamiliar voice had Keelie pulling back. Zane resisted at first, his arm lingering on her waist just long enough to let her know he'd rather keep her where she was.

But then, he let her go and they both turned to look at the speaker.

The woman was unfamiliar, her chestnut hair swept into a complicated twist, a pair of chic, sexy glasses perched on an upturned nose. She had catlike green eyes and a pale, creamy complexion. The suit she wore was a brighter green than her eyes and she had that turned out kind of look that Keelie spent *hours* trying to accomplish.

The woman studied Zach for a long moment before shifting her gaze to Keelie.

"You still don't know how to talk to people very well, do you?"

Keelie blinked, the familiarity in those words catching her off guard.

"Do I . . ."

She moved closer, light slanting across her face, and for a moment, it washed away the soft, peaches-and-cream hue, while casting her eyes into shadow.

No.

"I can't tell you how happy I was to see somebody finally have the balls to do this," the woman said, pausing to look down the hall that led to the courtroom where Price Vissing was currently undergoing a very, very unpleasant trial.

Somehow, things had shifted in the public eye and he wasn't coming out smelling as sweet as he usually did.

She continued her perusal of the empty hall before turning her head to look back at Keelie. "You would have done it, wouldn't you?"

"Done what?" Keelie asked, her voice shaking a little.

Zane slid his hand up, curved it over the back of her neck, a solid, steady warmth. It didn't *quite* stop her shaking. But she took comfort in knowing he was there. Close enough to hold. To lean on.

"Testified." As she came closer, her heels clicked on the floor. "I did hear you that day. Mom thinks I didn't, but I did. I was just . . . depressed."

"Son of a bitch . . . Toria."

Victoria Kingsley angled her head, smiled. "Actually, it's just Tori now. I kind of outgrew the goth thing a long time ago." Then, as a sad smile curled her lips, she said again, "I did hear you. While you were down there, talking to Mom. I heard what you said. Part of me wanted to listen, wanted to tell Mom we should try. But every other part . . ." She stopped and looked around. "I couldn't do this. Not then. And I've felt guilty, every day since. How many women did he hurt because I was too afraid to stand up?"

"It's not your fault."

Tori looked at her, lifting a brow. "And how many times have you told yourself you didn't do enough, Katie?"

"Keelie." It jumped to her lips before she could stop it. Turning her head, she stared out one of the tall windows. "It's Keelie now. I . . . I had my name changed when I was eighteen. I didn't want my mom, any of them trying to track me down."

"I can't say I blame you." Green eyes narrowed, Tori said, "You never answered me."

Keelie looked back at her. "You always did know me better than I'd like. It took me a long time to figure it out, though. We tried—you tried to tell the cops. I tried to tell them, told your mother I'd tell what I'd seen. None of them listened. At the end of it all, he was the one who took what he had no right to take."

"Yeah." Tori wrapped her arms around herself, shivering a little. A haunted look drifted across her face.

Keelie could have kicked herself, but when she would have said something, offered an apology, Tori looked back at her, a strange smile on her lips. "At the end of it all, it's on Price. I let him take too much, even after that night. Gave him too much—wasted years, refusing to look at myself. It wasn't just him. It was how the cops twisted everything around, how my dad took the money, tried to convince me it wasn't as bad as I thought. The son of a bitch."

If Keelie could have found that man and hurt him, she would have.

"My dad's dead," Tori said, offering the words like she knew what Keelie was thinking.

"Yeah?"

"Yup. He'd been drinking for a while anyway—that's why Mom left him. But he hit it harder and harder after that. One day, it was snowing. He was sitting outside drinking. Fell asleep. Temps dropped down into the teens. They found him a few days later. He froze to death. Sitting on his porch, wearing a T-shirt and jeans." She paused, looked away. "I guess he finally realized it was worse than he wanted to think."

Then she shrugged, the movement almost birdlike, as if she were settling feathers into place. She looked at Zane, sizing him up. Tori had always been petite and Zane had more than a foot on her. She merely lifted a brow and then looked Keelie. "You two fit."

Keelie looked up at him, found herself smiling. "Yeah. We do."

Zane had been quiet until that moment, but now he held out a hand. "Zane Barnes."

Tori accepted, shook his hand once. "I know that name."

* * *

Zane studied the woman, probably as thoroughly as she studied him. "Do you now?" he asked as she pulled her hand free.

"Yeah. I run a rape crisis center here in town, Joan's House."

Next to him, Keelie stiffened, almost imperceptibly.

Tori kept on talking, her voice calm, easy. "There was a bequest made a while back and when it came, there was also a framed print of your work. A picture of the shrine of Joan of Arc at Beauvais."

Zane managed, barely, not to turn his head and look at Keelie.

She'd asked him if it was okay to print that out. Not all of his images had been posted online but she'd seen that one once, when he was showing Zach some pictures from a trip to Europe. She emailed him about it, months later. Asked if she could get a copy to print and frame.

He'd sent her the framed picture he'd had on his wall instead.

"It's hanging on the wall in the community area," Tori said. "There's no religious affiliation. Some of the girls go to the church across the street. Others . . . not so much. But we talk about Joan. A lot. The peasant who became a warrior. We've all got some hidden strength inside us. That's what Joan's House is about—finding it."

"Sounds like a good place," Zane said softly, sliding his hand down, closing it around Keelie's.

"It is. We do a lot of good there. We'll be able to keep doing it for a long time." Then she turned her head to Keelie, lifted a brow. "I wasn't able to send you a thank-you card, but . . . well, thanks."

Then she turned, headed off down the hall.

Keelie busied herself staring at her shoes.

Zane didn't see the point in saying anything.

Then there wasn't any time. The sound of heels clicking had them both looking up. It wasn't Tori.

No. It was time for Keelie to face her stepbrother on the stand. A witness for the prosecution, a rebuttal witness. He'd claimed never to have touched a woman in violence. Keelie knew otherwise.

As they started down the hallway, he squeezed her hand. "You'll do fine," he said calmly.

"I know." She nodded, smiled. Then she looked up at him. "And when we're done, maybe you can think about dealing with some of your secrets."

He grimaced. Then, tugging her to a stop for just a moment, he pressed a kiss to her lips. "I love you."

"I know. I love you, too."

Turn the page for a preview
of Shiloh Walker's

BUSTED

*Coming May 2015
from Berkley Sensation!*

Week One

The first time Trey Barnes saw her it caught him by surprise.

Not because he knew her.

Not because of anything she did.

But because it had been six years since a woman had caused this kind of reaction in him.

Six years.

So it was a punch in the gut when he walked into the Norfolk library for the kids' reading program and saw *her*. His tongue all but glued itself to his mouth and his brain threatened to do a slow meltdown.

The woman was kneeling down in the middle of a circle of kids, a smile on her mouth. A mouth slicked wine-red and he suddenly found himself dying of thirst.

It had also been six years since he'd touched a drop of alcohol, but in that moment, he found himself imagining a glass of wine. Wine . . . wine-red lips, wine-red sheets, and that long body, skin just a few shades lighter than milk chocolate.

"Come on, Daddy!" Clayton jerked on his hand. "Let's go! I want to go play."

His son's voice dragged him out of the fantasy, rich and lush as it was, and he shook his head a little to clear it. A heavy fullness lingered in his loins and he was glad he'd gotten used to looking like a bum. The untucked shirt had fit him well enough when he bought it years ago, but the weight he'd lost after Aliesha's death had stayed off, so the shirt hung loose on his rangy frame. Loose enough that he figured it would hide the hard-on that had yet to subside.

A few minutes surrounded by chattering preschoolers ought to do it, he thought.

Clayton let go of his hand as he got closer and he reached up, nudged his sunglasses down. As he'd retreated farther and farther into hermit mode, fewer people recognized him, but he rarely went anywhere without something to hide his face. Between the hair he rarely remembered to cut and the sunglasses, people didn't often recognize him these days.

A shrill shriek split the air as two kids started to fight over a book.

That's going to do it, he mused. Blood that had burned so hot a minute before dropped back into the normal zone.

Only to jump right back up into the danger zone.

Miz Sexy Librarian was standing in front of the two kids. And *fuck* . . . her voice was a wet dream.

"Now I *know* you two weren't raised to treat books that way. Do you do that at home?"

Two pint-sized little blond heads tipped back to stare up at her. Trey barely noticed them because his gaze was riveted on the plump, round curve of her ass. How could he *not* notice that ass? She wore a long, skinny skirt that went down a few inches below her knees and her stockings were the kind with a seam that ran up the backs of her legs.

He passed a hand over his mouth.

Hell of a way to realize he could still get aroused—in the middle of the children's section of the very public, very busy

Norfolk library. Gritting his teeth, he focused on the ceiling. Would counting sheep help?

"Hello."

That whiskey-smooth drawl was like a silken hand stroking down his back . . . or other things. He cleared his throat. *Speak, dumb-ass.*

"Hi!"

Saved by the Clayton-meister.

Mentally blowing out a breath, he watched as his son rocked back and forth on his heels, smiling up at the woman.

"Are you here for the program?" she asked.

"I am!" Clayton stuck out his hand. "I'm Clay. I love books. My dad tells me stories. All the time. Sometimes he even makes them up. He gets paid to do that, too."

Despite the total insanity of the moment, Trey found himself biting back a laugh.

That boy, in so many ways, had been a bright and strong light in what would have been nothing but a pit of misery for far too long.

Oh, honey . . . come to mama.

Ressa Bliss would have been licking her chops if she had been anywhere remotely private.

Long, almost too lean, with a heavy growth of stubble and a mouth made for kissing, biting . . . other things . . .

He wore a pair of dark glasses that hid too much of his face, and she wanted to reach up, pull them off.

Because she wanted to too much, she focused on the boy instead.

She shook his hand, much of what he'd just said running together in her head. She'd caught his name, though. "Well, hello, Clay. It's lovely to meet you."

He grinned at her, displaying a tooth that looked like it might fall out at any second—literally. She thought it might be hanging in there by luck alone.

Clayton caught the man's hand in his and leaned against him. "This is my daddy."

She slid Mr. Beautiful a look. "Hello, Clayton's daddy."

He gave her a one-sided smile. "Hi." Then he crouched in front of his son. "So. Program lasts for fifty minutes. I'll be over in the grown-ups area if you need me."

"That area is boring." Clayton wrinkled up his nose.

"Well, if I stay here, I'll just play." A real grin covered his face now and Ressa felt her heart melt. Since he was distracted, she shot a look at his hands—ring? Did he have one?

Crap. Some sort of gloves covered his hands from knuckle to well up over his wrists. No way to tell.

Clayton leaned in and wrapped his arms around his father's neck. "Love you."

And her heart melted even more as he turned his face into his son's neck. "Love you, too, buddy. Have fun."

A man like that was most certainly *not* unattached.

But she still stole one last quick glance as he walked away.

The back was every bit as fine as the front.